PRAISE FOR *SCENT OF EVIL* AND ARCHER MAYOR

OTHER BOOKS BY ARCHER MAYOR

OPEN SEASON

BORDERLINES

SCENT OF EVIL

THE SKELETON'S KNEE

THE DARK ROOT

FRUITS OF THE POISONOUS TREE

SCENT OF EVIL

ARCHER MAYOR

THE MYSTERIOUS PRESS

Published by Warner Books

A Time Warner Company

MYSTERIOUS PRESS EDITION

Copyright © 1992 by Archer Mayor
All rights reserved.

Cover design by Julia Kushnirsky
Cover illustration by Chris Gall

The Mysterious Press name and logo are registered trademarks of Warner Books, Inc.

 Mysterious Press Books are published by Warner Books, Inc.
1271 Avenue of the Americas
New York, NY 10020

Visit our Web site at
www.warnerbooks.com

 A Time Warner Company

Printed in the United States of America

Originally published in hardcover by The Mysterious Press.
First Printed in Paperback: June, 1993
Reissued: December, 1996
10 9 8 7

To Mary O'Boyle, II
For her trust, her encouragement, and her friendship.
They were the fuel that kept me going,
as they have been for many others.
My deepest thanks.

CHAPTER

I

A human hand stuck out of the fresh dirt like a pale succulent plant, except this plant was wearing a silver ring, which twinkled fiercely in the burning sun.

"Want us to check it out?"

I turned at the quiet voice, looking over my shoulder to the top of the embankment. Two young men in white shirts with "Rescue, Inc." shoulder patches stood above me. The taller one had a medical kit in his hand. Behind them, only half visible from where I stood, was a large, boxy ambulance, its flashing lights anemic in the bright sun.

I shielded my eyes with my hand, feeling the sweat on my forehead. It was the hottest recorded August in Vermont history, with no reprieve in the forecast. I motioned to a fresh path in the slope connecting the street to the narrow dirt ledge we were occupying. "Maybe just one of you. Try to keep on the path so you don't add to the footprints."

The tall paramedic who had spoken sidestepped carefully down the path and joined me and Detective-Sergeant Klesczewski on the ledge. Klesczewski and I stepped back from the funnel-shaped hole in which the hand was nestled. The medic got to his knees and reached down to the bottom of the hole. I could see the sweat glistening on the hairs of his arm, and the damp impression his shoulder blades and spine made on his uniform shirt.

He felt for a pulse, checked for capillary refill by pressing the pale fingernails, and finally manipulated the fingers themselves. Even I could see they were as stiff as wood and clean. If the heavy ring was any indication, it meant we might be dealing with a man of means. Fancy rings are uncommon among Vermont men—they get in the way when you're working with your hands, and can be downright dangerous around machinery. More to the point, however, the possibility that wealth was a factor here, and therefore publicity, made me particularly unhappy.

The medic got up and shook his head. "Sorry."

The tone in his voice made me look at him more carefully. His gold name tag said John Huller. He was somewhere in his mid-twenties, with blond hair, a fair complexion, and eyes pale and sad. I regretted we'd had to call him and his partner in on this. For them, trying to save lives was often difficult enough; confirming obvious deaths seemed unnecessarily trite. Unfortunately, that was protocol.

I nodded to Huller. "Rigor mortis in the fingers?"

"Yes."

I mulled that over. On average, rigor was complete in six to twelve hours, nearer to six in this heat, with flaccidity returning in twenty-four to forty-eight hours—again, the hotter, the sooner. Since daylight seems to inhibit most clandestine grave diggers, I had to assume the hand with the ring, and whoever was attached to it, had been planted last night.

"Okay. Thanks for coming."

I watched Huller scramble up the embankment. This part of Canal Street crossed what originally had been a broad swale descending from the hills behind us to Whetstone Brook below. Some town fathers, well over a hundred years ago, had terraced that gap with an earthen embankment, on which Canal Street had then been built, buttressed by a stone retaining wall on the low side. Unfortunately, engineering arrogance had failed to heed the small spring that was buried under this wide balcony of dirt and rubble, and nature, three weeks ago, had finally reasserted itself. The old retaining wall had crumbled from spring-fed erosion, taking a good two-hundred-foot section of Canal Street with it.

The people of Brattleboro had become thoroughly riled—not a rarity in this outspoken town—and amid pointed questions as to why the road crew had patched ever-widening cracks in the road over the years without looking for their cause, the Department of Public Works had quickly set about replacing the old retaining wall with a heavily reinforced concrete dam, capable of shoring up an eight-lane freeway.

It was on this half-completed dam—or rather the leveled dirt fill packed in behind it—that I now stood with Klesczewski. The dam still had about eight feet to go before it reached the level of the street above.

I took out my handkerchief and mopped the sweat from my brow. From our manmade terrace, we could look down across the brook, over the warehouses lining Flat Street, and the trees interspersed throughout, and up the opposite slope to where Elliot Street was hidden by the town's typically intermixed hodgepodge of residences and small businesses. Despite the openness and proximity of running water, there wasn't the slightest hint of a breeze. The whole lumpy, hilly, topsy-turvy town might as well have been stretched out flat on an Arizona frying pan.

"I take it the state's attorney and the medical examiner have been contacted?"

Ron Klesczewski let out a small snort. "You can take it their offices have been notified. And Tyler should be here any minute with his toys."

J. P. Tyler was as close as our Police Department got to a forensics team. He did what print lifting, photographing, and chemical analysis he could, given the tools and training we could afford. What he couldn't handle we sent either to the State Police Lab in Waterbury or to the F.B.I. in Washington.

Klesczewski was still talking. "I took the liberty of telling Dispatch to round up all the detectives and to activate the night-patrol shift early for a neighborhood canvass."

I smiled at that. "All the detectives" came to two besides

Klesczewski, Tyler, and myself, who headed the squad. On the other hand, the uniformed night shift consisted of six people, including the shift sergeant. Adding them to the five-man day shift and ourselves would create a good-sized crew for Klesczewski's proposed door-to-door canvass of potential witnesses. I only hoped someone wouldn't knock over a bank at the far end of town in the meantime.

Ron Klesczewski had reached the same conclusion I had concerning the time of death. "I take it we're asking about something happening last night."

"That's what it looks like. Who found him?"

Ron pointed up the embankment to a man sitting on the running board of a large dump truck, smoking a cigarette in the shade. There were other workers around, but they were clustered farther off, as if the smoker had acquired some dubious aroma. "Name's Ernie Wallers. He was doing the soil borings, to make sure they'd compacted the earth hard enough, when he hit . . . that." He checked his watch. "We were called only about fifteen minutes ago."

"He's the one who dug the hole, too?"

"Yeah. The foreman said it kind of bummed him out."

Even from fifty feet, I could see Wallers's cigarette was clamped in the fist of one hand. "Bummed out" was the most lighthearted label I would have hung on him.

"You talk to him yet?" I asked.

"No. Lavoie was the responding officer—he talked to him a bit and gave me the gist of it. I thought you might like the first real crack."

Ron Klesczewski had been made my number-two man only five months ago. He deserved the promotion, and had proved more valuable than I might have guessed, especially in managing the office, but he still had a bit of the blushing bride in him—a shyness about seeming too bold.

I patted him on the shoulder as I eased by, heading for the path up to the road. "Thanks, Ron. Did Lavoie take pictures of all this?"

"Yeah—a whole roll."

Lavoie was good with a camera—J.P. wouldn't have to worry about the results. "You better tell Tyler that when he comes—it'll save time. I'd like this guy dug up as soon as possible."

"You got it."

I'd left my jacket in the car, but even so I was soaked with perspiration, especially after struggling up the loose-dirt embankment. Like many a native Vermonter, I didn't do well in the heat. I paused to catch my breath on the road. There was no traffic to worry about—the street had been closed for weeks, which made keeping the press and the general population at bay much easier—a luxury I'd soon be without. A death of this sort in a town the size of Brattleboro, with an average of one homicide every three years, would be front-page news for days, and that was only if we cleared it up fast.

I approached Ernie Wallers casually, taking time to wipe a spot on the truck's running board before sitting next to him. It felt good to be out of the sun.

"Pretty bad deal, huh?"

He shook his head, his eyes on the ground in front of him. "Sure as hell didn't make my day."

"I'm Lieutenant Joe Gunther, from the Police Department. You're Ernie Wallers, right?"

He gave me a cursory glance and a slight nod. "The guy was murdered, wasn't he?"

"Dunno yet. It's a pretty good guess. I hear you were taking soil samples when you found him; what made you dig him up? Didn't he just feel like a rock or something?"

Wallers straightened slightly and took a deep drag on his cigarette, which was burning perilously close to his fingers. "No way. We're putting clean fill in there—I would've dug it out if it had been a rock. Besides, it was a little soft when I pushed. I didn't know what the hell it was—just that it wasn't supposed to be there."

I looked around. "What do you use for your soil borings?"

He pointed to a long, thin cylinder, a little thicker than a walking stick. One end of it was protruding from the back of a nearby pickup truck.

"You pound that in, or twist it?"

"Twisting's best. That's what I was doing."

I made a mental note to have Tyler check out the end of

the probe, and to match whatever he found to the mark it would have left on the body. "Did you notice anything unusual about the dirt before you went for a sample—like footprints or any signs of digging?"

He shook his head. "Just the opposite. I tested there because it looked cleaner than anywhere else. There were footprints—we walk back and forth along there all the time—but not as many, like they'd only been put there today."

"And that layer of dirt has been there longer than that?"

"Yeah." Wallers's voice was picking up interest, now that I'd warmed him up. He got to his feet and I followed him over to the jagged edge of the road. He pointed to the two-hundred-foot-long ledge below us. "The way this works, we build up a few feet of wall, and then we fill in behind it, from left to right. Then we tamp it down with a compactor, do some borings to make sure the soil is compressed to within specs, and start all over again. We'd compacted the spot I was testing around mid-morning yesterday. It took us the rest of the day to finish that layer to the far end, and today we've just been building wall. So we've been walking on that particular dirt for almost two days."

"Why did you think that one spot was cleaner?"

He shrugged. "I don't know. I didn't give it any thought; not then. It just caught my eye, so I drilled it. I have to do a bunch of borings along the whole length of this thing anyway, so it doesn't much matter where I do them."

"Can you think back and remember if any of the footprints looked unusual or out of place?"

He smiled. "You mean before I dug that hole and covered them all up?"

I didn't answer. It was a rhetorical question for him, and spilled milk for me—at least he'd been curious enough to dig in the first place, and smart enough to stop once he'd uncovered the hand.

Wallers bent his head and thought for a moment, his eyes half closed in concentration. I was pleased with his deliberate cooperation. In over thirty years as a policeman in this town, I'd encountered every conceivable reaction to questioning like this, from obsequious babbling to a wild punch.

Thoughtfulness was a cherished rarity, especially at the start of a felony crime investigation.

He rubbed the back of his neck and gave a rueful smile. "I don't know. The more I think about it, the less sure I am."

"About what?"

"Well, I think there was something different. We all wear construction boots, with lug soles." He made an impression in the dust to prove the point. "Maybe there were others there that were smooth, like yours."

I stepped back, so that my print was next to his. He studied them both for a moment. "I can't say for sure. Maybe I'm making it up with all the excitement. It was like an impulsive thing to bore right there, you know? I wasn't really paying attention."

I squeezed his elbow. "You've been very helpful. Sorry this had to happen."

He gave a little humorless laugh. "Something I can tell my grandchildren some day."

I left him and walked back to where Klesczewski was gathering an ever-growing collection of police officers, patrolmen, necktied detectives, and a group of men and women who had obviously been called away either from home or from the off-duty, part-time jobs many of them held down to buttress their meager municipal wages.

"Everyone here?" I asked him.

"Close enough to start handing out assignments."

I nodded and glanced over the embankment. Tyler—short, thin, bespectacled, and in constant nervous motion—was organizing a small team of policemen/archaeologists to grid, sketch, collect, bag, and label the dirt covering the body. It would take them hours to dig down four feet, and days to sift the dirt and completely analyze what they found.

I turned my back on the construction site and the Whetstone Brook valley beyond it. Across Canal Street, the topography was just the reverse. Behind a low, four-business block of buildings fronting the street and a residential alleyway in back, the ground rose steeply to a wooded plateau which looked deceptively unpopulated. It actually held almost a fourth of the city, but from where I stood, I could just see the roofs of a couple of the older homes high against the skyline—the rest looked like wooded wilderness.

"Not a great place for finding casual eyewitnesses, is it?"

Ron Klesczewski was standing next to me, scanning the same view. He was right. The street had been blocked off for days; the four businesses opposite the scene were closed at night, as were the warehouses on the other side of Whetstone Brook. To the right of the small block of businesses was a school, to the left were four similar weather-beaten homes of dissimilar colors. On our side of Canal, there was a destitute apartment building clinging to the slope at one end of the retaining wall, and tiny Ed's Diner at the other end, neither of which had many windows facing the gap between them. Last but not least, this was one of the town's most rundown sections, populated by people whose pride ran more on what they wouldn't tell the police than on what they could.

I sighed and turned toward the hot and sweating group clustered in the dusty middle of the street. "Looks like we have a murder. It's an educated guess that it occurred sometime last night. Go for the obvious places"—I pointed at the dilapidated apartment building and the four small houses opposite it—"but don't miss the possibility that people were out strolling, that windows were open, that things might have been heard but not seen."

I aimed my fingers across the narrow valley at the buildings clinging to the slope below Elliot Street. "And check over there. It looks far away, but some people have binoculars and telescopes. On a hot night, they tend to hang around the windows, trying to catch the cool air. The highrise is good for that."

The highrise was actually the Elliot Street Apartments, a seven-story, modern brick federal housing project, whose broad but distant front directly faced us. I'd found in the past it had many of the same advantages of a first-class intelligence listening post—it was tall, centrally located, had balconies facing every which way, and was jammed with aspiring spies.

"One thing to remember, for those of you who haven't

done too many of these canvasses: We don't have anything so far. The trick is to make people open up, to give you what they've got. Don't rush them, don't finish their sentences for them, let them gossip if necessary. Somebody might know somebody who knows somebody who saw something, and we won't find that last somebody unless we're all ears right now. Good luck. Ron will give you specific assignments."

I broke away from the huddle and crossed to where State's Attorney James Dunn was getting out of his car. By Vermont law, an appointed representative from the SA's office is supposed to make an appearance at the scene of a possible homicide. Usually, it's the low man on the SA's totem pole. In Brattleboro, it's usually The Man Himself.

James Dunn was tall, pale, thin, and arrogant—a stone gargoyle who'd given up his perch to settle disdainfully among us mere mortals. He was good at his job, knew the law inside out, played no favorites, and kept his private passions to himself, except for this one—he loved to see the bodies. No matter the hour or the weather, if we ever came upon a corpse, or even someone close to being one, James— never Jim—Dunn made the show. He never got in the way and was occasionally useful, but I thought this morbid appetite a little odd. And it often made me wonder about his social life.

"You found a hand?" he asked, with a single raised eyebrow.

"A right hand; buried behind the retaining wall. We're assuming it was put there last night."

He slammed his car door and took long, elegant strides toward the embankment. He was also a bit of a dandy—a lifelong bachelor with an affinity for English clothes. Even in this heat, he wore a dark and natty suit, and refused to yield even the slightest sheen of sweat. "Is the hand attached to anyone?"

"Presumably. We're finding that out now."

J.P., whether following established technique or simply giving in to curiosity, had dug another funnel in the dirt, similar to the one that encased the hand. At the bottom of this one was a man's face.

Tyler was delicately whisking away granules of dirt from the body's mouth, nose, and half-open eyes with a camel's-hair brush when we arrived at the edge of the road. He leaned back upon hearing us and glanced up. "Look familiar?"

My own mother wouldn't have looked familiar. Flat and one-dimensional at the bottom of the hole, the pale face looked more like an ancient ceremonial ivory mask, waiting to be discovered and hung on some museum wall.

Both Dunn and I shook our heads to Tyler's question. He resumed his excavating.

I heard Detective-Sergeant Dennis DeFlorio, his voice small and tinny, calling me on the radio I had hooked to my belt. "Go ahead," I answered.

"You still on Canal Street?"

"Ten-four."

"Can you meet me on the south end of Clark?"

Clark was the short, horseshoe-shaped residential alley-way behind the small block of businesses facing Canal. Its one-way entrance cut between the businesses and the school to the block's right, and its outlet appeared back on Canal several hundred yards closer to downtown. Its only function was to provide access to some browbeaten apartments that were shoved hard against the steep wooded slope I'd been studying earlier. As elsewhere in this geographically topsy-turvy town, every square inch of flat land had buildings clustered on it like cows bunched together on hillocks during a flood.

I started down Clark Street and found DeFlorio coming toward me, his round face red and glistening. The opposite of James Dunn, Dennis was short and fat, given to soiled ties, loose shirttails, and to buckling his belt somewhere out of sight under his belly.

"What's up?"

"Well, I figured if I lived here, Clark being the dump it is, I'd be out taking a walk on a hot night, just to get away, you know? Like last night."

The one slightly irritating thing about Dennis was his propensity to beat around the bush, as if every declaratory sentence had to be prefaced by an enticing roll of the drum.

"So where did that lead you?"

He looked surprised at my thick-headedness. "I know nobody could of seen or heard anything from here, but I figured I'd ask anyway, especially to see if my theory was right."

"And it was."

"Yeah. I think I nailed down the time of death." He flipped open the cop's ubiquitous notebook he held in his soft, damp hand. "A guy named Phil Didry said he was walking along Canal around three this morning when he saw a police car parked with the engine running, right where the body is buried."

"One of our cars?"

"Yeah—I figure someone on the graveyard shift. All we got to do is find out who it was, and we'll have a pretty good idea when the body got planted."

I looked quizzically into his beaming face. "I don't follow you."

DeFlorio's smile faded slightly. "Don't you see? We can ask him what it looked like—the dirt. If it was disturbed, then the burial happened before three; if it wasn't, then it happened later."

"Dennis, the dirt never did look disturbed."

He looked at me blankly, trying to register this anomaly.

"Did your witness see the policeman?"

"No. I don't think he wanted to hang around. None of these people are too pure, you know."

"So what makes you think our patrolman was over the embankment? He might have dropped into Ed's Diner for a coffee."

DeFlorio made a fast mental run for safety. "I know that—I just meant on the off chance that if he did take a look, it would help nail down the time."

I pursed my lips and nodded thoughtfully. "It's an excellent point, Dennis. We'll check it out."

I shook my head as DeFlorio retreated back up the street to shake out some more gems. Not that his witness wasn't a good find, but DeFlorio's conclusions rubbed in a fact as painfully obvious to me as it seemed inconceivable to Hollywood: Cops are neither routinely corrupt nor preternaturally heroic, and damn few of them are endowed with the instincts of a Sherlock Holmes. They put in their hours, spending half of those doing paperwork and the other half dealing with cranky citizens, and then they go home.

In Brattleboro, their problems are compounded. The pay approaches the absurd and—where a homicide or bank robbery comes around once in a blue moon—the boredom can be mind-numbing. It was not an environment to attract either geniuses or careerists. Observations like that, however, can cut close to the bone. I'm no genius either, but no one could say I hadn't made this business a career. It's all I've done professionally since getting out of the service in the mid–nineteen fifties. Of course, my introduction to police work was different. The pay when I entered wasn't so balefully lopsided, and the neighborhood foot-patrol cop was a popular and respected figure in a small, almost provincial town where crimes were infrequent, unsophisticated, and easy to solve, and the need for a detective squad didn't even exist. We'd also had to contend with a quarter of today's paperwork. By the time it had all begun to change, I'd found myself too settled in to do otherwise.

Klesczewski met me back on Canal, where I noticed James Dunn was still hovering at the edge of the road, like a raptor looking for mice far below.

"What did Dennis want?"

"He found someone who saw one of our patrol cars parked out here around three this morning."

Klesczewski raised his eyebrows. "That might be handy. You know who it was?"

"Not yet. I'll get hold of George Capullo later." Capullo was the sergeant for the graveyard shift, and the one who handed out assignments.

"Well, I got something, too. It's not much, but I figured you ought to take a look." I thought back to the way DeFlorio had delivered his report; had it been Klesczewski, he would have escorted me to meet the witness and forced me to interview him all over again, just so nothing was left out. It had never surprised me the two men generally kept their distance from one another.

I followed Klesczewski toward Ed's Diner and the concrete barricade the road crew had set up weeks ago, which we were now using as a police line to keep out the public. My heart sank a little as we drew near, for standing on the other side of the listless yellow police line we'd strung across the road was the *Brattleboro Reformer*'s "courts and cops" reporter, Stanley Katz.

My relationship with Katz was emblematic of all that was wrong between the press and the police. We didn't like each other, didn't trust each other, and each of us was generally convinced the world would be a better place without the other. Stanley couldn't hear the time of day from me without smelling a cover-up, and I couldn't read beyond his byline on an article without feeling that he'd hyped up the gore and screwed up the facts. The irony was that we knew neither perception was accurate, but our reactions were chemical, not rational, a fact to which we'd finally become resigned.

Katz's narrow face broke into a wide grin at our approach. "Who belongs to the hand, Lieutenant?"

"I don't know, Stanley," I said, as I squeezed between two of the concrete barricades and under the rope. Kleszewski, who couldn't tolerate even speaking to Katz, was heading around the corner of Ed's and down across the sloping Elm Street Bridge.

I saw WBRT news reporter Ted McDonald drive up, park haphazardly near the curb, and struggle to get his massive bulk and tape recorder out of the radio station's undersized car in one failed fluid movement. His eyes focused on me like a dog's on dinner.

"Joe," he shouted cheerfully.

I waved to him and heard Katz's quiet groan. That gave me a gentle pang of pleasure. McDonald was a good old boy, born and raised in Brattleboro, as faithful to the town and its denizens as he was to the flag, and a throwback to the less complicated days I'd been thinking of mere moments ago. In his hourly four-minute news spots, he pretty much reported what he saw and what we told him, with no hype and no prejudicial inflections, which to me was eminently acceptable. Katz had once told me he thought McDonald was a dim-witted, stoolie woodchuck, the last part of which was a derogatory name given local rural folk. Katz was from Connecticut, which we woodchucks saw as a condemnation speaking for itself.

I waited for Ted to join us, enjoying Katz's heightening but resigned disgust.

McDonald's face was beet red and dripping with sweat. He began fumbling with his tape recorder, but stopped when I shook my head. "Sorry, Ted, it's still too early. We've found a body behind the retaining wall, but we haven't even finished digging it up. We have no who, when, how, or why to give you."

Katz gave a condescending smile to the older reporter. "It's obviously a murder—they just haven't determined the cause."

McDonald's face brightened, but I smiled and shook my head. "Don't let him jerk you around. Nobody's said it was a murder—right now, it's an unexplained death."

Katz fell in beside me as I set off to rejoin Klesczewski. "But he was murdered, right?" Ted lumbered silently behind, noisily pushing buttons on his machine.

"We don't know that."

"You think he died of natural causes and buried himself? Very considerate."

"It's early on, Stanley. Once we've exhumed the body and the medical examiner has had a chance to take a look, we or the state's attorney's office will issue a statement."

"How was he killed?" Ted asked.

"We've got a hand sticking out of the dirt. We'd like to see the rest of the body first."

"So he *was* killed." Katz smiled.

"He's dead—that's all we know. We don't know who he is, we don't know how he died, and we don't know if he was killed. We don't know anything at the moment."

"So what are you doing now?"

We were halfway across the bridge, which sloped steeply from Canal to the Whetstone Brook's low north bank. Below us, Klesczewski had already jumped the guardrail at the far end of the bridge and was sidestepping down to the edge of the river. I let out a sigh. The sun and the conversation were giving me a headache. "I'm trying to patiently explain that I have nothing to say."

Katz tried a more benign approach. "How about off the record? What does the guy look like? What did Dunn have to say?"

"Nothing. I'm not ducking you, guys. I just don't have anything."

"How about the age of the body? I mean, is it half rotted or does it look fresh?"

I lifted one leg over the guardrail in order to join Klesczewski. "I got to go to work. Talk to you later."

Ted, who by now had gotten the message and was undoing all his button pushing, muttered, "Thanks, Joe."

Katz made to follow me.

I placed my hand gently against his chest. "Where're you going, Stanley?"

I half expected some small lecture on the rights of a free press, but even Katz had grown beyond that. Besides, we both knew the unwritten rules of the game, and despite our sparring, we observed them. He gave me an infectious grin. "Thought I'd go fishing?"

I shook my head, unable to suppress a smile myself. "Nice try."

I left him on the street and climbed down the bank to where Klesczewski was moodily staring at the water, waiting. "So—what have you got?"

"It's over here." He led the way under the bridge, keeping to the rocks to avoid disturbing the damp soil.

Once in the shade, I paused and blinked to get used to the low light. It was suddenly delightfully cool, with the sound of water splashing off the concrete bridge that arched overhead, and the shadows flickering with reflected spots of sunlight. There was a slight but permeating odor of rotting vegetation.

"Nice place."

Klesczewski pointed to the narrow wedge where the bank met the underside of the bridge, some six feet up from the water's edge. "You're not the only one who thinks so."

Running parallel to the brook, a small shelf had been scooped out of the embankment, and on it was a two-inch-

thick mattress of old newspapers. Scattered around the shelf
was an assortment of everyday trash—bottles, food wrappers,
odd scraps of paper, most of it fairly fresh.

"The Dew Drop Inn, complete with air-conditioning—
and recently occupied."

Kleszczewski nodded. "That's not all." He retraced our
steps to the opening, so we were half in the shade and half
back in the glare. He pointed again to the ground.

I squatted down, keeping my hands on my knees. Resting
on top of the moist, pungent earth was an unusually fat,
chewed-up wad of gum, still pink and clean.

"What do you think?" I asked.

Kleszczewski looked vaguely uncomfortable. He hadn't
led me all the way down here to hear me ask that. But he
had led me, so I knew he'd reached some conclusions.

"Somebody's living here, or at least they were, up to a
few hours ago. Maybe they saw something."

I looked again at the gum, poking at it with a pen I'd
removed from my pocket. It was dry, but not rock hard, and
its cleanliness attested to its having been spat out within the
last half day. "We can't afford a twenty-four-hour watch on
this place, but tell Patrol to keep an eye peeled for anybody
coming back here in the next few days. I'd like to talk to the
gum chewer."

I glanced over my shoulder, straight across the water, and
up the opposite bank to where I could see Tyler and his team
bent over their work. He didn't know it yet, but Tyler's day
was going to be full of excavating. At least here, he'd be in
the shade.

CHAPTER
2

BY late afternoon we were alone, the body and I, in the cool basement embalming room of the McCloskey Funeral Home on Forest Street. Along the walls were a sink and counters, a roll-around cart with a variety of nonsterile surgical instruments whose role here I didn't want to know, and shelves stocked with row after row of identical plastic bottles filled with variously colored liquids, designed to be injected into bodies to give the skin a perking up. I was sitting in the corner on a metal folding chair. The corpse lay faceup on a fiberglass table, the bottom of which sloped slightly, so that any fluids accumulating at his feet could be washed down a drainpipe which paralleled one of the table legs.

Not that there were any fluids. The black-rubber body bag had been completely unzipped, revealing the body still fully clothed in a pair of pale blue slacks and a polo shirt, and covered with dirt. He looked like a well-dressed tunnel digger who'd chosen this incongruous spot to catch a couple of minutes of shut-eye.

The door-to-door canvass for witnesses was continuing, Dunn had finally returned to his office, and Tyler and his crew had switched from the retaining wall to under the bridge. I was waiting for the regional medical examiner,

Alfred Gould, to get off the phone and start giving my roommate an external examination.

The autopsy would not be done in Brattleboro. Beverly Hillstrom, the state's chief medical examiner, would do that in Burlington, where her office was located. Usually, in a homicide, Hillstrom traveled to the scene, wishing to keep the preliminary autopsy and the crime scene as close to one another as possible. But timing was a problem here; she'd made it clear that if we wanted results within the next forty-eight hours, the body would have to go north, soon.

It was an irritant. After all, we didn't know who this man was, and we didn't know what, or who, had killed him. All we had was the body, and little time to pick up a fresh scent. Still, I wasn't begrudging the point. Although Hillstrom had almost single-handedly made Vermont's one of the best M.E. systems around, only her laboratory had all the proper facilities for a complete job. So I had negotiated a compromise: Gould was to do a preliminary once-over before shipping the body north. It was the best deal I could get.

Alfred Gould walked in, looking starchy and official in a white lab coat he'd borrowed from the funeral director. Examinations of this type were also done at Memorial Hospital, but McCloskey's was far better for keeping out of sight of the press and other curiosity-seekers.

Gould smiled at me. "You look half asleep."

I laughed and got to my feet. "It's the air-conditioning—first cool air I've felt in days. I'd move a bed down here if it weren't for the company. You all set with Hillstrom?" I'd given him the phone after bargaining with her, so they could work out the details.

He was standing by the table now, his fingertips resting lightly on its edge, like a piano player preparing for a difficult solo. In the normal world, he shared a successful family practice with two other doctors. But I had only seen him in his medical-examiner capacity, and it made me feel odd to think of him working on live patients.

He nodded distractedly to my question. "Yeah. She's busy right now on another case, but she'll be ready in three hours or so."

The trip up to Burlington took three hours. "So how

long're you going to spend on this?'' I was disappointed. Time flies when you're struggling to get clothes off a body, or turning it over to check for previously unseen wounds, especially when it's as stiff as a board. It didn't leave us much time to actually examine anything.

His eyes were sweeping back and forth across the body. "Thirty minutes at most. She can only fit it in today if we get it to her fast. It doesn't matter; it looks pretty straightforward. I basically just want to draw some blood, lift his prints, and check for anything obvious."

Gould had appeared at the Canal Street scene shortly after Tyler had finished his exhumation. He'd looked at the pupils, checked the temperature in and outside of the body, felt the jawline and extremities for rigor, and examined the man's neck. It had taken all of seven minutes, and only because he'd moved slowly. I was growing anxious to know what little he knew, but I knew better than to rush him. Past experience had taught me he liked to keep his findings to himself until he was absolutely satisfied they were accurate. So, suppressing my impatience, I stuck to quietly assisting him as he awkwardly stripped his uncooperative patient.

Dead bodies don't bother me much, at least not emotionally. The horrifying realization that a once-vibrant human being can be reduced to a corpse in an instant had been beaten into me repeatedly during the Korean War. As a teenage warrior, I had seen friends and strangers shot, maimed, burned, blown up, and frozen to death, until the shock and my tears had evaporated. Now, instead of the horror, I can't help but see a corpse as a Chinese puzzle box.

Preliminary forensic examinations, like the one I was attending now, tend to open a few of the more obvious hidden compartments, answering the broader questions about the time and method of death. But the classic exams, the ones done by the true artists of the profession, can reveal far more, even, sometimes, the feelings, the motivations, and the calculations that once drove an individual through life. Hillstrom I considered such an artist.

The man Alfred Gould and I were undressing was not bad looking. Of medium height and build, he was probably in his late twenties, with a strong upper torso and only the faint beginnings of a soft waistline. His hair had been carefully barbered, his fingernails were neat and evenly clipped, and, as I'd suspected at the grave site, he was clean under his earth-soiled clothes, as might be a man who showered every day. The silver ring on his right hand was matched by a thin silver chain around his neck.

Twenty-five minutes after we'd begun, Gould muttered a small "huh." The body was on its side, and Gould was peering closely at something near the dorsal side of the right shoulder, out of my line of sight. While Gould had conducted his examination, I'd been noting details I thought might come in handy later, like the pale outline of a watch across the body's left wrist—a watch now missing—and the labels from his clothing, from L. L. Bean and Land's End, both upwardly mobile catalog stores. I'd also noted the bloodless dime-sized puncture Ernie Wallers's soil-boring tool had left on the corpse's right forearm.

I raised my eyebrows at Gould from across the body. "What?"

He smiled. "I appreciate your self-restraint, Joe. One of these days, I'm going to walk out of the room without saying a word, just to see if you'll wait a few days for the written report."

"I'd shoot you in the foot first. What did you find?"

He straightened and motioned to me to come around the table and look. What I found was a small reddish patch of skin on the shoulder, a perfect circle about a half inch in diameter.

"A bee sting?"

"I'd say an injection site; it's called a 'wheal.'"

I looked up at him. "So he OD'd on something?"

He shook his head. "My guess is that he died of acute cerebral ischemia." He smiled at my expression. "Which means the blood flow to his brain was shut off suddenly."

"Strangled." I had noticed two bruises on either side of the body's windpipe, but none of the standard transverse markings common to hanging, garroting, or throttling. Also, his face was pale and normal-looking, rather than bloated and flushed, as I'd come to expect in day-old strangulations.

"Not in the sense you mean. He didn't die of asphyxiation. The way I read it, his assailant placed a thumb on either side of his larynx and applied sudden pressure, completely blocking off both carotid arteries. He might also have hit the carotid sinuses and triggered what you'd call a heart attack. Either way, it was a pretty painful way to go, and slow, too. The face looks normal because the carotid veins weren't cut off at the same time, so no blood built up in the head to make his features discolor.''

Gould had placed his hands gently on my throat to demonstrate. I removed them, feeling slightly squeamish. "So the murderer was facing him."

"Presumably."

"Wouldn't this guy have put up a fight?"

"He may have tried. That may be where the injection fits in. Its location makes it all but impossible that the victim injected himself.'' Gould lifted one of the lifeless arms and turned it stiffly so I could see the inside of the wrist. "Also, there's a slight red band here, and a corroborating one on the outside of the other wrist, both of which suggest they were bound together at one point, probably just prior to death.''

I bent over and studied the mark on the other arm. Now that I knew what I was looking for, I noticed a neat rectangular pattern of hair had been removed from the back of the wrist, just where the watch had once been. "Tape?"

"I think so. I've made a note to Hillstrom to have the skin at those points analyzed for residual adhesive.''

I straightened and looked thoughtfully at the body for a minute. Tyler had yet to carefully examine the dirt he'd gathered at the grave site, but I already knew he'd found nothing as obvious as a piece of torn tape.

"There's something else," Gould added. "Normally, if a body were laid flat on its back after death and covered with dirt, the lividity—the postmortem pooling of the blood—would be equally distributed along all the low points—the shoulder blades, the buttocks, the calves, the heels, and the undersides of both arms."

"And here they aren't."

Gould rolled the body all the way over. "It's not crystal clear, but I see most of the pooling having occurred in the buttocks, thighs, and feet, and not at all along the upper torso—''

"As if he'd been sitting in a chair," I finished for him.

He returned his uncomplaining patient to its previous position. "Yup. Of course, it's all conjectural, including the injection, which could indeed be an insect bite."

My fingers strayed to the blue pants we'd removed. "I better have the State Police Crime Lab check these for adhesive, too."

Gould looked puzzled for a moment and then nodded, understanding. We both shared the mental image of how this man had died, sitting in a chair, his hands taped behind his back, his legs taped to the chair legs. The man opposite him—his killer—must have carefully positioned his thumbs over the fat carotids, feeling the life blood pumping underneath just seconds before he pressed down with all his might, shutting off the flow, starving the brain, backing the blood up to the nearby heart, jamming it to a halt, forcing the blood back further to flood the lungs. I wondered what had killed him first—the brain, the heart, or had he drowned in his own blood?

"You said the death was slow as well as painful. How long would this have taken?"

"If I'm right on the cause of death, his assailant had to have kept his thumbs in position for almost five minutes to do the job right."

"Would a shot of something play in with that? He must've been flopping around like a landed fish, even tied down."

"You mean a sedative? That's what I was thinking, actually. The killer gives this guy an injection to calm him down, maybe even knock him cold, and then goes to work without a struggle. The fact that the wrists show only adhesive and no abrasions or bruising indicate he didn't put up a fight." Gould made a sour face and shook his head. "But then, why bother cutting off the blood supply? Why not just overdose him and be done with it?"

I looked at the body again, those questions and more running around my brain. He looked fine for a corpse—a little in need of the bottled tints lining the far wall, of course. I wished I could peel back his eyelid and see reflected there the last image of his life. "How long do you think he was in the chair after he died?"

Gould stuck his lower lip out slightly. "Hard to say. Lividity generally becomes permanently fixed after eight to twelve hours, but that's not set in stone—variations can be huge. Best I could say is that he sat for several hours after he died, and before he was moved to a supine position."

So he was killed somewhere else, before being dumped behind the Canal Street retaining wall. "Can you tell if he was gagged?"

Gould shook his head. "I looked. I don't think so, but anything's possible." He glanced at his watch.

"I know—you got to go."

"Well—he has to. I'm just going back to my office. But I don't want to keep Hillstrom waiting."

I headed toward the door to arrange for a patrolman to accompany the body to Burlington. "I know, Al. Thanks for your help."

●　　●　　●　　●

I paused at Tony Brandt's open door, allowing some of the pipe smoke to filter out before I wandered blindly in, hoping I'd find his guest chair before falling over his desk in the smog. He glanced up from his computer keyboard and squinted at me as I settled down.

"Why the hell don't you open a window?" I asked him.

"Wouldn't make any difference." He pulled the omnipresent pipe from his mouth to make sure it was still burning brightly.

"Maybe not with the heat, but it might help with this stuff." I waved my hand through the tendrils of smoke.

There was the sudden shriek of a circular handsaw ripping through plywood. Brandt motioned to the door and I reluctantly rose and shut it against the noise, my day-long headache struggling for new heights. The Police Department's previous rabbit warren of offices was being totally remodeled. Walls were coming down, work spaces redefined, lighting replaced, and central air-conditioning being put in. Unfortunately, some logistical genius had arranged to have the window air conditioners removed before the central system had been completed, leaving us all to swelter at the peak of the summer's heat amid the pounding of hammers, the screaming of power tools, and the continuous swirl of sawdust.

I paused to open a window before sitting back down. Brandt made no comment. He'd been chief for the past nine years, on our force for ten years before that. Aside from Deputy Police Chief Billy Manierre and myself, he'd spent more years as a cop than any of us.

Not that he looked the role. I'd seen a television documentary recently about the Manhatten Project. It had shown all those tweedy professor types—skinny, aquiline, and bespectacled, with thinning hair—scurrying around the New Mexican desert in search of the perfect bang, and I could have sworn I saw Tony Brandt six different times. But where rocket scientists of lore are reputed to be sloppily dressed, absent-minded, and insensitive of other people's feelings, Brandt was neat, organized, tough as nails, and fully aware of the emotional buttons we all carry within us.

He fixed me now with a long look, his head slightly back, the blue rectangle of his computer screen reflecting off his wire-rim glasses. "So—we found a man in a grave."

I spoke distinctly, to cover the noise. "Yes. We don't know who yet. There was no wallet or ID. He's young, looks pretty well off, and Gould says he was killed by having his blood supply cut off to the brain." I put my thumbs against my throat to illustrate. Brandt's frown deepened.

"Either that or he was overdosed with something. We found a probable needle mark. Gould also thinks he was killed elsewhere, in a chair, and left there for a few hours before being moved to where we found him."

"And no one saw the planting."

"Not that we know of yet. Klesczewski's reviewing the canvass reports. There're a few people we missed that we're following up on, and there's the off chance a bum was living under the Elm Street Bridge who might have seen something. I'm having people check the flop house to see if we can get a line on him. Also, at around 3:00 A.M., one of our patrol cars was seen parked at the embankment. George Capullo says that would have been John Woll, but I haven't been able to locate him yet."

There was a slight pause. Brandt's pale gray eyes were looking out the window. A few months ago, he had requested funding from the selectmen to purchase beepers for all off-duty officers, not just the detectives and the upper ranks, as was now the case. He'd argued that both the private ambulance service in town and the Municipal Fire Department were so equipped, as were most of the surrounding-area fire and rescue squads, but he'd been turned down. We would therefore have to either wait for Woll to show up for his midnight shift, or hope he just happened to wander in early.

"There's no obvious motive at this point," I continued. "While the wallet and a watch seem to be missing, there was a fancy silver ring and a neck chain that would have been worth something to a thief. Plus, it sounds a little complicated for a simple robbery."

"So what is it?" Brandt rarely gave opinions himself. He sat as Sage on the Hill at times like these, welcoming all to divulge what they knew. Some of the younger officers found this an irritating trait and accused him of trying to look wiser than he was. I, on the other hand, took it at face value. I'd spent several months in his chair recently, as temporary chief, and I knew what his role was like—not being able to investigate anything personally, being chained to the desk, and yet being accountable in the public's eye for everything that came out of the department.

I let a minute float by before answering. "My gut tells me we're going to have problems with this one. There might be all sorts of reasons for wanting to bury a man you just killed, but I don't know why anyone would pick that spot."

Brandt's right eyebrow rose. "Seems perfect to me."

" 'Seems perfect.' That's the trouble with it. This is one of the most rural states in the whole country. Even Brattleboro has as much countryside as concrete. If I'd discreetly murdered someone in my basement, and had waited several hours to put him in my car at night so I could dump him, I sure as hell wouldn't head for Canal Street. I'd go out of town, find some forgotten ravine where I could work in peace, and bury my man for keeps."

"Maybe you don't have a car."

I pondered that one. "Which makes me local to the scene, having to carry the body from my basement to Canal Street on my shoulder."

Without a word being spoken, we both rejected that one.

"So why was it put there?" he finally asked.

"So someone would find it."

CHAPTER
3

THE carpenter had finished for the day by the time I left Brandt's office. I noticed the offending saw, lying tilted and silent on a sawhorse, its nerve-jangling screech as neutered as the unplugged electric cord curled up on the floor beneath it. I went down a short, interior hallway to the men's room to treat my headache with some cool water on the face.

It wasn't just the Police Department that was being revamped, but the entire Municipal Building. A half year earlier, the ribbon had been cut on the new District Court Building across the street and all the judges, clerks, secretaries, and sheriff's men who had once shared our quarters had taken their paraphernalia and abandoned us like a departing storm. In the sudden void, we survivors—the Police Department, the town manager, the planning director, the finance director, the town attorney, the listers, the town clerk, and all the others—had crept warily out of the nooks and crannies into which we'd been stuffed for decades and had begun to explore a vast new domain.

Unfortunately—in the short run—with freedom had come remodeling, and, department by department, the building was being torn apart. I knew it was for the eventual good, but at the moment I couldn't imagine a grimmer place to work, a point that was driven home by the notice on the sink of the men's room: "Disconnected for renovation—please go upstairs."

I sighed, mopped my forehead with my warm, soggy handkerchief, and crossed the main corridor to the unmarked door of the detectives' bureau, located opposite the department's administrative and patrol offices. At least now, though still looking like a battlefield and feeling like a banana republic, the building was quiet.

I found Ron Klesczewski with Harriet Fritter, the detective-unit clerk and, for me, a gift from a bureaucratically sensitive god. They were standing over Ron's desk, shuffling through the results of the canvass. Here, all construction had been completed. An erstwhile maze of cubbyhole offices had yielded to two large rooms, the first of which was circled by four smaller ones—a lockup evidence room; an interrogation room with a small viewing closet; a lab; and an office for me. This first large room—the squad room—also held a cluster of four desks in its middle, cloistered from one another by head-high sound-absorbent panels. The second large room beyond served as a meeting/training area, with a VCR, a TV, some equipment lockers, and a conference table. All of it was pretty basic, but compared to what we'd had—once the air-conditioning was in place—it would be heaven on earth.

"Anything new?"

Klesczewski looked up. "Not yet. Enough people were wandering around last night, but it seems they all had their eyes closed. I called Hillstrom's office to see if the autopsy had been done yet, but they're still at it."

I tried to keep the irritation out of my voice. "Who did you talk to?"

"A secretary, I guess—I got her name here somewhere." He reached for the note pad near his phone.

I shook my head to stop him. "It doesn't matter. I just hoped you hadn't gotten Hillstrom herself. The last thing we want is to breathe down her neck—nothing pisses her off more. She'll call us when she's finished—she always does."

Klesczewski's face reddened and I realized I shouldn't have spoken in front of Harriet. Even if she didn't give a damn, his were the tender feelings of a man in his twenties, quickly stung by criticism.

"Sorry," he muttered.

"Don't worry about it. You didn't know. Can you leave that for a minute?"

His face cleared slightly. "Sure."

I crossed over to my office, which occupied a corner of the squad room, and closed the door behind us. All these offices had once all been taller than they were wide, in traditional turn-of-the-century style, leading some smart ass to suggest that we nail our desks to the walls to take advantage of the wasted space. The current remodelers had realized that for generations of winters we'd been warming the ceilings while the people below them froze. So now we had false ceilings, which were currently keeping the summer's heat nice and tight around our heads.

My office was, nevertheless, aesthetically appealing—ten by twelve, nice paint job, newly installed fluorescent lighting I never used, and three tall, hard-to-open, wire-covered windows that now stretched up to somewhere beyond the Styrofoam grid overhead. I sat behind my battered wooden schoolteacher's desk and parked my foot in the lower drawer. I motioned to Klesczewski to grab one of the two molded-plastic chairs, noticing as I did so the pink phone-message slip before me. "Call Gail," it read.

"So, where're we at?" I picked up the phone slip and began idly folding and unfolding it.

Klesczewski cleared his throat. "Nothing obvious in the canvass results, but I'm hoping we can find some inconsistency somewhere—a crack we can pry open maybe."

I nodded. It was a good analogy. Canvasses rarely gave us a man holding a bloody knife in one hand and a written confession in the other, but they did supply us with people's alibis before much thought and refinement had been put into them, a point that often played in our favor if a particular alibi later came under scrutiny.

Klesczewski continued. "Tyler's digging through his dirt, along with a couple of people from the afternoon shift. There'll be overtime filed."

"That's okay."

"DeFlorio's still out there, catching the home-from-work crowd."

"That makes me think of something," I interrupted. "We better look into people from outside the neighborhood who use that route to go to and from work."

"Night-shift types?"

"Yeah. You got late-night grocery stores and restaurants both above and below that section of Canal. It's conceivable somebody saw something while they were passing through."

"They'd have to have been on foot."

"Not necessarily. You get a pretty good view from the Elm Street Bridge, if you happen to look that way. What's Martens doing?"

Sammie, actually Samantha, Martens was the junior-most member of the detective squad, promoted from patrolman after Willy Kunkle lost the use of his arm the year before in a shooting spree with a maniac the local press had dubbed the "Ski-Mask Avenger." That same case had turned the town on its ear, causing Brandt to leave for a while and putting me in his chair in the interim. It was old news now, but, through no fault of her own, seeing Sammie Martens in plainclothes always reminded me of how out of control a case can become. I hoped I wasn't attending the birth of an instant replay.

"I put Martens on finding whoever was under the bridge. She's supposed to be combing the flophouses and dives."

I wrinkled my nose, which brought a smile to Klesczewski's face. We had both paid our dues traveling the dark side of Brattleboro's otherwise appealing working-class facade, and we could easily envision Martens holding her breath and watching where she stepped as she navigated the hallways of some of the town's dreary, ancient, and pestilent rooming houses.

I locked my hands behind my neck, feeling how slippery with perspiration they were. This heat was like nothing any of us could remember—an invisible fog of damp, suffocating, eye-watering steam straight from the equator. Stepping out of a cool shower in the morning, I couldn't even start toweling off without feeling my own sweat mingling with the water on my body.

It also got inside you, causing the mind to drift. I refocused on Klesczewski. "You have any feel for what we've got?"

He scratched his temple. I noticed his hair was dark with dampness. "Not really."

"No preliminary observations?"

He pursed his lips, then shook his head. "I guess I'll wait for some of the lab results."

I nodded. It was a legitimate choice, and one fitting the man. It hadn't been a test, or a way for me to expound on my own theory that the body had been planted for discovery. I'd spare him that. I just wanted him to know I was interested—that there was an outlet for something beyond the pure accumulation of facts, where the use of inventive brainstorming would be rewarded. One of the disadvantages of being on a police force that often served young people as a stepping stone to better jobs was that few of them took the time to get their noses out of the paperwork and give their intuition some exercise.

Klesczewski left me. I stared at the now-limp phone message in my hand. I was supposed to have dinner with Gail tonight, dinner and maybe more. I often stayed over on such evenings. Over the years, Gail Zigman and I had become best friends who had only then become lovers, an evolution that had stood us in good stead during rough times.

I called her at home, from where she did much of her work as a realtor. She laughed when she heard my voice. "My God, the rumors must be right."

"How do you mean?"

"That the body you found is causing problems. You sound like you're on a short break from the rack." Her tone darkened slightly. "It's not somebody I know, is it?"

I shook my head in wonder. For its size, which isn't inconsiderable, Brattleboro had the social infrastructure of an isolated mountain village. You could kick a man on one end of town and hear his fifth cousin, four times removed, yell "ouch" on the other. "Gail, we don't even have a name on him yet, much less whether he was a friend of yours. How did you find out about this, anyway?"

She chuckled again. "It's been several hours already; Ted McDonald's made it old news almost. Besides, I'm well connected."

That she was, being not only a realtor but also one of five town selectmen. In both capacities, she was frequently one of my primary news sources, as I suppose I was one of hers. "So what about the body is giving us problems?"

"Oh, nothing specific. I just heard there were complications, that the midnight oil was going to burn."

"Well, that much is true. I can't make it for dinner."

"I hope not. I put it in the freezer two hours ago. Do me a favor though, will you?"

"What's that?"

"Don't replace my dinner with Cheetos and Coke, okay?"

I laughed. "I promise—nothing that glows in the dark."

She snorted. "I bet, and try to get some sleep."

"Yes, mother."

I hung up, crumpled the pink phone message up, and dropped it into the trash can by my desk, the smile on my face fading as the realities at hand began to settle back around me.

Some of those realities, I knew, might end up involving Gail and me, assuming my dour instincts about this case proved accurate. As selectman and chief of detectives, respectively, we could, in times of crises, occupy opposite corners, with her peers clamoring for information, and mine playing close to the chest. And we were not, as I often wished, that detached from our jobs. Experience had shown us that our basic philosophical differences— hers far-left-leaning, mine stuck in the middle—could put a serious strain on our intimacy when the pressure was on.

I crossed the room to where Tyler had set up a makeshift laboratory in what had once been a good-sized janitor's closet. I knew the room was occupied because all the boxes that normally lived in it were neatly piled outside.

"Who is it?" Tyler answered my knock. I could hear the strain in his normally placid voice.

"Joe."

"Come on in."

I opened the door cautiously and was immediately assaulted

by a cloying wave of moist, sweat-anointed heat. The overworked suction fan in the ceiling screeched in an effort to make the air breathable. A second motor, attached to a large vacuum cleaner hooked to the drain of a special "dry sink," was also howling, trying to keep the dust out of the air, with marginal results. The noise made me wince in pain. J. P. Tyler and two other men were jammed inside a space in which one person could comfortably operate. They were standing at the two-wall counter, sifting dirt through fine-gauge wire meshes into the dry sink. On the floor, several more dirt-filled, labeled garbage bags awaited processing.

Tyler's face was dripping with perspiration and covered with a fine layer of dust.

"Jesus, you guys look like miners." I stood in the open doorway, not being able or willing to actually enter the small room.

Tyler's two equally grimy companions gave me acknowledging looks. Tyler, however, seemed totally oblivious. He wiped one cheek with the back of his rubber-gloved hand, thereby turning dust into a muddy smear, and gave me a broad smile—the lab man in his element. He looked around, as if suddenly discovering where he was. "Yeah. Tight quarters."

"It's boiling in here, and noisy."

"Oh, I guess it is." He glanced over at the other two. "Why don't we take a small break?"

The other two filed past me, no doubt wondering where in their job descriptions they'd missed having to play in dirt in a hundred-degree, hundred-decibel closed box.

Tyler tore a paper towel from a wall dispenser and wiped his face. "Well, we're getting a few things."

"Like what?"

"A Camel cigarette butt so far, and some dirt that seems like it came from somewhere else."

"All that dirt came from somewhere else."

He smiled ruefully, utterly unoffended—a reaction I could usually count on. Tyler was so lost in his own view of the world that irony, along with most other subtle forms of communication, affected him the way a mouse fart does a high wind. This made him both an excellent technical man and a lousy judge of human character. I hoped, definitely for our sake, and perhaps even for his, that he would never be promoted or hired away from the small niche in police work he so perfectly inhabited.

"You're probably right," he admitted. "But I thought I might keep a few samples to compare with whatever Hillstrom or the crime lab in Waterbury might come up with. You know, from the shoes and fingernails and whatever."

I nodded, remembering how clean I thought the dead man's fingernails had been at the funeral home. I wasn't too optimistic. "Did the photos come back yet?"

Harriet Fritter had overheard us. "Yes, they did. I put them in J.P.'s top drawer. There was another envelope with ten copies of the head shot. I gave those to Billy to be distributed to the patrol."

Harriet was the robust, widowed mother of five, grand-mother of eight, and great-grandmother of an infant girl. She seemed born to the task of making order out of chaos and, in the managing of her burgeoning brood, had turned discretion into the Eleventh Commandment. She'd come to us one year ago, looking for a challenging way to fill her hours, and had proved to be a paper-management wizard, an ability which had allowed me to stay being a cop instead of becoming an office jockey. If anyone asked me who really headed the detective bureau, I was hard pressed to deny her the honor.

Tyler tore off his rubber gloves and crossed over to his partitioned cubicle, right next to Klesczewski's, wiping his sweaty hands on his apron. He opened the top drawer of his desk and removed a fat manila envelope. "Needless to say, I haven't looked at them yet."

He poured out about seventy eight-by-ten glossies—two film rolls' worth, one taken by Patrolman Pierre Lavoie right after the construction crew called us in, the other taken by Tyler during the excavation, detailing its progress.

I pulled out one near the top of the pile. "This is what caught Ernie Wallers's eye—these smooth footprints." Wallers had been afraid he'd covered them all when he'd dug the hole down to the dead man's hand, but the photo I was holding showed at least one print, clean and in sharp focus, with a ruler laid alongside for reference. Lavoie had been very thorough.

Tyler looked at the picture carefully, his face peaceful and content. When there was none of this kind of work to be done, he was just another detective, digging into burglaries, car thefts, assaults, or anything else that came our way. To him, those times represented the desert between oases.

"Looks like one of those comfort-tread shoes; soft crepe sole running flat from toe to heel."

I thought of the print I'd made for Ernie Wallers in the dust. It had been similar, smooth and even, with no cut where standard soles curved away from the ground to make way for a hard, half-round heel. "Like what cops wear."

"Cops, nurses, ambulance attendants, people with bad feet. Here's where we found the cigarette." He showed me a photo of a patch of earth to the right of the partially uncovered body.

"I don't see anything."

"It's not there; this is an early shot. I'm just saying that's where it was—some two inches or so below the surface, meaning it was tossed there partway through the burial."

"Or placed to look that way."

He gave me an odd look. "You have a devious mind."

I couldn't deny it. I'd always thought it was an occupational hazard. "What'd you find under the bridge?"

"Haven't had time to analyze it yet. One thing, though—the guy obviously loved gum, and he wasn't particular. What you and Ron found was the latest sample, but he made lots of deposits. The neat thing is, he always lumped three sticks together to make a bigger wad."

"Three sticks at once? That's enough to choke on."

Tyler wrinkled his nose. "Yeah. The point being, it's a personality trait—something he always does. I thought you might like that as a tidbit till I can really look into the rest of it."

The phone buzzed on Harriet's desk. She left Ron's cubicle, picked it up, and motioned to me to grab it on Tyler's extension.

"Gunther."

"Hi, Joe." I recognized Billy Manierre's softly paternal voice. "John Woll just walked in—said he heard about the body on the radio. I showed him the photograph. Turns out he knew the guy."

I thanked him and hung up the phone. It should have been good news, which of course it was. But I didn't feel elated. Somehow, in my subconscious, a warning bell sounded in the distance. Perhaps it was the coincidence that the same officer who could identify our John Doe was also the one whose squad car was last seen parked near his grave.

CHAPTER 4

JOHN Woll and Billy Manierre were in the patrol lieutenants' office on the other side of the building's main corridor. Like my office, it had a rectangular window looking into the larger room outside—the patrol division's so-called officers' room. Unlike my office, it had only that window, being an interior room, and its view was one of utter confusion and bedlam. For while the lieutenants' office had been completed just the week before, the officers' room still looked like a practice hall for aspiring carpenters.

I stepped over piles of two-by-fours, tangles of extension cords, and around several stranded sawhorses to get to the office door. During the renovation, the patrol division had been relocated across the hall to our side of the building, in a large, dark room with no long-range purpose. Eventually, one corner of it was slated to become Billy Manierre's office, but for the moment, Billy had commandeered his present abode, despite its being both isolated from the rest of us and located smack-dab in the eye of the renovator's storm. I noticed as I crossed the threshold that the wall-to-wall carpeting, still smelling strongly of its chemical origins, was embedded with a snowlike trail of sawdust.

Billy Manierre, big-bellied, white-haired, and patrician in the deputy chief's dark-blue uniform he preferred over street clothes, filled the fanciest tilt-back, swivel office chair in the department, an item we were all convinced he'd intercepted on its way to the equally fancy new Court Building across the street. Opposite him sat John Woll—late twenties, narrow-bodied, thin-haired, wearing a permanent expression of weariness that made him look fifteen years older. He'd been on the force two years, was hardworking if uninspired, and was liked by just about everybody.

I perched on the corner of Billy's desk, noticing the photograph of the dead man lying next to me. "So, you knew this man?"

Woll nodded. "I went to school with him. His name was Charlie Jardine."

"What school?"

"Here—Brattleboro Union High."

"What year was he, same as you?"

"Yeah, '81."

I paused to pick up the photograph. Woll's answers were perfectly straightforward, but somehow terse. Given the circumstances—his being the one man in the department with important knowledge—I would have expected more excitement from him. Instead, he was waiting for the questions, apparently unwilling to supply what should have been a torrent of information, both trivial and vital.

"Were you friends?"

"More like acquaintances."

Again, I expected more and got nothing. "Did you keep up with him? Did he live around here?"

"Yeah, he lived in town—I'm not sure where."

"What did he do?"

Woll shifted in his chair. Throughout, his eyes had kept to the carpet. This wasn't unusual. He avoided eye contact as a rule, and generally appeared uncomfortable with superior officers. In fact, he was somewhat reserved with everybody. But I was still hearing the echoes of that distant alarm bell.

Woll very quietly cleared his throat. "I don't know exactly. We didn't keep up. But I think he invested in things."

"Stocks?"

"Stocks, bonds; probably more. I don't know for sure."

"Successful?"

"I guess."

"When we found him, he was wearing a fancy silver ring and a chain around his neck. Does that sound right?"

He nodded. "Yeah, he was sort of flashy—popular with women."

"Was he married?"

"No."

The answer was both abrupt and curiously final, and I wondered why. But I didn't ask—I didn't want to make this too personal. Not yet.

"When was the last time you saw him?"

John Woll shook his head and let out a sigh. "Oh, gee. I don't know. I'd see him around town, you know? In a car or walking on the sidewalk. But I haven't talked to him in years. We weren't friends or anything."

I lightened my tone of voice. "Well, it won't take long to get some kind of line on him. I gather you were on patrol last night near where Jardine's body was found."

Woll shrugged. "The embankment? I drove by there a couple of times, like always—even went down it once, but I didn't see anything."

"You went down it? Why?"

He looked at me, his eyes wide. Now that we were off Jardine in particular, Woll seemed more at ease, and more willing to talk. "It was strange. I thought I saw a light—something flickering just out of sight. So I got out to take a look. There was a road flare . . . you know that flat sort of path between the dirt slope and the unfinished retaining wall, the space they're filling in? That's where it was lying, kind of tucked under the wall like it had been thrown there. I went down to investigate, but that's all there was. I looked around with my flashlight, but I didn't find anything. I finally figured someone must've lit it and chucked it over the side—like a prank, you know? Teenagers."

"What did you do with the flare?"

"Stubbed it out and left it there. I couldn't see anybody. No point putting it in the car—it would've just smelled it up."

"Did you radio it in?"

"Oh, sure."

Out of the corner of my eye, I saw Billy nod slightly, confirming the claim. Obviously, he'd checked the night-dispatcher's log but hadn't gotten around to telling me yet.

Woll was watching us both. "Was Jardine found right there—right where the flare was?"

"We didn't find a flare."

There was a long, drawn-out silence. "I left it there," Woll finally said in a near whisper.

"You said you patrolled that part of Canal a couple of times last night. Was it about three o'clock when you checked out the flare?"

Woll looked at me in surprise. "Yeah, how did you? . . . Oh, the log."

"No—you were seen by a witness."

I was watching for a reaction—some show of fear or doubt, some flicker of culpability. The lack of one made me berate myself. I too liked John Woll, and had put in a good word when Brandt considered putting him on the payroll. He'd previously worked for us for several summers as a part-time "special officer" and I'd been impressed by his conscientiousness. During this questioning, however, I hadn't looked at him in that light. The coincidence of his knowing Jardine had loomed too large. Now, as I watched his open expression, the guilt was mine.

"John, when you were on that ledge looking around, did you notice what the ground looked like? The guy who found the body said there were fewer footprints where Jardine was buried."

He thought a moment and then shook his head. "I wasn't looking for prints, you know? I thought there might be someone hiding down there, or maybe some dead flares, or something. I didn't think to check for tracks. Like I said, I finally just figured somebody had tossed the thing there."

"How long a flare was it?" I asked.

"Twenty minutes."

"Was it set up, or just lying there?"

"Lying, like I said. If it'd been set up, I might have

checked for footprints. That would've looked suspicious, as if it'd been carefully placed there."

"Could you tell how long it had been burning?"

"Not really. It wasn't petering out, though."

I stood up and wandered over to the window. It had finally turned dark outside, and the officer's room was shrouded in gloom. It promised to be a real obstacle course on the way out of here, since the overhead lights hadn't been hooked up yet.

My view of the room was suddenly pierced by a small burst of light—the glassy reflection of Woll's lighter behind me being put to the end of a cigarette. I turned to look at him as the flame died and he inhaled.

He misread my interest and quickly blew out a cloud of smoke. "I'm sorry. Is it okay to smoke?"

"I don't mind. Billy?"

Manierre nodded. As Woll tucked the pack of cigarettes back into his breast pocket, I noticed they were Camels, the same brand Tyler had found in the dirt.

"John, did you ever get the feeling the flare had been put there to lure you to the ledge?"

"To get at my car, you mean? I didn't see anything wrong when I got back to it."

"No. I meant the opposite—that someone had wanted you on that ledge specifically."

"No. Why would they?"

Why indeed? I scratched my head. I was making too much out of this. Hell, I'd been around this town for so many years, it was amazing I didn't know Charlie Jardine, too. I couldn't walk down a single block without saying hi to half-a-dozen people most of the time. Was it any big deal, therefore, that John Woll had gone to school with the murder victim almost ten years ago? And he was probably right about the flare—it would have been the perfect prank to throw a lit flare over an embankment just as a police car was coming up the street.

But if that was true, then why had the flare been removed later? And why was Woll so reticent about Charlie Jardine? And why had a butt of his brand of cigarette been found in the grave?

I turned to face both men, Billy Manierre still looking like a silent Buddha in his chair. "Okay, John, thanks for coming in early. If you think of anything more about Jardine that might be helpful, let me know."

Woll stood up and crossed over to the door. "Sure will, Lieutenant. See you later."

I stood watching the door after he'd closed it behind him. Manierre's soothing, low voice hung in the air. "What're you thinking, Joe?"

I looked over my shoulder at him. "That maybe I've been in this business too long."

"I doubt that."

I sat in the chair Woll had occupied. "What did you think of that little chat—the first part?"

"He didn't look too comfortable. That might have been you."

"Me? Why?"

"John's not a tough guy—he might have felt you were putting him under the hot lights."

"I was a bit. I think he's holding back on Jardine."

Billy tilted his head to one side. "Wouldn't be the first time."

"What's that mean?"

"It means he holds back in general—that's partly why everyone likes him. The rest of us wander around gossiping about whoever's not in the room. Willy Kunkle was always a prime target for that, remember? But John's not that way. He minds his own business. I think you'll find out that maybe Jardine and John had it out over a girl in high school or something, and that John still feels bad about it. That would fit him like a glove, by the way. John's a bit of a brooder."

"He had a drinking problem once, didn't he?"

"That's what I mean. He's a good worker, though."

"Yeah. I was just remembering I recommended him to Tony."

"We all did, Joe. He's a good man."

I let out a sigh. "I guess that's the problem with a case like this. You think if you get the pin back into the grenade fast enough, maybe the damn thing won't go off."

"Well, I seriously doubt John Woll is your pin. Besides, he wouldn't be stupid enough to transport and dump a body while he was on patrol."

"I know, I know. It was just a coincidence I wanted to check out."

Billy stood up and stretched. "Well, I think I'll cross the hall and check on the troops."

I stayed in my chair. "Sure. And thanks."

Billy disappeared into the gloom beyond his door with the confidence of a man who knew his way through a mine field by heart.

CHAPTER 5

AT nine o'clock that evening, Klesczewski, Patrolman Jerry Mayhew, and I met up with Patrol Sergeant Al Santos at Fifty-five Marlboro Avenue, the residence of Charles J. Jardine. Santos had been on guard at Jardine's house ever since I'd sent him to find out whether the dead man whose photo we had was the Jardine listed in the phone book. Forty-five minutes after Santos had radioed in that a neighbor had confirmed the identity, we'd secured a signed search warrant.

It was a modest house, very neat and tidy, one-and-a-half stories tall with two peaked dormers and a similarly designed small roof over the front door. The trim and clapboards were painted different shades of gray-blue, offsetting one another nicely. The small square lawn had been mowed and edged. The houses up and down the wide street were comparable in size and appearance—a symmetry Levittown had made famous forty years before—although Jardine's was remarkably immaculate.

A little known grid of six short, intersecting streets surrounded by two cemeteries, a wooded ravine, and the Brattleboro Union High School, this section of Brattleboro looked airlifted from a quiet midwestern suburb. It was located on perhaps the highest point of land around, on the southern edge of town, which added to its air of serenity.

There was a sense of space here, unlike in the rest of Brattleboro, where most of the homes had a pushed-together look, the way a child hurriedly gathers his blocks together in a haphazard jumble on a bunched-up blanket.

Santos pulled a key from his pocket. "Neighbor had it—in case of an emergency. Apparently Jardine lived alone."

I looked beyond Santos to the house next door. A man in a baseball cap and shorts—and nothing else—was hovering on his front porch, shifting his weight from one foot to the other as if he'd been denying nature's call in fear of missing our arrival. My glance got him going like a starter's gun. He bustled through the screen door, came down his porch steps, and crossed over to us, his sunburned belly jiggling with every step. Absurd at it was, I envied him his attire. Despite the hour, it was still suffocatingly hot, and my pants and shirt clung to me like an unwelcome embrace.

"So what happened to Charlie?" The man smiled awkwardly and removed his hat, as if to reveal his honesty.

"I'm Lieutenant Gunther. Are you his neighbor?"

"Ned Beaumont—I lent this officer the key." He stuck out his hand. I could tell before I shook it what a spongy, unpleasant experience it would be.

I unobtrusively wiped my hand on the seat of my pants. I noticed he did the same with his. "Thanks, Mr. Beaumont. I'm afraid we can't say much right now—too early yet."

"Was he murdered? Was he the guy they talked about on the radio? I can't believe it."

I liked Beaumont's open face. His attitude, like his gut, was without guile. This was big news on the block and he had been the supplier of Jardine's key—a position of some importance to him. I saw no harm in catering to that, and hoped for some fringe benefits. "He may have been. We don't know for sure, and we're hoping to keep his name out of the limelight for as long as possible."

"Oh, sure; mum's the word. Wow. Murdered. Who did it?"

"We don't know that either. Where did he work, Mr. Beaumont?"

"ABC Investments. He was one of the partners."

I'd never heard of the firm; it sounded custom named for

a first listing in the *Yellow Pages*. "Did you know him well?"

"Not too well—just as a neighbor, you know? This was his parents' house; they're dead now. They were the ones who gave me the key, a long time ago, you know how neighbors do sometimes. He seemed like a real nice guy . . . How was he murdered?"

"An autopsy's being done on him right now so we can find out. When was the last time you saw him?"

Beaumont looked thoughtful, absentmindedly rubbing his stomach. "I guess it was yesterday morning. We go to work about the same time."

"Did you notice any activity at the house last night— lights, music, his car in the driveway?"

Beaumont smiled ruefully, perhaps with a touch of envy. "Charlie was a bachelor. Him not being home at night wasn't all that unusual."

"So nothing all night long?"

He glanced at the house. "Just the way it looks now."

"What was he like as a neighbor?"

Again, the thoughtful stomach-rubbing. "Nice. He was quiet—no loud parties or anything. He minded his own business; wasn't too outgoing, if you know what I mean. It wasn't that he kept to himself so much—he'd say hi when we saw each other and ask about the family, but he never had us over and never accepted our invites for a barbecue or whatever. But he was nice about it. I figured he just liked his privacy."

"Did you ever see any of his friends?"

Beaumont leered slightly. "Sometimes he'd have a lady friend over. He had real good taste."

"Did you know any of them by name?"

"Oh, he never introduced them. I would just happen to notice now and then, through the window or when I was in the yard."

"When was the last time he had a guest, that you know of?"

"Oh, I don't know. A week, maybe."

"A woman?"

"Yeah. Sometimes men would come by too, by the way."

"What did this woman look like?"

"Blonde—short hair . . . I guess they call it a page boy. She was real cute. Not much up here"—he patted his own fleshy chest—"but good-looking. She'd been by a few times before."

"You've never seen her anywhere else?"

"Nope, and I'd remember her—it was real blonde hair, almost silvery."

He looked at Jardine's house again and shook his head. "I can't believe he's dead."

I figured I wasn't going to learn too much more here, and I knew I could find Beaumont again if I needed him. Also, Santos had opened the door by now and Klesczewski was standing impatiently on the threshold. I stuck my hand out for another soft, warm, damp handshake. "I want to thank you for your help, Mr. Beaumont, and we appreciate your discretion. I'll keep in touch."

He opened his mouth to say something, but obviously thought better of it at the last moment. Instead, he backed away a few steps, gave us a half wave as Ron closed the door behind me, and muttered, "Anytime; mum's the word."

The inside of Jardine's house was surprisingly cool, and in the brief moment of quiet before we set to work, I could hear the muted hum of air-conditioning.

Santos noticed the same thing. "He must've been doin' all right to leave the AC on when he was at work." Santos was a transplant from Queens and had a thick New York accent—a detail that had startled more than one flatlander who'd had their vehicle stopped by him on the road.

"Could be a timer. Or maybe he thought he was coming right back," I muttered. Just because Beaumont hadn't seen Jardine at home since the previous morning didn't make it fact.

We divided our labor. Ron took the upstairs, Santos the basement, and Mayhew the garage. I took the ground floor, which consisted of a living room, a kitchen, a study which had once been a dining room, and a combination utilities and mud room.

It wasn't a terribly revealing environment, at least not on the surface. I'm a bachelor, too—a widower, actually—and my Oak Street apartment is like an old dog's kennel, filled with books and the bric-a-brac of a lifetime's memories. This home was store-bought, displaying more of J. C. Penney's current fashion statements than any of Jardine's character. The furniture went well with the wall paint, the calendar-art pictures, the fake-wool area rugs, and the occasional chunk of decorative antique farm equipment. Looking at it from the entryway, I thought the one thing none of this was designed for was a human being or two; it was perfect just the way it was—tastefully bland, neat, cool, and empty.

It also spoke of some quick money, and not a lot of it. None of what I was looking at would have been called "quality goods." Indeed, I'd seen similar interior decorating in upscale motels. From what John Woll had said vaguely about Jardine's occupation, coupled with his being "a partner" in ABC Investments, I guessed Jardine had benefited somehow from the 1980s feeding frenzy on Wall Street, albeit in a minor way.

The house's sterility allowed me to make quick work of the living room and kitchen, both of which were immaculate and lacking in telling detail. I discovered that Jardine should have checked more often under his sofa pillows for his missing change, that the last time he'd watched TV he'd been tuned to the Playboy channel, and that his culinary talents, although obviously not flashy, far outshined my own—meaning he made more of a meal than a pig-in-a-blanket and a can of fruit cocktail.

I'd been keeping my hopes high for what his office might yield, however, and after a quick look through Jardine's laundry—in which I found a woman's blouse—I settled in his desk chair to see if at last I could peel back a small corner of the blanket that shrouded this man's history.

First impressions were not encouraging; the top drawer was empty, a discovery I thought symbolic of the entire house.

The underlying question was, why? Was it that Jardine's moderate wealth had come so suddenly that he'd leapt from having nothing to a house full of furnishings without passing through those years in which the rest of us accumulate tons of junk? That didn't explain the parents Beaumont had mentioned. Jardine must have bent over backwards to eradicate all signs of their presence here, making an erstwhile family home into what looked like a weekend condo.

I hesitated before checking the other desk drawers, still lost in thought. There were other possibilities—a man without identification traced to a house without individuality. There was an almost ominous blandness to it all, the way aspects of real life are sometimes portrayed artificially on stage. I put that thought into a mental cubbyhole and began going through the rest of the drawers.

There I found the first signs of life—bank statements, insurance papers, credit-card receipts, utility and oil bills, IRS returns. I would immerse myself in all those later, fabricating a life from them as an archaeologist does from debris found in the dust. But at first glance, it all seemed utterly normal. Jardine had an income that averaged out to some forty-five thousand dollars a year. There were no gigantic debts, no large, unexplained deposits.

There was a Keith Clark desk calendar, one of those two-ringed plastic easels you can flip through, day by day. Again, it was mostly blank, barring the occasional cryptic note, like "R 2" or "G 730." Flipping through, I found concentrations of R's, G's, T's, S's, and more, with some extending throughout the year and others ending at the tail end of a clump. For the most part, whether bunched or spread out, they usually fell on Fridays or Saturdays. With Beaumont's appraisal of Jardine as a ladies' man, I was content to think for the moment that the initials stood for women's first names, some of whom were regulars, while others had apparently been brief and passionate affairs.

I leafed through the calendar a little more carefully a second time, focusing on a single discrepancy. Without exception, R had a single low digit next to it, usually a 2 or a 3, while all the others rated anywhere from 6 to 11, with the occasional 630, 730, and 830 thrown in for good measure. If these numbers stood for rendezvous times, then R had a fetish for either mid-afternoons or the dead of night.

The phone rang suddenly, causing me to drop the calendar in surprise. It stopped after the first ring, there was a click and a soft whirring sound, and then a gentle, modulated male voice filled the room: "Hi, this is Charlie's machine. Talk to it like you'd talk to me, and I'll get back to you as soon as I can."

There was a beep, a pause, then an irritated woman's voice muttered, "shit," and the line went dead.

I stared at the answering machine under the phone. A single beady red light was blinking on its front. I leaned forward and read the various labels imprinted in the black plastic. I couldn't remember if that light had been on when I'd sat down or not. I found a button marked "messages" and pushed it. Again the machine whirred, and I could hear the tape rewinding. There was another beep, and a woman's voice asked, "Charlie, I can't find one of my white blouses. Do you still have it? Call me before Thursday."

I pursed my lips. Why was it friends never identified themselves on the phone? Gail never did either. I was used to it now, of course, but at first it had thrown me for a loop, forcing my brain to scramble through its entire voice catalog in a desperate search for the right one, all while I tried to converse with utter self-confidence.

The machine spoke again—another female voice, hesitant, soft, almost fearful. "Charlie? I was wondering . . . I'd like to . . . call me, okay?"

A beep again and I heard the muted "shit" that had caught my attention to begin with.

I thought for a moment, still looking at the machine, and then reached for the telephone book nearby. I picked up the phone and dialed.

"ABC Investments."

"Hi. Is Mr. Jardine there?"

"The office is closed, sir. This is an answering service. May I take a message?"

"Oh, sure. Actually, it would be for his partner." I paused.

"Mr. Clyde."

I quickly flipped to the front of the phone book, talking while I did so. "Yeah, that's it—he's the one I really want to chat with." I found the listing. "Mr. Arthur Clyde."

The voice on the other end took on a slight edge. "That's what I said, sir—Mr. Clyde. What's the message?"

"I changed my mind—it's a little delicate. I think I'll wait until I see—" But the line had gone dead.

I smiled to myself and dialed again. A man answered—I could tell I'd woken him up.

I altered my voice. "Is this Arthur Clyde, of ABC Investments?"

"Yes." His tone became slightly wary.

"You around tomorrow? I was wondering if I could come by to discuss some investments I'd like to make."

The wariness yielded to controlled irritation. "I'm around, but I'd prefer that you called my secretary tomorrow at the office. She'll set up an appointment. Good night."

I hung up. Not knowing anything about Clyde or ABC, or even much about Jardine, I didn't want things to move too quickly. I wanted to learn what I could from Jardine's records before telling Clyde of his partner's death, and I knew that task might take me a good part of the night. The phone call had told me I had the right man, and that he'd be available in the morning. I turned to the sound of Ron Klesczewski coming into the office.

"Finding much?" he asked.

I shrugged. "I'd say the guy was a monk if it weren't for all the women on his answering machine. I've seen two-year-olds with more material possessions."

Klesczewski gave an uncharacteristic smirk. "He was no two-year-old, and I think his interests were way outside religion."

He crooked a finger at me and led the way upstairs. Given the layout of the house on the ground floor, I expected a conventional equivalent above. I was dead wrong. The entire second floor consisted of two enormous rooms—a bedroom and a bathroom, both of which had cathedral ceilings going right up to the apex of the roof.

The contrast didn't stop there. The rooms were not only disproportionately large, they were also as gaudily furnished as the downstairs was staid. The bed was circular, huge, and covered with a fake-fur coverlet and black satin sheets. It was a four-poster, but instead of supporting the traditional fabric canopy, the posts carried a round mirror reflecting back down on the bed.

There was also a fireplace—gas-fired for intimacy at the twist of a wrist and flanked by mirrored panels—and before it was an eight-foot-square fur rug with pillows. One wall had an elaborate stereo and TV system, controlled by a couple of remote units I saw parked on the half-round headboard of the bed, next to copies of *The Joy of Sex* and *The Sensual Massage*. The lighting was dim and indirect, as if designed for some Hollywood seduction scene. The walls were painted a dark, sensuous red.

The bathroom was similarly excessive, with thick rugs, a Jacuzzi, and a separate glass-walled shower stall so big it had several nozzles and a redwood bench inside. Again, mirrors predominated throughout.

"Jesus Christ," I muttered at last. "Looks like a whorehouse."

"Does seem he had a one-track mind. There's a ton of massage oils and weird creams in there, plus a couple of vibrators." He gestured to a cabinet over one of the two sinks.

"What else did you find?" I could tell from his expression that Klesczewski was feeling terribly proud of himself, especially knowing of my own slim pickings downstairs.

He smiled and led me back into the bedroom. Along another wall, next to the closet door, was a long, low set of drawers. Klesczewski pulled one all the way out and laid it on the floor. "Look at the back."

I did, and found taped there a Ziploc freezer bag filled with white powder.

"I didn't touch it, but I don't guess it's sugar." He paused and frowned. "I always thought coke was supposed to kill your sex drive."

"Maybe he wasn't the one using it."

Klesczewski looked slightly abashed. "Oh—right."

"Holy fuck."

We both turned to see Al Santos standing at the top of the stairs, looking around as if he'd just been exposed to the Sistine Chapel.

Ron laughed. "Yeah. Literally."

I placed a call to J. P. Tyler to let him know what we'd found, and asked him to come over and collect the cocaine. He could check the house more carefully tomorrow, but for now, I wanted at least that one piece of evidence under lock and key in the Municipal Building.

Santos and Mayhew took us on a tour of other parts of the house. It became apparent that a good deal of what I'd been missing in my search had merely been relegated to less traveled areas. Both the basement and the garage appeared more normal than the first floor. They were cluttered with skis and winter clothing and empty suitcases and automobile parts and boxes of conventional books. Somehow, that discovery set my mind at ease. I was no closer to finding out why or by whom Charlie Jardine had been killed, but at least now I felt he'd been a real—if slightly exotic—human being.

I had Mayhew relieve Santos baby-sitting the house. The graveyard shift would take over in a quarter hour in any case, since it was now almost midnight. The dread of the publicity and the bureaucratic hassles that had crept into me when we'd uncovered Jardine's body had by now been replaced by the familiar adrenaline of the hunt. Driving back to the Police Department with a boxful of evidence in my car trunk made me regret that in order to be halfway functional tomorrow, I would have to call it quits soon and go home to bed.

I parked near the department's private outside door, right beside where John Woll, now in uniform, was getting out of the passenger seat of his own car. His wife, Rose, leaned out the window as he circled around, and kissed him good-night.

I'd seen her before at department get-togethers, a pretty, slightly plump, dark-haired woman with an overly and permanently anxious face. I waved to her before I opened my trunk to retrieve the box.

She waved back and then called out to Woll, who was halfway up the steps to the entrance. "John, you forgot your lunch box."

He returned and took it from her, muttering a greeting to me. I stood at the back of my car, watching her drive away and hearing the door slam shut behind him, my heart hammering and my previous good mood destroyed.

The sense of dread I'd experienced earlier, of being in the way of some threat as implacable as fate, caught hold of me again. Only this time, recognition had made it abruptly more pressing; the urgency I felt now had less to do with solving a complex crime quickly, and more to do with the department's self-preservation.

The voice I had heard on Charlie Jardine's answering machine, the hesitant one who'd left no clear message, had belonged to Rose Woll.

CHAPTER

6

I didn't get to bed that night. I'd packed the answering machine's tape in the box I'd brought back from Jardine's place, and after I sent all the detectives home, I played it over and over in total silence, trying to hear in Rose Woll's voice things that weren't there to hear. I also leafed through Jardine's desk calendar, fighting the growing conviction that the *R*'s scribbled there stood for Rose, and that the hours opposite them were for two and three in the morning, when John Woll was on the midnight shift, as he had been for the last two years.

After about thirty minutes of this, I decided the only cure for the depression that now hung over me worse than the heat was to look at this mess analytically. I left my office to dig out Woll's personnel file.

Everyone's personnel files were kept locked inside the chief's office across the hall, available only to the chief and his deputy. Normally, access was only granted under their supervision, but I had asked Brandt earlier if an exception could be made in this one instance. Time, after all, was a crucial element here, and we both knew my penchant toward burning the midnight oil. He'd told me to be as discreet as possible and had handed me his keys.

The chief's office was located in the room next to the officers' room, in the corner of which Woll, Manierre, and I had met earlier. Now that both Brandt and Billy Manierre had gone home, however, the only other occupant on that entire side of the building was Dispatch, which was located in an open-doored corner room diagonally across from Brandt's glass-walled cubicle.

Using my own key, I entered the darkened officers' room from the hallway, risking my neck by tiptoeing across that carpenters' battlefield so I wouldn't have to use the primary entrance, whose lock was electronically controlled by the dispatcher.

I waited at the interconnecting threshold, around the corner from the dispatcher's open door, until I heard him acknowledging someone on the radio, which he could only do by turning his back to me. I then quickly crossed over to the chief's office, unseen and unheard. I was not taking Brandt's admonition to be discreet lightly. Not much happened in the department that didn't become common knowledge within a day. Being caught going through the personnel files in the dead of night would have been like dropping a lit match into a bucket of gasoline.

Using the parking-lot lights filtering through the window, I located the cabinet I was after and opened the appropriate drawer. I found John Woll's file by using a small flashlight I always carried in my pocket. It was a bizarre sensation, skulking around my own place of employment like a second-story man, all for the sake of discretion. By the nervous sweat that was beading my forehead, I might as well have been lifting someone's silverware.

As I eased the file drawer shut, I noticed a dilapidated oscillating fan sitting on top of the cabinet. The temptation was more than I could resist. If I was slated for an entire night in my hot coffin of an office, at least I could have the air being pushed around a bit. I tucked the fan under my arm and started to make my getaway.

I was halfway across the officers' room, feeling the euphoric rush of the successful thief, when the far door opened, a hand groped along the bare-stud wall, and the entire place was flooded in blinding light. I froze in double shock, not only because I'd been caught, but because I had no idea the lights had been connected.

As it turned out, that revelation served me well, for I blurted out without thinking, "The goddamn lights work."

Buddy, the night janitor, stared at me in startled amazement. "Oh . . . hi, Lieutenant. Yeah—they hooked 'em up this afternoon."

I chuckled and shook my head, relieved that my secretive ordeal was abruptly over. "I've been poking through here like a blind man, for Christ's sake."

Buddy was carrying two buckets full of sponges, rags, solvents, and whatnot, destined to maintain the dispatch office's brand-new luster. "What're you doin' here so late?" He suddenly looked down at the floor, as if the words had blurted out before he could stop them.

He was almost in his thirties, a somewhat scrawny-looking man with a pile of curly hair on his head and a pathetically wispy Vandyke. He'd been the night janitor for years, telling me once that he liked the privacy and the hours because they allowed him time to read. Indeed, he always had a paperback stuck in his back pocket, although I'd never been curious enough to find out what kind of books he preferred. He was generally quiet, sometimes painfully shy, and, I thought, apparently perfectly suited to his solitary job.

"Actually, I was about to commit a theft." I waggled the fan that was still tucked under my arm.

His eyes grew round. "That thing? If you don't mind me saying, that's not much of a theft—too noisy." He hesitated, while a nervous smile spread across his face. "You know, Lieutenant, if it's a fan you want, I could get you one as quiet as a whisper."

"From where?" I couldn't deny I was interested. I'd heard the chief's fan in action, and understood why he never had it on. My lifting it had been an act of pure desperation.

He gave me a lopsided grin, relieved at my lack of outrage. " 'Don't ask me no questions and I won't tell you no lies'; isn't that what they say?"

I hesitated. "How about a temporary loan, from someone who won't miss it?"

"Oh, sure. That's just what I had in mind. Be right

back.'' He piled his belongings along the wall and headed out the door.

"I'll be in my office," I called after him, and placed Brandt's fan on a nearby windowsill.

I returned to my own corner of the building. Under cooler circumstances, I actually enjoyed working here in the middle of the night. It wasn't only the silence that made it appealing, although the still phones and absence of people were definite plusses; it was also the odd satisfaction of being up when almost everyone else was asleep. I felt in the middle of the night as if I were capable of deeds unachievable in the daylight—as if I were endowed with ethereal powers.

Buddy found me as I was sorting through the contents of Woll's file, separating the bureaucratic confetti from the reports that might tell me something.

"Here you go.'' He wiped a large blue-and-white plastic fan clean with a rag from his pocket and placed it on my desk, fastidiously moving aside a large ashtray filled with paper clips. The fan was enormous and looked brand new. "Even goes back and forth, and it's got three speeds.''

He got down on his knees and plugged it into a baseboard outlet. The fan began swinging its mechanical head back and forth, as if sighing in resignation at the plainness of its surroundings. It was admittedly the fanciest thing in my office.

"See? Quiet as a whisper.'' He was grinning like a sweepstakes winner. Helping the chief of detectives in an interagency theft had obviously made his day. He slightly readjusted the fan's position.

"It's great, Buddy. I owe you one. What do I do with it after tonight?''

"No one's the poorer, I promise.''

"And you won't tell me where you got it.''

Again, he looked at the floor and grinned. "Nope. I tell you what—if anyone misses it, I'll take it back. It'll never happen, though. That okay with you?''

"I'm happy, Buddy. Thanks again.''

I waited until he'd left before I sat down to survey what I'd collected. The fan kept shaking its head mournfully, drying the sweat on the back of my hands and making the heat almost bearable. I pulled the ashtray full of paper clips near to me in case I wanted to mark any pages.

John Woll, as he'd told Billy and me, had graduated from high school ten years earlier. During his senior year, he'd been enrolled in the Law Enforcement and Fire Sciences Program at school and had won a scholarship to college, where he apparently intended to continue his police studies, hoping later to qualify for the F.B.I. While not a stellar student, he was inordinately "well rounded"; a hardworking perfectionist with a broad interest in extracurricular activities. Plans changed, however, for reasons I couldn't decipher from the files. The following fall, after marrying Rose, he dropped his college plans, forfeiting the scholarship, and signed up as a special officer with our department. Specials were one of those bureaucratic wonders—a compromise between the budget watchers and the people crying for more cops on the beat. They were allowed to work only a limited number of hours a week and were therefore excluded from the benefit package offered to their full-time colleagues. Also, they only had to take sixty-two hours of training at the Police Academy, instead of the standard fourteen-week course. The result, as I saw it, was a street cop with little training and no sense of job security—a wonderful entity worthy of the minds that had created it.

Whether because of this, or from the same mysterious pressures that had changed his college goals, John's job evaluations started issuing warning signs eighteen months into the job. He was still praised for his pleasant demeanor and his ability to steer clear of any inner-office bickering, but an undefinable uncertainty began entering the evaluators' comments; phrases like "vague on the future," "gung ho with little follow-up," and "workaholic habits, but not much to show for it," appeared in clumps at this point in his career. One evaluator suggested a counselor be brought in to identify what he thought might be escalating personal problems. That was never done. John Woll quit too soon after that entry appeared.

He went full time at a local manufacturing plant he'd been working at during his off hours with us, a place that turned out the elastic found in diapers and golf balls and women's underwear. I knew the building—long, low, and noisy, where every surface was covered by a thin veil of white powdery talc, used to keep the hot rubber from sticking in its course through the huge, high-temperature machines that kneaded it, cooked it, and transformed it from raw, brown rubber blocks into paper-thin elastic strips. It was a mind-numbing environment: the floor-shaking hum of the machines and the air-cleaning equipment relieved only here and there by the tinny sounds of rock 'n roll emanating from transistor radios.

The pay was good, the environment stultifying. The psychological nose dive that had swept John Woll from the Police Department continued unabated in the new job. He began to drink noticeably.

He was never stopped for driving under the influence, or for creating a public nuisance; to anyone's knowledge, he never broke any law as a result of his boozing. But he was caught nevertheless. His shift supervisor smelled liquor on his breath, discovered a bottle among his personal effects, gave him several warnings, and finally found him polishing off a pint in the men's room. He was ordered to either get some alcohol counseling or leave. He chose the counseling.

The recommendations accompanying his reapplication to the Police Department four years later were glowing. After the showdown with his supervisor, Woll began turning his life around. He signed up for company-sponsored "self-betterment" classes, made a few highly praised suggestions on improving management-worker relations, and finally ended up as a night supervisor himself. Whatever role his wife, Rose, played in all this was again not clear from what I was reading, but the overall picture was of a man wrestling his devils down to the mat.

When he did reapply to be a cop, we put him through an alcohol screening process, which he passed with flying colors. The good will he'd left behind combined well with his Cinderella comeback. He took the full Police Academy course and we welcomed him with open arms, no questions asked.

Until now. I closed the file.

For the rest of the night, I studied the documents I'd

removed from Charlie Jardine's house, arranging them in chronological order, trying to get a feel for the subcurrents of his life. What I found showed a combination of steady progression and good luck. Fortunately for me, he was a creature of habit, keeping to the same bank since high school, saving all his IRS returns back to the first one filed. There was no padding, nothing in the collection of a personal nature, like letters, diaries, or personal memos. But the dry, clear-cut residue of a paper-shuffling society more than made up the difference.

Jardine had not graduated from high school with the career goals of John Woll. Where John had turned a teenage interest in law enforcement into immediate employment by the Police Department, Charlie had stayed at home with his parents, at the same address I'd visited hours earlier, and had drifted about for a couple of years. His W-2 forms indicated a series of short-lived jobs in and around Brattleboro, at restaurants, car washes, gas stations, and finally, five years ago, at a lawyer's office as a "gofer." That had been the turning point.

I knew the law firm: Morris, McGill. It dealt mostly in corporate and criminal law, and represented much of the town's upper crust—that part which didn't deal directly with firms in New York or Boston. It was the biggest outfit around and its gloss obviously began to rub off on young Jardine. He started playing the stock market, gently at first, then with increased confidence. He set up an account at a brokerage house. For several years, he kept the same lowly position, but his bank and tax records reflected considerably more ambition and success than the job description implied.

His parents died within six months of one another and he inherited eighty-five thousand dollars and the house on Marlboro Avenue, free and clear. Now, suddenly situated, financially secure, and filled with an intoxicating sense that the golden ring was his at last, the one-time office boy made a direct leap to entrepreneur—he became founder, part owner, and partner in ABC Investments.

That had been a little over one year ago, which helped explain why the name of the firm had meant nothing to me when Beaumont had first mentioned it.

I sat back in my chair and rubbed my eyes. Despite the fan, I felt sticky and unwashed. The inside of my mouth tasted bitter and I was sure my breath could wilt flowers at twenty yards.

I wondered what connection these two young men shared, besides possibly the wife of one of them. Had they both known Rose in school? That was likely. Had she dated them both? Simultaneously? If so, had their triangle ended on a sour note, as most triangles do?

I crossed my hands on my stomach and stared at the reams of scattered paperwork covering my desk, much of it highlighted with my large pool of paper clips. Despite John having been at the site of Charlie's grave, and his wife's appearance on Charlie's tape machine, I didn't want to jump to any jealousy-fueled conclusions. I had dealt with people who sought revenge for infidelity. They fit a general type, albeit with rare exceptions, and John Woll was not of that type. He had none of the insecure and possessive qualities that found an outlet in violence upon others. Aside from the self-destructiveness that had marked his early twenties, his career as a cop had been spurred by his own harsh self-criticism. None of us could ever be as hard on him as he was on himself.

I was brought out of my reverie by a gentle tap on the door. Sammie Martens poked her head in. "Morning, Joe."

I looked at my watch. It was six o'clock. "Christ, Sammie, I just sent you home."

"I got some sleep. I wanted to come in early to give you my report. You seemed a little distracted last night."

I motioned to her to come in and sit. Hers wasn't the only report I'd stifled. Once I'd connected the voice on Jardine's machine to Rose Woll, I hadn't been in the mood to play lieutenant. I'd sent everybody home, whether that had suited them or not. "Let me ask you something, Sammie."

She sat down with her report folder on her lap. "Shoot."

"You're aware of the male stud's vision of what a woman wants most, aren't you?"

She couldn't suppress a little smile. As one of the few policewomen in the department, and the only one on the detective squad, she'd had more than her fair exposure to the convoluted and fragile male libido. "Muscles, macho, and fast fucks?"

I chuckled at that. Her flat-footedness was refreshing, especially coming from a woman as slight and demure in appearance as she. "How about mirrors over the bed and in front of a fur rug?"

She hesitated a moment, gauging the nature of the question. Her gender had also exposed her to an excess of sexual innuendo and outright abuse. I was gratified when she answered me directly, and with less than an innocent glint in her eye. "Depends who's on the bottom."

That was half of what I'd been thinking earlier.

Sammie crossed her legs and hooked an arm over the back of her chair. "What's this all about?"

Leaving out all mention of Rose Woll, I explained to her what we'd found at Jardine's place, coupled with the assumption that the initials in his calendar belonged to women. She shrugged at that. "They might all be women—some of them might be men, too. Brattleboro would be a good place for it."

And that was the second half of my little voice's chorus. Our city's homosexual population was impressively large, a point I was pleased she'd thought of too. It was helpful knowing I wasn't theorizing in a total void. There was one point she didn't mention, however, and which had always struck me when beds and mirrors were combined: To me, the mirrors not only reflected self-made erotica; they could also confirm one partner's domination over his or her mate, a significantly less sensual but all too human ambition. It put a definite chill on the image of Charlie Jardine as Casanova.

I got up and stretched. That was the downside to the early stages of an investigation: Nearly everything looks plausible. "Okay, what did you find out last night?"

Sammie opened her folder and began detailing her search for whoever might have spent the night under the Elm Street Bridge. She'd covered all the obvious bases—the flophouses and the halfway homes, the cheap hotels and the informal rooming establishments the Fire Department hoped would never catch fire. Windham County called itself the

"Gateway to Vermont"; some contended that with every gate you get a doormat, which accounted for Brattleboro's highly mixed population.

Indeed, from retired hippies to sawmill operators, from fancy doctors to drug pushers, and from established gentry to homeless unemployables seeking the nation's third-highest welfare check, Brattleboro had it all. Considering that it boasted only a meager twelve thousand inhabitants, that deeply varied demography was to me the city's biggest asset. It had made what might have been a sleepy, boring town just the opposite.

It also, however, made it a good place to hide, and from Sammie's conclusion, that's exactly what was happening. "I think maybe he's spooked."

"Why?" I asked.

"He'd been there a while—you could tell from the junk. The newspapers he used for the bed go back several weeks. So do the expiration dates on some of the food wrappers. Plus there're all sorts of cigarette butts and gum wads that indicate the regular life-style of a single person. A succession of bums wouldn't have been that consistent."

"So who spooked him, us or what he saw?"

Her face turned grim. "That's more than a rhetorical question. Late last night, just before you told us to punch out, one of the people I interviewed told me another guy had offered him five hundred dollars for the same information."

I sat up straight. "What guy?"

"He never saw him. My informant—Toby—hangs out on Elliot Street. He said he was leaving the Bushnell Apartment block and had ducked down that steep alleyway to the east—the one with the steps leading down—to do a little private drinking, when some man came up behind him, told him not to turn around, and said he'd pay five hundred bucks to whoever would take him to the latest tenant under the Elm Street Bridge."

"The latest tenant? He said that?"

She apologized. "No—those are my words. Toby said he'd look around; the guy said he'd be back in touch and then he disappeared. Toby told me it'd been like talking to a ghost. He even climbed back up to street level to double-check, although that doesn't mean much—he's a pretty slow mover. In any case, to answer your question, it sounds like our bum has all sorts of reasons to make himself scarce.''

I thought back to yesterday afternoon, when I'd stood where our homeless quarry had, on the bank of the river, looking up at the retaining wall. Was he running from us or some killer, or were they one and the same? After all, how did the killer know about the bum in the first place, unless he was in the Police Department?

Whatever the case, I couldn't argue the major point. If I was that bum, I'd be hiding in a hole so deep no one would ever find me.

CHAPTER 7

THIS time, I did bother to climb the stairs to the building's upstairs bathroom. I stripped off my shirt, tied it around my waist so I wouldn't get my pants too wet, and splashed as much cold water as I could on my face and torso to feel halfway revived. I then brushed my teeth, gargled some mouthwash, and put on a shirt I kept in reserve in one of my lower desk drawers. Gail had once commented that the Municipal Building had become a home away from home to me. She didn't know the half of it.

Whatever lift my sink bath supplied me evaporated before I was halfway to Brandt's office. The cool water of moments ago was replaced by the day's first prickly sheen of sweat. I didn't need a forecast to know our heat wave was still entrenched.

Nor did I need a watch to know it was early in the day—the air in Brandt's office, although as stale as a bar on a Sunday morning, was still smoke-free. The chief was remedying that by holding a lighter to his pipe as I walked into the room and dropped Well's file on his desk.

Gray clouds ballooned from his mouth as he glanced at the file, reading the name on the tab. I sat in the chair opposite his desk.

He blew some smoke toward the ceiling and leaned back,

propping one foot on the rim of his wastebasket. "Billy mentioned the three of you had gotten together."

It wasn't a breach of confidentiality. Billy's loyalty to the chief was similar to mine. I knew that what he told Brandt would be kept private between them. "Yeah. That was before I heard Rose Woll's voice on Jardine's telephone tape machine."

A deep crease appeared between Brandt's eyes. "They knew each other?"

"Apparently. The file didn't tell me anything new; it did remind me that John's had his rough times."

Brandt was quiet for a few moments, gazing vacantly out the window and letting loose rhythmically spaced puffs of smoke. He didn't even twitch when the circular saw outside awoke with a scream that sent me lurching to slam the door. He waited until I'd sat back down. "You better fill me in."

I did so, not only on John Woll, but also on our search of Charlie Jardine's house. The mention of the bedroom setup and the cocaine deepened Brandt's frown. During the "Ski-Mask Avenger" case of the year before, my best friend and predecessor as chief of detectives, Frank Murphy, had swept an apparently innocuous piece of evidence under the rug in an effort to streamline his investigation—a detail that had only loomed large after Murphy had lost his life and the department had been excoriated by the press and the selectmen. The specter of that mess was obviously beginning to stir in Brandt's mind.

When I'd finished, he removed the pipe from his mouth and examined it carefully, as if curious to know how it had gotten there. "Do you think Woll's involved?"

"I think it bears a careful look."

"That's not what the press will give it."

Especially the newspaper, I thought. The *Brattleboro Reformer* had been bought by a large midwestern media group, which had promptly fired the old editor and replaced him with a *USA Today* graduate with a passion for colorful, bite-sized news bits. His first executive decision had been to change the paper's logo from black to bright red. The Police Department's objections weren't restricted to the esthetic,

however. Stan Katz, whom the old editor had kept somewhat in check, had now been issued a license to kill.

"You want me to keep the double-Woll connection to
Jardine under my hat for a while?"

"Yeah. No reports, no memos. If it blows, we'll own up
to it, but not until then."

"Does that include the state's attorney?"

"Yeah."

That sent a chill down my spine. I too remembered how
the shit had hit the fan as a result of Murphy's tidying up of
the evidence. I couldn't argue with Brandt's short-term
desire to simplify all of our lives, but I worried about the
cost of such streamlining further down the road. For the
second time in just a few hours, my concerns wandered
from the strictly professional. I worried how a decision like
this might play between Gail and me later on. "Is that
wise?"

Brandt fixed me with his pale eyes. "You going to talk to
the Wolls soon?"

"To her, certainly. Then it depends."

"All right. Let's keep it quiet, at least till we see what she
says. Could be someone else has a voice just like hers.
Maybe I'll tell Dunn then. As for John, I want a pretty good
idea of his role here before his name becomes public
knowledge. So far, all we've caught him doing is his job."

I got up. "It's your call." I thought he was being a little
harsh on Dunn, and perhaps foolhardy. Odd as he was, I'd
never known the SA to leak information—or to overlook a
slight.

Brandt caught my tone of voice. "Think I'm being
paranoid?"

I shrugged, still troubled, not wanting my personal concerns to cloud my judgment. "You know the stakes more
than anyone. I won't deny information leaks out of here like
a sieve. Still . . . I'll let you know what I find out."

•　•　•

The detective squad does not hold to a regimented schedule. There is no roll call, no single hour at which all

members punch in. Usually, they show up at half-hour intervals, a system which allows them to leave in the same order, and thereby have the office staffed by at least one person until eight o'clock at night. As a result, on any given morning, I'm lucky to find even one of them in attendance when I usually come in at seven-thirty.

This morning, it was seven-ten, and the entire squad was ready and waiting.

I led the way into the conference room and sat at the head of the long table, waiting until everyone had found chairs, arranged their coffee, doughnuts, and note pads, and had finished the last one-liners.

I gained their attention by tapping my pencil on the edge of the table. "You all did nice work yesterday. Starting cold, we got an identity, a residence, and some inroads on a possible witness. The medical examiner should be coming through with some more on the cause of death either today or tomorrow, and maybe J.P.'s dirt-sifting will add something."

DeFlorio pretended to wipe some of that dirt off his pad. "It already has."

"I spent a few hours going through Jardine's papers last night. I've listed his various jobs and what years he held them, along with how much he made, who he banked with, and those places where he seemed to shop most often, at least according to his credit-card slips and canceled checks."

Harriet Fritter handed out copies of a fact sheet I'd deposited on her desk earlier.

"Charlie Jardine left a pretty good paper trail, but not much personal information. We didn't find any letters, diaries, or tapes. It seems, however, that he did have at least one unusual kink to his personality." I went on to describe what we'd found at his house, especially the upstairs, omitting only the fact that I'd tied a name to one of the voices on the answering machine.

"I didn't ask you yesterday, but do any of you have anything on your case loads you cannot move to the back burners?"

I actually knew their case loads pretty well, so the question was largely rhetorical. Still, it seemed a friendly idea to let them decide for themselves. No one said a word.

"Okay." I looked at each of them as I went around the table. "Sammie, I want you to stick to finding whoever was under that bridge. Ron, dig into Jardine's background—what he was like at school, who he hung out with. You might want to get Lavoie to help you; he's probably dying to get out of uniform. Dennis, expand the canvass to Jardine's neighborhood; check for anyone who saw him the last day he was alive. His next-door neighbor, Ned Beaumont, might be a place to start. By the way, I'm going to hit his business partner, so I'll tell you what I find there. J.P., just keep sifting, and let me know as soon as you get anything back on that cocaine. I'll have Harriet photocopy whatever bits of Jardine's paperwork you might find useful."

"As you can see from the handout, Jardine's last place of employment before going solo with ABC was Morris, McGill. I'm going to dig into them, too. Okay—questions, comments, ideas?"

For the next fifteen minutes, there was a round-robin discussion, each person letting fly their impressions of the case so the others could benefit—or not—from the experience. At this early stage, it wasn't very constructive, but I was heartened by the general enthusiasm.

I motioned to Ron Klesczewski to stay back as they all finally filed out the door. "You probably saw in this morning's dailies that John Woll was driving the patrol car that was parked on Canal."

Klesczewski nodded. The dailies were a summary of the preceding day's activities, distributed at the start of every shift.

"Well, you might find in your travels through Jardine's past that he and Woll went to high school together."

Ron gave me a rigidly neutral look. "Oh, yeah?"

"I've already talked to him about it. John says they were just acquaintances, but let me know if you find out differently. The thing is, keep it subtle. I think the chief's a little twitchy."

"Sure. By the way, you didn't find any old phone bills in Jardine's files, did you? It might be a way to find out who his friends were."

I didn't let it show on my face, but inwardly I cursed

Brandt's decision to keep the Wolls' connection to Jardine a secret. It hadn't been more than an hour, and already I was having to lie to my own men about it. Perhaps with a touch of malevolence, I passed the buck: "I found 'em, but the chief's got them now. I'll see if I can prod him a little."

"Thanks." Klesczewski gathered his things and left. It was true that any calls Jardine might have made to Rose or John Woll would have been local and not on any bill. For that matter, I didn't even know if Rose had made more than the one call I'd overheard. But I hadn't had a chance to analyze those bills myself to see if he'd ever called her or John at any recognizable long-distance number, and I didn't want Klesczewski to get that lucky. It was that bit of subterfuge that left a bad taste in my mouth, and sharpened my concern. Keeping this connection a secret could well end up alienating me from my entire squad.

•   •   •

Main Street in downtown Brattleboro is a throwback to New England's late–nineteenth-century industrial era, its double row of solid, ornate, red-brick buildings a tribute to capitalism's smug sense of immortality, here largely founded on the Estey family's parlor-organ empire that had made the town the organ capital of the nation for almost a hundred years. Over recent decades, however, those monuments have yielded their own irony, for while the ground floors have catered to an ever-changing succession of retail businesses, the floors above either become noisy, smelly, peeling, low-rent apartments, or professional offices for hopeful but underfinanced entrepreneurs. ABC Investments was on the third floor of number 103, several doors down from the 1930s Art Deco Paramount movie house.

Number 103 was a walkup, like most of its brethren, cored by a wide, linoleum-skinned staircase. If the exteriors facing Main Street combined antique charm and stolid optimism, the interiors of these buildings went deeper. Dark, soiled, sagging, and retrofitted with a crosshatching of pipes and cables to meet modern safety codes and conveniences, these hundred-year-old walls and lofty, cobwebbed ceilings spoke of pure endurance. Once I was within their embrace, their concession to economic survival was revealed by the sounds of typing from behind one door, contrasting with the snarls of a domestic dispute from another.

"ABC Investments Corp." was carefully painted on the frosted-glass upper panel of an otherwise dark wooden door. I entered to the angry buzzing of a dot-matrix printer churning out an endless ream of paper, and into a solid mass of blessed air-conditioning.

A hefty young blonde woman turned from the machine as I closed the door. "May I help you?" She smiled.

"I'm here to see Mr. Clyde."

Her eyes widened a fraction, but she was no less friendly. "Oh? Did you have an appointment?"

"No, I'm from the police; Lieutenant Gunther."

That killed the smile. "Oh, dear." She worked her way around the desk and crossed over to one of two closed doors on the west side of the reception area. She knocked briefly and disappeared.

Jardine and Clyde had gone to some lengths to distance themselves from their stairwell's appearance. A lower false ceiling had been emplaced, the walls painted and decorated with soothing southwestern prints; the floor was covered with a thick wall-to-wall carpet. The furniture also was new and impressively weighty—as recent as, but a step above, what I'd seen at Jardine's house. Maybe Clyde had been the one to shop for the business.

That hunch was confirmed when the receptionist returned to usher me into Clyde's office. The room, with two large windows overlooking Main, was quintessential transplanted old Bostonian—lots of burnished wood, padded leather, and glass-paneled bookcases—as incongruous in this building as if it had been on shipboard.

Behind a massive antique partner's desk was a large, white-haired man in a seersucker suit and a red bow tie, looking vaguely like Spencer Tracy in *Inherit the Wind*, except for the face, which was square, florid, and utterly without expression.

"Have a seat." The man's voice was not unpleasant, but

it too lacked any warmth. He hadn't offered his hand, or moved from his chair in greeting, so I followed his suggestion and sat.

But that was all I did. This was not an outgoing man, at least not with strangers, so I thought I might encourage him to talk by keeping my mouth shut. There was also an element here, perhaps a combination of the stuffy furnishings and the coldness of their owner, that rubbed my plebeian fur the wrong way.

The silence lasted a very long thirty seconds. He finally sighed, his brow furrowing, and said, "I'm told you're from the police."

I nodded. "Joe Gunther. I was wondering if you could tell me when you last saw your partner."

There was another pause, this one quite calculated. Clyde's eyes were as impassive as ever, but I could almost hear his brain whirring at high speed, analyzing the implications of my question. People who deal with other people's money often have good reason to conjure up private paranoid fantasies. My guess was that I had pushed this man to abruptly struggle with a few of his.

"The day before yesterday. Why do you ask?"

"Was that in the evening—quitting time—or earlier?"

"I last saw him when we closed for the day. Do you plan to tell me why you're asking these questions?"

I tried to sense something more than simple growing irritation in his voice, but I couldn't, either because he'd had too much practice avoiding the truth or because he was being honest. I reached into my pocket and extracted one of the head shots of Charlie Jardine that Tyler had taken. I tossed it onto Clyde's desk. "If that's him, we found him in a shallow grave yesterday, on Canal Street."

I don't know what I'd expected with that melodramatic and tasteless ploy. Whether it was the lack of sleep or the air-conditioning that had lulled my common decency, I was thoroughly embarrassed by the reaction I got. Clyde leaned back in his chair as if I'd pushed him, his mouth half open, his eyes wide with shock, his face suddenly pale. "My God, that can't be."

I half rose from my chair. I had guessed Clyde to be a

well-preserved seventy years old. Now he looked a hundred. "Are you okay?"

He blinked a couple of times and touched his forehead. "I read about 'an unidentified body' in the newspaper this morning. I told my wife how I'd hoped we'd left this kind of thing behind us in Boston. It never occurred to me . . ." He pushed his chair away from the table and leaned forward, his elbows on his knees. "Charlie . . . My God."

When he looked up at me again, I felt like the first three minutes of our meeting had taken place in a dream. The man before me now was old, tired, sad, and perhaps a little frightened. His suit, like his surroundings, looked less like the trappings of establishment arrogance and more like the shell protecting what was left of the ancient turtle within.

"What happened?"

I retrieved the photograph. "We don't know. We're trying to look into every corner of his past to find out."

He shook his head and stood up, rubbing his hands across his stomach. He suddenly stabbed a button on his intercom. "Ginny—get me a glass of water."

He stood with his back to me, looking out the window. Ginny came in, nervously glancing at both of us, and placed a glass on the desk. "Will that be all, Mr. Clyde?"

"Yes, thank you." He waited until she'd left before turning around. He drained the glass, wiped his mouth with a handkerchief from his back pocket, and took a deep breath. I was watching a process of reconstruction so determined, it was like seeing a house rebuild itself brick by brick. He even seemed to reinflate slightly inside his clothes.

When he finally regained his seat, he was almost as I'd first seen him, albeit minutely frayed. "How may I help you?"

It had been an impressive full circle, a roller-coaster ride from utter control, out over an emotional abyss, and back again. "First, an odd question: What was he wearing when you last saw him?"

Clyde's eyebrows rose slightly. He paused to remember. "Pale tan suit, white shirt, and some light-patterned tie."

So he'd gone home to change before getting himself killed. Not only had we found him in different, more casual clothes, but I also remembered the suit hanging in the laundry room, presumably for some touching up or ironing. Also, since we had found no automatic timer at the house, it reinforced the theory that the air-conditioning had been turned on in the house by Jardine in expectation of his own return that night.

"When did you first meet Jardine?"

"About a year and a half ago. Tucker Wentworth introduced us."

Tucker Wentworth was the senior partner of Morris, McGill, Jardine's prior employer for five years. "Why did he do that?"

That brought a faint, humorless smile to Clyde's lips. "Because he knew I was becoming bored. I come from Boston, Mr. Gunther, where for my entire professional life I was an investment broker. My wife and I moved up here when I retired, I half believing in her notions of a bucolic life of gardening, reading, and long summer strolls. But within a few months I was about ready to murder her and lay waste to the countryside. The sight of flowers almost made me ill. I needed something to stimulate my mind. Tucker seemed to think Charlie might be the answer."

"With this business?" I waved my hand around the room.

"Yes. It's not much, but it did the trick. My background was in analysis; Charlie had a propensity for sales, which I loathe. Tucker suggested we could make a workable odd couple—two men steering a canoe straight by paddling on opposite sides of the boat. That was his image, incidentally. Canoeing is quite a pastime with him."

By now, all signs of shock had seemingly vanished from Clyde's countenance. He even interrupted himself to offer me coffee. I turned him down. "What did you know about Charlie Jardine?"

"At first? Nothing. In fact, on first meeting him, I thought Tucker had lost his mind. Charlie's style and mine are . . . were pretty far apart. But there was no dishonesty there; we openly discussed how we could and could not work together. Perhaps it was that immediate frankness that appealed to me. There were never any bones made about how I disliked what Charlie did—you know, selling the product—or how he thought the nuts and bolts were 'a drag,' to use his phrase.''

"So you hit it off, despite your differences?"

Again the humorless smile. "You make it sound like a blind date. No, it was a gradual process, stimulated by both Tucker's prodding and my wife's insistence that I start a garden."

"But Charlie was a pretty genial guy?"

He tapped his chin with the tips of his fingers. "In an artificial sort of way. He reminded me of a good many of the young sharks I saw in the city. Let's say that while the source of our mutual interest was shared, our motivations were quite different."

It seemed the farther we got from the shock of Charlie's death, the cooler Clyde's demeanor became. I also was struck that he wasn't bending over backwards to burnish Charlie's memory, as one typically does with the dearly departed.

"Meaning you both liked investments, but while he was in it for the money, you just wanted to stay out of your wife's garden?"

This time he actually chuckled. "That's certainly accurate, although I like making money, too."

"What were his qualifications?"

Clyde's eyebrows shot up. "Ah, yes. Well, that was the rub, as I saw it, when Tucker first approached me. Charlie didn't really have any experience. A local high-school graduate, an undistinguished string of short-lived, low-paying jobs—not very promising. But that was on paper. In person, Charlie could be quite persuasive, and Tucker had taught him well."

"Tucker knows a lot about stocks?"

Clyde gave me a quizzical look, one usually reserved for people fresh off the fruit truck. "You could say that."

"I'm afraid someone in my position wouldn't know much about that."

"Of course. Well, Tucker Wentworth is extremely qualified. His background encompasses not only corporate law, but investment banking as well, a career he pursued prior to moving here twenty years ago. Charlie couldn't have found a better tutor in the entire southern half of the state.''

"So it was really Wentworth's recommendation that won you over."

Clyde became abruptly guarded. "Among other things."

"Like what? Did he help fund ABC?"

"I'm not sure that we're not going off on an irrelevant tangent here."

The ponderous double negative made me smile. "Meaning that's none of my business."

Clyde looked uncomfortable. "I don't wish to be uncooperative, but I do have certain confidentialities I must maintain. I'm sure these matters have nothing to do with Charlie's death."

I couldn't have disagreed more, but I wasn't about to admit it. Until I had a subpoena in my hand allowing me to grab all of Jardine's papers, I wasn't going to display the slightest interest in them. "You're probably right. Somebody did kill him, though. Was there anything about his personal life that might have led to that?"

Clyde shrugged and made a face. "Ours was a business relationship, based on mutual advantage. Tucker Wentworth may have known him well; I did not. I don't even know where he lives . . . or lived."

"You never saw one another outside the office?"

"Well, yes, I'd see him on occasion, maybe to meet a prospective client at a bar, or maybe even in the street on a Saturday or something. It's a small town, after all, but we didn't socialize."

"You didn't know any of his friends?"

"Only Tucker."

"Did he talk about himself much? His family, background, likes, dislikes, ambitions, what have you?"

The other man sighed and gave a surreptitious glance to his watch, a gesture carefully designed to catch my eye. "He may have tried at first, but I wasn't interested. My vested interest was in his ability to bring in the accounts, not in his past history and pipe dreams."

"And he was bringing in the accounts."

"Yes. Considering that starting a business of this nature

can be slow, he did remarkably well. He could win people's confidence quickly, like any good salesman."

Dismissive disclaimers like that one had littered this discussion like falling leaves. Arthur Clyde was an old-time aristocratic snob, and I began thinking Charlie had been well served by not sharing his thoughts with him. On the other hand, maybe there was more to it than just snobbism. "You didn't like Charlie much, did you?"

Of the options available to him, Clyde chose the least appropriate. He gave a false smile and a good-old-boy wave of the hand. "Charlie was a charming person; people instinctively warmed to him."

"But you didn't," I persisted.

The smile crystalized. "That wasn't the basis of our arrangement. Our backgrounds were entirely different."

I let it go; he apparently wasn't going to break down and confess to anything. "I understand; we run into that in the Police Department, too, sometimes. So you just kept it professional, right?"

His face had regained its previous haughty rigidity. "It did seem the best way to go."

I pushed on the arms of my chair and stood up. "Well, I'll leave you be. If you think of anything that might help us out—some personal or business detail that might tie in to Charlie's death, even vaguely—give me a call."

Again, he didn't get up, didn't offer his hand. "I'll help in any way I can."

Especially after I get that subpoena, I thought, as I showed myself out.

CHAPTER
8

I paused at the building's entrance, blinking away the bright sunlight and trying to reacclimate to the heat. I was wondering how many such brutal contrasts would eventually lead to pneumonia when I recognized Ted McDonald's official, antenna-festooned WBRT car parked diagonally across the street. McDonald was just pulling his bulk out from behind the wheel, his eyes fixed on the upper windows of the building I'd just left. I recalled then seeing a small "ABC Investments" sign perched on the sill behind Arthur Clyde's desk. That meant the cat was out of the bag—that either Brandt had held a press conference revealing Jardine's name, or McDonald's old-boy network had yielded him another golden nugget.

I was still standing in the shade of the doorway, I hoped unobtrusively. I waited until McDonald ducked back into his car to retrieve his recording gear, and then I cut north, away from him and toward the Paramount Theater.

My next planned move had been to visit Rose Woll at her job in the Vermont National Bank Building, the front entrance of which was directly beyond McDonald's car. Now, dreading any encounter with the press, I thought a flanking maneuver was in order.

I strolled to the pedestrian crossing where High Street dead-ends into Main, and waited for the traffic to stop.

Leaning against the far side of the lamp post, I peered back at McDonald jaywalking in a beeline to Jardine's office. I let out a sigh of disappointment.

From my current vantage point, it was a straight shot to the Dunkin Donuts on the opposite corner, which, given my sudden change of mood and my gastronomic proclivity, was an extremely inviting harbor. It was also a necessary one, as I saw it. I hadn't eaten since the night before and, like Pavlov's dog, that fact hit home with a jolt as soon as I saw the pink and orange sign. Sacrificing all to camouflage police business from the media, I ordered a coffee, a Bavarian creme, a double honey-dipped chocolate, and an orange juice. By the time I finished, I figured I'd have a clear shot at the bank's rear entrance via the Harmony parking lot.

Even if there hadn't been a press conference, I wasn't too surprised McDonald had put the name to Jardine's body. I sometimes thought both he and Katz had more connections inside the Police Department than I did. Any fact that became part of almost any document usually found its way into their hands sooner or later, regardless of the restraints put upon it, which is why Brandt had stressed we keep the Wolls' involvement in all this to ourselves.

The irony was that most cops pride themselves on keeping their mouths shut. Among themselves, however—and the greater fraternity of deputy sheriffs, state policemen, state's-attorney investigators and prosecutors—they often felt free to talk confidential shop. It was the same age-old human impulse that had given "I've Got a Secret" high ratings for years. And given the sheer number of people that were finally involved in this grapevine, I was more often surprised when McDonald and his colleagues actually missed a story now and then.

The Harmony parking lot occupies the entire center of Brattleboro's primary business block and is entered through a low, narrow, vaulted tunnel, reminiscent of the entrance to a medieval castle. Inside, the encircling buildings form a near-solid courtyardlike wall. There's an abrupt lessening of the hustle-bustle here; the strong, weathered, ugly backs of the buildings, the recently planted trees among the parking meter islands, and the presence of a café poised on the roof of a single-story outcropping all lend to a feeling of cloistered serenity.

From the parking lot, I cut a diagonal path to the bank's back door.

Rose Woll worked in customer relations, a small cluster of desks in the corner of the bank's recently revamped lobby. There were few people needing help this morning, and all of them were at tellers' windows, so Rose was sitting at her desk alone, staring at a computer display. I noticed as I approached that her hands were in her lap, idle, and that her eyes were vacant and unmoving. The computer might as well have been off.

"Rose?"

She jumped in her seat and looked at me, her face pale. "Lieutenant."

"Are you all right?"

"Of course." But a sudden trickle of tears down her face made a lie of it.

"Can we go somewhere to talk?"

She nodded without speaking or getting up. I gestured to a neighboring desk where one of her colleagues was watching us with keen interest, a sheaf of papers still clutched in her hands. "Can you cover for her for a while?"

"Of course. Is there anything I can do to help?"

"No. I think we'll be okay. She just needs a couple of minutes." I circled the desk and took Rose by the elbow. She got up and led the way to the back of the lobby and a short hallway lined with doors. Behind one of them was a small, empty cubicle with a counter and two chairs, presumably designed for pawing through safety boxes in privacy.

"Tell me about Charlie Jardine, Rose."

She was wiping her cheeks with the back of her hand, her body shuddering with her sobs. I didn't know her well—she was one of many spouses I saw primarily at department picnics. But her emotional state encouraged an intimacy we'd never shared.

I reached over and took her hand away from her face. Her eyes focused on mine. "Did you love him?"

She left her hand in mine and gave an exaggerated shrug,

her face contorted with sorrow. "I don't know. I did, but he wasn't . . . it never would have worked. We always knew that. But he . . ." She left the sentence unfinished.

"Did John tell you about his death?"

She nodded silently.

"Did he know about you two?"

She dropped my hand and wiped both her eyes then, shutting off the tears and struggling for composure. "He's always known. We were all friends in high school."

"John and he were close?" I was remembering Woll's vague comments about Jardine the night before.

"I was the link. I dated them both."

I was so used to these kinds of interviews evolving slowly that her immediate intimacy startled me. I changed gears to keep her going. "So they were really rivals."

She shook her head emphatically. "They weren't rivals. I just couldn't decide. They were so different; I was the only thing they had in common."

"Who pursued who in the long run? Did you really want Charlie and end up with John?" Even with my scant knowledge of the three, that would have seemed believable.

"That makes it sound so bad. I chose John. I love him very much. I knew he would be dependable, and that Charlie would always be chasing rainbows."

A practical choice, I thought, and a surprising one, given Rose's naive appearance. Of course, sometimes appearances are cultivated to good purpose. "Sounds like he hit the pot of gold anyhow."

"That was later. Back then, he was wild and funny and caring. A 'reckless dreamer,' I called him, but undependable." She half smiled.

Her face had cleared somewhat, still stained with tears and flushed. She was no beauty, but she emanated a tangible sensuality with an open, innocent face and a body given to suggestive fullness.

"You married John because he was safe."

She took offence, but only slightly. "I married him because I loved him."

I didn't respond. Speaking to her was like watching for

movement at the bottom of a stream, an effort thwarted by shadows, reflections, and self-doubt.

"And he was dependable," she added.

"Why did John drop his scholarship and his chance to go to college?"

Her eyes welled up again and her lip quivered. She was emotional enough right now for any reminiscence to cause tears, no matter how trivial, so I had no idea what had set her off. I played it safe by silently taking up her hand again and giving it an encouraging squeeze.

She returned the gesture and smiled sadly. "I was pregnant."

That was certainly not trivial, nor had it appeared in any paperwork I'd studied. "And you lost the baby later?"

Silently, wiping her cheeks again, she nodded.

"I'm sorry, Rose." I let a moment pass for that to sink in, but I had to keep going. "So what happened between you and Charlie?"

"He understood. We kept in touch. We were always friends."

All of which told me nothing. Her show of openness had been reduced to three telegraphic sentences, closed doors I had to get through by presuming I already knew what lay behind them. I felt now that my night's reading was yielding benefits. "Until John began drinking."

She became very still, looking at me in wonder, a prior acquaintance who now seemed to know a great deal about her. "He got so wrapped up in himself. I kept asking him what was bothering him, but he wouldn't talk."

"Did Charlie know about the drinking?"

"Not until I told him. After school, he and John never saw each other."

"So when you said John knew about you and Charlie, you didn't mean as lovers."

"No . . . Well, yes, in high school . . . And just recently, but not in between."

There was an awkward silence. I changed tack to safer water, keeping her reference to "recently" in the back of my mind. "What do you think made John hit the bottle? Work? Being a special officer instead of full time?"

Still, she looked distracted, too caught up in the intimacy

of her troubles to want to share them, especially with me. "Being part time . . . that was part of it."

I racked my brain to come up with something else, remembering what I knew about John, thinking about what Rose had told me. I was casting on that water, trying to coax something to the surface. "And you were the other part?"

She sighed so deeply her body shuddered. "Yes."

"Fights?"

She nodded.

"About what?"

Her eyes had strayed to the counter top and now remained fixed there, as if captivated by its cold, white, featureless surface. "Oh, you know . . ."

That was stretching things a bit, but I gave it another stab. "Married life wasn't all it was cracked up to be?"

"John is so good. So hardworking, forgiving, generous—"

I was getting the gist of it by now. "But boring."

That stopped her cold.

"Did you begin your affair with Charlie before or after John began to drink?"

Her expression turned to a pout, reminding me how powerful self-delusions can become. "It wasn't an affair. It was like I needed something only Charlie could give, like therapy."

"Something to keep your marriage together."

I hadn't kept the skepticism from my voice—a calculated risk. She brought her face up sharply and glared at me for a moment. I remained impassive, as if this entire conversation were merely a rerun for me, the veteran of a thousand broken hearts. She finally acknowledged the point, albeit defiantly. "It helped me, and our marriage still works."

"So when did John hit the bottle, before or after?" I wanted to establish cause and effect here, to make sure I had the sequence of events down accurately.

She seemed to think about that for a while, perhaps cautioned by the way I was forcing the issue. I was grateful she'd chosen to take this conversation more as a counseling session than as part of a murder investigation.

"Before. That was part of the reason I called Charlie; I was starting to climb the walls."

"But now you think maybe your feelings for Charlie, and your dissatisfaction with John, helped turn John toward the bottle?"

Once again, she began crying. "It was like he was the only one whose problems counted. I thought if I could take care of my needs, then I could help John with his. I could be strong for him like he'd been for me before."

"When you were pregnant, you mean?"

"Yes."

I paused for a moment, and then took another gamble. "Were you carrying Charlie's baby?"

She froze, her eyes focused on some middle space. Her lips moved slightly, but a full fifteen seconds elapsed before she answered: "No, of course not."

It was a straightforward denial, but I found the hesitation significant. I chipped away from another angle. "Didn't things get a little complicated once Charlie began to do well? I mean, initially, you'd chosen John because you were in trouble and he was supportive and dependable. But it didn't take long before you returned to Charlie for both support and sex. What happened when Charlie began looking more dependable than John?"

I wasn't surprised she became angry. In fact, I wondered why she'd taken so long. "That never happened. Charlie was making a lot of money, that's all. But he was seeing other women, too. John would never have done that. If I'd moved in with Charlie, it wouldn't have lasted a month. John's always been the rock in my life; I would never leave him—not for what Charlie had to offer."

"Rose, how long did you think you could have your cake and eat it too?" I blurted unintentionally.

She looked stricken.

I played the card she'd dealt me earlier, partly to cover my outburst. "You said John had found out about you two just recently?"

She blinked a couple of times, her shoulders slumping. "Last night he told me he did. He'd never let on. He said he understood what I'd done with Charlie. I explained to him that my heart was all his, and that Charlie had just been something I'd needed to keep it all together, like a safety pin to close a coat."

I thought, instead of the grenade pin I'd mentioned earlier to Billy Manierre. "How did John tell you about Jardine's death?"

"He was very sweet, very gentle."

Given John's brooding character, I found that hard to believe. The choice, therefore, was either that she was lying, or kidding herself, or that John was being more manipulative than I thought. That idea turned me cold.

"Did he say how he'd found out about Charlie's death?"

She looked surprised. "He said you'd told him, you and Billy. Didn't you?"

"We talked. Were you and Charlie seeing each other up to the end?"

"Oh, no. After John turned his life around, it ended between Charlie and me. I started thinking that if he could do it, then so could I."

A deadly quiet settled in my brain, her lie confirming my earlier suspicions. "I heard your voice on Charlie's telephone tape machine last night, Rose."

Her cheeks turned bright red, but she looked at me defiantly. "So? We were still friends."

But from her yearning tone on the tape, I knew she was still hooked on Jardine for something; even if I paid her the benefit of the doubt and agreed that sex was no longer the attraction, that still left one obvious alternative.

"Rose, do you have any idea why Charlie was killed?"

She curled in on herself slightly, her hands back in her lap, her chin on her chest. The room was still for a while. Finally, she shook her head. Her voice was almost a whisper. "All night, I thought about that. He never hurt anybody."

"When you took cocaine with him, did he ever say where he got it? That crowd plays pretty rough."

It had been a ham-handed ploy, and it didn't work. After what I thought was a telling pause—just enough to ruin what should have been innocent spontaneity—Rose gave me a wide-eyed look. "We didn't do cocaine. Charlie never wanted anything to do with that stuff."

My patience was wearing thin. She was naive, true enough, but also selfish, clever, and manipulative, much like Charlie Jardine was beginning to sound. I decided I'd better quit before I gave myself away.

I got to my feet, the fuse-equipped secret Brandt and I shared at the forefront of my mind. If McDonald, Katz, and company got hold of this in its present, nebulous, volatile form, there would be hell to pay. "I hope all this hasn't been too much of a strain, Rose. Right now, we're all trying to keep you and John out of this; you might want to keep a low profile."

She stood and I opened the door for her. "Sure, Lieutenant. Thanks."

In the hallway, a bank officer whom I knew, and whom I thought worked upstairs, came swinging out of the men's room in front of us. "Hey, Joe, how're you doing? Oh, oh." He playfully checked Rose's wrists for handcuffs. "You're not busting our customer-relations people, are you? A simple nasty letter would have done the trick."

Rose and I both handed him weak smiles. He waved and walked on.

So much for the low profile.

CHAPTER
9

MAXINE Paroddy, the morning-shift dispatcher, rolled her office chair across the small room and handed me a phone message through the slot below the bullet-proof glass separating her from the entrance hall. "Call Gail," she said.

I glanced at the pink slip. "There wasn't something from the medical examiner's office, was there?"

"Not on this shift. You heard the radio yet?"

"Why?"

"WBRT got hold of Jardine's name somehow."

A small pop of disappointment went off in my chest; so much for any press conference. "I was afraid of that. I saw McDonald lurking." I crossed the hall to the detective bureau. Jardine's identity was no deep, dark secret, and would have been released soon in any case, but McDonald's scooping the information early made me feel like a man holding a stray kitten, surrounded by a pack of gathering mongrels. I didn't doubt they'd be joined by others before too long.

I closed the door to my office and sat at my desk, eyeing the phone and thinking of Gail. I'd been looking forward to our planned dinner the night before with the enthusiasm of a teenager hoping he'd get lucky. It astounded me that, after so many years, such moments of intense sensual anticipation should hit me so hard . . . and that being deprived of one should make me all the more eager for a rematch. For years after my wife's death, I never dreamed that the vitality of my courtship days would ever come my way again.

Now, however, my eagerness was tainted with my growing concerns about the case, and I became downright alarmed when her opening words today were: "You're in deep shit now."

"Why?" I suddenly knew she was speaking as a selectman, and that Brandt's and my little conspiracy to keep Woll's name under wraps had been revealed.

"First, you never went to bed; I have that on high authority. That means you've probably been fueling yourself with enough chemical by-products to drop a horse."

I thought back to the Dunkin Donuts, my brain flooding with relief. "Horses are overbred—makes 'em weak. What's the second reason?"

"I got a call from Mrs. Morse. She's beginning to twitch."

Barbara Morse was the chair of the board of selectmen, and one of Gail's major opponents on most issues. Everyone called her "Mrs." Morse with the same cringing optimism that they call obnoxious, willful children "sweetheart"; it was an unconscious peace offering made before each and every encounter. I put the relief on hold.

"What does she have to twitch about? The body's barely cold." I heard the wariness in my own voice.

"You heard the radio?"

"I've heard about the radio. What are they saying?"

"That a young, successful local businessman has been found dead and that the police are totally stymied. That's my shorthand, of course." Her voice dropped slightly. "I met him once, at a chamber-of-commerce thing. He was a bit like a used-car salesman, but it's odd knowing someone who's been killed that way."

Depends on what you do for a living, I thought. "What does Mrs. Morse's twitching mean for us?"

"Not too much right now. Most of us are reacting just like you did: It's too early to start getting hysterical. Still, she's working the phone, wondering out loud if the town's going to be turned inside out like it was by your friend in the ski mask, and whether we should be better prepared, just in case. I don't think she's getting far. On the other hand, it won't take much to make the board overreact, once they've built up enough steam."

I let out a sigh; it was depressing, but predictable—so far. Nevertheless, her comments did make me feel the first twinges of guilt. I was indeed keeping her in the dark, because of her official position, which made me feel doubly uncomfortable when I asked, "Do you want to know if you should fasten your seat belt?"

"Nope. I'm calling to ask if you'd like yesterday's dinner tonight. I just wanted to let you know the drums were beginning to beat."

I chuckled at that, off the hook again. "What's on the menu—sliced tofu on sprouts flambé?" Gail was an unbending vegetarian.

"Worse."

"You got a date . . . and thanks for the warning."

"My pleasure. See you soon."

I hung up and turned on my pilfered fan, both to cut through the heat and to soothe my conflicting emotions.

The state medical examiner, Beverly Hillstrom, and I had become fast friends over time. We were both wary of pat answers and distrustful of the expedience that often pushes through red tape. We had more than once compared notes privately just to make sure her findings hadn't suffered in translation from her office to mine. But, as I'd reminded Klesczewski, I always waited until I had those findings in hand before I called. Until now.

"Hello, Lieutenant." Her voice was cool and pleasant, as usual. There were times that second adjective slipped, allowing the first to freeze the air. But this time I'd caught her in her office, presumably grateful for a paperwork interruption. "What can I do for you, as if I couldn't guess?"

"Ouch. I tried leaving you alone as long as possible, but I'm afraid my sweaty palms got the better of me."

She chuckled. Despite our friendship, we always referred to one another by title. Somehow, I'd felt early on that was a line she preferred to leave in place, for whatever reasons.

"Well, I take it that Dr. Gould told you what he told me."

"Acute cerebral ischemia?"

"Correct. That was definitely the cause of death."

"Do you also agree with his hypothesis that the victim was taped to a chair and, quote-unquote, strangled by having his arteries shut off?"

"I find that entirely consistent."

"What about the possible injection site? Was he shot up with anything?"

Again, I heard her soft laughter. "I give you high marks. A more impulsive man would have made that his first question. It was an injection site—we definitely ruled out an insect bite—and it's also the reason you don't have my report yet. I could fill out the death certificate now and be satisfied it was correct, but I agree with you and Dr. Gould that something about this whole thing is off-key."

There was a pause. I could hear classical music in the background being reduced to a murmur. "So I took the liberty of contacting Dr. Isadòr Gramm, who works for the Department of Health on environmental matters."

"Like pollution?"

"Yes. Primarily his focus, and most of his funding is EPA. But he is also one of the only board-certified forensic toxicologists in New England, which makes him an invaluable resource. We've worked together in the past and I respect him immensely." Her choice of words, especially when coupled with that almost aloof tone, always made me think Dr. Hillstrom was just two steps away from bursting into Old English.

"How long will it take him to find something?" I asked, knowing full well how scientists, given an intricate puzzle, love to play with it for an eternity.

She didn't pick up on my suspicious tone, or didn't choose to. "That depends on what process of elimination he employs. He obviously has to compare our sample to known entities in order to come up with an identification. That's quite a list, as you can imagine. I think, however, that you'll be pleasantly surprised. This is an inspired researcher, and we have already given him a leg up."

"How so?"

"Well, the histamine wheal—that's the red halo around the injection site—is uncharacteristic of either heroin or cocaine, and the urinalysis revealed only cocaine metabolites, or leftovers, if you will, indicating the victim's last usage was several days ago. Furthermore, I removed a large tissue section at the injection site for Dr. Gramm's use, which should be a big help to him."

"So, the bottom line is what? A month?"

"At the outside. I'm not going to push him, since he's doing this as a courtesy, but I have seen him when his interest is piqued. If that happens, results will be forthcoming much faster."

I looked up and saw Tyler hovering outside my office door. I motioned him to enter and sit. "Let's hope he's piqued half to death, then. I really appreciate it, Doctor. I promise I'll sit tight till I hear from you."

"Not to worry, Lieutenant. It's always a pleasure."

I hung up and looked at Tyler. "What've you got?"

He leaned forward and placed one of our own fingerprint index cards on my desk. I twirled it around and read, "Millard 'Milly' Crawford."

"Mr. Crawford's thumb print was flat-dab in the middle of the cocaine envelope you found at Jardine's place."

I read the card more carefully. Milly Crawford was a regular client, an erstwhile car thief, dealer in stolen goods, and—recently—a drug dealer. I knew him personally, of course; few of these guys become regulars without also becoming acquaintances with everyone on the force. But I had never had much to do with him. "Nice work."

"That ain't all." Tyler pulled his notebook from his pocket and thumbed through several pages. "The cigarette we found in the grave had saliva on it. We managed to type it—the guy was a secretor, lucky for us. It's AB, which is pretty rare; only about ten percent of the population is AB, so that might come in handy somewhere down the road."

Not too far down, I thought. I remembered from his file that John Woll's blood type was AB.

Tyler flipped a page. "And last but not least, we found out that the woman's blouse you found in Jardine's laundry was probably bought at a store called One Hundred Main, which is, predictably, on Main Street.''

"Yeah, I know it—been open about six months."

"Right. They import very upscale stuff, like that blouse, which, it turns out, is a rare designer item."

"You don't know yet who bought it, though?"

"No. I called the distributor in New Jersey, which led me to One Hundred Main. I called them, too, but only to ask if they'd sold any of the blouses. I figured you'd want to send somebody down there to get the details.''

"How many had they sold?"

He grinned and held up one finger.

I nodded. "Lucky again. Anything else?"

He got up. "That's it. I should be hearing from Waterbury about the specific makeup of the cocaine later this afternoon, but I doubt it'll be worth much. Unless it was stepped on with something weird like Tylenol or boric acid, it won't really help identify the manufacturer.''

"Stepping on" cocaine meant cutting it with some cheap powdery substitute so dealers could swell both inventory and profits. In the movies, they always use powdered sugar or milk; real dealers know those are too sweet and detectable. "Do you know what Milly Crawford's preference is?"

Tyler went back to his notebook. "I wrote that down somewhere . . . Last time we arrested him, he had several jars of Coke Buster in his apartment. I think that's mannitol with a sexy name, but everyone uses it—you can buy it under that trade name in any head shop.''

I stopped him as he reached the door. "By the way, does Crawford still live at the same place?"

"Yup. Has been for years."

I waited until he'd closed the door, pulled a set of keys from my pocket, and unlocked the only drawer in my desk I kept secure. There I had an extra gun and some ammunition— strictly against the rules—some private papers, and my "snitch book"—an address book filled with the names of Brattleboro's nether world, some of whom were paradoxically pillars of the community. But whether they were high or low on the social ladder, or had criminal records or not, they were here if I'd ever thought they might be useful, and if I had some information on them that could be used as leverage. You never knew, for example, when an almost perfectly legit dealer in wrecked cars and scrap iron might be the innocent connection between a crook and his victim.

In this instance, however, my target wasn't even remotely innocent. "Dummy" Fredericks, whose true given name was Alphonse, was one of society's true leeches. At the ripe old age of thirty-two, he had benefited from just about every parking spot the establishment had ever conceived for the wayward. From reform school to prison, from halfway houses to alcohol wards, from methadone programs to mental-health clinics, Dummy had made the rounds. I expected that if anyone filled with altruism and grant money ever opened a treatment center for deranged, left-handed, bald, Argentine-born Lithuanians with severe chemical imbalances, Dummy would find some way to qualify.

I found him, after a couple of false starts, at one of the local detox houses. "Hi, Dummy, it's Joe Gunther."

There was a long pause during which I could hear, and from past experience almost smell, his rank breathing. Personal hygiene had never been one of Dummy's great interests. "What d'ya want?"

"I want to give you twenty bucks."

"What for?" Small talk had never been too big either.

"So you can buy some dope for me."

"Can I get my ass shot off?"

"Only if you try. The dealer's a friend of yours."

"Why should I burn a friend?"

"I was using the term loosely. Besides, you'd burn your mother for twenty bucks."

"She's dead. Who is it?"

"Will you do it?"

"For forty."

"Thirty if you do it right now, as soon as you hang up. I'll meet you at Mortimer's mother with the thirty and the buy cash. Deal?"

Another pause. "You guys must really be in a rush."

"Come on, Dummy, don't live up to your name. You don't want to do it, I'll call the next guy on my list."

"Jesus, I didn't say I wouldn't do it. Who is it?"

"Milly Crawford."

"That asshole? Shit, you could've had it cheaper."

"Sure, you would've done it for free, right? We got a deal?"

"Yeah—Mortimer's mother."

I hung up and tapped my fingers on the desk top nervously. There was one thing that needed doing before I headed back out. I called in Harriet Fritter and dictated enough information for her to prepare an affidavit for a duces tecum—a "produce the records"—search warrant for Charlie Jardine's business files. Then I crossed the hallway to clear my deal with Dummy Fredericks with Brandt. He listened to my rationale, pulled out the money in old, mixed bills from the "informant fund," recorded their serial numbers, and had me sign on the dotted line.

• • •

"Mortimer's mother" was a century-old gravestone set far to the back of Morningside Cemetery, out of sight from the street but with a good, long view all around. The inscription read:

POTTER, HELENE 1810–1883
Here lies Mortimer's mother,
Dead at the age of seventy-three.
All her life she compared to no other.
Now she's at peace and so is he.

It had been Dummy's and my meeting place for years, as well as a good spot to reflect on familial entanglements and the value of having the last word. I sat down in the shade cast by the headstone and waited.

Dummy's role in all this hinged on the ever-growing rules and regs that kept us from jumping on the bad guys from impulse alone. We had Milly's print on the bag of cocaine, that bag had been tied to a homicide victim, and Milly's history was a long and documented treatise on criminal behavior. Nevertheless, we still had to establish that Milly hadn't recently become a saint and that he was still up to his old habits. Only then could a warrant be issued to search his place for something that might tie him to Jardine's death. In this light, the Dummy Frederickses of this world, for all their lack of esthetic appeal, had become crucial police adjuncts.

I half thought I smelled him before I saw him cresting the low grassy rise between South Main Street and our meeting place. He was dressed in a sweat-soaked, tie-dyed T-shirt and baggy Bermuda shorts of such incredible filthiness that I suddenly wondered if I might not be exposing myself to some environmental hazard.

A broken-toothed grin split his grimy, unshaven face. "Hi, Joe."

"Hey, Dummy. Staying out of trouble?"

"I'm seeing you—can't be too good."

I pulled out the envelope into which I'd put the buy money and waved it under his nose. "You know the drill—as soon as you accept this, we're joined at the hip. You go straight from my car to Milly's place, make the buy, come straight back to my car, and hand over the goods and any change. You driving?"

"Yup." He was looking pleased with the prospect of cutting a reasonable transaction with Milly and pocketing the aforementioned change. He might get away with it, too, but only if he could find a hiding place between Milly's apartment and my car, because I would search him there; using him didn't mean I had to trust him.

"All right, I'll drive you back to your car when we're through, then. Take your shirt off."

He looked affronted. "Here? Come on."

"Off, or no deal." I could have patted him down, but I was reluctant to touch him without rubber gloves.

Still he demurred. "What am I making out of this?"

"Thirty bucks, as agreed."

"Forget it."

I glowered. "I don't have time for this—it's too goddamn hot. Thirty-five or get the hell out of here."

With an expression of great distaste, he peeled the grungy T-shirt over his head, revealing a vast expanse of soft, pale, blotchy flesh. While the search after the buy would be to check for his ripping me off, this one was for James Dunn, indirectly. I had to be able to later state categorically, under oath, that Dummy had carried no other cash and no drugs whatsoever into the meet with Milly.

He dropped the shirt onto the grass and I gingerly examined it. "Okay, drop the pants."

"I will not."

I sighed at his modesty. This was the same man we had once busted for walking naked down Main Street at ten on a Friday night. Of course, he'd been slimmer then. "Believe me, Dummy, I like this a hell of a lot less than you do." I waved the money again. "And I'm not getting a cut of the pie."

He dropped the shorts, muttering, "I should be gettin' more," revealing an absolute lack of underclothing. He looked around nervously, as if expecting a girl-scout troop to crest the hill at any moment. "Hurry up."

I poked at the shorts, turning the pockets inside out, and had him turn around. Satisfied at last, I separated one hundred dollars from the rest of the money and had him sign a receipt for it. The thirty-five extra I'd hang onto until after the buy. "All right. We'll ride together, I'll find a parking place within sight of Milly's front door, and you do your thing, okay? You screw up, and I'll bring Kunkle out of retirement just to flatten you."

Willy Kunkle, recently retired with a damaged right arm, had been the department's narcotics specialist. He'd also had a notoriously cranky personality, from which the likes of Dummy Fredericks had suffered repeatedly. Dummy grinned, hopping on one foot as he got back into his pants, the cash like a bouquet of flowers in his fist. "Don't give it another thought."

Milly lived on a short, horseshoe-shaped street called Horton Place, right off Canal. It was narrow and one-way and lined with tall, old, skinny wooden apartment buildings made spindly by the presence of railed balconies across the front of every floor. I parked inconspicuously at the mouth of the street, where I could see Milly's third-floor apartment by merely slumping in my seat. I radioed Maxine Paroddy at Dispatch to let her know where I was, if not what I was up to, and then settled down to wait a few minutes, feeling my shirt slowly gluing to the Naugahyde cover of the seat. I wanted to see what was up in the neighborhood before letting Dummy go. He sat quietly beside me, smelling up the car.

After about five minutes of watching a perfectly normal residential block, I decided to go ahead. I nodded to Dummy and saw him shamble up the steps to the front door and disappear. This was not the stuff of Don Johnson and "Miami Vice." There were no stakeouts, no guns, no surreptitious mutterings over portable radios, not even any backup. Drug dealers in Brattleboro probably made annually what car-wash attendants did; they just didn't have to work as hard. Occasionally, we did go the full nine yards, including putting on bullet-proof vests—we even had our own SWAT, or "Special Reaction Team"—but we did that more in practice than in real life. What they did with monotonous regularity in South Florida and other drug-infested hot spots, we did once in a blue moon. Encounters like the one I was attending between Milly and Dummy had all the built-in tension of watching two rummies on a park bench lean against each other for support.

All of which explains why it took me five long seconds to react when Dummy suddenly appeared at the third-floor balcony of Milly Crawford's apartment, waving two blood-covered hands and shouting, "He's been shot. Joe, he's bleeding all over the place."

I finally bolted up in my seat, grabbed the radio, told Maxine to send backup and to dispatch Rescue, Inc., for a gunshot wound, and began running for the building.

While I ran, I wondered what had gone wrong—why had Milly been shot just as I was about to round him up? With the adrenaline came a feeling that this investigation had just been torn violently from my hands, and was about to be scattered in the sun-parched wind.

CHAPTER
10

I climbed the inner staircase two steps at a time, my back to the wall, my revolver drawn, my eyes fixed as far ahead up the stairs as I could see. Dummy's voice was echoing down, high-pitched and thin, a wail of despair. "Come on, Joe, he's bleedin' bad. Hurry, hurry."

I watched for shadows moving, for doors slightly open, for the scrape of a shoe around a blind corner. But, as expected, I saw and heard nothing aside from Dummy and a growing chorus of startled or angry murmurs from behind the apartments I passed. At the third floor, Dummy came down several steps and reached for me, trying to pull me along. "Hurry, Joe, there's blood everywhere." His red-smeared hands left skid marks on my shirt as I shook him off.

"Dummy, stay out here and be quiet. Do you understand?"

He was breathing hard, the sweat literally pouring off his nose. He nodded as I parked him in a corner of the landing.

"One thing. Did you see or hear anyone when you found him, either in the apartment or out here?"

"I don't know." He put both his hands in his hair, as if holding himself down. "I don't remember."

"All right, all right. Stay put, okay?"

I stepped over Milly's threshold, pushing the door back until it banged against the wall. I ignored the body stretched out before me, despite the wet gurgly breathing emanating from it, and scanned the small room. Empty. I quickly went around the periphery, checking a closet and behind the couch. The bedroom door was open. I poked my head around it and ducked back fast, waiting for some response. Silence. I checked again, slower this time, and then entered the room, searching it and the bathroom. Satisfied the apartment was empty, I pulled my radio from my belt and announced the fact. Through the open windows, I could hear a growing orchestra of sirens converging on the building.

Milly Crawford—all three hundred pounds of him—lay flat on his back in the middle of the floor like a beached walrus, with what looked like the lower half of his face blown away. I holstered my gun and knelt by his side in the pool of blood that surrounded his upper torso. Large pink bubbles foamed from his mouth and poured down both sides of his face. Now that I was closer to him, I could see his mouth and chin were intact; the blood had made me think the damage was greater. Nevertheless, he was obviously drowning in the stuff. I grabbed his shoulders and strained against his weight to roll him toward me and drain his airway; as I did so, I saw the cause of his bleeding: There was a ragged hole in his cheek. I lifted his head and checked the other side. Sure enough, there was another hole—the entrance wound of a bullet that had passed clean through. I put his head back on its side and heard the breathing clear up a bit.

But I was baffled. A shot through the cheek doesn't kill a man, but by the looks of him, Milly didn't have long for the world. I checked the rest of his body and found that one side of his T-shirt was also saturated with blood. I tore it open to find a small, neat hole about halfway down the left side of his rib cage.

I tried to remember what I could of the first-aid classes we took every year. The blood was still flowing, as far as I could tell, and there was that snorelike gurgling, but it was sounding less and less like breathing and more like a death rattle. I felt for a pulse on the side of his neck. Nothing. Probably doing it wrong. I swore at my own laziness in maintaining only the minimal medical requirements set down by the department.

I knew he needed mouth-to-mouth. The ABCs, that's what they drummed into you—airway, breathing, circulation. They'd never mentioned his face would be covered with blood. I pulled out my handkerchief and wiped at Milly's mouth, then I made a doughnut out of it and placed it around his lips to form a barrier of sorts, so we wouldn't actually touch. My stomach was already beginning to turn over as I flopped him back the way I'd found him and bent forward to try to resuscitate him. My head was encircled by the stench of sweat and of alcohol-tinged bad breath as I placed my mouth over his, feeling his whiskers stab my chin and upper lip through the handkerchief. I blew a single breath. Blood sprayed from both holes in his fat cheeks, and a large red bubble grew from his chest, along with a small hissing sound. I pulled back abruptly, my head swimming with nausea, fighting the urge to retch. I could hear the pounding of feet on the wooden stairs below. I rolled Milly back onto his side with considerable effort just as two cops and three white-shirted members of Rescue, Inc., burst through the door.

I lurched to my feet and turned to the policemen, wiping my mouth repeatedly with the back of my hand. "Check the rest of the building, up and down, and seal the block. Whoever did this can't be far."

Just moments ago, I and my handkerchief had been feeling so utterly alone; now, the room was suddenly jammed with equipment and people who knew how to use it. A drug kit was opened, a heart monitor turned on and electrodes attached, an oxygen tank appeared from a small duffel bag and was hooked to a bag valve mask. John Huller, the tall, blond paramedic I'd met at Charlie Jardine's grave, put down the radio with which he'd been talking to the hospital, paused briefly to look at my blood-spattered face, and dug out a combination face and eye shield that he quickly slipped on before getting down on his hands and knees by Milly's head. There, holding a long plastic tube in one hand, he paused to consult with the other two EMTs, checking on Milly's vitals. He also checked his patient's back for an exit wound. There was none.

"You have the gun? Know what caliber?" he asked me. "No."

Huller bent low and looked into Milly's mouth with a small flashlight. He let out a little grunt and reached in with the gloved fingers of his free hand, pulling out a yellow, blood-streaked tooth.

"There's got to be two more in here somewhere," he said quietly, groping around.

The hand reappeared with another tooth and some fragments. Huller muttered, "I guess we can forget the laryngoscope," to himself and reached for a portable suction machine with which he vacuumed Milly's mouth. I could see several more small fragments go chasing up the suction tube. Satisfied, Huller put aside the machine and reached deep into Milly's throat, feeling presumably for the trachea. As he did so, his mask was showered with a fine red spray. He quickly inserted the plastic tube along the passage opened by his fingers and attached the end protruding from Milly's mouth to a bright blue "ambu" bag—an artificial lung. Another of the medics, a slim, dark-haired woman with incredibly long fingers and a name tag reading "Brenda Merritt," pressed a stethoscope to the dying man's chest and nodded. Huller compressed the bag several times as his colleague listened to both sides of the chest.

"Nothing on the left," Brenda said.

He nodded. "Lot of resistance. Must be a tension-pneumo."

While this was going on, the third member of the team had tied a tourniquet to Milly's biceps and was examining the lower arm for a vein. I stood transfixed, fascinated by the cold chaos of it all, the seeming randomness of actions that quickly coalesced into a recognizable unified effort, all with very few words spoken.

"Get another line going. I'm going to decompress the chest."

Brenda tied a tourniquet around Milly's other arm and began mimicking what her male counterpart had been doing earlier, looking for a vein.

Huller, in the meantime, had pulled a long, fat, over-the-needle catheter out of one of the kits, along with an extra latex glove. He quickly cut one of the fingers off the glove and nicked the closed end of it, forming a small slit. He then felt along Milly's left ribs, below his armpit, poised with the needle to make sure of his landmark, and then stuck it in. Nothing happened for an instant as the needle buried itself deeper and deeper into the fleshy skin. Huller's face was absolutely calm and still. Abruptly, he withdrew the needle, leaving its enveloping catheter in place. There was a loud hissing sound and again blood came spraying, this time out the end of the catheter. After the hissing ebbed, Huller attached the finger of the glove to the end of the catheter with some tape.

He glanced up at my perplexed expression. "Flutter valve; lets the air out, won't let it back in." He listened to Milly's chest as the male EMT worked the ambu bag, and nodded with satisfaction. He didn't look happy with what the monitoring equipment was telling him, however. "Let's put the MAST on him."

Both colleagues looked at him quickly. Brenda asked quietly, "With a chest?"

"I think we've got volume problems somewhere. We have little to lose anyhow, especially if he codes."

While Huller went back to his radio to give medical control an update, Brenda cracked open a square plastic box, the lower half of which had three dials with stopcocks, the upper half a cumbersome pair of inflatable nylon-coated trousers. A foot pump and three colorful rubber tubes also sprang out like jacks-in-the-box. The Medical Anti-Shock Trousers, or MAST, were quickly slipped over Milly's legs and abdomen, velcroed shut, and inflated with the foot pump. The principle, I knew from seeing the pants used before, was to restrict the patient's blood flow to where it was most needed. The slight disagreement I'd noticed must have stemmed from the obvious fact that if Milly's fluids were restricted to his upper body, then they would obviously add to the leakage in his chest, possibly further compromising the lung. Apparently it was a judgment call, and nobody was arguing.

By the time they were loading Milly onto a wooden

backboard, therefore, he had two large-bore IVs in his arms, had been intubated and encased in pneumatic trousers, and was being given one-hundred-percent oxygen. I didn't know what to make of the erratic squiggles on the heart monitor's small green video screen, but I figured that any signs there meant the heart was doing something.

That changed on the first floor. Milly's enormous weight hadn't made getting him downstairs an easy thing, especially with several bags of IV solution to juggle and an ambu bag that needed constant deflation. Six of us had struggled, risking the collapse of the staircase, to deny gravity's excessive interest in our load. The trip had been jarring and clumsy, interrupted by long pauses during which we'd fumbled for better positions, our hands as wet with perspiration as if we'd just plunged them in salt water.

At the bottom, Brenda had announced in a calm voice, "We have asystole."

That was double-Dutch to me, but it had an electric effect on her colleagues. Milly's backboard was slammed flat on the floor, and the male EMT prepared to administer sternal compressions. Asystole meant Milly had flat-lined on us.

Huller just watched and waited, breathing hard from his exertions, his uniform soaked and sticking to him, but his face forever quiet and reflective. From the start, his expression had never shown more animation than that of a passenger staring out the window of a bus. He, however, was staring at the heart monitor.

"That's not right. Check the leads."

The EMT froze above Milly's chest. Brenda ran her hands over the three electrodes stuck to Milly's body. The one that was supposed to be attached to his waist was half undone and went dangling. She quickly reattached it.

Huller paused, waiting for the green squiggles on the screen to settle down. "We have V-tach. Prepare to defibrillate."

He hit a switch on the monitor, a loud whine escaped from the machine, and a bright red light turned on. He took two paddles which were wired to the machine, spread some goo on them and applied them to Milly's chest.

"Clear. All clear."

There was a moment's pause, then Huller hit the buttons on the paddles. Milly's chest twitched, sending fat shock waves across his enormous white belly.

Huller watched the screen. He shook his head. "Again."

The machine wound itself up, Huller placed the paddles, shouted "clear," and again Milly spasmed.

"Okay. We got something here. Let's move him fast."

The cluster of us carried the backboard out into the street and deposited it onto the waiting ambulance stretcher. Klesczewski was standing on the porch and began walking next to me.

"Ron, find Dummy Fredericks and empty his pockets. I had a buy planned for a hundred dollars that didn't go down. Get him to tell you what he saw or heard when he found Milly—he couldn't have been lying there more than a couple of minutes. If he cooperates, give him this." I reached into my wallet and handed him the allotted money plus another twenty of my own. "I told the patrol boys to search the area; I don't expect much, but see how they did and report back to me at the hospital. Whoever plugged Milly did it fast and dirty, probably to stop us from talking with him. I want to find out why, if I can, so I'm going to stick to him like glue till he talks or he dies."

Milly had already been loaded into the back of the ambulance. I could see Huller, now wearing a pair of headphones with a microphone, inject something into the IV line, presumably on orders from the hospital.

"Mind if I ride along?"

Huller glanced over at me. "Nope. I thought you would anyway."

I pulled myself up and looked back at Ron. "You better send someone to get a search warrant for Milly's apartment. I don't know what we'll find up there, but I don't want some lawyer making us eat it later."

Klesczewski nodded, gave me a thumbs-up, and slammed the door.

The ride to the hospital was short and nerve-wracking. Even with my ignorant eye, I could see something was going seriously wrong. As Huller continued watching the monitor intently, simultaneously holding his stethoscope over Milly's exhausted heart, I could see the fat man physically changing before me. He began to turn blue from the nipples up, large veins loomed on his engorged neck, and one of the other monitoring machines they'd hooked up once they were on board started beeping dismally.

Huller spoke into his headset. "BMH from Rescue One. I think we have cardiac tamponade."

He glanced out the window in response to some inaudible query. "We're ten-seven your facilities right now."

Indeed, the ambulance lurched slightly as it climbed over the small hump marking the hospital's driveway. Whatever plans Huller might have had up his sleeve to deal with this latest crisis were obviously put on hold. Rather than dealing with Milly's heart, he and his team began unhooking the IV bags and the oxygen tubing from the walls of the ambulance, preparing themselves for a quick exit.

Huller addressed me as he worked. "When we stop, as soon as those back doors open, jump out and clear away. We'll be moving fast."

"What's happening?"

"Cardiac tamponade. The sac around the heart has filled with blood and is squeezing the heart so tight it can't beat. We're going to have to drain it as soon as we get inside."

I stared at the subject of all this attention: deaf, dumb, and beyond my reach, perhaps permanently. I was half tempted to slap his cheeks, to wake him up for an instant only, just long enough to get a name out of him at least. But it was looking increasingly doubtful that Milly would chat with anyone ever again.

I did as I was told. As soon as the doors opened onto the hospital loading dock, I cut left and stayed out of the way. Meeting us was what looked like a complete surgical team, led by Dr. James Franklin, whose reputation as a general surgeon was matched only by his famous good humor.

"My God, he's fat. Roll him into number three."

I followed them all in, feeling like a balloon trailing a group of eager kids.

"How long's he been like this?" Franklin asked Huller.

Huller checked his watch. "Two minutes."

Franklin snapped on a pair of latex gloves. "Okay—let's cut to the chase. Got that syringe ready?"

Milly had been rapidly transferred by eight straining people from the stretcher to the bed. Franklin, flanked by two nurses, used his stethoscope briefly and was then handed the largest syringe I'd ever set eyes on. He felt Milly's chest gently with his fingers, searching for a landmark before suddenly inserting the needle. He pulled back the plunger slightly, allowing a small amount of bright red blood to enter the syringe chamber; he withdrew the needle just a hair and tried again. This time, the chamber filled with dark blood, and Franklin began pulling on the plunger in earnest.

"All right. Nice call, Mr. Huller. You ought to go into the oil business."

Milly's various tubes and wires had been reattached to hospital equipment, and after Franklin had withdrawn eighty-five milliliters of blood, the heart monitor's green line began to scribe a more regular pattern than before.

"Okay. That's bought us some time." He paused to check some of the digital numbers glowing on various machines clustered around the bed. "He's got an acceptable BP, and by miracle of miracles, we have an OR available. Ruth, you want to get hold of the blood bank and have the first four units set up, stat? Okay, boys and girls, let's get him moving." He noticed me standing by on his way out and stopped dead in his tracks. "My God, Joe, you look disgusting. He belong to you?"

"I guess."

"What's his name?"

"Milly Crawford."

"And you don't know what caliber hit him, right?"

"Nope; 'fraid not."

Franklin nodded. "Well, we'll dig around a little and find out. You coming?"

"If that's all right."

"Absolutely. Clean yourself up and grab some greens." He looked over my shoulder behind me. "Harry'll show you." He shook his head at me again. "You look worse than your fat friend." He vanished down the hallway through a pair of double doors, his team in pursuit, clustered around Milly's rolling bed, carrying IV solutions, equipment, and the ever-present ambu bag. They looked like ants carting off their enormous, somnolent queen into the bowels of the anthill.

A tall, unsmiling male orderly was standing in the hall. "Come with me," he muttered, and led the way through various twists and turns to a locker room. Franklin had not been kidding; looking at myself in the mirror there, I wondered if I had more of Milly's blood than he did. I washed thoroughly and changed into a set of "greens," struggling for an inordinate amount of time with a pair of seemingly too-small paper slippers I'd been instructed to slip over my street shoes.

Harry, looking as morose as a basset hound, pointed at the blood-soaked clothes at my feet. "You got other stuff to wear?"

"No."

"Better keep the greens, then. Those are gross."

I couldn't argue the point, so I simply nodded and followed him to the operating room.

CHAPTER

11

HARRY had explained to me that Dr. Franklin called an available operating room "a miracle" because they were usually heavily booked and, at three, grand total, in short supply. Number two was open because electricians had been replacing the fluorescent tubes in the ceiling, a mundane fact that explained the inordinately dramatic scene that greeted me as I walked through the room's swinging door.

Operating rooms routinely share three attributes: they are clean, they are more or less filled with exotic and arcane machinery, depending on the budget of the hospital, and they are as bright as the Sahara at noon. The one I entered had the equipment, but that was it.

Milly had been shifted from the rolling bed to the operating table in the center of the room. He was naked, huge, pale, and blood-streaked, his dirty white body glowing with the reflected brilliance of a trio of tripod-mounted flood lamps. But where the rest of the room would have been lit normally by overhead flourescents, this one was dark, its distant corners almost indistinguishable to my eyes, as yet unaccustomed to the gloom. On first impression, it seemed Milly, dazzlingly suspended, was floating in dark space, asleep and utterly passive, attended to by a flurry of some eight green-clad satellites, all laying out instruments, hooking up equipment, and generally preparing for the doctor's arrival. He looked so out of place, his soft, spongy flesh overflowing the narrow table, one arm dangling off to one side, punctured by an IV line attached to a blood bag hooked to a nearby stand. His head was extended back, his torn mouth open and filled with a thick tube hooked to the oxygen equipment and an ambu bag, still being rhythmically squeezed by a technician. I noticed how shockingly yellow his gnarled toenails looked in contrast to his almost bloodless skin.

A far door banged open with a brief flash of light and Franklin stormed in, mask already in place, tailed by a smaller, thinner man, also in scrub greens. Franklin went straight to the tray on which the surgical tools were being laid out, and without waiting for sterility-insuring assistance, ripped open a package of latex gloves and snapped them onto his still-damp hands, muttering to the smaller man, "Don't wait for a nurse. They're busy and there's no time." His former jaunty tone had been cooled by concentration.

He grabbed a scalpel from the tray and positioned himself to Milly's left side, the nurses and technicians still moving about, some of them with their gowns still untied in the back, one of them beginning to drape the body with large, dark-green squares of cloth.

Franklin waved her away. "Later. I want to go in now. Vitals?" he asked the woman at the head of the patient.

She nodded. "Systolic seventy, pulse fifty. Things are slowing down again."

"Okay, Mr. Crawford, time to see if we can help you out a little." Franklin placed the point of the blade on Milly's sternum, just above his nipple line, and in one smooth, almost theatrical movement, sliced a deep incision from the front of the chest, across the left rib cage, and all the way to where the back met the table top, about eighteen inches long.

"*Finochetto*," he barked.

A glistening steel apparatus with a crank on one end appeared from the surrounding gloom. Franklin's surgical assistant fit the device between two of Milly's ribs and began to turn the crank. There was a sound of wet tearing, a few sharp snaps, and finally several loud cracks as the ribs, one by one, were pried apart.

I had moved through the shadows to where I was now standing behind the two surgeons, and as the ribs yielded to the spreader, I saw a sudden frothing of pink bubbles from the lung beneath the ribs, followed by a brief, explosive cascade of blood that poured from the wound and splashed off the table, soaking both men's pants and covering the floor. A nurse threw down a thick green sheet that both men trampled beneath their feet, absorbing some of the blood and reducing the risk of slipping.

Milly's left lung, suddenly unrestrained, expanded a good six inches from the huge hole in his chest. It was streaked with blood, somewhat pink, but heavily marked with dull gray stripes and clusters of black spots. "Look at that— heavy smoker. As if your diet wasn't enough to kill you," Franklin muttered. "Give me a lap pad. Vitals?"

"Systolic fifty, pulse thirty. Almost off the charts."

"Come on, fella, don't crap out on me now. Keep that suction coming." Franklin squeezed the lung, now held in the lap pad, and followed it as it deflated up into the chest cavity, his entire hand and half his forearm disappearing from view as he bent over and shoved the lung up and out of the way for a clear view of the heart's left side, snipping away at thin connecting tissue with his other hand as he went.

"Move the light so I can see inside." Franklin paused and spoke to his assistant over his shoulder: "Walt, I want you to move to my other side and hold this lung out of the way."

Walt quickly accommodated this request, allowing me a brief unimpeded view of the wound and what it revealed. Milly's chest was now totally empty, easily hollow enough to fit two footballs. Its bottom was like a water-filled grotto, the water being thick, dark-red blood, and was constantly being drained by two large-bore suction catheters hooked to a sizeable transparent jug, now about half full. At the back of the grotto, high up against its far wall, a fat, bulging swelling—a sack of red flesh—was straining against its contents, some of which was dribbling down the wall to the pool below.

"Systolic forty, Doctor. He's almost gone."

"Not yet, he's not. Walt, push it further up, but watch out for the major vessels." Franklin took up his scalpel again, reached in, and sliced the bulging sack on the far wall.

"Suction here."

More dark blood poured out as from a burst water balloon, along with several small clots. The suction tube made a sound like some obnoxious child overworking his straw at the end of a satisfying ice-cream soda.

"Blood pressure rising."

"All right, nice goin', Mr. Crawford," Franklin muttered to himself. "Get some more light in here."

Both Franklin and Walt now had their hands in the chest, and yet there was still enough room for me to see the heart itself, visible through the opened pericardial sac, rhythmically squirming like a fist in a pink mitten, closing and opening, closing and opening. With each contraction, a small spurt of blood arched out into the grotto.

Franklin was speaking to Walt, both of them with their heads almost inside the chest. "All right, can you see it? A hole in the ventricular wall . . . right there. It just missed the L.A.D. coronary artery. See? It's a little hard with all this fat. Just follow the spurts."

He stuck a red hand out at the nurse next to him. "Four-oh cardiovascular and a big needle, single-ended."

Equipped with his sewing kit, he reached back into the cavity, made a couple of quick sutures, and stopped the bleeding. "Okay, the hole's been placated; how's he doin'?"

The technician at the head answered. "Systolic ninety-five, pulse sixty. Nice job, Doctor."

Franklin withdrew both his hands and straightened. "Nice job, Mr. Crawford. With any luck, maybe you can go back home and die of a heart attack, like you deserve."

One of the nurses laughed. The tension eased measurably. I could sense not victory—the chest was still wide open, after all—but certainly a growing optimism. If death had not yet blinked, it was beginning to yield.

"All right, let's heat up some saline and clean up a little here. You people have really let things go to the dogs."

This drew a couple of more timid laughs, and the team shifted into gear. The grotto, now deprived of its primary liquid source, was suctioned almost dry, more blood bags were hung and fed into the IV tubing, crimson-soaked pads were removed from the cavity and hung out for later counting and collection, and Franklin's requested hot saline, warmed to just above body temperature in a nearby microwave oven, was applied to swab Milly's interior.

Walt was still in place, still bent over holding the lung out of the way. My back hurt just looking at him. "Dr. Franklin, where's the bullet then?"

There was a skipped beat in the room. No one had forgotten the bullet, but with the flush of success, it had slipped to second billing. That changed with Walt's question.

Franklin looked over to one of the nurses. "Let's do a portable film."

She left the room, returning soon with another technician in tow, both of them lugging a large X-ray machine on wheels, whose odd, birdlike shape was made even more alarming by its appearing from the peripheral gloom. Everyone pitched in to gingerly hoist Milly up high enough so a film plate could be slid underneath him; the exposure was made, and the technician and his machine exited.

The results were delivered a few minutes later, and Franklin held the film up to one of the flood lights so Walt could see it from his stooped position.

"There it is, lodged against the spine. That'll probably take care of his walking days."

"What did it go through to get there?" Walt asked in a soft voice.

Franklin used his scalpel as a pointer, trying to trace the course of the bullet, muttering anatomical landmarks as he went. He finally paused, let a few seconds of silence pass, and then muttered, "damn."

"What?" The nurse's voice was nervous, not wanting to hear that victory might still elude them.

"It looks like the bullet passed through the back wall of the left atrium."

Dead silence greeted this piece of news.

"Vitals are improving," the woman with the ambu bag said hopefully.

"That's because we're still feeding him blood. There's a hole there, I'm afraid. Let's just cross our fingers it's a simple in-and-out. We might pull this off yet, people. Come on, hope springs eternal."

The tension I'd noticed easing earlier returned with force. The room was so still, the quietest mutterings between both surgeons were easily overheard.

Franklin was back with both his hands inside the chest. "Okay, it's going to be tight back here. We got pulmonary veins, the artery, and the bronchus to contend with, all jammed in together. Maybe the bullet whacked the bunch of them, and their being so tight together has stopped a major bleed, or maybe the exit is just beyond by a hair and we're sitting pretty. Here, hold this clear while I rotate the heart. Little more . . . ah, there we go. We've got some arterial blood here. Little more . . . hold it there . . . oh, SHIT."

There was a sudden whooshing sound, followed by a cascading of liquid. Bright-scarlet blood, as if poured from a garden hose, abruptly filled the chest to overflowing, and splashed noisily onto the already soaking floor.

"Lap pad, now." Franklin shoved the pad deep into the chest, and looked without speaking at the oxygen therapist.

"BP falling, pulse falling."

Franklin was now talking to himself. "Looked like the whole back of the atrial wall gave away. Crawford, you bastard, if you'd taken better care of yourself, you might have had a stronger heart. What the fuck do you expect me to do, goddamn it?" He kept looking into the chest. "Keep up the suction and hang more blood."

"Twenty beats per minute," the woman's voice intoned, in the quiet, gloomy room to her motionless audience. Her gradual countdown took five minutes, during which not another voice was heard. "Ten . . . two. . . . There's been one in the last two minutes." And finally: "No cardiac activity."

In the stillness greeting this statement, Franklin straightened for the last time. He peeled off his gloves and dropped them on Milly's stomach, pulled off his hat and mask, and, walking away into the dark, let them both fall to the floor as he vanished stoop-shouldered through the door.

There were a few half mutterings as people followed his example, some to go back to tend to the living, others to get the necessary equipment to clean up the mess.

In less than a minute, I was alone with Milly Crawford, as I had been when I'd first found him in his apartment. His eyes were half open, staring unblinking into the hot, bright lamps. The fat tube protruded from his mouth, silent and without purpose. His body, where it wasn't covered by the stained green sheets, was as white as marble, and would soon be as cold.

"You know who did it?" Harry stepped out from the surrounding darkness, his eyes sad and his voice gentle.

"I was hoping to ask him."

"I'm sorry."

I shifted my gaze back to Milly. "So am I."

CHAPTER

12

K LESCZEWSKI couldn't stop smiling at my lime-
green attire.

"No Doctor Kildare jokes."

He shook his head. We were standing at the threshold to Milly's ransacked apartment. The pool of blood had congealed and now looked more like a huge spread of dried blackberry jam. Without a body at its center, it took on a horrifying, suggestive aspect, one which prompted me to keep my eyes instead on Tyler and his men as they picked their way from one end of the apartment to the other, scrutinizing and photographing every square inch.

"I take it you didn't find the shooter."

Ron shook his head. "We're still interviewing, but it looks like a clean getaway. I'm not even sure which direction he took."

I turned and glanced up the hall stairs, not surprised at this bit of news. As spontaneous as I guessed Milly's murder to have been, it hadn't struck me as a crime of passion, where the killer would be found, blood-soaked and distraught, lurking around some nearby corner. Milly's death had been rushed and risky, but planned all the same; that much I could feel in my bones. "How many ways out are there?"

He followed my glance upstairs. "Well, that's one of

them. The door to the roof is wide open, for ventilation, and the roof connects to buildings on either side. There're front and back doors to the place, plus a cellar with a bulkhead entrance. The guy had his pick."

"Assuming he left at all." Here I was playing the devil's advocate, virtually positive the killer was long gone.

"That's what we're checking on now, door to door. We sealed the area. The same landlord owns all three buildings, so we're using him as a passkey. If the killer is here, we should find him, unless he lives here."

I raised my eyebrows at him silently. He looked slightly uncomfortable. "Well, you know, if the killer's one of the neighbors, then we'll find him at home, looking perfectly normal."

I nodded distractedly and sat on one of the steps behind me. Klesczewski felt the need to explain further, his latent insecurity surfacing. "It's possible this all happened because of a fight between neighbors, especially with someone like Milly. I wouldn't want him next door."

I didn't argue the point. Statistically, Klesczewski was right, not that it altered my private opinion any. "Did anyone hear shots?"

"No—no one, and a couple of them were pretty close by, one right across the street at the same height, open window to open window, and another directly downstairs. I don't think they're trying to duck us, by the way; must've been a silencer."

I was suddenly aware of the suffocating heat in the stairwell. Glancing at Klesczewski's face, I saw it was beaded with sweat. "Is there any shade on the roof?"

He took it in stride, long used to my wandering mind. "Some."

"Good." I got up and began climbing the tired, sagging stairs. I could hear him following, judging his earlier observation. "I guess a silencer isn't the kind of thing you bring to a neighborly dispute."

I didn't rub the point in; it was just the kind of thinking I was trying to encourage in him. "Did Dummy come up with anything more?"

"No, and he's not real happy with you, either. Says you

can take him off your list of born suckers. This is the last time he does our work for us."

"Did you pay him off?" The environment suited the conversation. Now free to look around, instead of ducking potential bullets and watching people die, I became aware of the drab surroundings—the splintered, bare-wood floors, the dark-lit walls, stained waist-high by the touch of countless unwashed and unsteady fingers. I wondered briefly how many times I had traveled hallways similar to this, and how many more lay ahead.

"Yeah. It didn't make much of a dent, though. He said you were a lying bastard for setting him up and that I was cheap."

The door to the roof was on the fourth floor, at the top of a steep half ladder, half staircase. I continued climbing toward the glaring, white-hot rectangle of light. "I did tell him there was no risk."

Klesczewski let out a laugh. "He heard that part, all right."

I'd just reached the top step when both our radios squawked. I recognized DeFlorio's voice asking Klesczewski where I was.

"We're both on the roof."

"Chief's here."

I looked around briefly and keyed my own radio. "Send him up."

Klesczewski frowned as he hooked his radio back onto his belt.

"You're not surprised he showed up, are you?"

He shrugged. "No, I suppose not."

But he wasn't happy. Unlike when a general appears through the smoke of battle, the arrival of the police chief was not inspiring to the troops. Most department members were uncomfortable around Brandt, seeing him as their political leader, with his own separate arena in which to wage war. His presence among them, especially at a crime scene, gave rise to both self-doubt and resentment that they weren't being trusted to do their jobs. The fact that Brandt had patrolled more streets and stuck his nose into more potential trouble than any two of them combined meant next to nothing to them. He was the Big Cheese, and best avoided. Having been in his shoes, even for a scant few months, I could sympathize with his peculiar isolation.

"Why don't you get back to it? I'll stay put and find out what he wants."

Klesczewski didn't need urging. He let out a quick okay and was gone.

The heat on the roof, especially when reflected off its flat tar-and-gravel coating, was no less intense than what it had been in the stairwell, but the location's openness was a help psychologically. In fact, although the steep bluff that skirted a good portion of lower Canal Street, and which forced Horton Place to double back on itself like a horseshoe, loomed just a hundred feet to my back, the building itself was tall enough to compete with the treetops. Looking northwest along the axis of the Whetstone Brook valley to the distant hills beyond West Brattleboro, I imagined being a raft-borne sailor on a choppy green sea. The verdant stretch of tree crowns was punctuated by oddly shaped rooftops, which, in my craving for cool air, I chose to see as parodies of icebergs. Not that the illusion was wholly satisfactory; I ended up seeking the more palpable comfort of a large maple's half circle of shade near the rear edge of the roof. There I waited, dimly aware of the city's murmur below and around me, reflecting on the events of the last few hours.

Brandt found me five minutes later and gestured at my borrowed scrub suit. "I take it Milly didn't make it."

I shook my head. "Ron and I were just discussing that whoever hit him probably used a silencer. Also, the slug they dug out of him in the operating room looked like a .38 or a 9 millimeter."

Brandt grunted. "What did McDermott tell you?"

That came from left field. I gave him a dumb look. "Fred McDermott? I haven't seen him in over a week."

"Oh. DeFlorio mentioned he was here when the shooting started. I thought you might have talked to him."

Fred McDermott was the town's building inspector, a position which made him intimately familiar with most of the firetraps and health hazards in the city. I wasn't surprised he'd been seen in a kindling pile like this, but the timing was unusual. "No. I haven't even seen DeFlorio yet."

"Well, no big deal. From what I gather, he had nothing to offer." Brandt moved into the shade next to me and waved his arm to encompass the three adjoining roofs. "So, you think he got away over the top?"

"It's possible."

Brandt caught my tone. "But you don't think so."

I didn't share my men's distrust of Tony Brandt. He was reserved. He didn't laugh it up with the boys or ask to be treated as a pal. Although politically versed, he lacked the instinctive glibness that marks the common breed of politician. I saw him rather as a policeman who'd chosen to be a chief because he wanted to prove the two weren't mutually exclusive. That was a subtlety lost on the department's younger members, too concentrated on their swagger and pride. But to cops like Billy Manierre and me, Brandt's attempt to keep the cop in him alive while playing the bureaucrat's role was an asset; it supplied us with a trusted sounding board which could tell us how our ideas might play to either a professional or a political audience.

I therefore had no qualms about sharing my doubts with him. Besides, with what we knew about the Wolls, we shared a secret, which by definition made us conspirators.

"No, I don't, although it sounds reasonable enough." I paused and moved to the edge of the roof. Brandt remained silent. Below me, police cars were parked helter-skelter, like badly aligned toys. "If I wanted to kill someone who lived near the top floor of this building, I'd make my escape over the roofs. It would lessen the chances of anyone seeing me twice and it would allow me two neighboring buildings with all their exits to choose from."

Brandt still didn't speak, being used to my ramblings.

"The silencer, assuming there was one, indicates premeditation, which would tie in to a preplanned escape route." I crossed over to the opposite edge and looked over into the tangle of weeds, bushes, and sun-bleached grass that consti tuted the backyards of the buildings.

"But the timing bothers me, and makes me think this

wasn't as premeditated as it looks." I turned and faced Brandt. "We haven't heard from Milly Crawford in months—almost a year. He hasn't come up in any of the local criminal street gossip, as far as I know. So we've got to assume he's been leading his normal low-life existence. Then, all of a sudden, his name pops up, we set up a way to bust him, and he gets himself killed, all in the space of a few hours. Nice and neat."

Brandt finally spoke up. "How does that connect to a rooftop escape?"

"Not enough time to preplan it. How would you know if the rooftop door would be open, or at least be unlocked? How about the doors leading down in the other two buildings? Also, you need to know the route from beginning to end, and the habits of the people living here. You need to hang around for a while, find out how things work, work out as many of the intangibles as possible."

"And you don't think that happened here?"

"Nope. I think this was an act of desperation, done at the last second to stop us from talking to Milly, but not by a hothead. Whoever it was kept his cool. That tells me we're facing a planner by nature; someone who thinks before he jumps, even on short notice."

The radio muttered my name from the back pocket of my green pants.

"Go ahead."

"You might want to come down here and check this out. Second floor."

I glanced at Brandt, who shrugged and followed me back into the gloomy, stifling stairwell.

We found several officers, including Ron Klesczewski, gathered on the second-story landing. With them was a red-faced, sullen man with a peeved expression and a large set of keys on a ring.

"This is Mr. Blossom," Klesczewski said, with a palpable touch of sarcasm. "He's the landlord here and has been kind enough to open whatever doors need opening."

Blossom and I nodded curtly to one another. I could see from his face that proffering a handshake would only invite a rebuke and probably a smirk to match.

Kleszczewski indicated an apartment door labeled "21." "No one was home, so we asked Mr. Blossom to do the honors, and found out the jamb was busted."

Brandt gave me a look and bent down to study the door. It opened to the inside and was held shut by a simple keyed doorknob. The interior jamb, where the lock's catch plate had been mounted, had been splintered by a heavy force coming against the outside of the door.

I pointed at several small wooden shards lying on the inside of the threshold, evidence that the breakage was recent. Brandt grunted, "The exposed wood looks fresh, too."

The whole setup made me feel slightly hollow.

I didn't want to say too much in front of Blossom, whom I regarded as little more than a loudspeaker to the neighborhood and the press, which couldn't be far off. I turned back to Kleszczewski. "Better seal this off and get Tyler on it as soon as possible. Be easier all around if he got it done before the tenant comes back home."

Brandt motioned to me to follow him downstairs. "So what do you make of it?" he asked, once we were out of earshot, heading out the front door of the building.

"Pure guesswork?" I said, with an artificial brightness. "Sure."

"Then I think I probably came close enough to the killer to touch him. Either he broke open that door to hide when Dummy came upstairs, which he really didn't have any reason to do unless they know each other, or he was in Milly's room when Dummy walked in, ducked downstairs when I was being called from the balcony, and hid behind that door as I was coming up."

Brandt was silent as we both crossed the street, walking toward Canal. He spoke up as I stopped by my car. "You're also saying someone in the police department told the killer about Milly, right?"

"It looks that way."

He frowned. "Just like he told him about a bum being under that bridge."

I didn't respond.

"Which means we're back to John Woll."

"Or we're being led back to him."

Brandt pursed his lips, considering that much more complicated possibility. "By who?"

"Take your pick. A lot of people had access to Milly's identity, just as soon as we did. Tyler dug his card out of the fingerprint file; he made no secret of his pleasure to me, and I doubt he did to anyone else he met on his way to my office. And you gave the paperwork I filled out for the money to your secretary, didn't you?"

"Yes."

"She's out in the open, near where half the department and a good many visitors pass by on the way to the coffee machine or the copier or whatever. Anybody could have paused there to say hi, glanced at the paperwork, and put it all together."

Brandt shook his head. "That one's slim."

"Okay, but I also told Dispatch where I was when I parked here. Someone familiar with how we work could figure it out, especially if Jardine was buried so we would find him. It would further reinforce the theory that this whole investigation is being manipulated somehow."

"But that points to police involvement again, doesn't it?"

I doggedly refused to be cornered, if only to stave off becoming too tunnel-visioned. "Not necessarily. Look, someone could have been tailing me. He sees me meet Dummy, follows me here, realizes Milly's been blown, and goes upstairs to kill him just before Dummy arrives to make the buy. There was a five-minute gap while Dummy and I just watched the front of the building from the car. Same thing identifying the bum angle. We spent a few hours crawling under a bridge that's obviously served as somebody's home. What conclusions would you draw, as a reasonably bright onlooker?"

Brandt stared at the sidewalk. He had my sympathies. Not only did he have two homicides in two days—with the attending heat from both media and selectmen—he also had a chief detective who seemed ready to embrace any theory that popped into his head.

In the brief silence, I almost hated counterbalancing my own broad view of the case with John Woll's latest coffin nail; but there it was, as hard as evidence could get. "One other piece of bad news," I said, as I circled my car and opened the driver's door. "The saliva on the cigarette butt found in Jardine's grave was AB, same as John Woll's. It's a pretty rare type."

Brandt absorbed that glumly. "Which brings up the most obvious possibility of all—that Woll knocked off Milly."

"True. Tell Ron to look into that, would you? Have him check on John's whereabouts today." I slid behind the wheel and started the engine.

"Where're you going?"

"To change my clothes." I ignored his look of irritation and backed the car around to face Canal.

Reasonably, I should have stayed at the scene and looked over the shoulders of my men. But they knew what they were doing. I, on the other hand, needed no more than fifteen minutes of meditative quiet, just enough to distance myself from Milly's grotesque and bloody passing, and my own unknowing escape from his killer. I needed a touch of the routine, a familiar setting in which I could shift gears and begin to move forward again.

My apartment is on the corner of High and Oak, just a stroll up the hill from the center of town. It's actually a pretty ritzy neighborhood, with lots of Victorian homes, heavy on stained glass and gingerbread moulding, made all the more exclusive for being a stroll away from the business district. Gail had once pointed out that, were it not for the building's appearance, I couldn't afford to live there. It was true that home wasn't much to look at. It too had once been Victorian, but a bargain-basement remodeler had pretty much butchered whatever grace it might have had. Now it was just large, lumpy, and painted urine yellow. Also, its location, within immediate earshot of High Street's grinding gears or squealing brakes, helped keep the rent low and the yuppies away.

I lived on the top floor in a ramshackle place, comfortably old and dusty, as filled with dark wood, ancient overstuffed furniture, and low ceilings as Gail's place was open and airy and modern. Indeed, its one striking architectural feature was its massive number of books; they lined my walls, were piled in odd corners, and covered much of my furniture. An obsession planted by my educationally minded mother, reading books had become my primary off-duty pastime, besides spending time with Gail. The apartment had therefore become, over the years, a cavelike shelter against the outside world, a museum of my past, my passions, and my deep-rooted pleasure in solitude.

I stripped off the hospital greens, turned on the various fans I'd acquired of late, and settled in my nest of choice, an enormous, comforting, bulging armchair, surrounded by a cluster of lights, books, side tables, and a mismatched ottoman, all of which normally tended to most of my needs.

I didn't use any of them now, however. This time, their proximity was enough. I stared out across the worn carpet to the battered coffee table with its neat stacks of mail, to the nondescript sofa against the wall of books beyond, and I thought.

A quarter hour later, resolved if not refreshed, I got up and began dressing. If I was to pursue the theory that this entire investigation was being manipulated to incriminate either the department generally or John Woll personally, I had to do more than stand around and watch that process take place. My job now was to focus less on the "who" in both these murders, and more on the "why."

Which brought me back to Charlie Jardine. Unlike Milly Crawford's, his death had been planned, carefully executed, and intensely personal.

CHAPTER

13

THE law firm of Morris, McGill is the biggest one in town. It occupies one of the few wooden structures near the downtown *T* intersection of High and Main, a long single block down from my own apartment, at exactly the point where High Street's descent into Main is at its steepest. This geographical detail helps create the unfortunate impression that the building is being crushed between its stalwart brick neighbor below, and the equally heavy but seemingly less surefooted monstrosity above.

No one I knew had any idea who Morris or McGill were. The firm had been a longstanding establishment when I'd first come to Brattleboro in the fifties, so presumably the founding partners were a part of ancient history, if they existed at all. It brought to mind that Brattleboro itself had been named for William Brattle, a Harvard-educated theologist/speculator who died as a colonel for the losing side in the Revolutionary War before ever visiting his namesake.

The receptionist/secretary who greeted me exuded crisp efficiency. I asked to see Tucker Wentworth.

Her expression became professionally crestfallen. "Oh, I'm sorry. Mr. Wentworth is out of the office."

"Is he due back anytime soon?"

"I'm afraid he's out of town. Would you like to leave a message with his secretary?"

"No, that's all right. How about Jack Plummer?"

"Mr. Plummer's in. Do you have an appointment?"

The sudden inanity of the question stalled me for a second. I pulled out my badge and showed it to her. "If he's free, tell him Joe Gunther would like a couple of minutes."

She nodded quickly, got out from behind her desk, and trotted up the flight of stairs along the wall. The building, in keeping with its awkward exterior, was equally odd inside. Like a series of stacked hallways, it was built narrow and deep, which allowed for very few offices with windows, since only the front and the back were free of the two brick behemoths on either side.

The receptionist returned and told me I could go up. Jack Plummer and I had known one another for twenty years. He was a fastidious man, plump and bald as an egg, given to bow ties, French meals, and front-row seats at the nearby Marlboro Music Festival every summer. Our connection, needless to say, was not social. As one of the town's highest-paid criminal lawyers, which, in truth, wasn't saying too terribly much, he had gleefully grilled me on many occasions in court, a relationship which had in turn led, paradoxically, to a pretty sound friendship.

His office was on the third floor, facing High Street, and took up the entire breadth of the building. He was also, this announced, the senior partner of the firm. The door was open, and his secretary waved me in without a word.

Jack was tilted back in his chair with his feet parked on his windowsill—fastidious but not prissy. He was also not one to beat around the bush. "I take it you're here to discuss Charlie Jardine."

"Very good."

He waved it away. "Hardly; the whole town is beginning to hum about your problems. Plus, you're a little behind the eight ball. Stan Katz has already come and gone."

That struck a sour note. "Really? When?" Katz would be twice as fired up since McDonald had beaten him to the punch identifying Jardine.

"I don't know; an hour or two ago."

"Sent to you by Arthur Clyde?" I wondered how deep he'd dug already.

"He didn't say. He is an amazingly unappealing little man, isn't he?"

"Katz? Yeah. What did you tell him?"

"Nothing. He asked if Jardine had worked here. I said yes. He asked if I'd known him. I said no. It went downhill from there. Only lasted a few minutes. He's probably wining and wooing half my staff by now, looking for the scuttlebutt."

"Which is what, exactly?"

"About Charlie?" Plummer looked thoughtful for a few moments. "Not much, really. Interesting guy in a way. One of the few people I ever met who defied categorization."

"How do you mean?"

"Well, he was like a bottomless pit. You could shovel things into him and never hear it land, but you could never get much out of him."

"Kept to himself, then?"

"No, no. He was all over the place. The guy was an office boy, for Christ's sake; that's a job leading nowhere, generally held by nobodies. They pick up mail, deliver memos, go out for pizza, buy stationery supplies. Their curiosity is satisfied by catching a glimpse down some secretary's blouse. Charlie attacked this place like it was a natural stepping stone to fame and fortune—a training ground. He read everything he could, asked questions of all of us, even took me out to lunch once just to grill me about criminal law. And his curiosity wasn't restricted to just the lawyers. I'd hear him asking the girls about how the computers worked, or how our contract with the Xerox people was set up. I don't doubt he interviewed the janitor on the merits of Ty-D-Bol."

"He didn't show any preferences?"

"Oh, sure, eventually he turned Tucker into his favorite port of call, but even then he didn't lose sight of the rest of us. Amazing drive. I wasn't surprised he finally succeeded."

"By getting Wentworth to sponsor him with Clyde?"

Plummer hesitated. "Yeah, well, I meant before that—by getting Tucker to turn him into a sort of protégé. Tucker's a pretty private man, and I don't think at first he was too impressed being hounded by the guy who delivered his morning mail. But Charlie was pretty irrepressible; even

Tucker had to finally respect that. Jardine had the get-up-and-go we all have envied in other people at one point or another in our lives. When someone like that asks for help, it's pretty hard to resist."

"Did it become a personal friendship?"

Again Plummer paused before speaking. "I sensed they were certainly friendly, given their age difference, but I couldn't say much beyond that. As I mentioned, Tucker's pretty private, and I don't know if any of us ever found out what really made Charlie tick, so what they thought about one another is a little hard to guess. But, like you said, Tucker did sponsor him with Clyde, which isn't something he would have done lightly."

"Is Tucker really so sharp that Charlie would have picked up so much?"

Plummer laughed. "Tucker Wentworth is a natural. Business finance, in all its aspects, is to him what the sea is to a fish: home."

"So—no offense—but what's he doing here?"

Plummer laughed. "Oh, shit, he's just like the rest of us, practicing on-the-job retirement." The smile faded from his face. "Actually, his stimulus for leaving the fast lane wasn't so self-serving. Some twenty years ago, his wife died, I don't know from what. He doesn't speak of it, but I've heard it was a painful experience. In any case, he had a young daughter whom I supposed he'd never really focused on, and I think it hit him that what he'd been working for all this time had nothing to do with reality. So he stepped back, signed on with us, and began paddling in calmer waters. His daughter and he are very close, he lives in a huge, fancy home with a view of the West River Valley that'll break your jaw, and he's become a kind of distant elder statesman in his field. Life has become heaven on earth, from what I can tell."

"So he kept up with his past work—I mean, he didn't lose touch being out here instead of in New York?"

Jack Plummer leaned over and patted his telephone. "Welcome to the twentieth century, Joe. Between this, the computer, and the fax, all Tucker Wentworth missed out on were the power lunches and the attending heartburn. He'd already culled a lifetime's worth of contacts. All he had to do when he joined us was maintain them.''

I gave him a skeptical look.

He held up both his hands. "He's an elder statesman. He doesn't need to earn his stripes in the fast lane anymore; nor does he need to know all the nitty-gritty about who's screwing who. He can play a more general game now, and be just as successful. He can also afford to be generous, which does Morris, McGill good, and obviously didn't hurt our friend Charlie Jardine.''

"So what made that relationship click?''

Plummer shrugged. "Who knows? The son he never had? Some shared interest I know nothing about? Usually it's a little thing, some initial connection. It grows from there; I don't know why.''

"What did they do? Spend hours together in the office doing a *My Fair Lady* imitation?''

Plummer laughed again. "If they did, they kept their singing low. Yeah, they spent time together, but they both had their own work to do. I used to see Charlie doing a lot of reading in his spare time, presumably homework Tucker had assigned him. I guess they spent non–office hours together, too, but I don't know for sure. You have to understand that Charlie was amazingly bright. He soaked up information like a blotter. I think a lot of his education from Tucker consisted of just being pointed in the right direction. That's probably what made it so gratifying to Tucker—it was easy and rewarding. The American Dream.''

I mulled over all he had said for a few moments. "I take it Wentworth knows about his death by now?''

Plummer shook his head sorrowfully. "I guess so; everyone else does. He was in this morning, but he's out of town until tomorrow night on business. I'm sure he heard the news on the radio, though.''

"So Katz hasn't talked with him?''

"Not here. That doesn't mean he didn't drive his car through the poor bastard's front door before Tucker left.''

I couldn't resist asking, "What about McDonald? Did he come by?''

Plummer smiled. "Better manners. He called, but I stiffed him, too."

I got to my feet. "Will you let me know if anything comes up I might be interested in?"

"Sure, if I think it's fair to Tucker."

I nodded. "Okay. Oh, there was something else. Do you know if Wentworth helped finance ABC Investments?"

Plummer looked thoughtful. "Finance it? I haven't the slightest idea. I don't doubt he steered some business their way, but that would stand to reason. You'll have to ask him. If he did supply the financing, it'll be in the public record—by law."

"And what about Arthur Clyde? Do you know him?"

"Nope. I think I've seen him in the building a couple of times, when he was visiting Tucker, but I'm not even sure I'd recognize him if he walked in the door right now."

"Okay. Thanks, Jack."

"You bet. Give my best to Gail."

Jack Plummer's information had been full, detailed, and enlightening, but all it had done for me was to render Jardine's portrait even murkier.

Charlie Jardine had come across as a young eager-beaver—bright, a quick learner, full of intelligent questions—a man on the go. Had that jibed with everything else I knew of his past and personality, I really would have been flummoxed by his grisly demise, but the contrasts kept my interest keen. For example, what did a golly-gee, supermotivated gofer have in common with Rose Woll's portrait of a reckless, irresponsible, sexual sybarite?

And why had a man of minimal education and a dead-end future suddenly shifted gears? Which button had been pushed? Was it the death of his parents and the sudden inheritance? Had there been a bond there that had held him captive, which when severed had allowed him to soar? Or had his apparent aimlessness fresh out of high school merely been the signs of a man finding a foothold? And why the obsession to separate sex from emotion—the manipulativeness implied by all those mirrors and oils and the cocaine? Despite Rose Woll's appreciation of him, Charlie seemed to me as sensual as an expert lathe operator, producing brilliant, complex results by coldly mechanical means.

People do not get themselves systematically executed like Charlie had without having gotten someone extremely pissed off. And despite his business partner, his employer, and one of his girl friends all agreeing that the dead man had been a very nice guy, I couldn't shake Plummer's image of Jardine as a deep and unyielding emotional well.

The paradox was, I found all that strangely heartening. It made me feel that in pursuing Charlie Jardine, I was following the right track.

The mood didn't last. As I walked down High Street, Stan Katz poked his nose out of the Dunkin Donuts. "I was wondering when you'd get back."

I looked at him incredulously. "You've been staking me out?"

He grinned. "Sure. You think you guys are the only ones who do that?"

"I thought you'd have better things to do. Christ, we came up with a fresh corpse for you. Why aren't you hanging around down there, or did McDonald beat you out again?"

He gave me a sour expression. "I knew about Jardine before he did; I just don't have a public outlet every hour on the hour. Besides, it's no big deal—who cares when a body is ID'd? You people would have 'fessed up soon enough anyhow."

He shifted gears, barely bothering to sound nonchalant. "I heard somebody call the stiff 'Milly,' but that didn't mean anything to me."

"Millard Crawford, called Milly for short. You can find out more about him in the court records. He was a regular customer. Shot at close range."

Katz stared at me, his eyes narrowed. "What're you up to?"

"Meaning?"

"Usually it's 'no comment,' or 'talk to the SA.' Why so chatty?"

I turned to cross the street. "Fine. No comment, then."

He reached out and touched my elbow. "No, no. Don't get your shorts in a twist. I was just surprised, that's all."

"You know, Stanley, I'm not uncooperative just for fun. But you nag and nag and nag like a kid who doesn't know when to quit. You should learn to win people over."

He was shaking his head, unconvinced by my contrived

irritation. "That's not it. You want me to chase after Crawford instead of Jardine. Why aren't you at today's murder scene right now?"

The clever son of a bitch had me there. That was exactly why I'd given him Milly's name. "Wouldn't do any good. Besides, I was the first one there; rode in the ambulance with the guy. Tyler and his boys're doing the technical stuff now. I'll get into it later."

He ignored me, correctly sensing he was on the right track. "In the interest of fair play, I was thinking I should get some comments from you about Jardine before I file my story."

"Sure." He'd turned tables on me. Now I was the one wondering what card he had up his sleeve. We may have been natural antagonists, but I had to admit he was tough, determined, and damned good at his job; all qualities I would have admired if he'd been a cop.

"For example, you just went to Morris, McGill, where Jardine was once employed, to investigate the highly unusual connection between that firm and ABC Investments."

"Really? I thought I went there to hear them laugh about how they told you to take a hike."

"I also know that you people think Crawford and Jardine were connected, and that you were about to question Crawford before he was killed."

I smiled at him. "You didn't even know Crawford's name two minutes ago."

He flared. "The name of the guy's irrelevant; I heard you tell Dispatch you were parked at Horton Place just before all hell broke loose. You were there to interview somebody, only it turns out somebody beat you to it. Crawford and Jardine are part of a pattern."

I was impressed. Based on a few overheard radio comments, and a knowledge of how we worked, he was close to hitting the nail on the head. It almost saddened me to have to play the charade out to its humdrum conclusion.

"Write what you will, Stanley, but I wouldn't stick my neck out too far, if I were you. You could end up looking pretty foolish." Or we could, I thought privately.

•　　•　　•

One Hundred Main, as the boutique was called, was right where Tyler had said it belonged. The lettering of the sign was pseudo–Art Deeo, and the windows picked up the theme, with flapper-clad mannikins holding 1920s props. Inside, the decor and the cool air exuded exclusiveness and ritzy class. I couldn't for the life of me figure out why anyone would have such a store in Brattleboro.

A tall, gray-haired woman in elegant clothes slid up the counter toward me, her penciled-in eyebrows arched in inquiry. "May I help you?"

"I'm Lieutenant Gunther from the Police Department. One of my men called earlier about a blouse you sold."

The eyebrows came down, as did the sophisticated manner and the mid-Atlantic accent. "Oh, yeah. The Riviera—that's what we call it."

She walked back along the counter to the cash register. "I dug it out of the files. Wasn't hard; it's the only one we've sold. Real expensive." She began pawing through a drawer.

"You do a lot of business?"

"No. I think the place is a tax dodge, if you ask me. Still, it's a job. Ah, here it is." She handed me a sales slip.

Attached to it was a credit-card receipt. She'd been right; the blouse had cost one hundred and ninety-five dollars. More interesting, though, was the name on the receipt.

"Did you make the sale?"

"Yeah. She was perfect for it. Looked great."

"Can you describe her?"

"Sure. About my height, slim, not too much up top—that's what made the blouse look so good on her—and she had very blonde hair."

I thought back to Ned Beaumont's description of Jardine's last female visitor. "Almost silvery, cut in a page boy?"

"That's right."

I looked at the receipt again, studying the signature: Blaire Wentworth. So Charlie Jardine's interest in Tucker Wentworth included his daughter. Maybe Stan Katz was on to something, after all.

CHAPTER

14

FROM the soft mutterings emanating from my portable radio as I crossed the street, I knew that part of the team digging in and around Milly's apartment had returned to the Municipal Building. Not only was I curious to find out what they'd discovered, I also wanted to make sure I'd overturned every rock available to me before I confronted the Wentworths.

My trip to those rocks, however, was interrupted as I walked through the Police Department's doors. Gary Nadeau, the town attorney, was approaching down the hallway, a long-suffering expression on his face. "I'd like to talk to you."

The town attorney, unlike Brandt or Town Manager Tom Wilson, has no employment contract to protect him. He is appointed by the selectmen and confirmed by town meeting in March of every year. His job, therefore, hangs on the good graces of any three of the five selectmen. It is a political thread always ready to snap.

Over the years, there have been aggressive town attorneys, who made it their business to collect as much dirt on the selectmen as possible in order to keep them muzzled; passive types, who did their jobs and kept a packed bag always ready under their rented beds; and supposedly self-preserving types, who believed survival was based on toadying

135

up to the bosses. The last, to my thinking, was the least reliable variety, and matched Gary Nadeau to a gnat's eyelash.

I was, unfortunately, a minority, for Gary had the reputation of being a ready listener and a good old boy, which made him the repository—and the conduit, as I saw it—of a lot of information he didn't need to have.

"What's on your mind, Gary?"

He lightly grabbed my elbow—a gesture I've never liked— and steered me toward one of the walls, as if seeking earthquake protection. "Well, it's a favor, actually, about something that really doesn't come under my jurisdiction."

I let him dangle in silence.

"It's these killings. I've been getting some heat from, you know, the big brass. They want to know what's going on. Could you give me something to tell them, just to get them off my back?"

I made a big show of shaking my head in commiseration, as if I were receiving news of his pet beagle's death. "I wish I could; there's just not much to tell yet."

He tossed that away with a nervous wave of his hand. "I heard one of our officers was near the place where Jardine was found."

I deadpanned. That information was generally available, but to pick it out specifically meant someone was paying very close attention, and I doubted it was just Nadeau. "It was a routine patrol—unconnected."

He lumbered on—Mr. Casual. "Well, I wondered, you know, because if one of your personnel was somehow involved, I should be informed, since personnel matters do come under my umbrella."

"When there's a legal problem, yes."

There was a long pause, during which I stayed absolutely still, the better to offset Nadeau's nervous twitches. He finally gave it up with a sigh, shoved his hands into his pockets, and gave me an idiotically false grin. "Right. Well, thanks for the chat. Keep in touch."

"Glad I could help," I said, moving across the hall toward Brandt's side of the building, my course changed by this little noninterview.

The usual cacophonous symphony of hammers, saws, and drills outside the chief's office had been reduced to single, identifiable outbursts. The carpenters were winding down, putting up trim and fitting hardware to doors. It wouldn't be long before their efforts were restricted to the officers' room only.

Brandt removed his oral fog machine. "What've you got on Milly?"

"I don't know yet. I was on my way to find out when Gary grabbed me in the hallway. He's snooping for the 'big brass,' as he calls them—asked me about John's cruiser being seen near Jardine's grave. I don't think he's on to anything, but I thought you should know. By the way, I just found out that woman's blouse we found at Jardine's belonged to Blaire Wentworth."

"Tucker's daughter?" He mulled that over for a few seconds. "Curiouser and curiouser."

I reopened the door. "Yup. I'll let you know about Milly."

Brandt suddenly held up his hand. "Hold it. You wanted to know about John Woll's whereabouts while Milly was being shot?"

"Yeah," I answered cautiously.

"Not good, I'm afraid. He told me he went for a drive in the country, to get some fresh air. He didn't stop anywhere, and he didn't see anyone he knew. Sorry." He looked at me for a quiet moment before going back to his computer and his smoke production.

J. P. Tyler was hunched over his desk, sorting through piles of various-sized Ziploc bags. I looked around the room and saw only Klesczewski sitting at the long table in the meeting room, doing some paperwork. "Hi, J. P. —you two the only ones back?"

Tyler looked over his shoulder. "Yeah. Dennis and the others are still interviewing. I think you were right about how the killer got out, by the way. Lucky he didn't plug you when you went by."

I didn't comment, but it was a sobering thought. It lent credibility to my growing concern that the person behind all this, even while forced to act fast, was still coolly following an agenda. Killing me on the stairway would have been easy and uncomplicating—one less cop was surely an asset. My being left to live was therefore paradoxically chilling: It made me all the more fearful of what our nemesis was up to.

I nodded at the pile on Tyler's desk. "What'd you come up with?"

He straightened, his eyes bright. This was one happy man. "This is just the small stuff. I don't know how it ties in with Milly's murder, but we have just fallen into the biggest coke stash this department's ever seen. I locked most of it in the evidence room."

I stared at him. "How much?"

"I haven't checked through it all yet, but I'd say about a kilo. There's also a couple of bags of pills and a shitload of grass—maybe another five pounds. Milly was running a small factory out of there."

I shook my head. "That doesn't fit; Milly was a small-timer."

Tyler shrugged. "Maybe he was just starting out. Only a couple of the coke bags had been opened and cut, at least by him. We'll have to have some purity tests done to figure out how much he stepped on, and how pure the stuff was he hadn't got to yet."

I suppose I should have been delighted. Considering what Katz had planned for us in tomorrow's paper— "Police Baffled"—this was publicity made in heaven: "Police Close Down Drug Wholesaler." Instead, my mind was suddenly filled with questions and doubts. There was no way in hell anyone was going to convince me that Milly Crawford had suddenly become a big-time drug lord. The quantities Tyler had mentioned, depending on the purity, could be worth one hundred and fifty thousand dollars at the street level, and would have cost Milly maybe fifty or sixty thousand to purchase. It was the kind of money he'd only had in his dreams.

Furthermore, that kind of transaction took brains, perseverance, and good connections. Nothing in Milly's history fit that picture. He'd been a small-time opportunist, content to fence shoplifted items for resale to flea-market vendors.

He'd stolen an occasional car, sold a little dope, committed a petty burglary or two. The only expertise he'd acquired over the years was an inside-out knowledge of who was doing what to whom among Brattleboro's low-rent criminals.

Which, of course, had a certain value of its own.

I thought of Charlie Jardine, suddenly rich in inherited chips, on the brink of becoming a big man in town, a regular at the Rotary lunches. He had the money and the perseverance. Maybe Milly had built up some valuable connections, which would have made the two of them a very compatible team.

"You didn't run across any interesting paperwork, did you?" I asked Tyler.

He laughed, still in a good mood. "Like receipts?"

"I found something." Klesczewski's voice floated in from the other room.

I stepped away from Tyler's cubicle and went over to the doorway. Klesczewski was sitting before a small scrap of dirty paper, his note pad, and an open copy of the *Johnson Directory*, or "crisscross book"—a reference linking telephone numbers to individuals, their addresses, and their professions.

He picked up the scrap and waved it at me. "I found this in the apartment. It's a list of five phone numbers."

I took it from him and looked at it, my heart skipping a beat at the last number on the list. I kept my voice neutral. "Why don't you bring the book into my office so we can kick this around?"

He looked at me oddly for a moment and then nodded. His voice matched mine. "Sure—you got the fan."

As we passed Tyler, he was back pawing through his envelopes, cataloging them into his evidence book, seemingly oblivious of our strange little dance.

Klesczewski closed my office door behind him. "I guess you recognized John Woll's number."

I didn't answer, but pulled a sheaf of papers from my desk and handed them over to him. "Yeah, I did. Those are Jardine's phone records."

He glanced at them and sat in the plastic guest chair. "Chief finally let go of them, huh?"

I took a deep breath, in part relieved to finally share a burden I'd borne only reluctantly from the beginning. "Not exactly. He and I were sitting on them for a while. We were afraid one of them might connect Jardine to John and/or Rose Woll."

Klesczewski looked down at the records in his hand again. "Holy shit." His voice was low and full of disappointment.

"We weren't sure we'd find anything, or what it'd mean if we did, but we wanted to tread carefully, since it wouldn't have been the only thing linking them all together. I'm sorry, Ron. It wasn't exactly kosher."

Klesczewski shook his head, his cop's self-protective and perhaps self-serving instincts immediately grasping the rationale. "Oh, hell, that doesn't matter; the press would have a field day with this. What'd you think's going on?"

I turned on the fan, sat on the edge of my desk, and told him about recognizing Rose Woll's voice on the tape, interviewing John, and my conversation with Rose that morning at the bank. He kept silent throughout, reacting only with an occasional shake of his head.

I ended by pointing at the phone records. "That's just pure paranoia, I suppose; only long-distance calls show up . . ."

He waved it off. "You think she was lying about ending the affair?"

"Maybe. She might have been into him for the drugs only. I think it was a bit of both. She doesn't seem to have a great grasp on reality."

"You think John killed Jardine?"

"The evidence suggests it, circumstantially. You were supposed to check Jardine's background this morning; did you get anywhere on that?"

He looked mildly embarrassed, for no good reason. "No. I made a few phone calls, but I spent most of this morning clearing my desk of any stuff that had to be done in the next few days. Then, of course, the Milly thing came up."

"Well, work Rose and John into any questions you ask. But go lightly, okay? If somebody like Katz or McDonald picks up on this, the shit'll really hit the fan. So," I added regretfully, expanding both the conspiracy and the risk of discovery, "nothing on paper about them either; just keep it verbal between you, the chief, and me. Sorry I'm putting you in such a position."

"It's okay." He paused, and then asked the obvious: "Have you talked to John about all this?"

I shook my head. "If he's guilty, he could use the interview to find out how much we have on him. If he's innocent, it would just make him think we're out to get him. Either way, this case'll rest on all the evidence we can dig up, and I want as much of that as possible before sitting down with John."

I handed the scrap of paper back to him. "So who do those other phone numbers belong to?"

He opened his note pad. "Kenny Thomas, Paula Atwater, Jake Hanson, and Mark Cappelli."

None of them rang a bell with me.

"According to the crisscross, the first two work at the Putney Road Bank, Hanson isn't listed as doing anything, and Cappelli works for E-Z Hauling."

"As what?"

"Cappelli? Doesn't say."

I thought about that for a moment; any mention of drugs usually brings to mind transportation. "Did Lavoie say he could help you out on some of this?"

"Yeah, he jumped at it, like you said."

"Why don't you have him nail down exactly what these people do for a living? He can also find out who's around that remembers Jardine from high school. But I want you to do all the actual interviews, both the ones on that list and the general ones, okay? Just in case either one of the Wolls crops up. And do Cappelli first, if you can; the trucking angle interests me."

"What about Milly Crawford?"

"Dennis can head that up. Personally, I think they're both the same case anyhow. I just don't have any way to prove it for the moment."

Kleszewski stood up and smiled back at me from the door. "Well, I'll see what I can do about that."

I sat quietly for a few seconds, thinking about John Woll

and his wife. Whatever their involvement, it wouldn't be too much longer before their world was blown sky-high, unless I either defused the bomb beneath them, detonated it myself, or watched the press do the latter, regardless of the facts. I crossed the hall to Brandt's office.

"What's up? You look worried."

"I am," I admitted. "I've brought Ron into our little secret about John and Rose. He found a piece of paper with John's home number written on it in Milly's apartment, along with four other people's."

"Who?"

"We don't know yet; just names. Nobody notorious. The point is, we now have ties to John in both murders. In fact, he's the only common denominator."

"He is or Rose is."

"Okay. One or the other or both; whichever it is, the SA is going to be royally pissed if he discovers we've been sitting on this for days, just hoping it'll go away, and he'll be right if it turns out the Wolls are dirty."

"You think they are?"

"She's not playing straight, I'm pretty sure of that. As for John, I don't know; it's not looking good. But that might be exactly what we're supposed to think."

"All right." Brandt removed his pipe and placed both his hands behind his head. "What do you suggest?"

"We've got to follow the trail to the Wolls, even if the scent's suspicious."

"A search warrant?"

I shook my head. "I doubt we'd get it. We don't actually have anything truly incriminating against either one of them—it's all circumstantial."

I moved over to the window and stared out at the parking lot through the steel grille attached to the frame. As with most such locations in this town, the municipal lot had both predictable urban neighbors, such as the almost windowless State of Vermont District Office Building, and a few more off-beat reminders that Vermonters make poor urbanites: Parked under a shade tree just beyond our chain-link fence was a weary but serviceable wooden fishing boat, mounted on a trailer and ready to roll as soon as its owner knocked off work.

I turned back to face Brandt. "Hypothetical question: Why would John kill Jardine or Milly?"

"Jardine for adultery and supplying his wife with drugs; Milly for being the source of the drugs."

"So why did Milly have his name on a piece of paper?"

Brandt smiled. "It's Rose's number, too."

I tapped my forehead gently against the grille. This whole damn thing was driving me crazy; not just the complexity of the case, but the duplicitous role I'd taken on. "I just lectured Ron on the rationale for not confronting John with all this right now, but I have to admit, it's a temptation to kick the apple cart over to see what we end up with."

Brandt smiled in sympathy, but still he held firm. "Let's see what those other names on Milly's list are first, to establish if there's a connection. It would be nice having that under our belts before confronting him."

I sighed my agreement and headed for the door, pausing as I got there. "By the way, some good news. Tyler tells me we grabbed our biggest dope stash ever in Milly's apartment. That ought to play well."

"We may need it." The weariness in his voice told me I wasn't the only one feeling the stress. And I had a feeling the worst was yet to come.

CHAPTER
15

LATE that afternoon, I pried Billy Manierre out of his reclusive lair in the corner of the future officers' room and asked him to attend a full meeting of all investigators, including those few patrolmen who'd already been assigned to help us out. My motive, of course, was pure greed—I needed more manpower, and wanted Billy to rearrange his three shifts to supply me.

Despite my gut feeling that the Jardine and Crawford murders were connected, and perhaps even committed by the same person, I had to treat them as separate cases. After all, the only tie linking them was a thumb print on a Ziploc bag and John Woll's telephone number—and the latter was a secret only three of us shared.

Not that my request of Billy would have been any different had I chosen to lump the two cases together. Either way, I still had four areas that needed lots of plain old conventional police work: the Jardine grave site, the scenic dwelling under the Elm Street Bridge, Jardine's house, and Milly's apartment.

Billy, as usual, was the soul of generosity. By slimming down the patrol shifts, pulling in all his special officers, and assigning his parking-enforcement crew to wider duties, he met my request while still attending to his own requirements. It would all be reflected in the overtime budget, of course, but that was always a predictable battle in any case.

With the meeting concluded and its participants scattered, I sat alone in the conference room, amid the fetid, motionless air, surveying a long table littered with stub-choked ashtrays, half-empty coffee cups, and crumpled bits of litter. I was suddenly drained of all energy and felt as rooted to my chair as if my legs had been anesthetized. I glanced at my watch. I was due at Gail's for dinner in twenty minutes.

Ordinarily, I might have called her and begged off, choosing to collapse in my own bed to see if ten hours of sleep might offset thirty-six in overdrive. But I didn't want to do that. Tonight I needed her company both for the creature comforts it offered and to dampen the guilt I'd been feeling by seeing her as a selectman first and a discreet and trusted friend second.

So I cranked myself out of the chair, clocked out, told Dispatch where I could be reached, and shuffled out to the parking lot.

Gail Zigman and I had met six years ago at an open-air community meeting hosted by Vermont's Pat Leahy, a US Senator with a penchant for consulting his conscience before running off at the mouth. She had just been elected selectman and was well known around town both as a successful realtor and a member of damn near every left-leaning, charitably disposed board the town could dish up. I had heard of her, but didn't even know what she looked like until she sat down next to me and introduced herself. It was a late-summer evening, with a tinge of fall coolness in the air, and I ended up lending her my jacket and admiring her clean profile out of the corner of my eye.

It hadn't been a romance at first glance. Indeed, she'd left that meeting with other people, thanking me for the use of the jacket. But I saw her again on some other occasion, got to talk with her, and found her mind, like her profile, equally free of distracting lumps and bulges.

Our courtship was leisurely. She'd never married, I'd been widowed for quite some time. We were both therefore very comfortable in our respective bachelorhoods, and in no rush to complicate things. But we discovered over time that we had become best friends, turning to one another for advice and companionship over lunch or dinner. Becoming lovers, finally, was a natural extension of that friendship.

Mine had not been an overly populated life. My brother, Leo, and I had been born and brought up on a farm near Thetford Hill, about halfway up the eastern side of the state. Our father had been a silent, hardworking man, considerably older than our mother, who had dedicated herself to supplying her family with virtually all its essential needs, including many of its cultural ones. She did this with such success that Leo and I were content most of the time to stay put on the farm.

As teenagers, we never felt any yearning to escape to the neighborhood watering holes, an isolationist tendency that followed both of us through the years. Leo, several years my junior, never did marry, and still lived on the farm with our now wheelchair-bound mother, working as a butcher and dividing his extracurricular interests between classic cars of the fifties and fabulously endowed young women with very short attention spans.

I, on the other hand, had become, for a time, a nomad, fighting in the Korean War, attending but not graduating from college in California, sampling the early stirrings of what would revolutionize the sixties. I returned to Vermont with an enormous library of eclectic tastes, more questions than I could handle, and was gradually tamed, first by Frank Murphy, who lured me to Brattleboro and the Police Department, and then by Ellen, whom I met and married shortly thereafter.

Ellen's death, eight years later, nipped that renascent taste for interdependence in the bud, driving me back to my solitude and my books. Meeting Gail many years later was thus a seriously mixed blessing, and had posed the first real threat to my by-now stolid bachelor ways.

Not that she ever pushed for marriage, or even cohabitation. She too had become used to a single life. Still, relationships by their very nature must evolve, and I often feared ours would eventually collapse precisely because neither one of us wanted it to change.

It nearly had ended the previous fall. I'd gone up to

Gannet, in Vermont's remote Northeast Kingdom area, for what I'd hoped would be a working vacation. It had turned out to be a grueling murder investigation. I'd emerged from the traumatic Gannet case, dedicated to patching things up between us.

That optimism had benefited us both. We still lived apart, still pursued our separate interests, but now, having leapt this hurdle of self-doubt together, we'd come to trust one another more deeply, which is why the John Woll time bomb, and the obvious effect its explosion would have on the board of selectmen, chewed at me so constantly.

Gail lived in West Brattleboro, on the other side of Interstate 91, on Meadowbrook Road. Her home had once been an apple barn, isolated at the top of a hill, the lesser of several outbuildings belonging to the Morrison Farm. Now that barn was Morrison's only tribute, the farm having been sold and subdivided, and all the other buildings demolished.

She'd renovated it, of course, filling it with a dizzying array of platforms and catwalks, all interconnected by enough stairways to satisfy an aerobics instructor. The core of the building she'd left open, so it soared some twenty feet to the rafters. In the winter, the whole place could be heated with the single wood stove in the center of the first floor. In the summer, the heat rose to the high ceiling and was vented through large skylights there, encouraged by two broad Hunter fans that continually moved the air.

I drove up her steep, long driveway, leaving the gloom of the gully and the road behind and becoming increasingly exposed to the sunset-lit view that surrounded her house. As I got out of the car, I felt bathed in the light of the pink-tinged bluish clouds overhead, stretching all the way to the blazing, mountainous horizon.

Gail, barefoot, in shorts and an abbreviated T-shirt that exposed her tanned stomach, lay stretched on a metal-and-plastic lawn chair on the second-floor deck that surrounded three sides of the building. Stepping onto the deck, I walked over to her and kissed her without saying a word. Her lips tasted of salt.

She shifted her gaze from the dazzling sunset and smiled at me. "You are a sight for sore eyes."

I settled into the chair next to hers, feeling as I did so the last of my energy giving out. "I feel like I've been hit by a truck."

She reached out and took my hand in hers. "How's it all going, Joe?"

"Well, it ain't no back-bedroom crime of passion. I have the sinking sensation we'll be tearing at this for a while, and that before it's all over, there'll be more bodies to bury, literally and otherwise."

She looked at me with her brow furrowed. "Why do you say that?"

I waved my free hand toward downtown Brattleboro, invisible behind a masking cloak of distant green trees and hills. "Somebody down there has a serious grudge, and I don't think he's half close to getting it off his chest."

"And you haven't the slightest idea who he is?"

I shook my head, tempted to tell her anyway. "I have ideas, but that's all."

She looked confused. "So you have a suspect, but you don't know if he's the right guy?"

I changed my mind and slid away from the truth. "You got it."

I told her about Gary Nadeau making a grab for some inside information. I put it in joking terms, but she only half smiled.

"Luman Jackson was behind that; I can almost guarantee it. Mrs. Morse finally found someone she could get hysterical with."

That was not good news; nor was it surprising. Jackson was vice-chairman of the board of selectmen. Once a teacher at the local high school, he'd retired several years back and had decided to right the wrongs he'd claimed had been foisted on the town by its incompetent leaders. Now, no less incompetent himself, he was a brooding, occasionally raging presence on the board, using manipulation, accusation, and sometimes outright blackmail to get his way. I guessed Gary Nadeau was deep in his pocket, and I knew Town Manager Tom Wilson would usually yield rather than stand on principle. I also sensed that a good many other people in town government had become Jackson's stoolies out of fear for their jobs. He was the man Tony Brandt most frequently locked horns with, and was without doubt one of the primary reasons Brandt had chosen his current strategy.

I kept my voice neutral. "He's getting worked up, is he?"

Gail hesitated before answering. "Well, he's certainly doing that, but that's nothing new. He hates Brandt and would love to see him canned. But I sense something else here. Usually, he gets this glint in his eye when he's really onto something, but this time it's not as obviously calculating; it's more emotional. Nothing positive, though; just a feeling."

I thought of John Woll. "No innuendos to go on?"

She shook her head. "Just the glint, so far, although it seems worse than usual."

I glanced over at her, her eyes closed, her skin made dark by the blush of the fading sun. She looked very peaceful and in control, not at all awed by the threat of what she'd just forecast. She came from a generation that had cut its teeth protesting the Vietnam War, defending the underprivileged, decrying complacency and the status quo. Her past had prepared her well for her service on the board. People like Luman Jackson were not taken personally, or blown out of proportion. She dealt with their actions, and avoided the dirt. It was an admirably clear-sighted approach, but I knew it must take its toll. Gail was no saint, after all, and had been known to have a nasty temper when properly irked. I knew that from personal experience.

"Has Luman leaned on you over this thing, because of me?"

"Oh, a bit." She opened her eyes and turned toward me. We were still holding hands. "Not enough to make any difference. Luman lives his life as a conspiracy, so he sees everyone else conspiring against him. To him, you and I aren't a couple; we're a plot, a dark and private conduit between the selectmen and the PD. So, sure, he leans on me sometimes, making insinuating remarks, but that's all he can do. It amounts to a lot of hot air. It might be different if we were creeping around trying to keep this a secret; he would love that. But we're not, so I wouldn't worry.''

That made me feel great.

An alarm jangled by her side. "Ah, dinner beckons.''

She got up and I followed her into the house. It was cooler than the deck. The fans overhead were whirling at top speed, making the dozens of plants look like they were enjoying a breezy day by the sea.

The kitchen had once been in a separate room, but Gail had since torn down the wall between it and the central core of the house. In fact, the bathroom was the only totally walled-off enclosure left in the building. I noticed that nothing was on the stove and that the oven knob was set at zero. "What was the alarm bell for?''

Gail went over to the icebox and pulled out a large earthenware bowl. "Cold soup; I had to refrigerate it for a couple of hours.'' She kept adding to a pile of things on the counter, all from the icebox. "Also cold fruit salad, cold celery and cheese, cold ice tea, and, in the freezer, cold ice cream. It's a thematic meal.'' She was a lacto-vegetarian, eating no fish, fowl, flesh, or eggs.

I looked suspiciously at the cheese on the celery. "What is that?''

"A mixture of bleu and cream cheese. Sorry, they were out of Cheez Whiz.''

"You should switch stores. And this?'' I sniffed at the soup, which had no odor whatsoever.

"Carrot soup mixed with orange juice.''

"My God. Is that legal?''

Laughing, she dipped a spoon into the gluey orange substance and held it out for me to taste. I scooped a bit off the end of the spoon with my lips. It was delicious. "Oh, that's awful.'' I finished the spoonful.

We ate under the fans, on the thick wool rug, our plates, bowls, and glasses spread out as if at a picnic. The sun had set, and the lighting came from indirect, hidden sources, mostly tucked behind the plants to project the giant shadows of their leaves across the ceiling and walls. It was all I had hoped it would be earlier, when I'd opted to come despite my exhaustion. Now, that deadness at my center had been smoothed to mere fatigue and I was feeling whole again, and more hopeful that with time and a few breaks, what had seemed chaos to me earlier would sort itself out.

Gail got up, walked over to me, and told me to take off my shirt and roll over onto my stomach. She then sat on my haunches and began working her fingers into my back, locating the knotted muscles and setting them loose. She was very good, trained in this as she was in the other extensions of her naturalist philosophy.

After some fifteen minutes of pure bliss, I rolled over onto my back and looked up at her, still straddling my hips. Her face was shining with perspiration. "You do good work."

"I'd take that as a compliment if I didn't know you're only half conscious."

I laid my hands high on her bare thighs, which were hot and slippery from her exertion. "Christ, you worked up a sweat."

She smiled at me, and in one fluid movement removed her T-shirt. She was wearing nothing underneath. "That's not all."

•   •   •

When the phone rang, I listened to the answering machine giving its predictable message. Then I heard Sammie Martens's voice: "Lieutenant, I hate to bother you, but if you're there, could you either pick up or call me at the office right away? Thanks."

Gail, now naked, had dozed off on top of me. We were still on the rug, still intertwined and slightly sticky with sweat. I slid out from under her and glanced at my watch as I answered. At most, I'd been asleep a couple of hours. It wasn't quite midnight. "What's up, Sammie?"

"Sorry, Joe, but I think I've got the man we've been looking for, the one who spent the night under the Elm Street Bridge."

CHAPTER

16

EVER since Sammie had reported that Toby, her home-less informant, had been offered five hundred dollars by some mystery man to locate the bridge dweller, I'd told her to concentrate solely on finding him. Despite the growing work load, and the help she could have given by fulfilling other duties, my instinct was that the killer was stalking that bum, and that if we didn't find him first, we never would. Her phone call gave me hope that we were close to a major breakthrough.

Buddy Schultz almost dropped his mop when I banged through the back entrance to the Municipal Center. "Holy cow, Lieutenant. You almost scared me to death. Somethin' up?"

"Just a little late-night work. Sorry I startled you."

He shook his head in wonder. Compared to his other tenants, the Police Department was probably a prime source of entertainment. He made me feel almost sorry I couldn't tell him of a major riot breaking out.

Sammie was waiting for me in my office, which, when I entered, I wished she hadn't been. I was instantly assaulted by the overwhelming odor of cheap wine, stale sweat, and what could only be described as rotting animal matter, all of it emanating from a tattered pile of humanity which was parked on one of my two guest chairs.

Sammie rose as I entered. "Hi, Lieutenant. This is Milo. Milo, Lieutenant Joe Gunther."

Milo looked as if he'd fallen asleep, a gesture I envied him. I wondered myself how much longer I could keep functioning without some sleep. I sat on the edge of my desk, my fingers unconsciously dabbling in the large ashtray filled with paper clips. "Hello, Milo. How're you doin'?"

He looked at me with one yellow, watery eye. The other one had a whitish glaze and didn't seem to function. "Okay." His voice was low and gravelly, as if he had a severely sore throat.

"Sammie tells me you used to live under the Elm Street Bridge. That right?"

He thought about that. In fact, all his responses were delayed by long pauses, although I became less convinced as we went along that thoughtfulness had much to do with it.

"Yup."

"Were you living there the night before last?"

"Before last? Sure."

"How long had you been living there?"

The eye, which had wandered to the floor, slid back up and fixed me again, watching me carefully. "How long? I don't know."

"A few days? A few weeks?"

"A while." Behind his caked, multistained beard, I caught the hint of a smile.

"And three nights ago—the night before last—did anything happen that struck you as unusual?"

He was wearing a raincoat, and he removed one hand from its pocket to scratch at his forehead, which was grimy and spotted with scabs. His fingernails were snaggled and black. "Like what?"

I had to be careful here. If I suggested a possibility he found acceptable, some defense lawyer down the line could accuse me of creating the very story I wanted to hear. "How did you sleep that night, Milo? Did you sleep through the night?"

"I woke up to piss." He glanced at Sammie to check for a reaction, but she was busy scribbling on her note pad.

"Did you see or hear anything unusual during that time?"

"I pissed in the water. I like the sound it makes."

"I meant something outside the area in which you were sleeping."

"Like what?" Again the sly smile.

I looked at Milo for a moment's silence, wondering about that smile. Then I circled my desk, pulled out the file Tyler had put together on the bridge site, and resumed my perch. "I don't know; how about gunshots? Hear any of those?"

"Nope."

I feigned surprise. "You're kidding. No shots? Something like a backfire, maybe?"

His brow furrowed. "I never read nothin' about gunshots."

"I'm asking what you heard, Milo."

His face closed down to an obstinate mask. "No. No shots."

"What did you make your bed out of?"

"I was under the bridge. There wasn't no bed."

"But you slept on something. What was it?"

"You know what it was. You found it. Don't you believe me or somethin'? I was under that bridge."

"I believe you, Milo, but the bedding was missing. We need to know what it was you used as a bed."

Sammie had stopped writing and was looking at me strangely.

Milo's eyes shifted back and forth several times, his lips tight. "Cardboard. I slept on cardboard boxes."

"Not newspapers? I thought you guys liked newspaper."

"It tears."

"So, no newspaper at all."

"No." His voice was defiant.

"Why'd you sleep so near the water? Weren't you afraid of getting wet, or of rolling over into the stream in your sleep?"

"No." More doubtful now.

"I would have tucked myself right up under the bridge, maybe dug a shelf so I'd be high and dry. Why didn't you do that?"

"Too much work." He didn't believe it anymore than I did.

"You smoke, Milo?"

"Why?"

"We found some butts. They yours?"

"Yeah."

"You smoke a lot, huh."

"Yeah. A lot." His confidence was returning.

"Bullshit." I tossed the file onto the desk. It made a little slapping sound in the quiet room. Milo watched it as if it might fly off and attack him, but it already had.

"Why're you telling us this, Milo? You were nowhere near that bridge."

He bristled. "Was too."

"Whoever was living there had been there for weeks, well over a month. The bed was made of newspaper. It was tucked up onto a shelf right under the angle of the bridge, six feet from the water, and there wasn't a butt to be seen that was under two months old. Why are you here, Milo?"

He went back to staring at the floor, his hands jammed into his pockets. Sammie was looking embarrassed.

"You're not in any trouble, you know. You haven't broken any laws. The worst you've done is waste my time and make Detective Martens feel bad. You could fix that by telling us why you came to us. Did someone tell you to?"

He didn't answer.

"You done talking to us, Milo?"

Still no response.

I tried one last time. I reached into my pocket and pulled out a five-dollar bill and extended it to him. He shifted his gaze to the bill. "Take it."

He hesitated.

"No strings. I don't know why you tried to jerk us around. I know word's gotten out we're looking for whoever was under that bridge, so maybe you thought it would be a lark to be him. Maybe someone threatened you or paid you off to do this. Beats me. But understand something, Milo. Whoever really was under that bridge had better watch his ass, because there's someone looking for him, the same guy who's killed two other people. So spread the word around. Tell whoever it is to come to us, or we'll all be going to his funeral."

Again, there was a long silence in the room.

"Is that all?" he muttered.

"Yeah. You can leave if you'd like. Call us if you want to talk more."

Milo rose to his feet, pulling the five dollars from between my fingers as he did so. He shambled out the door silently, leaving it open behind him.

Sammie looked at me with a crestfallen expression. "I'm really sorry."

"Don't be. Somebody tells you he's somebody else, you believe it. It's natural."

"You didn't."

"At first I did. You would've tumbled to him eventually; his story was pretty leaky. Anyway, maybe it'll do some good. If he spreads the word around, we might get lucky." I got up and stretched. "Well, I'm hitting the hay. Tell Dispatch I'll be at home, will you?"

Twenty minutes later, as I walked around opening windows and turning on fans in my apartment, I mulled over what we had so far. Two dead bodies, one an up-and-coming successful businessman with an unconventional past history and a hyperactive interest in sex and drugs; the other a lowbrow hustler and petty thief found in possession of enough narcotics to make a big-time dealer proud. Was Jardine financing Milly Crawford? Did Milly kill Jardine and then get killed in turn? If so, then by whom? Did John Woll kill Jardine out of jealousy? It made sense, but it didn't explain the connection between Milly and Woll, unless, of course, drugs were the motive, and not jealousy. There had been cases where cops had been used as protection by drug dealers, but that didn't seem to fit here. John Woll was a low-ranking patrolman, and had not, as far as I knew, had anything to do with drug investigations within the department.

Plus there was the assumption that John, if dirty, had transported Jardine's body in his patrol car, while on duty, to bury it in full view of any potential passerby. If he'd been that stupid, then why should I believe he was now cunning enough to kill Milly and stalk whatever bum might have seen him from under the bridge? Why so paranoid now if he'd been so careless and nonchalant initially?

And what of Tucker Wentworth and Arthur Clyde? What had two older, successful, veteran financiers seen in a local high-school graduate with an undistinguished string of minimum-wage service jobs in his wake? Were they as successful as they appeared? Had the lure of drug money caught their interest and led them to employ both Jardine and Milly Crawford as part of their organization? If so, then what had gone wrong? From all appearances, Milly hadn't really begun to tap into his chemical treasure trove—he'd been nipped in the bud and his product left for us to collect. His murder, I still felt, had been a risky, unplanned affair, committed to shut him up fast, not because he'd been guilty of any transgression. What had it been that he could have told us?

And then there was Blaire Wentworth, reputedly a devoted daughter, and apparently one of Jardine's lovers. Where did she fit? And was Rose Woll as innocent and unrealistic as she seemed?

I lay on top of my bed, naked, the two fans I'd placed on either side of me moving just enough air to keep me from soaking the sheets with sweat. As much as I needed sleep, I knew my mind would not shut down easily. It would keep working, mulling over the angles, applying less and less logic as my thoughts became more like dreams.

Indeed, when I finally did fall asleep, it was to the image of Luman Jackson, laughing maniacally, dragging the entire Police Department into court for "willfully ignoring the wishes of a town father," while a shadowy figure, his hands red with blood, faded gradually to the extreme limit of my vision, and then vanished.

CHAPTER 17

THE morning edition of the *Brattleboro Reformer* proved worse than I'd imagined. The body we had dug up the day before was identified as Charlie Jardine, Milly Crawford's murder was described as having taken place under our noses, and the drug seizure came across less as a coup, and more as dumb luck.

The editorial didn't help. It bemoaned a world in which a small, almost rural town like Brattleboro could become the target of drug traffic, and questioned the Police Department's ability to stem the potential "coming tide." The hand-wringing prose reflected the paper's new scarlet banner, and made me nostalgic for the tough-minded but clear-sighted *Reformer* of old.

Indeed, both the neighboring *Keene Sentinel* and *Greenfield Reporter*, which had also clarioned our troubles across their front pages, seemed downright muted in comparison.

On the other hand, Katz's vague promise of more shocking revelations were conspicuously absent. Both ABC Investments and Morris, McGill were mentioned, but only as places of employment. Either Stanley had shied away, or he was biding his time. I wasn't putting money on the first.

Predictably, the mood in the squad room was thunderous. Dennis DeFlorio was sputtering as he read one of the ten copies of the *Reformer* that were scattered around like oversized confetti: "'Police were noncommittal about the timing of their arrival at the murder scene, but from their promptness and from overheard radio transmissions between mobile police units and their dispatcher, it was apparent one or more of them had been positioned near Horton Place before Mr. Crawford was killed, for reasons unexplained. Later, one police officer was overheard saying, "He really pulled the rug out from under us," referring apparently to the murderer.' Can you believe this shit? I bet that son of a bitch quoted himself."

They were all there, including Sammie Martens, who looked like she hadn't gotten any sleep at all. I walked to the door of the meeting room and gestured to everyone to follow me. Harriet brought up the rear, yellow legal pad in hand.

I sat at the head of the table and waited for them to settle down. "We're going to have to ignore the press reports as much as possible. With the change of management at the *Reformer*, I think we'll all be seeing some pretty sensational stuff, a lot of which is going to get under our skin. This is the first time something this big has come their way, and the local editor is trying to satisfy his midwestern bosses. So, either get used to it or change subscriptions." I didn't add that if the politicians got warmed up, the press would be the least of our problems.

"At least Ted's playing it straight," someone muttered.

That much was true. On my short drive in, I'd tuned in to several radio reports. McDonald, the only local newscaster, had been his usual brief, straight, and to-the-point self. I guessed it helped when you had no time to editorialize. Ted, unlike Stan Katz, didn't have the luxury of a single story and thirty column inches to fill. To McDonald, we were merely the lead item in a four-minute summary, including the weather. Indeed, I often thought that my colleagues' preference for McDonald over Katz was based solely on Ted's inability to take up as much of their time with his reporting. Personally, while I found him by far the more unpleasant of the two, Katz got my nod as the better journalist. It was an opinion, however, that wild horses couldn't drag out of me in public.

I pointed the end of my pencil at Dennis. "What's the bottom line on the Milly canvass?"

Dennis gave a sour expression. "Whoever killed him really did pull the rug out from under us. We've interviewed everyone who lives on that street, and nobody saw a thing. A few people heard things, like Dummy shouting and you coming upstairs. A woman right below Milly's place said she heard footsteps just before the shouting, but she didn't pay any attention to it until later, after all hell had broken loose."

"No one heard the door to number 21 being broken?" I asked.

"Not specifically. Like I said, people heard things, but they can't, or won't, peg them down."

"J.P.?"

Tyler cleared his throat. "From the evidence, it appears the shooter nailed Milly with a silenced nine millimeter as he opened the door. He then hid in the apartment until Dummy went to the balcony, raced downstairs, broke into number 21 until you passed him on the way up, and escaped. It was a highly risky operation, successful only out of dumb luck."

"And a pair of brass balls," DeFlorio muttered.

"That's a good point," I interjected. "It did take balls, which brings up the major question here: Why did he kill Milly when he did?"

There was silence around the table, as when a teacher asks a question so apparently moronic that no one dares answer for fear it's a trap. "So we couldn't get to him first," Ron finally said in a soft voice.

"That's what I think, which might mean Milly could have fingered Jardine's killer. Remember: That's why we were there, to ask Milly about his involvement with Jardine. Does anybody here have a problem linking these two cases together?"

"I don't have a problem with it, but I don't think we should ignore the possibility that it was sheer coincidence."

That was Tyler, of course, applying the scientific leveler. I pointed my pencil at him. "What have you got on the dope?"

"It's a little early to tell. The total amount of cocaine was two pounds, just under a kilo; there were nine and a half pounds of marijuana, about four point five kilos; and there were two plastic bags of Bennies, Nebbies, and Blue Birds, all mixed together."

"What are Blue Birds?" Harriet asked, taking notes.

"Amytal—it's a barbiturate. I sent the coke north for analysis, but from what I tested, I'd say Milly's import was about eighty-percent pure, and if the sample we found at Jardine's came from Milly, then he was stepping on it hard, like down to twenty-five or thirty percent. Of course, in this market, he could do that and get away with it. They're used to shitty stuff."

"How many one-ounce packets could he make that way?" I asked.

"One hundred, maybe more, but he wouldn't sell it that way, not at two thousand dollars per ounce. He'd sell it by the gram, for maybe fifty to a hundred bucks. In those quantities, he could supply twenty-eight hundred customers."

"And make two hundred and eighty thousand dollars?" Dennis whistled.

Tyler hesitated. "Well, that would be on the fat side, and I'm guessing a lot here. Still, he would have cleaned up."

"I take it you got the results back on the Jardine sample?" I asked.

Tyler shook a sheet of paper before him. "This morning."

"Is there any way you can prove Milly processed it?"

"Not prove like in a court of law, but I'm pretty sure he did. It was cut in the same proportion as the few prepared samples we found at Milly's apartment, and they were both cut with mannitol."

The numbers Tyler had rattled off put a depressing pall on the group. Kilos of cocaine were what Tubbs and Crockett played with on "Miami Vice," complete with fast boats, submachine guns, and rock-and-roll theme music. Earlier, the mere mention of a single kilo in Brattleboro, Vermont, would have struck a similar fictional chord.

I turned to Klesczewski. "Ron, you're our resident expert in drug affairs. Why would Milly need that much? There aren't twenty-eight hundred coke sniffers in this town."

"There probably are throughout the state."

Again there was silence. The suggestion had been obvious, and the fact that I hadn't thought of it revealed how hesitant I was to truly grasp the significance of all this.

Ron continued. "You might want to talk to Willy Kunkle, Joe. He knew the drug scene inside out when he was here. I'm just learning still."

I nodded. He was right. Kunkle had made the town's underbelly his specialty, applying his mercurial moods and brutal methods where we could see them least. In the office, he'd been a dark beast of sorts, sour and distrustful, supposedly given to hitting his now-divorced wife during his off hours. Many of his fellow officers had been delighted when a sniper's bullet permanently disabled him and forced him into retirement. But Ron was right. In his way, Kunkle was an educated man, and I would have to visit him. Later.

"All right," I said. "Here're a few things to think about, then. Milly Crawford was sitting on enough coke to make him a wealthy man. Where and how did he get it, along with the money to buy it in the first place? Someone killed him just before we could talk to him. Why? Furthermore, assuming the drugs were part of the reason he was killed, why were they left in his apartment? Why was his death more important to his killer than a quarter-million-dollars' worth of dope? Was Jardine the money man and Milly the processor? If so, then who killed them—a third partner wanting more, or a competitor? Keep all that in mind as we go along, as well as J.P.'s suggestion that we may be dealing with two separate, unrelated homicides whose coincidences are screwing us up. It's not impossible that while Milly and Jardine were somehow linked, Jardine's killer might merely have been a jealous husband who knew nothing about his dope dealing."

There were some murmurs at that, and some comments about both cases in general. I wrapped up the meeting by asking what else might be worth sharing before we broke up.

Harriet handed me some legal paperwork. "This is the affidavit for a search warrant for Jardine's business records. I had Sue Davis at the SA's office review it; she wasn't thrilled, but said that was the judge's business. So," she smiled sweetly, "you have an appointment with Judge Harrowsmith in twenty minutes across the street."

I thanked her, took the papers, and checked my watch. "Ron, are you and Dennis available to grab those papers as soon as I get the warrant?"

They both nodded.

"Okay. We'll meet back here in half an hour. I want Dennis to dig into that stuff as soon as you get it. Harriet, maybe you can help out. Call Justin Willette if you run into anything that throws you. He's in the book under stockbrokers; he's helped us in the past."

We all rose and began filing out of the room. I stopped Ron Klesczewski at the door. "How did you manage with those four names on Milly's list?"

"I got a line on Mark Cappelli at E-Z Hauling. He's a truck driver, due back from a trip later this morning. I was planning to meet him when he arrived."

"I might join you, if that's all right."

He seemed pleased. "Sure. Thomas and Atwater are still at the bank—the one listed in the directory—and I figured we could chase them down at our convenience. Hanson I still don't know."

"How about Jardine's phone records?"

"I've got a list going. Nothing I can nail directly to . . ." His voice dropped and he looked around for eavesdroppers. "You know . . . John, but there're about fifteen numbers that crop up regularly; most of them are women, but about a third are men."

I shook my head. Even considering the number of people I'd come to know outside this town over the decades, I would have been hard put to collect a list that big from my long-distance phone records. Ron was going to have his work cut out for him interviewing them all, with or without help. "Is Blaire Wentworth one of them?" I remembered Plummer saying the Wentworths lived outside of Brattleboro.

He looked surprised. "Yeah. How did you know that?"

"She's the owner of the blouse. I should have mentioned that at the meeting; it'll be in my daily report Harriet is typing up. I'm going to see if I can chase her down after I see Harrowsmith, so you can cross her off your list.''

He grimaced. "Thanks a heap. She's probably the best-looking in the bunch.''

"I hope so.''

The District Courthouse had been built on the sharp point of the isosceles triangle formed by Park Place at the base, and Putney Road and Linden Street on the sides; it was also right across Linden from the Municipal Building. Despite certain similarities, such as the fact that they were both built of red brick and had oversized dormers defining their rooflines, the new Courthouse was as different from its former abode as Charles Dickens is from Harold Robbins. Where the older building exuded a sense of creaky antiquity and cooped-up dusty nooks and crannies, the newer one looked fresh and airy and sunlit.

Which it was, for the most part. It was also a rabbit warren of hallways, offices, and dozens upon dozens of doors. Keeping the public from the staff, and both of them from the inhabitants of the holding cells, necessitated a staggering number of locked barriers. I walked and/or parlayed my way through six or seven of these before I was ushered into the antiseptic wool, wood, and whitewalled retreat of the Honorable Alfred J. Harrowsmith.

He greeted me noncommittally and read through the affidavit. Watching his profile—bushy eyebrows, hawk nose supporting half glasses, a strong lantern jaw over a skinny, sinewy neck—I felt like a small boy in knee socks presenting a report card to his grandfather. The rules all but require the requesting officer to present the affidavit in person so he can answer any questions the judge might have, although it is wise to have already anticipated those questions in the wording of the application. The goal of the process is to establish that "more probably than not,'' there is justification for the issuing of a warrant. In other words, fifty-one percent or more probable cause. I was hoping I had that much.

Harrowsmith stopped reading, looked ahead for a moment as if collecting his thoughts, and then turned to me. "Any reason to suspect that Mr. Jardine's business dealings had anything to do with his death?''

"Suspect? Absolutely, but we can't be certain till we look at his records. Certainly the connections between Jardine and Wentworth grow stronger the more we dig, and Wentworth played a major part in the creation of ABC Investments. He introduced the two partners and might have had a hand in supplying some of the start-up funds.''

I knew I'd stumbled as soon as the words came out. "Might? I might have invested in that myself, or I might even have murdered Mr. Jardine. Why else should I sign this? Right now, it sounds like a fishing trip.''

Knowing Harrowsmith, I actually took hope from his words. Had he thought the request was trash, I would already be standing on the curb. "Your Honor, as I pointed out on page two, the circumstances surrounding the birth of ABC Investments are extremely suspicious, more so than any other aspect of Mr. Jardine's life.'' I'd omitted any prejudicial references to Charlie's bedroom and the coke. "From being a one-time glorified bottle-washer, Mr. Jardine was abruptly catapulted to becoming the protégé of a finance hotshot, hooked up to a veteran stockbroker, and encouraged to set up shop for himself in a business he didn't seem to know existed just a few years earlier. We strongly suspect the roots of his death can be located in those business files.''

Harrowsmith grunted. "You realize this warrant has to stand on its own merits, not on whether your suspicions are borne out later.''

"Yes, sir, I realize that.''

"And that if it doesn't, chances are good it'll be suppressed by a later judge and all the evidence you collected under it thrown out.''

I didn't answer. He stared at me for a moment, and finally signed his name. "I can live with seeing one of my warrants suppressed. You better think how you can live with seeing your whole case destroyed in court because you jumped too fast.''

I thanked him and took the warrant. He had a good point. Too many cops thought that if they got the proper paperwork, their asses were covered and their cases were sanctified. But this instance didn't weigh as heavily on me as Harrowsmith thought. Unless we found a letter written by the killer telling Jardine his days were numbered, I seriously doubted his business papers would hold any earth-shattering news. What I was hoping for was a crowbar—some piece of information I could use to pry either Clyde or Wentworth or whoever else cropped up off balance.

But I would leave the finding of that crowbar to Ron, Justin Willette, if he agreed to help, and Dennis, to whom I delivered the warrant, while I went instead to the Brattleboro Museum and Art Center, where Blaire Wentworth, according to the woman who answered her home phone, was working as a volunteer.

The BMAC, as it was locally known, was a converted railway station, built of solid stone on the bank overlooking the railroad tracks and the river below. Its front entrance, with a stolidly attractive wrought-iron and glass awning, was located on the Canal Street level; its rear, with the platform still serving the once-a-night Montrealer, was two flights lower down.

I found Blaire Wentworth at a desk on the middle level, in a dark and narrow hallway, typing some correspondence. Behind her, extending into the gloom, were piles of boxes pushed to one side so that the corridor was reduced to half its already restricted width. There was a single strip of dusty fluorescent tubing overhead. Despite knowing where we were in the building's overall scheme, I felt we were meeting in the fourth sub-basement of some large and ancient penitentiary.

"Miss Wentworth?"

She looked up from her typing, her almost platinum-white hair shining in the light. "Yes?"

She was stunningly attractive, which made me instantly think back to Klesczewski's comment. Her eyes were pale blue, her cheekbones high, her mouth full and mobile, quick to smile. She was slim and angular and stylishly dressed and reminded me of a racing yacht ready to unfurl its sails to the wind. There was no air-conditioning in the hall, but she looked cool and fresh. Seeing her that way made me wonder how I looked, which was rarely a concern of mine.

"My name is Lieutenant Joe Gunther. I'm with the Police Department."

She stuck out her hand, but stayed seated. "I've heard of you."

Her voice was subdued, which made me study her more closely. Indeed, behind the initial impression of fashion-model imperturbability, I sensed she was at once tense, sad, and very tired—a woman grieving.

I jumped in with both feet, spurred by her appearance and my own pure instinct. "I'm sorry for your loss."

She looked at me for a long few seconds, her face unchanged by the sudden turmoil of thoughts I was convinced were crowding her brain. This was no Rose Woll. Behind the distress was a mind in motion, analyzing the reasons for my presence and pondering the appropriate responses. The intelligence in those very attractive eyes sharpened my own mental focus; I instantly sensed that unless I was lucky, I wasn't going to leave this interview with more than she wanted to give me.

"Thank you," she finally answered, in a neutral voice. "I will miss him."

There were no questions concerning who we were talking about, or how I had known to come see her, or even how I knew she'd be in the bowels of this building.

"How long had you known Charlie?"

"Four years."

She still hadn't moved from her seat, nor had she offered me one, which would have been difficult in any case. I gingerly parked myself on one of the wooden crates, my back against the wall.

"You knew him well?"

She pursed her lips before speaking. "You know most of the answers to your questions before you ask them, don't you?"

I had to smile at that. "Sometimes. So you were lovers."

"Friends and lovers."

I nodded. "A good combination. Maybe you can help me

out a little then. I'm trying to get a handle on Charlie—find out what made him tick.''

"Life made him tick, Lieutenant, and that's over with. What do you really want to know?'' The tiredness I'd seen in her eyes earlier tainted the harsh tone, making it more despairing than hostile. In fact, I half sensed a double meaning to her question, as if she were undecided whether to thwart me or pump me for whatever information I might be holding.

I decided to work from the outside in. "I want to know who killed him and why.''

Her face tightened. "I can't help you then.''

"Maybe not directly, but you can tell me something about his habits, his other friends, his general life-style. People rarely kill strangers; they kill people they know. The more I can learn about Charlie's life, the better my chances are of finding out why he died, and who did it.''

"That won't do him much good, will it?''

Now it was my turn to be irritated. "Come on, Miss Wentworth, his death doesn't mitigate finding his killer, you know that. I'm not preaching revenge or justice here; just about righting a wrong.''

"Not putting 'an animal behind bars'?'' She was taunting me.

I looked at her straight, making sure my voice stayed calm and quiet. "I have no idea what kind of person killed him. People kill out of love sometimes.''

She smiled bitterly and shook her head. "I guess they do, at that.''

"Might that have happened to Charlie?''

She leaned her elbows on the desk and covered her face with her hands. Her body seemed to withdraw into itself, shrinking a little in the process. It made her look suddenly frail. With that strikingly youthful face out of sight, I could easily imagine this same body on an eighty-year-old, thin, stoop-shouldered, and powerless. It was a jarring view of a far distant future.

She straightened and rubbed her eyes. She hadn't been crying, I realized, but perhaps reorganizing her thoughts or merely taking a break to settle down. In any case, some of her immediate defenses were noticeably lowered. "I don't know what happened to Charlie, Lieutenant. One moment he was there, the next he was dead."

"So you didn't feel there was anything preying on his mind, some threat he didn't want to talk about?"

"Not a thing. He was perfectly normal."

"When did you last see him?"

She hesitated. "Three, four days ago."

"Like a day before he died?"

"Two days. We spent the night at his place, and went our separate ways the next morning. Then I called him at home that night, and that was the last time we ever spoke." Her voice sounded hollow at the end. I wondered if she kept herself this bottled up when she was alone, and whether she'd allowed herself to truly grieve at all so far.

"And he sounded fine then?"

"Absolutely fine."

"You left a blouse at his place."

She paused a couple of seconds, thrown perhaps by the sudden shift, and then she smiled sadly. "Yes."

"Did you have a complete change of clothing there, for when you stayed over?"

"No. Some oil had spilled on that blouse. Charlie had cleaned it up, but it was wet and he said he'd hand wash it later, so I left it there. I took one of his shirts instead. He was much better at that kind of thing than I am."

"You mean washing?"

"Washing, cooking, all those things. I have a maid come in. He loved doing it himself. He had a very domestic strain in him."

"Were you aware of other women in his life?"

"Of course. That was no secret."

"And no problem, either?"

She was surprised. "You mean jealousy? You think he was killed by a jealous lover?"

"It happens."

She laughed, shaking her head. "Not with Charlie. That kind of possessiveness never came into it."

"Maybe not with you; it might have with others. That's not something you can easily control."

I expected her to keep rejecting the idea, convincing herself that her experience with Charlie had been shared by all his women, but her intelligence willed out, and her expression sobered. "It's hard to imagine, but I suppose you're right."

"Did you know any of these other women?"

She opened her mouth to speak, hesitated, and then said no.

"What were you about to say?"

"Nothing . . . oh, just that we hadn't formed a club or anything. Maybe there is some jealousy there after all."

"You sometimes thought about him making love to another woman?"

She shrugged. "Sometimes. I wasn't faithful to him either, you know."

"But it bothered you where it didn't seem to bother him?"

"I know it didn't bother him. That was one of the ground rules. With Charlie, it was like an exchange. He would give you probably the best sex you'd ever had, but only if that's where it stopped: no love, no commitment, no expectations."

"Sounds pretty cold."

She shrugged. "Maybe, but it was honest, and he delivered on his end."

My inner vision blurred slightly, imagining this woman being gratified sexually like another might be pampered by a good hairdresser.

"What did he get out of it?"

It was a pretty tactless comment, blurted without thought, but she merely smiled. "I wasn't a disinterested party, Lieutenant. I played, too."

I reddened. "Of course. It just sounded . . . I don't know . . . almost commercial."

"His payment was in power. I think he liked manipulating a woman's passion, making her lose control. Sometimes he wouldn't even join in; he'd just gratify me and then quit."

"Like he was doing a job," I reiterated.

She didn't take offence at my perseverance. She merely

corrected me. "No. It was as if while my pleasure was sexual, his was psychological."

"But it was sexual, too, wasn't it?"

"Of course, most of the time. But he transcended plain sex. In a way, if I had any jealousy, it was of his pleasure, because of its utter privacy. I felt he was enjoying something beyond what I could ever feel. I'd see him sometimes, watching us making love in one of those mirrors, totally absorbed, as if I didn't matter, just my body."

"Did you two do drugs together?"

"Sometimes." The answer was hard and defiant.

I kept my voice unchanged. "We found some cocaine in the house. Is that what you used?"

"A little."

"Where did he keep it?"

"You just said you found it."

I continued to avoid the emotional edge she was skirting, hoping to pull her back, to show her there was no danger from me. "Yes, but we might have missed a place. I want to make sure we got it all."

"It was taped to the back of a drawer; in the bedroom."

"Okay. Same stuff then. Ever do any grass or pills?"

"No. We weren't into drugs. The coke was to relax, like having a beer."

I resisted arguing the point. "You don't happen to know where he bought the coke, do you?"

She shook her head.

"But he always had some?"

"Yes. Not much; just that one baggie."

"How did you two meet?"

She smiled. "At my father's office. Charlie worked there before he set up his own company. I guess you know that."

I nodded. "So you just bumped into him?"

"Well, at first, yes. But they spent a lot of time together, so I got to know him pretty well that way."

I was a little confused by the phrasing. "You mean they were in the office together when you came to visit?"

"No. I saw Charlie at the office—around the building, that is—but he'd come over to my father's house, too, for dinner or whatever. They loved to talk."

"Where do you live, Miss Wentworth?"

"At my father's. Actually, it's a separate building, a small cottage, but we usually have breakfast together, and lots of dinners. My mother died a long time ago."

"Did your father know of your involvement with Jardine?"

"No. Does he have to find out?" For the first time, I sensed real distress. She leaned forward in her chair, her eyes fixed on mine, her face rigid with sudden tension.

"I can only say I won't tell him."

"What's that mean?"

"It means the media is on the prowl and a lot of people are involved in this investigation. It might get out, even if I bent over backwards to stop it."

"And you wouldn't do that." She sounded both bitter and resigned, already anticipating how to pick up the pieces before anything was broken.

"I can try, assuming I discover you've been straight with me."

"I've answered your questions, haven't I?"

There was an element of the rebellious child in this woman, despite her mature and sophisticated appearance. The revelations that she more or less still lived at home, worked as a volunteer, and went about buying two-hundred-dollar shirts, all helped to reveal a pretty self-indulgent person, free from the constraints of a job, a mortgage, or any worries about money. It made me wonder how free she felt from telling the truth. It also thinned out her natural beauty in my eyes, making it more superficial; no doubt that was partly my working-class prejudices at work.

"I hear your father was a big help to Charlie, training him, setting him up in business. Why did he do that?"

"He liked him."

"There must have been more to it than that. Your father put a lot of money into ABC Investments."

"He has a lot to give."

I didn't actually know if Wentworth had put a plugged nickel into Jardine's business, but I'd been hoping for a different reaction than the one I got. Obviously, the father-Charlie part of this conversation was pretty barren land.

"How did Charlie help your father?"

She tossed her head impatiently. "Oh, you know—the father-son bit, I suppose."

The tone was disinterested, but I wasn't convinced. From the start, I'd felt Blaire Wentworth was holding more in her hand than she was willing to reveal. Indeed, in a few minutes, she had metamorphosed in my eyes from a cautious mourner to a careful player. I decided to return to what had been a more fruitful topic. "Did Charlie talk about his past much?"

"No. Well, it was selective."

"How so?"

"He loved to talk about high school. He said that was the most fun he'd ever had. I think it's because that's where he discovered sex. He was seriously into that."

"Did he mention friends or enemies? Any times he got into trouble?"

"Just the usual—the kind of scrapes we all got into. Nothing serious."

"How about a girl named Rose. Did he ever talk about her?"

"Rose?" She shook her head. "Never heard of her."

I looked at her; she looked back, her eyes wide and expressionless. Her answer had been immediate, clear, and to the point, and for all those reasons utterly unbelievable.

Abruptly, I decided to call it quits. I rose from my wooden box, thanked her for her time, and left. Blaire Wentworth had plenty more information, but for whatever reasons, she obviously didn't want to share it with me, at least not yet.

CHAPTER

18

"**H**OW did it go with Arthur Clyde?"

"I think it surprised the shit out of him," Klesczewski said. "If there's anything incriminating in all that junk, I think we'll find it, 'cause he didn't strike me as someone who'd swept his dirt under the rug. He looked totally stunned, and got madder than hell."

"Did you call in Willette to help sort it out?"

"Yeah. Dennis and him are working on it now. Better them than me."

I looked over at him. He seemed more relaxed than I'd seen him in a long time; in fact, since his elevation to second-in-command. If nothing else, I thought, this double homicide and its attending chaos was going to make him more comfortable with taking initiative. That was a personal vindication for me, since Brandt had voiced serious reservations about my decision. He'd favored Tyler—an obvious choice and, I'd thought, a perfect opportunity to see the Peter Principle at work.

E-Z Hauling had its truck depot on the Old Ferry Road, somewhat of a no-man's land on the edge of town where the north Putney Road becomes Route 5 heading toward Putney and Westminster. The area has been taken over by a mismatched scattering of metal buildings, some modest in size, housing conventional businesses like American Stratford

174

typesetters, others so enormous as to defy the imagination, like the seven-acre main shipping and receiving terminal and the four-and-a-half-acre freezer building of C&S Wholesale Grocers, arguably the largest business in the whole state of Vermont, and one of the ten most profitable companies in New England. In between were operations like Pepsi-Cola Bottling, Northeast Cooperatives—a health-food distributor—UPS, Boise Cascade, and various trucking firms. It was no scenic wonderland, but considering it was designed to keep the majority of the area's heavy truck traffic away from downtown, I'd always thought both planners and developers had done a halfway decent job. Nothing could alter a metal building's basic lack of aesthetic appeal, especially if it approached the Pentagon in size, but site location, lots of trees, and self-deprecating paint jobs helped.

Klesczewski slowed at the traffic light and turned right onto Old Ferry, paralleling the length of the main C&S building, which occupied the inside corner of the intersection. E-Z Hauling owned a small lot at the top of a low crest about a quarter mile up the road, also on the right, with a view of the C&S freezer building's roof.

"What's this guy's name again?" I asked.

"Cappelli, Mark Cappelli." Ron checked his watch. "The dispatcher wasn't too clear on when he'd be pulling in; just said sometime late this morning."

It was now 11:35. Ron had bumped into me just as I'd handed Harriet my notes on the Blaire Wentworth interview. The chance to get out of the office and play second fiddle while Klesczewski dealt with Cappelli was too attractive to pass up. Not only would it give me a breather and let me see Ron at work, it would allow me time to think over, once again, the growing pile of evidence in both cases.

"What did you learn about that other guy, the one who didn't have a profession listed?"

Klesczewski drove through the gate and pulled up opposite a battered metal door in a totally windowless corrugated wall. The door was labeled "Office." "Jake Hanson. Not much. I found out through the town clerk that he owns a couple of old warehouses on Birge Street. My guess is he lives off the rent."

We got out of the car. I always felt I should wear a jacket around town, if for no other reason than to hide the gun on my belt, but as I twisted around, trying to pluck the fabric free of my sweat-soaked back, I cursed my sense of etiquette. Ron had no such scruples; he left his coat in the car.

The gum-snapping girl in the office directed us around to the back, where the trucks were parked. It turned out the building was mostly a glorified garage, with three large, open bay doors revealing spaces where trucks could be pulled in for repair and maintenance. About six eighteen-wheelers were parked, side by side, in the rear lot.

We stepped into the slightly cooler shade of the garage, blinking away the sun's brightness. At the back of the bay, only visible as a shadow, a man's figure moved back and forth along an extended workbench.

Ron, squinting as I was, spoke up beside me. "Excuse me. Could you tell us where to find Mark Cappelli?"

My vision, adjusting more rapidly now, saw the figure twist around and freeze for a moment, its face pale against the dark back wall. Whoever the guy was, he seemed more focused on Klesczewski than on me, which made me instantly think of Ron's gun, hanging out in plain view. "Better tell him we're cops."

He never got the words out. There was a metallic scraping sound from the bench as the figure ahead of us made a violent movement, and I suddenly sensed more than saw something spinning toward our heads. I instinctively raised my right arm and began to duck and turn away. A burst of pain whacked my forearm, numbing my hand, and a crescent wrench clanged at my feet.

Ron seemed riveted in place, staring at me doubled over in agony, my arm tucked into the pit of my stomach. "Son of a bitch. Are you okay?"

"No, I'm not fucking okay—damn."

Crouching, we both recovered quickly and fanned out to either side of where we'd been, but the dark outline at the bench had vanished. I glanced at Ron, his gun out and ready. I'd left mine in its holster, since I still had no sensation in my lower arm and couldn't shoot worth a damn with my left hand. "See anything?"

He scrutinized the gloom as if concentration alone could give him the vision he lacked. "Cappelli, come on out. We're from—"

Again, he was cut short as a gunshot shattered the gloom and sent both of us flat on the grease-stained ground. No more flying tools, I thought; now we were getting serious. There was the sound of running feet and the clang of a metal door.

"Over there—to the left."

"Watch it, Ron. He may not be gone." I was sweating freely now, the pain in my arm superseded by an adrenalin rush that made my heart pound and my pupils dilate.

My vision of the garage now entirely cleared, I could see a line of oil drums running parallel with part of the bench, forming an aisle to a doorway mounted in the left-side wall. I gestured to Klesczewski to circle out to where the drums met the wall, while I made an approach more in line with the aisle, so that by merely poking my head out, I might see all the way to the door. I too now had my gun cradled in my still-tingling right hand.

The aisle was empty. I straightened from the crouch I'd unconsciously assumed. "He's gone."

Ron vaulted over the drums and beat me to the door, turning the knob, kicking it open, and tucking himself behind the jamb, all in one fluid movement. We were looking into the same office we'd visited upon our arrival. The gum-chewing secretary was standing between us and the front door, her mouth open at the sight of our weapons.

"Oh, my God." She backed up several steps, caught her desk with the backs of her thighs, and went tumbling head over heels, vanishing on the far side with a crash and a flash of upturned legs.

I checked the office quickly as Klesczewski ran up to the desk. "We're cops. Where did that man go?"

The girl, from the floor, pointed toward the front door.

"Was that Cappelli?" I shouted, already moving.

She answered yes, as we made for the exit.

Outside, we saw Cappelli disentangling himself from three strands of barbed wire strung along the top of a low chain-link fence separating E-Z's yard from the C&S lot.

The huge, dark-brown freezer building just beyond loomed like Jonah's whale, lying ready to swallow our man whole.

I ran across toward the fence, yelling to Ron. "Drive to the far entrance. Radio everyone and get 'em out here . . . And give them a description."

I began struggling with the fence, just six feet tall, trying to keep my hands free of the barbs while scrambling for toeholds in the wire. Ahead, I could see our quarry, now almost at the bottom of the grassy slope between me and C&S's tarmac apron. Cappelli was of medium height, broad-shouldered, with long black hair and a mustache. He was wearing jeans, work boots, and a bright-red T-shirt with black lettering on the back. I couldn't see a gun and presumed he'd pocketed it for convenience. I hoped Ron had noticed as much for his description to the troops.

Cursing my own clumsiness, I finally stripped off my jacket, laid it across the top of the fence to absorb the barbs, and half fell into the grass on the far side just as Cappelli vanished around the corner of the distant building. Running downhill, I forgot radio protocol as I unclipped my portable from my belt: "Ron, he's gone into the freezer. Try to seal off the perimeter gates somehow and then block the connecting tunnel into the main warehouse. Maybe security can help."

The two C&S buildings are gigantic rectangles when seen from the top, linked by a thin, umbilical-like surface tunnel for forklifts. The long southeastern walls of both buildings house rows of some fifty loading bays each—square holes punched into the wall about four feet off the ground to accommodate the thousands of trucks that back up to them every week. The rest of the thirty-five-to forty-foot-tall walls, including the one I was skirting at a dead run, are relatively free of doors or windows, and enclose a dizzying array of gigantic rooms, some two hundred and fifty by three hundred feet, which are interlaced with thirty-five-foot-tall racks. Loaded with boxed produce, they look like solid walls. Both buildings are manned twenty-four hours a day by a total of some six hundred stockpilers and machinery operators, all motivated by an incentive-pay system to keep twenty-one thousand products moving toward retailers over a good part of New England as fast as possible. Where

Cappelli had just disappeared, in other words, was like an entire town under one single three-hundred-and-ten-thousand-square-foot roof—not a bad place to hide, and a bitch to control.

I skidded around the corner, almost in time to be killed by a fast-moving tractor, and found Cappelli had vanished from sight. It was perfectly possible he had disappeared into one of the cabs or was hiding behind the wheels of one of the many eighteen-wheelers backed up to the building, but my instincts told me otherwise.

I double-stepped up a short flight of concrete stairs to a door marked Authorized Personnel Only, pulled it open, and slipped inside.

The shock left me breathless for a moment. From blazing, white-hot, suffocating daylight, I had stepped into a huge, artificially lit, cold cave. The sudden contrast made me feel I'd been transported forward in time, to the gloom of late fall, and the unexpected cool air was like a splash of water in the face.

The room was approximately one hundred feet long, forty feet wide, and another forty feet tall. There were two enormous doorways in the long concrete wall opposite the row of loading doors, both of which were blocked off by overlapping strips of heavy plastic hanging from above. Behind them was the freezer room, almost one hundred thousand square feet of it.

I was in the dock area, where piles of boxed frozen goods were stacked on pallets, either fresh from or ready for the truck bodies that extended like dead-end doorless hallways from the open loading bays. Blinking away the outside brightness, I scanned the large room, looking for Cappelli's distinctive red shirt.

"Hey. What's up?"

I whirled around. A man dressed in insulated overalls, gloves, and a wool cap stood slightly behind one of the stacks along the wall, a clipboard in his hands. His eyes widened at the sight of the gun strapped to my belt.

"I'm a cop. Did you see a guy in a red T-shirt run in here?"

"Yeah. He went in there. I thought—"

He pointed toward the plastic-curtained door to the freezer. Just then, a lightning-bright muzzle flash exploded and crashed against the metal walls around us. The bullet tore the clipboard from my guide's hands just as I threw myself against him and sent us both sprawling behind some boxes.

"Holy shit. What the hell is going on?" His cap had slid over one ear, and he looked like the village drunk, propped up against his cardboard shelter.

"I'm going in there. As soon as you think it's safe, get out and take as many people with you as you can. Don't waste time doing it and don't be a hero. Just spread the word and get the hell out. I got troops on the way."

He nodded dumbly, his eyes wide, as I got to my knees and peered around my barricade. The shadow I'd seen behind the muzzle flash was gone.

Tucked low, I scuttled from pallet to pallet, working a zigzag course toward the freezer door. Finally, with my back against its cold concrete edge, I pulled out my radio. "Ron, you there?"

I released the key button and waited. Some two seconds of static came back at me.

"Ron? Do you copy?"

More static.

"I can't read you. Maybe it's the building. I'm about to go into the main freezer room." As I replaced the radio on my belt clip, I noticed its side had been badly gouged, presumably from my nose dive to the cement floor. That probably accounted for the static; it also meant I was all by myself.

I leaned around the edge of the doorway and peeled back one of the plastic strips, shivering as the blast of cold air hit my sweat-soaked shirt. I was about to slip through the narrow opening when I heard a sudden loud whining bearing down on me. I looked around frantically and then spun back as the plastic strips burst around me, yielding to a fast-moving forklift that missed me by two inches.

"Get the fuck out of the way, you moron. I almost killed you." The operator stopped abruptly, his eyes like his predecessor's, glued to my gun.

I gave him the same set of instructions, adding that he

should run to the far end of the building as quickly as possible to get the cops.

He did so, abandoning the fully loaded forklift.

I stepped onto the tiny driver's platform at the back of the machine and studied the controls for a moment. Then, crouching down, I operated the reverse and backed through the curtain as fast as I could.

On the other side was a wide traffic lane, running parallel to the cement wall and at right angles to an endless row of three-story-high stocking racks. I drove fast and straight toward the nearest aisle, using the machine and its speed as cover. It almost wasn't enough. Another bullet whacked into the control panel, showering my head with shattered plastic. I jumped for the temporary safety of the aisle just before the forklift crashed into one of the racks.

The sudden silence was electrifying. With the forklift stilled, I became aware of the all-encompassing low-toned rumble of the refrigeration compressors, as seemingly permanent and pervasive as the sound of a distant sea.

I picked myself up off the icy floor and began to look for a way west, through the middle of the towering racks, and in the direction of the last shot. I was now beginning to feel the cold. My breath hovered before my face. Overhead, ominous icy stalactites reached down from the steel cross-bracing and water-sprinkler pipes high above, reminders of how briefly I could survive in this environment. I began to shiver as I squeezed between two stacked loads on the bottom shelf and wriggled my way into the next aisle.

Aisle by aisle I progressed, slowly, cautiously, and without sound, looking up and to the sides, never knowing where Cappelli might be lurking, not even sure he was still in the freezer. My hands and feet became numb. My shivering developed into an uncontrollable shaking. My jaw muscles began to ache from clamping my chattering teeth together.

I decided to speed things up a bit by running to the far end of one of the aisles and proceeding up the distant traffic lane, thereby sparing myself the additional discomfort of sliding between the frozen boxes.

It was the shortcut Cappelli was waiting for. I rounded

the first aisle without mishap or reward, but as I dashed across the open space for the sanctuary of the next line of racks, now almost sure I was alone, I heard the faintest of sounds overhead and looked up just in time to see several boxes come hurtling down on me, the flash of Cappelli's T-shirt behind them.

I twisted out of the way, tripped and landed on my back, my revolver going off accidentally. There was a loud metallic crack following the blast and one of the overhead water pipes blew up. I watched in slow terror as a fountain of freezing water sprang free and came at me, a huge, expanding, life-threatening shower. As I rolled over to catch the brunt of it with my back, I wondered incongruously why Cappelli hadn't simply shot me. The answer, of course, lay in my hand. He, like I, had no feeling left in his fingers, and no ability to willfully pull the trigger.

The water hit me like icy lava, burning my body and changing my entire focus from pursuit to survival. At first crawling, then staggering to my feet, and finally lurching down the hundred-foot aisle, I made a beeline for the exit, fully aware that any caution now would mean my freezing to death. As I ran, I could feel my clothes stiffening against my skin.

Cappelli must have been in the same situation. About halfway down the aisle, I saw another flash of red before me as he darted across the opening, making for one of the huge curtained doors. He was a good fifty feet ahead, and long gone by the time I half fell between the long plastic strips.

I looked around, standing in the open, my hair and eyebrows glistening with ice, my gun hanging useless at the end of an arm without feeling. Several heads were visible peering over the tops of various boxes.

"Where did he go?" I asked in my head, but not in fact. My mouth was numb, and the sounds from it made no sense.

Someone nevertheless pointed to another curtained opening which separated the cold portion of the building from what the workers called "Phase B," a second hundred-thousand-square-foot addition that was slated to become a freezer, but which for the time being was uncooled.

With none of the caution I'd displayed earlier, I stumbled through the connecting archway into Phase B.

The shock of coming from the cold into the warm was not as brutal as the reverse. My body was so numb, it took a while to adjust, but I was aware of the change, and of the salvation it represented. That mere instinct sharpened my senses.

"Where?" I asked the first person I met.

Word had obviously gotten out, however filtered. Here, as in the freezer, the steady whirring of forklifts had been quieted by the crisis Cappelli and I represented, but the sense of threat had suffered in translation, or had been diminished by our weather-beaten appearance. In any case, the workers were just standing around, looking baffled.

"What're you guys doing?" The man I'd addressed was wearing jeans and a white T-shirt that said, "Five hundred thousand cows can't be all wrong—Visit Vermont."

"Where did the man in the red shirt go?"

"Into the tunnel." He pointed to the far end of the room.

The tunnel was a ten-foot by ten-foot boxed-in metal corridor that connected the freezer building to the main warehouse. It was restricted to forklifts only and designed to allow them free access to both buildings regardless of the weather. Unfortunately, it wasn't short or straight. Despite the proximity of the buildings, they were on sharply different levels, so, to avoid too harsh an incline, the tunnel had been built as a long, gradually descending V, with a one-hundred-sixty-degree switchback crimping the middle. I ran toward it, feeling more limber with each step, knowing that as soon as I was in its embrace, I'd stick out like a target in a shooting gallery. Again, I tried my radio, and again I got no results.

The first fifteen feet were no problem, since they were a straight shot from the building to the top of the V's first leg. At the corner, however, things literally and otherwise went downhill. I glanced at the convex mirror mounted in the far corner, but the distortion was too great to distinguish much detail. Cappelli could be tucked alongside one of the hundreds of metal ribs that held the tunnel roof up and not be seen until I stuck my nose out.

I did stick it out, briefly, and saw nothing, just a hundred feet of gray corridor stretching away like a near-bottomless well. I began walking down it, keeping to the middle, ready to move right or left, depending on his angle of fire. I flexed the fingers of my right hand. At least now I could fire back.

But again, he didn't shoot. As I was about twenty feet shy of the switchback, I thought I saw a movement in the second distant mirror. I moved to the left, progressing now from protective rib to protective rib, so tense I thought I could hear my socks rubbing my pants legs. My eyes were glued to the mirror, willing its image to flatten out and enlarge, to tell me more of what lay hidden just a few feet away now.

There was another movement, along the wall, tiny and distorted; an arm, holding a revolver.

"Stop where you are and throw your gun out. This is the police."

I froze. It was Kleszczewski.

"Ron?"

"Lieutenant?" In the mirror, several bodies appeared from behind the metal wall supports, all but Kleszczewski's in police uniforms.

"He didn't get away, did he?" I asked as we met at the hairpin corner.

Kleszczewski looked totally frazzled. "No, no. We don't have him yet, but I'm sure he's still in the building. Why didn't you use your radio?"

I patted his shoulder, more grateful than I cared to admit for his company, as we all four jogged back toward the main building. "It's broken. How many troops do you have now, and where are they positioned?"

"Eight or so, including some of the local security people. I put some of them outside, along sightlines near the perimeter fence, just to make sure he didn't slip out between us."

"That's great."

"I'm trying to get the building evacuated, but the P.A. system failed, and I only found someone who'd take responsibility a few minutes ago. Half the people are still unaware of what the hell's going on."

"Well, I chased him this far. He's got to be in the main warehouse. Let's keep the evacuation going, lock the place up, and send in the Special Reaction guys. Should be just a matter of time, as long as he doesn't squirt out somewhere between now and then."

We'd arrived at the tunnel's far end, into a room that totally dwarfed the two I'd been in before, covering almost seven acres of floor space, and reaching four stories up. As Ron had mentioned, the bustle of forklifts, "hi-lo's," and manual loaders had been only slightly reduced at best, although I could see several men in white shirts and ties using bullhorns, trying their best to wind things down.

"There aren't many doors on the northwest side," Ron continued, "and I think I got them all covered. It's the loading dock and all these damn bays that have me worried. I never figured it would be that complicated to shut a place down."

We heard a startled shout and a gunshot from one of the most distant of those bays.

"Oh, shit," Ron muttered, and began to sprint down the length of the loading dock, cutting right and left around stacks of produce like a football player going for a touchdown.

I paused a moment. A forklift operator clutched his arm as Mark Cappelli bolted through a crack between one of the bay doors toward a truck backing up to the bay. I ran out another door, set on heading him off outside.

Unfortunately, I was still several hundred feet away and had a long line of trucks to get around. I was about fifty feet from where I thought Cappelli had left the warehouse when I heard a loud crash and the roar of a diesel engine in distress.

The noise had been caused by a Freightliner cab-over being driven away from its box without the support legs being dropped. I rounded my last obstacle in time to see the box lying with its nose in the tarmac like some religious penitent. The cab, shuddering and belching black smoke as Cappelli slammed it through its gears to gain speed, was already peeling away. He was headed west, against the prescribed traffic flow, bound for the far corner of the building and the entrance gates leading out to Ferry Road.

A trucker, his mouth half stuffed with a sandwich, was gesticulating near the front of the box. "He stole my cab, for Christ's sake; that's my fucking truck."

I saw Ron standing at the edge of the adjacent loading door. "Where's your car?"

"Follow me." He bent down and swung me up onto the dock before leading me through the entrails of the building on a roughly diagonal tack to the building's dressed-up front door to the west. As we both burst out onto the parking lot, Cappelli's fire-breathing behemoth screamed around the far corner, heading for the closed front gate.

"Guess we better let 'em know what's happening," I said, as we piled into his car, just as the truck blew through the gate with a shriek of complaining metal. Leaving parallel crescents of black burnt rubber on the pavement, Cappelli slewed onto Ferry Road, heading toward the Putney Road traffic light. In a squeal of spinning tires, Ron backed out of his parking space and gave chase, while I began giving orders over the radio.

We had two major problems: We didn't have enough time to get roadblocks properly organized, and we didn't know which way Cappelli would take. If he turned right at the light, he could go north up Route 5 to grab the interstate at Putney, or try to vanish along the byways crisscrossing the hills around Dummerston, the next township. If he turned left, which I suspected he would, his choices were downtown Brattleboro, a couple of miles straight ahead, Route 9 East into New Hampshire, or I–91's Exit Three, both located at the crossroads less than a mile down the road. I told Dispatch to contact the Vermont State Police and the Windham County Sheriff's Department for anything north of our position, the New Hampshire cops for anything east, and ordered all available units to converge on Exit Three.

Another disadvantage was that most of our patrol units were behind Klesczewski and me, which left precious little to put between the truck and the open road. As Cappelli skidded through the light and drove south, I modified my instructions over the mike.

"This is Oh-three. I want all available units to move onto I–91, north and southbound. Rolling roadblocks." I hung up the radio. "Ron, you better let at least one of the patrol units by. We aren't exactly legal here."

He slowed slightly and waved one of our tailgaters on, but only one; he wasn't about to concede the chase, despite the rule that high-speed pursuits and roadblocks were only to be performed by recognizable patrol units.

"Why put everybody on the interstate?" he asked. The crossroads were coming up with amazing speed. I noticed both my feet were pressed flat against the floor.

"Gut call. It's a wide-open road. That's what I'd do."

As if I'd willed it, the Freightliner slid into the crowded intersection, sideswiped several cars, and peeled off toward I–91. Another police unit screaming up the Putney Road from downtown almost added to the wreckage, barely missing us and a man who'd leapt from his vehicle to check the damage. I looked over my shoulder as Ron swept around the corner. That put three units behind us and one in front. I wondered what was left to stop Cappelli. I also wondered how much hell I was going to catch for putting this demolition derby into action.

As soon as I saw the truck commit to the first on-ramp, I grabbed the radio again. "All units from Oh-three. The truck's heading north on the interstate. All units respond accordingly."

But I shook my head as soon as I'd delivered the message.

Klesczewski saw me. "What?" he half shouted over the noise of the engine and the sirens.

"Why would he head north?"

"Why not?"

It was a legitimate response. Neither choice was rational, nor was the whole premise, for that matter. How Cappelli hoped to escape, driving a Freightliner with a bunch of cops on his tail, was beyond me. But if he was stupid enough to think he could, he was stupid enough to think that heading south toward Massachusetts and beyond held more options than tearing up the pavement for a hundred miles toward Canada.

I grabbed the mike again. "All units from Oh-three. Who's on the interstate now?"

"Oh-three from One-five. I'm just north of Exit Two right now."

"Set up a roadblock southbound just below the West River Bridge."

"I thought he was heading north." The voice was high-pitched with incredulity.

"He is. I think he'll turn around."

"Oh-three from One-two. I'm coming onto Exit Two from West Bratt. Want me to join One-five?"

"Ten-four."

Klesczewski's face was tight with concentration as he tried to keep out of the ditch rounding the corner of the on-ramp. "You better be right, or we're going to look like a bunch of assholes."

I grinned at this rare profanity; in fact, I knew that soon, especially in the eyes of several of our town leaders, we would earn the label regardless of today's results.

Cappelli's truck was swerving slightly from side to side, making it impossible for the patrol car behind him to pass. As he drew abreast of the interstate at the top of the ramp, he added to the obstacle course by clipping a Subaru station wagon and causing it to twirl into a series of multiple pirouettes, which made all of us slam on our brakes to avoid joining in. Thus shielded, Cappelli cut into a controlled slide and sliced across the emergency U-turn lane a bare hundred feet away from the ramp. He was going for the southbound route.

The unit immediately behind him missed the U-turn completely, since it had veered to the wrong side of the dizzying Subaru and was hurtling north in the far breakdown lane. Klesczewski was luckier, as were the two units behind us.

"One-two and One-five from Oh-three. He's headed your way."

The thousand-foot-long West River Bridge, one hundred feet above the water and now just a mile ahead of us, was undergoing repairs. The entire southbound span was closed, and traffic had been rerouted to one half of the northbound span, which was split down the middle by a row of heavy concrete dividers. The speed limit, for good reason, was forty. We were going ninety-five.

The approach to the bridge is a slightly descending slope. Units Twelve and Fifteen, their blue lights twinkling fiercely, were clearly visible on either side of the single southern lane at the far end of the bridge. Real roadblocks, unlike those in the movies, should always allow an exit. They are supposed to show the bad guys that escape is fruitless, not to provide them with photogenic opportunities to create mayhem. At midpoint on the bridge, in the gap that separated the two spans, workmen were operating acetylene torches from a long wooden platform, suspended by cables from the railing above. The flames from their torches looked like minuscule chips of sunlight.

"Ease up a little, Ron, the switch-over is bumpy."

Klesczewski slowed down. Cappelli did not. His truck hit the thin, ripply asphalt overlay linking the southbound lane to its half of the northbound bridge, bounced once, and began to twist sideways, spewing several small rooster tails of burning rubber.

"Holy Christ, he's going over." Klesczewski slammed on the brakes hard, making my seat belt cut across my chest.

The truck hit the bridge sideways, with its rear wheels in the lane, its middle straddling the guardrail, and its cab hanging over the gap between the two spans. I could see the looks of horror on the faces of the workmen on the platform as the Freightliner screamed toward them, riding the guard-rail sideways like some bizarre huge toy run amuck. Now, added to the black smoke from the burning tires and the diesel exhaust, there was a shower of flaming sparks cascading from where the railing cut the truck undercarriage as it slid.

Slowly, as if tantalizing us, the cab began to peel forward off the chassis, exposing the engine beneath and throwing the whole disastrous mess off balance. For a moment, the truck's wheels left the pavement and then, with the last of its momentum, it flipped on the guardrail like an acrobat somersaulting on a tightrope. The cab flew high in the air, its driver catapulting through its front window like a champagne cork. The chassis settled back onto the road, a smoking, twisted wreck, while Cappelli and the cab landed with an explosion onto the wooden platform below the bridge. We watched transfixed as the cab, surrounded by debris, spun silently through the hundred feet down into the shallow river. The platform, hanging on by a single cable, swung in a wide arc, and below it, swinging in turn by his leg, which was tangled in the remains of the other cable, was Mark Cappelli. The workers, hooked to their safety harnesses, were glued to the metal undercarriage of the bridge like insects to flypaper.

There was a deathly quiet as Ron and I left the car and stepped out onto the bridge. All traffic had frozen in place, all the topside workers were as still as statues at the railing; the one sound I could hear distinctly for that brief moment was the gurgling of the water far below as it swirled around its newfound obstacle.

I began to run.

CHAPTER
19

IT took an endless thirty minutes to get Cappelli up onto the bridge, never knowing when the tangled cable around his leg might suddenly unravel. Finally, two members of the Special Reaction Team managed to rappel down to the hapless trucker, hook a harness to him, and have him pulled to safety. When he reached us, he was unconscious but alive, and for the second time in two days, I rode in the ambulance to baby-sit someone I hoped would wake up to answer my ever-growing questions.

It was not to be. Dr. Franklin met us at the emergency-room door, shaking his head and telling me his practice could survive without my supplying him extra patients. He assessed Cappelli's condition, had several X rays done, ordered a C-T scan, and told me to take a hike. Cappelli would not be waking up anytime soon, and when he did, Franklin and his neurosurgeon pals would have first dibs. Only then would I get a call. I arranged to have a uniformed officer stay at the hospital to keep a discreet eye on him anyway.

Ron Klesczewski was waiting for me in the hospital parking lot.

"We kill anyone in that free-for-all?" I asked.

"Nope, not even a flesh wound, but the powers that be are still pretty pissed. The motorist who almost got clipped at the intersection is pounding the chief's desk right now, unless he's left to get his lawyer, and Wilson is walking up and down the hallway as if he'd like to put a chain saw to someone's neck.''

"Mine, presumably."

Klesczewski started the car engine. "Oh, I don't know. He looked pretty undiscriminating to me; that's why I'm here."

It turned out Klesczewski had painted a rather rosy picture. When we pulled into the Municipal Center's parking lot, I recognized not only Stan Katz's car, but Ted McDonald's, as well as a station wagon advertising the *Keene Sentinel*, and one from the *Greenfield Recorder*. In a few hours, I didn't doubt Channel 31's broadcast truck and others would also be jockeying for space.

"Let me off at the back door." I pointed to the Police Department's private entrance, openable only by key, and leading to the hallway around the corner from Brandt's office. I wanted to talk with the chief first, to put together a coherent party line, always an improvement over "no comment."

That, at least, was the plan.

"Hi, Joe."

I turned, one hand on the doorknob, the other holding my key.

Stan Katz had been sitting in his car, waiting, typically bypassing the organized circus that was probably clogging the building's main corridor.

He rose from his seat and slammed the door. "I guess you guys thought you were being pretty clever keeping John Woll out of the limelight."

The shock was worse than I'd imagined. My heart skipped several beats, and a nervous sweat sprang out all over my body.

"What?" My voice sounded strangled to my own ears, and was obviously no clarion of innocence to Katz, for he smiled broadly.

"John Woll—patrolman, husband, and drunk. The same John Woll who went to high school with Charlie Jardine, whose wife had an affair with Charlie Jardine, and whose squad car was seen at the Canal Street dam about the same time Charlie Jardine was planted there."

I considered denying it, bluffing my way through the door and out of his reach, but I realized he'd quote me later as proof of a cover-up. I could talk to him about it; I'd had conversations with him in the past when I'd thought such honesty might serve to set him straight. But there too, he had me. I didn't know who else in the department he'd challenged, or how they might have responded. I also doubted that whatever I told him, even if I confessed all my sins for the past eight years, would have the slightest impact. This was a man with a long-sought-after bone, and he was savoring the flavor.

"Come on, Joe. You going to deny it? Woll is dirty and you've all been scrambling for cover, hoping for a miracle."

I stuck my key into the lock, more aware than ever of the crushing heat, and of the futility of trying to fight it. "No comment, Stanley."

"Is that a quote?" I heard him laugh as the door slammed shut behind me.

I stood there, in the hallway, overhearing the babble of the impromptu press conference in the main corridor. The chase after Cappelli was so fresh, and had taken so much out of me, that I had, for the moment, forgotten the time bomb Brandt and I had built through complicity. I had naturally assumed the media had gathered to catch the gore of a multiple-vehicle pursuit/smashup, and to ask some inane questions about how it tied into the current double-homicide investigation. I rubbed my eyes with the palms of my hands—obvious wishful thinking. Mundane, albeit attention-getting police action was no longer worthy of the spotlight. Now we had scandal. I could already envision how the headline would look under the *Reformer*'s scarlet banner.

What energy I had left from scrambling through the C&S warehouse drained away entirely, leaving me dour and depressed. The dance would begin in earnest now; the buffer between the Luman Jacksons of the board and the department would wither under the heat, and the entire investigation would likely become secondary to the defense of our jobs.

I turned the corner to Brandt's office and nodded to the carpenters who had broken for lunch. He was sitting at his desk, with the computer's large bluish eye keeping him company, but his attention was focused on the most distant window, in which a large box fan rattled noisily.

I entered the office and closed the door behind me. Only then did I notice the fan was sucking the air out, causing the door to push against my hand as I shut it. Although Brandt was smoking as usual, I realized the air was free of its perpetual smog.

"Goddamn computer. Couldn't take the smoke," he said around his pipe stem.

I sat gingerly in his guest chair. This was definitely an odd mood, perhaps classic denial, I thought. "Oh, yeah?"

"Repairman came this morning, said the pollution was gumming up the works. Said I should either quit or have air scrubbers installed." He nodded toward the fan. "What d'you think?"

I decided I'd play along. "As a scrubber? Be a little tough in the winter."

Brandt sighed, pushed his glasses up on his forehead, and rubbed his eyes. "So. I guess we fucked up on John Woll."

I let his words float in the air a moment. It was so tempting to mention that he'd fucked up, and that I'd merely been following orders, but the disgust following that notion soured my gut. What really weighed me down wasn't that we'd been caught in a stupid subterfuge, but that I'd ignored my own judgment and had gone along with the idea. Brandt had fucked up because he'd been caught; I had disappointed myself three times over: I'd ducked my own moral instincts, had helped spawn a lousy alternative, *and* I'd been caught. Furthermore, my earlier qualms about being secretive with Gail were now guaranteed to blossom into an awkward debate about trust.

I tried putting it all to the back of my mind. "I wonder how Katz tumbled to it?"

Brandt readjusted his glasses, leaned way back in his chair, and looked at me through half-closed eyes. He seemed to be taking it in stride. "The background checks. Who did you have digging into the high-school link between Jardine, John, and Rose?"

I thought back. So much had been going on lately, with a few people doing so many different things, it was hard to keep track. "I told Ron to get Lavoie to help him locate people who knew all three in high school, but I also told him to do the actual interviews himself, for discretion's sake.''

''Well, either something went wrong, or Katz is getting better. He apparently put the three names together and did some interviewing of his own. He also found out John was on patrol on Canal Street, no big secret, and that he'd had a problem with booze; again, common knowledge.''

He paused, took the pipe from his mouth and looked at it, as I'd seen him do a thousand times in the past. ''I read once that you can make nitroglycerin, or something like it, from common household products; you just have to know which ones to choose and how to mix 'em. Katz probably knows the formula.''

A depressing silence settled in the room.

''So why aren't you being drawn and quartered in the hallway?'' I finally asked.

He chuckled. ''My turn'll come. Right now, James Dunn, Tom Wilson, and Gary Nadeau are standing in for me.''

I shook my head, momentarily confused. ''What do they know about Woll?''

Brandt focused more sharply on me. ''You don't know what's been going on, do you? John Woll is Katz's private property for the moment; the other media boys don't know about him. But Stanley didn't want to play a story this big without official reactions, so he ran it by the three gentlemen in the hall for quotes, thinking they were all co-conspirators with us. Imagine the looks he got; he wound up giving them more information than they had to begin with. Tomorrow's reading should be nothing if not entertaining.''

He suddenly grinned at the thought. ''They were on their way down here to chew my ass when they ran into the microphones. So, right now, their brains boiling, they're being grilled over a high-speed chase they couldn't care less about. Now, that is irony.''

I stared at him, amazed at the workings of his mind. It was truly a revelation of why he was as comfortable in his job as I'd been miserable during my brief tenure as chief. While he may have forsaken the street for the office, he'd obviously come to grips with it with the same relish and dexterity. What I'd seen as a disaster, he saw as a change in tactics, and he was already thinking of how to make a profit from it. It now became clearer to me why the decision to keep Woll under wraps had come so easily to him. Sooner or later he'd known the shit would hit the fan; he'd just chosen to put it off, hoping it might miss him altogether. It had been a gambler's call, with a gambler's knowledge of the risks. The losses, as he apparently saw them now, were acceptable.

"So how many other people are in on our little secret?"

Brandt shrugged. "That's it, I think."

That was enough, I thought. Dunn, Wilson, and Nadeau were about as dissimilar as three personalities could get. Where normally a state's attorney, a town manager, and a town attorney should have had no problems either ignoring or cooperating with one another, each of these three had established a sense of turf only a pit bull could envy.

That last point prompted my next question. "So why all three together? Whose idea was that?"

He was now smiling broadly, a man in his element. "Mine. I figure the best way to survive this shoot-out is to have everyone firing at the same time, and at different targets."

That was all I wanted to hear. I pushed on the arms of my chair and stood up. "Well, I better make myself scarce. Don't want to be the only private in a field of generals—you guys'll kill me first, sure as hell."

He waved me back down. "Stay. We might as well clean the slate with one swipe."

The sudden swelling of voices from the hallway indicated the immediacy of my education. We both watched through Brandt's interior window as three men carefully picked their way across the carpenters' debris: Tom Wilson, small, enervated, and red-faced; James Dunn, his exterior as cool as ever, but with a hard set to his mouth this time; and hapless Gary Nadeau, naturally bringing up the rear, at the same time obsequious and officious, basking in the glory of reflected authority.

Brandt stood as they entered, smiling as the affable host. They remained grim, their eyes shifting from him to me to the two available chairs. Dunn showed no hesitation; this was more his arena than theirs, so he sat immediately. I had moved to lean against a filing cabinet, and Wilson took what had been my seat. Nadeau looked uncomfortable, and ended up standing by the door, as if foreseeing his fate in this company.

Dunn played up his insider's role by looking at me and ignoring the topic at the front of everyone's mind. "Is Cappelli going to make it?"

I shrugged. Obviously Brandt had been doing his homework, passing along the tidbits to Dunn. "Can't tell yet. He's still unconscious. I did get the impression he'd come out of it, though."

Nadeau nodded in a show of mock knowledge, but Wilson's already high blood pressure was no longer interested in such face-saving games. Nor was he interested in side issues. "Who the hell is Cappelli?"

Brandt smiled again, as did I. Tom Wilson may not have been our town manager of choice, but he was fairly free of pretense. "The driver who went off the bridge."

Wilson rolled his eyes, suddenly sidetracked. "Would someone mind telling me what the hell that was all about? And why did Dirty Harry here have to turn this place into a Hollywood back lot?" He glared at me.

I cleared my throat. "We went to interview him. He started shooting and ran for it."

"Interview him about what?" Nadeau's voice seemed out of place.

Dunn cut straight to the heart of Brandt's strategy. "I would suggest that's an inappropriate question. If we are all to remain in this room for this conversation, we'd better stick to general topics."

"General topics?" Wilson choked, back on course. "Weren't you aware of what was going on in that hallway? We've got two murders on our hands; our police force is so stretched out it can't even issue parking tickets; we've got high-speed chases; a pissed-off motorist who almost got killed by a hotshot cop; and I just got a call from the company that employs the bridge workers who almost went for a terminal swim in the river—they're wondering if police negligence might have had anything to do with that. And that's not the worst of it," he added, holding up a hand to stop any interruptions, none of which I saw forthcoming. "The worst of it is that that bastard Katz is crawling around asking what we know about a Brattleboro policeman killing one of our bright young local businessmen."

He fixed both Brandt and me with a baleful eye. "Do you two catch a certain theme going here? Did the word 'police' crop up a half-dozen times just then? We don't have any general topics, James; we have problems, and most of them seem to be coming from here."

Dunn stuck to his position. "Then I suggest we change the forum of this meeting. Tony should perhaps have separate conversations with each of us."

"I didn't ask for company here. I need some answers. Luman Jackson, as vice-chair of the selectmen—that means officially—has been blistering my ass. Christ, news of the car chase was still on the radio when he rang up last. I didn't even know what the hell he was talking about. That made me look stupid, and I am goddamned well not going to look stupid to an asshole like him just because you guys aren't talking. I don't give a flying fuck if it's appropriate or not; I want to know what's going on. Do we suspect that one of our own cops is a murderer?"

His face was beet red at the end of this tirade, and the rest of us watched in silence for a moment, as if more interested in seeing a blood vessel explode than in addressing his question.

This time, Brandt cleared his throat, but Dunn stepped in again, as unperturbed as before. "Wait, Tony. Tom, I understand the pressures being brought to bear here, but it would be entirely wrong to cater to them. Perhaps we can hone our own focus a bit. Gary, why are you here?"

Nadeau looked as if he'd just been discovered eavesdropping on grownups. "Katz came by my office, too. John Woll is a town employee, and I'm legal counsel where town employees are concerned. My problems may look minor compared to Tom's, but if Woll is seriously being considered as a murder suspect, I feel I should be intimately involved in the discussion."

"I disagree," Dunn stated flatly. "If there were charges pending against Woll, they would be criminal in nature. Your involvement in that case would be limited to writing the letter that suspends him from employment, and you would do that only once Chief Brandt and I had advised you to. Aside from Mr. Katz's innuendos, however, I have heard nothing to indicate that any of that is germane.''

Now we could watch Nadeau turn fuchsia. He didn't pull out a knife and stab James Dunn in the heart, as he understandably might have. Instead, he paused a moment to select his words. When they came out, I was impressed at their cogency, and at the restraint in his voice. "That may be true. It still remains that this high-speed pursuit has started talk of one lawsuit and might lead to another from the bridge people Tom mentioned. Both of those would land squarely in my lap, and both have their origins in the police investigation that led to that car chase."

The state's attorney took it in full stride with a wide smile. "Excellent. Then we have no problem. As soon as the Police Department and my office have determined Officer Woll's culpability in all this, we'll let you know. And we'll try to expedite matters quickly, so you might have time to head off any lawsuits."

There was a very long and awkward pause, during which Gary Nadeau let out a small breath of air through slightly flared nostrils. Finally, he put his hand on the doorknob. "All right. The sooner the better."

Dunn smiled. "Absolutely. It'll be among our highest priorities."

But the door had slammed halfway through the sentence.

"You're a prick," Wilson said.

"Perhaps, but I'm also correct. We haven't the slightest idea how much Katz has collected. To presume too much and allow Nadeau to take confidential information directly to the selectmen would be extremely ill-advised."

"I talk to the selectmen, too."

Dunn nodded. "That's true, and so some of what I said to Gary applies to you also. However, some of your concerns are legitimate, and I think we ought to give you some credibility for your next encounter with the press."

Wilson looked at him as if he wanted to scrape him off his shoe. "That's very big of you, James. I didn't see you looking too credible out there a few minutes ago."

"They were interested in car chases. It wasn't my concern. When Katz publishes what he knows about John Woll, we'll be faced with an entirely different situation. In fact, we might consider beating him to the punch, holding an official press conference, and blowing his exclusive.''

I was fascinated with what had transpired here. In some five minutes of razzle-dazzle, James Dunn had convinced both Wilson and Nadeau that he was the man with all the answers, and that Brandt, myself, and indeed the entire Police Department had been acting with both his knowledge and his blessing. That he might be just as ignorant as they were had never been allowed to cross their minds.

Brandt, probably having anticipated all this, played an equally cool and rational role in addressing Wilson. ''Let me try to put it in terms you can use without offending James's sense of legal propriety. John Woll is not under investigation as a murder suspect. His name has, however, come up in a few compromising places, which is precisely what got Katz all worked up.''

''Katz all but claimed Woll killed Jardine because Jardine and Woll's wife were fooling around,'' Tom protested.

Brandt passively downplayed it. ''They were all in high school together. In fact, John Woll is one of the few on our force who was born and brought up in this town. There are people around here who probably saw his first bowel movement—that kind of intimacy can work against you in bad times.''

''So he's clean and Katz is full of shit.''

For once, both Brandt and Dunn looked uncomfortable. Brandt answered, I thought because Dunn felt that once you'd strolled out onto the diving board, it was your responsibility to jump on your own.

''Not necessarily.''

Wilson leaned forward in his chair and held his head. ''What the hell have you guys got us into this time?''

Brandt's voice took on an edge. ''We are conducting a homicide investigation, in the process of which we are uncovering leads and building a list of suspects—a long list—one of whom is John Woll. The others include an unidentified homeless bum, all the way up to one of this town's top-drawer citizens. Right now, none of them is any more suspect than the others, but some make for better news copy. Am I communicating clearly enough who is getting who into what?''

Wilson straightened, conciliation in his voice. "All right, all right; poor choice of words. You might remember the last time we had a murder in this town, though; the press had a field day. I guess I'm a little gun-shy.''

Brandt stood up and leaned across his desk, staring into Wilson's face. His voice was icy calm, but I had never before seen him so angry. "Let's not forget who pulled whose fat from the fire that time, Tom. I went on a long vacation and let you and your pals upstairs make it look like I'd been suspended. That was a favor I didn't have to do. I'd appreciate your remembering that, without having to be reminded in a less private forum.''

He sat back down in total silence. I, like most, had been a little vague on what exactly had happened a year ago, although I'd been the one tapped to be acting chief in Brandt's place. This was the first time I'd heard the truth, and it left me stunned. Whatever Brandt's motivations for taking the heat for Wilson and the selectmen, it had translated into a political debt of staggering proportions. Brandt could reveal the truth and publicly humiliate his "bosses" anytime. I could only think they'd been out of their minds to let him do it, just as he'd been equally nuts to propose it. It was hardball politics on a level I'd never imagined, especially in Brattleboro.

Wilson looked at us all as if he'd suddenly acquired some noxious odor he wished he could deny. His tone was utterly muted when he spoke. "Of course we all appreciate your position, Tony. No offense. Maybe you could give me a little more to dole out. I think James's idea of a press conference before tomorrow might help us out a bit.''

Brandt smiled his most affable smile. "Sure. What's your pleasure?''

"Well, I don't know. How about enough on Woll to take the wind out of Katz's sails, but not so much that it looks too important. We could make the car chase the lead item, and mention the Woll lead as an incidental, something only a rag like the *Reformer* would bother with.''

The chief looked at me. "What about the chase, Joe?''

I cleared my throat, feeling like the only amateur in the room. "We have no explanation for its cause. We went to ask Mr. Cappelli some routine questions related to the two major investigations we have going, and he responded by shooting at us and running away. We never actually spoke. So, until we can talk to him, the whole thing's a mystery."

Wilson nodded, but he didn't sound happy. "Okay. See if you can dress it up a little." He stood up, shaking his head. "I'm not casting aspersions here, but I do wish for the good old days sometimes, when a crime wave in this town was two kids stealing hubcaps on a Friday night."

Brandt also rose, again the smiling host. "I know what you mean, Tom. Thanks for stopping by."

Wilson, wrapped in his own misery, wandered out the door, closing it softly behind him.

Two down, one to go, I thought.

Dunn was obviously thinking the same thing, with different numbers. He fixed Brandt with his arctic eyes. "I hope you won't put me in a position like that again any time soon."

Brandt was unimpressed. "I thought you did very well."

"Cute. How long were you two going to sit on John Woll? I take it, by the way, that until now, nobody else was in on this?"

"Just us and Klesczewski," Brandt admitted. He went on to explain about the list of names found in Milly's apartment, the one that included John Woll's name. He also went into what we knew of the John-Rose-Charlie triangle.

Dunn digested it all without comment to the end and then let out a small grunt. "I hope Tom Wilson's medical insurance covers strokes. I take it you're going to interview Woll right away."

Brandt surprised me with his answer. "We've already tried to set it up; I called right after Katz left my office. There's no answer at his home, and a patrol unit reported his car isn't in the driveway. Until Tom mentioned the press conference, I was going to wait until he showed up for duty tonight."

"Unless he reacted like Cappelli did and is now long gone."

Brandt shook his head. "He's already been given a chance to do that."

Dunn nodded, putting a temporary end to the business. "I take it that's all of it? No more surprises?"

Brandt smiled. "Not yet."

"Well, I may have one for you. Arthur Clyde is raising a stink about having his business records removed under warrant and he's petitioning the court for return of property, so if you haven't already, you better read that material fast. I talked to Harrowsmith about Joe's affidavit, and I think you're on safe ground, but keep in mind that anything you find in that stuff might turn into smoke down the line." He looked directly at me. "I tell you this so you can start looking elsewhere for corroborating evidence, and to remind you that we are the good guys here, trained in the law. I realize that Sue Davis of my office looked that affidavit over and gave it a lukewarm approval, but remember: Don't be too independent, or you'll end up looking stupid.

"Which reminds me." He swiveled back to Brandt. "If you get so much as one more hiccup that incriminates or implicates John Woll, I suggest you hand the whole thing over to my office and my investigator, or the entire department, and possibly the town, will be criminally charged for protecting one of its own, and I might be the one filing the charge. If that makes you unhappy, then bring in the State Police; but either way, don't get your butts in a crack. It'll hurt, and you won't be able to play political footsie with Wilson to get out of it."

He stood up and walked to the door. "By the way, what you pulled on Tom is the most cockamamie stunt I ever heard, Tony. I hope it gets you mileage, because you're going to need it."

As he left, one of the carpenters, his lunch break over, picked up a circular hand saw and pulled the trigger. The echoing scream sounded an appropriate grace note.

CHAPTER
20

NUMBER 18 Brannen Street was a three-story, ramshackle, weather-beaten pile of functional, turn-of-the-century architecture, originally called a "three-decker" and designed to house three middle-class families, whose original breadwinners undoubtedly had been employed by the Estey Organ Works, at that time Brattleboro's largest business and an instrument maker of international renown.

But the organ works had gone out of business in the mid-1950s, and by the looks of it, the life had gone out of this building long before then. It, and many others like it around town, had been cut up by landlords, abused by countless winters, and undermined by a mismanaged real-estate market. It was now a peeling, neglected, compartmentalized collection of six small, airless units, one of which was the home of Rose and John Woll.

I got out of my car and looked around. In the hot stillness of the early evening, with the sounds of birds and rushing water nearby, the locale was as pristine and charming as the building was not. Brannen, or Brennen, depending on which of the two street signs you read, is a short, two-hundred-foot loop off Williams, which meanders alongside the Whetstone Brook between a steep, verdant ravine wall on one side, and a small sylvan pasture on the other side of the water. It's one of those typically Brattleboro settings where, surrounded by a city of twelve thousand people, you can imagine yourself in the isolated foothills of the Green Mountains.

I slammed the car door and walked toward the back of the building. The Wolls occupied a rear apartment on the second floor, accessible by an ancient roofed staircase that clung to the exterior wall like an afterthought. I climbed it gingerly, uncertain of how much more use it could bear.

I wasn't here by invitation. As Brandt had mentioned, John Woll had not answered his phone all afternoon, and coming around the building, I could confirm his car wasn't parked in the drive. On the other hand, I'd remembered his wife had dropped him off on the evening I'd recognized her voice, and I thought it possible that his car might be on the blink.

The impulse that had led me here had been triggered by more than that simple deduction, however. With Katz hot on the Wolls' connection to Jardine, he had probably tried to confront the subject of this latest political whirlwind with what he knew. If he had, I understood why John Woll was no longer answering his phone.

For some cops, the uniform and the badge offer the security and social courage they lack as civilians; it gives them comfort, much as the military does. That's where I fit John Woll. He'd stumbled once a few years back, and had made the Police Department his lifeline. If I was right, and Katz had gotten to him, then, guilty or not, John Woll was now in free-fall.

I reached the second-floor landing and found the front door ajar. I knocked, the door widening slightly under my hand. "John? It's Joe Gunther."

There was no answer, but I thought I heard a small and distant sound, like protesting bed springs. I entered the apartment.

I was standing in a living room, brightly painted, neat as a pin, sparsely and inexpensively furnished. The windows were all open, and the dying light outside still caught the colorful hues of the thin cotton curtains. It was an unexpected, comforting cocoon, buried in a building with all the warmth of a rotting, beached ship.

"John?"

Again, there was that slight shifting sound. Someone was definitely in the back of the apartment. Despite the domestic tranquility of my surroundings, a growing apprehension seeped into my bones.

I didn't unholster my gun, there being no tangible reason to do so, but I did rest my hand on its butt as I sidled up the narrow, short hallway toward the back. I paused beside the first door on the right and peered in around the corner. It was a bathroom, fresh-smelling, cheery, and empty.

I moved to the next and last door, also on the right. John Woll, flat on his back across a double bed, lay staring at the ceiling of his bedroom. His hands were wrapped around a tall glass of amber liquid and ice cubes which rested on his stomach. I took some comfort from that; if he was still sensitive enough to want ice cubes in his drink, he couldn't be totally blitzed—not yet, at least.

"Hullo, John."

He sighed without speaking.

I entered the room and moved over to a worn wooden rocking chair in the corner, a poor man's antique, which creaked ominously under my weight. "You coming on duty tonight?"

That obviously struck him as an odd opener. He turned his head to look at me. "You gotta be kidding."

His voice was soft, but clear, with no hint of an alcoholic slur. It occurred to me then that the glass was still full, its exterior heavily beaded with droplets of condensation, its ice cubes small and few in number. He'd obviously been lying there, merely considering a dive off the wagon, for quite some time.

"You can, for tonight. We'll keep you around the office for the shift, away from the press." I hesitated, wondering how coy I should be. Not very, I finally decided. "It'll spare you lying around here all night, playing Russian roulette with that glass."

He gave me a long, impenetrable look, and then extended the glass out to me. "It's ginger ale."

My face reddening, I nevertheless took the glass and sipped from it. It was indeed ginger ale. I handed it back, not bothering to apologize. "The way things are piling up, Brandt's going to have to call in the state's attorney's office to look into the allegations against you pretty soon. Dunn read him the riot act a half hour ago."

He let out a half snort of derision.

A moment of silence elapsed while I pondered the timing of this conversation. Brandt, Klesczewski, and I had seen the evidence damning John Woll escalate over the last two and a half days. He, presumably, had suffered a different perspective, knowing from the start he had compromising ties to the victim of a homicide, and wondering when that fact would emerge to bring an end to his world as he knew it.

I was running out of time. James Dunn's office was poised to drive a wedge between the department and John Woll that neither party would be allowed later to breach. If we didn't talk now, we never would.

"John, when did you first find out about Rose and Charlie Jardine?"

After a brief pause he held up four fingers.

I took a guess. "Four years?"

"Yup." It was a whisper, almost a sigh.

From past observations, I guessed that wouldn't have been too long after the affair's beginning. I'd never heard of an affair yet where the third party hadn't pegged to the truth pretty quickly; I imagined it had a lot to do with body language, literally.

"What did you do about it?"

He shrugged, almost dumping some of the ginger ale onto his already damp shirt.

I came at it from another angle, looking for an opening I could widen. "How did Katz break the news?"

"He called."

"And what did he say?"

"He knew about Charlie and Rose." He gave a sudden half chuckle. "He asked if I killed Charlie—out of jealousy, I suppose."

"He's not the only one thinking that."

There was a long silence. Then he said, "Yeah, I guess not."

I leaned forward quickly and plucked the glass from between his fingers. He was startled at my speed and half sat up as I put the glass on the floor beside me.

"Sit up, John," I ordered, standing over him.

"What d'you want from me?"

"I'm trying to talk to you. Sit up."

He shifted over to the head of the bed, his back propped against the pillows, his legs crossed. He would have looked like a kid except for the face—pale, haggard, and as worn as an old man's.

"What did Katz tell you?"

He rubbed his forehead with his palm, jarred out of his self-pity. "He said he knew my patrol car had been parked near where Charlie was found later, that Rose and Charlie were having an affair, that I'd lied about seeing a flare over the embankment. He said the department was covering for me—that they'd known all this from the start but that they were protecting their own."

He paused.

"Anything else?"

"He knew about my drinking. Said he knew Rose had dated both of us in high school. That the department had hired me even though they knew I was a drunk."

"Was there more to the high-school connection, something else besides Rose that connected you and Charlie?"

He made a face. "Charlie was a loser—long hair, did dope, jerked the teachers around, not serious about anything. He was everything I hated."

"But Rose liked him."

"Yeah."

In the quiet following that half moan of a response, I noticed the room had darkened and cooled with the yielding sun, if only slightly. It lent a slightly confessional feeling to the setting. I played into it by sitting back down.

"I never could understand that," John added. "I still don't."

"Rose told me you only admitted knowing about the

affair a couple of days ago. Why'd you sit on it for four years, John?''

''Because now he was dead.''

''He wasn't for four years.''

He stared at the middle distance between us, lost in thought for a moment. ''I didn't want to force her to choose.''

''And killing him solved that.''

''Oh, Christ,'' he muttered, and dropped his chin down on his chest.

A surge of genuine pity washed over me suddenly. I had always liked John Woll, had respected his quiet, conscientious manner over the years, and the courage he'd summoned to beat his drinking problem. Now his life was a shambles. It was partially his own fault, of course, but other factors had played a part. That I was one of those factors gave me no pleasure.

But my job now was to peer into the inky murk of his life, to distinguish not why things had happened to him and Rose, but what those things were. At this late date, with the pressure building under me, I couldn't afford to worry about how ham-handed I was, or what damage I might do to what was left of their marriage. Besides, regardless of the other threads left dangling in this case, I couldn't overlook the possibility that Katz was right about John Woll.

''Why'd you lie to Billy and me when we asked you how well you knew Jardine?''

John looked up at me, a new strength in his voice. ''He was dead. It was over. I didn't know who killed him, but I wasn't surprised somebody had. I heard about his death and felt nothing but relief. With Charlie gone, Rose's temptation was gone, too. That's how I saw it. Charlie was Rose's addiction, like booze is to me. And now that it was gone, I didn't want to say anything that might mess that up.''

I didn't mention that the removal of something tempting didn't automatically cure an addiction.

''What about the flare over the embankment?'' I asked, curious whether he would stick to that part of his story.

''There was a flare.'' His fist clenched in emphasis. Despite his obvious distress, I far preferred it to the listlessness

I'd encountered upon entering this room. But I also knew it was probably a mere passing gust of wind.

"We never found it. We did find one of your cigarettes, though; in Jardine's grave, in fact."

His mouth fell open, a reaction I found in his favor.

"Do you smoke while you're on patrol?"

His face reddened. "Sure; sometimes."

"Were you smoking when you got out to check on the flare?"

"I don't know—Jesus—maybe."

I leaned forward in the chair for emphasis. "Not maybe, John. People are sharpening their knives for you; I need answers. I said the cigarette was in the grave; that means under the soil, buried with the body, and the saliva on it matches your blood type. So concentrate."

He closed his eyes, his legs still crossed, making him look vaguely meditative. I thought how much I'd hate to be in his shoes.

"I flicked it."

"Where?"

His eyes opened. "As I got out of the car. I took it out of my mouth, flicked it into the street, and reached for my flashlight."

"You're sure you flicked it into the street?"

"Yeah, because I remember the smoke stinging my eye as I got out."

"Did you see anyone while you were checking out the flare?"

He shook his head, a little mournfully.

"Did you go into Ed's Diner afterwards?"

"No. I just drove on."

I thought a moment. Something was wrong with all this; something I'd thought of while we'd been speaking of the cigarette. "If you only told Rose you knew about the affair two days ago, why did you assume they'd broken it off before then?"

He brought his fingers to his temples and held them there, as if staving off a migraine. "It was just a feeling; nothing specific. Jesus—I thought Charlie's death was the best thing that could have happened to us. Now everyone thinks I killed him.''

"Did you know Milly Crawford?''

His hands dropped from his temples. "Crawford? No. Why?''

"You know about him?''

"I heard his name mentioned, you know, at work.''

"Do the names Mark Cappelli, Jake Hanson, Kenny Thomas, or Paula Atwater ring any bells?''

He looked totally baffled. "I've never heard of them.''

I hesitated a moment, doubtful of the wisdom of what I was about to suggest. Given the case's dim prospects, however, I was getting desperate. "John, would you grant us a consent to search this apartment?''

"A consent . . . Holy Jesus, Lieutenant.'' He knitted his brows in concentration, trying to fit my request into the context of our conversation. If what he claimed was true, he was the victim of a damn good frame, and sitting by passively hardly seemed constructive. So I hoped he'd decide to take part in his own fate. On the other hand, I couldn't help wondering if now wasn't exactly the wrong time for him to act. Sometimes, the best defense against a frame is immobility.

"All right,'' he said finally.

I got up. "Come out to the car with me while I get the form.''

I kept a sampling of most of the paperwork we use in the field in my car. A "Consent to Search'' is a warrantless, spur-of-the-moment device allowing a police officer to examine a house or car without the rigamarole of submitting an affidavit to a judge. It is granted by the owner of the property to be searched, can be withdrawn at any point during the search, and is viewed with distaste by any prosecutor or judge. The problem is that the grantor, at any time following the search, can claim he or she was coerced into cooperating. If that claim sticks, which it tends to in Vermont, then anything found under the consent is inadmissable in court.

But I felt myself guided by a strong sense of inevitability. John Woll was being painted, step by step, into a corner, either by his own devices or by outside manipulation. The question no longer was would he fall, but who would push him. I flattered myself by thinking that if we did, it would be on the basis of carefully evaluated evidence, not the kind of innuendo and inference that fueled Katz's accounts.

Also, I wanted to search John's place myself before James Dunn took over the investigation, which I feared he might do at any moment. Once that happened, not only would all contact with John be off limits, but so would any hopes of finding Woll-related clues that might apply to the Crawford and Jardine homicides.

I retrieved the single-sheet Consent to Search form from a battered briefcase in my back seat, filled in the blanks, and handed it to John as we walked back to his apartment in the half-light of sunset. He read it through several times, shaking his head. "This is so unreal."

"I know. Right now you've got a few circumstantial things against you, enough to titillate the news crowd, but not enough for an indictment." I patted his shoulder, conscious of my opposing desires. If he were being framed, by someone who knew all the tricks, chances were good this search would do him more harm than good. My motivations, I realized, were now almost entirely selfish, despite my liking for John, or my sorrow at his predicament. "You don't have to sign that," I added halfheartedly.

He shrugged, and signed it on the bannister, taking matters into his own hands, or so I hoped.

It was awkward, having him stand around as I began poking through his belongings. I was used to being armed with judge-signed paperwork, accompanied by a complete search team and at least one uniformed man to escort the homeowner out the door and out of the way. With John watching, I felt more like a guest who'd suddenly been seized by an insane desire to ransack the place. I found myself gingerly shifting through the kitchen drawers and carefully replacing sofa cushions, so that any trace of my passage would be minimal.

My real interest was the bathroom and bedroom, where I'd found in the past most people tend to hide their secret pleasures. But I was holding them until last to make damn sure I covered the apartment thoroughly. Not that I had long to wait; the place was so small, it wasn't forty-five minutes later that I crossed the threshold into the bedroom.

Throughout this ordeal, John kept silent, standing away from me, watching me work without expression or comment. I checked occasionally, over my shoulder, to see if his demeanor had anything to tell me, but his face told me nothing.

I stood before the plain wooden dresser, noticing that here, as everywhere else in the apartment, gentle grace notes had been added to soften the plainness of the general surroundings. The dresser was draped with a colorful cotton runner that cascaded off either side of the top, and the shade of the light, which I switched on to chase away the gathering gloom, had a bright-red paper flower pinned to it, whose scarlet aura touched the near wall like a watercolorist's diluted paintbrush.

I pulled open one of the top half-drawers and discovered a neat row of rolled men's socks. This is where a search started yielding a mixed emotional bag, for while bedrooms were traditionally rich in compromising landmarks, you had to paw through condom packs, underwear, weird literature, and God knows what else, some of which one inhabitant of the room had been keeping secret from the other for years.

I sifted through the gathered socks and then reached in behind them, my fingers touching something smooth and metallic. Just then, the screen door in the front room opened and banged shut.

As I pulled out a large, very expensive looking gold watch from the back of the drawer, Rose entered the room, a quizzical expression forming on her face at the sight of me. The shiny band of the watch caught the lamplight, scattering it in tiny flecks across the ceiling.

"This yours?" I asked John.

He shook his head, looking puzzled.

Rose, at his shoulder, went white, her mouth falling open in shock. She moistened her lips and blinked. "It's Charlie's."

CHAPTER
21

K LESCZEWSKI appeared at the screen door, followed by Tyler and several other police officers, who filed past us into the apartment. Rose and John Woll sat side by side on the couch, looking as if they were being held at gunpoint. In fact, no one was paying any attention to them.

Tyler handed me the search warrant as he went by. His voice was flat to the point of rudeness. "Harrowsmith was not thrilled at the procedure."

"You mean that the warrant was triggered by a Consent to Search?"

He nodded curtly. "He had questions I couldn't answer."

I opened my mouth to respond, but he disappeared down the hall into the bedroom, his enormous evidence box tilting him to one side.

I looked to Klesczewski for an explanation. Tyler usually came to these scenes like a beagle to the hunt. This testy display was so rare as to be unique.

Klesczewski waited until the last of Tyler's team had gone by. "Everyone's heard that you and Brandt sat on the evidence against John. They're a little pissed off you didn't trust them, and more than a little pissed that the shit's going to hit the fan in the papers."

I noticed he'd severed himself from Brandt's and my

conspiracy, siding with the disgruntled lower deck as mutiny loomed on the horizon. I obviously had some major bridge-repairing to do.

That, however, would have to wait. I crossed over to the Wolls, Klesczewski in tow, and pulled an armchair around so that it was directly facing them. Ron parked himself on the corner of a sturdy coffee table, notebook in hand, slightly to one side.

I looked at Rose and tilted my head in Ron's direction. "You two know each other, don't you?"

She nodded silently.

"I want him to hear this conversation, since things have become more formalized with the search warrant. I also want him to read you your rights. You're not under arrest, of course, but I have to let you know you're under no obligation to talk to us."

They both barely nodded. I glanced at Ron, who recited their litany of rights by heart.

I resumed speaking when he'd finished. "The state's attorney will probably be taking over the investigation from us, at least as far as you and John are concerned. Otherwise people could complain of a conflict of interest. You understand that?"

Rose didn't look as though she understood anything. "You mean because of the watch?"

"Yeah. That, and other things. John was seen in an area where Charlie's body was later discovered, John's cigarette was found in Charlie's grave, and his footprints were in the soil around the grave site. In addition, you'd been having an affair with Charlie, about which John was aware, and there's a history of conflict between the three of you going back to high school, including your pregnancy. And now Charlie's watch, presumably the one that was missing from his wrist, is found in your apartment. It's all what they call circumstantial evidence, but it is beginning to stack up."

This time, they both nodded without a word. I hadn't mentioned Rose's call to Jardine, or John's admission that he'd known about the affair virtually from the start. Things were looking bad enough for him without rubbing them in.

"Did you know whose watch that was?" I asked John.

"No."

"How did it get into your sock drawer?"

"I don't know," he answered in a dull monotone.

"You'd never seen it before?"

"No."

"Rose, how did you know whose watch it was?"

She glanced furtively in John's direction, two incongruously bright patches of pink rising on her cheeks. "I recognized it."

"Very quickly. How come?"

She hesitated, touching her forehead gingerly with a fingertip, as if checking for a loose strand of hair. "I gave it to him."

I looked at John, no longer sure he was breathing. His eyes were fixed before him, locked onto my right kneecap, his face deathly pale.

Tyler gestured to me from the hallway. I grimaced, more than a little irritated at this obvious breach of interview protocol. "Hang on a sec, will you?"

I crossed over to Tyler, unable to read his expression. Without a word, he led me down the hallway to the bathroom. There, taped to the underside of the toilet-tank lid, was a small envelope of white powder.

"Shit," I muttered.

His voice held no satisfaction. "I thought you'd want to know."

I patted him on the shoulder. "Thanks J.P. I appreciate it."

I reentered the hallway, almost colliding with James Dunn. He did not look pleased.

"What the hell do you think you're doing?" His voice was a barely subdued hiss. I glanced over his shoulder at the Wolls. John was watching us.

"Let's take this outside," I muttered, and steered toward the front door.

We rattled down the rickety stairs and stopped around the corner, amid quite a cluster now of official-looking cars.

The state's attorney could barely contain his rage. "I told you, not two hours ago, that if anything additional was dug up against the Wolls, my office would take over the investigation. Am I dreaming, or does that ring a bell with you?"

"Look, I came by here to see how John was doing. I knew Katz must have contacted him; I also knew John had his problems with booze in the past. I wanted to see how he was holding up."

Dunn was not sympathetic. "Right, and the next thing we know, he's signing search consents and you're ordering up warrants to tear his house apart. You think I'm an idiot, Joe? You think I don't know you pulled a fast one on me? This is bullshit."

I felt my face flush. "Hold it just a goddamn minute. Your *request* to be informed is not an order; and I followed the paperwork here." I pulled out the consent form. "He signed this thing, and I made damned sure he knew what it meant. As soon as the watch surfaced, that was it; there was barely a word exchanged between us until the search warrant arrived to cover our butts."

Dunn raised his hands in frustration. "Oh, for Christ's sake. The consent form makes the fucking warrant useless. If the court throws out the first, which they almost always do, then they have to throw out the second." He took a deep breath. "What else have your people found?"

"Looks like some coke, taped to the inside of the toilet tank."

Dunn rolled his eyes. "Great. Perfect."

Again, I was washed with anger. "Look, James, if the consent form is such a live grenade, then why do we have it? It was one of *your* people that told us, and I quote, 'it is one of the weapons in our arsenal.' I admit they said it wasn't a first-choice thing, but that we could use it. What the hell's going on? Seems to me you'd be better off telling your own people to do their jobs before you start on mine."

We stared at each other like two bloody-nosed kids, breathing hard. Finally, Dunn lowered his head and took a deep breath. "All right. Consents aren't totally worthless, but they cause intense judicial scrutiny. It usually hinges on what they call 'the truly voluntary nature' of the consent. If the defense can raise a single hint of coercion during the process, then it's dead. It boils down to your word against theirs, and they have an attorney telling them just what to say. Maybe we'll get lucky; maybe Woll's lawyer'll be brain dead.''

He turned on his heel and stalked off toward the apartment. It hadn't been an apology, but I sensed the edge was off his anger. Furthermore, I couldn't blame him. In my own anger, I had forced him to justify the validity of consent forms, but I'd known what a feeble tool they were. Part of my irritation stemmed from my own sloppiness. It was a thought that gave me pause—it wasn't the first time I felt the pressures in this case were having an undermining effect on my judgment.

As I followed Dunn up the stairs, he turned to me and said, ''You realize the Wolls are mine, right now, this second, right? And everything having to do with them.'' He jerked his thumb toward the apartment.

''Right,'' I said tersely, and followed him inside to inform the troops.

•   •   •

''We have a problem,'' Brandt said later, as I entered his office.

''I know. Dunn's already told me: hands off the Wolls.''

Brandt shook his head. ''I was expecting that; I've already talked to his office. This concerns Mark Cappelli.''

''Oh, Christ. He didn't die on us, did he?''

''Figuratively. He woke up a couple of hours ago, but he won't say word one to us. He's instructed his lawyer to sue the department for reckless endangerment, among other things.''

''You're kidding. He shot at us, for Christ's sake.''

''In self-defense. He claims you never identified yourselves and that he thought you were hoods about to jump him. He saw Klesczewski's gun and, as his lawyer put it, moved to protect his own life.''

I sat on the edge of the low filing cabinet near the door and thought back. ''I don't think we did ID ourselves; he opened fire on us before we got close enough. But those were obviously police cars chasing him down I–91, and he sure as hell didn't have permission to steal that truck. Nor was he protecting himself when he shot that other guy, getting out of the building.''

Brandt shrugged. ''Doesn't matter; that's all food for the legal beagles. Chances are, before it's all done, he'll end up in the can. What counts for us right now is that he's dead as a witness. We won't find out why he was on Milly Crawford's list until after we've done a long, protracted dance with his nit-picker attorney. That could take weeks. We also lost out on a warrant to search his apartment. Harrowsmith said we were fishing.''

I ran my fingers through my sweat-dampened hair. ''So we are. By the way, Tyler found what looks like cocaine at Woll's apartment.''

Brandt made a face.

''Think Dunn'll issue an arrest?''

Brandt shook his head. ''Too early. He'd sooner put up with the political heat than lock John up and then try to cobble together a case before the judicial clock runs out. I'm afraid John's going to be hung out to dry for a while.''

I didn't point out the irony of the phrase. ''You going to hold the news conference to steal Katz's thunder?''

''Yeah, Dunn called from the Wolls' to arrange a time. We've missed the TV news hour, but we'll hit the radio guys and the papers.''

I pushed myself to my feet, feeling drained. ''Well, I think I'll check in with the troops.''

Brandt stopped me at the door. ''You look a little flattened.''

I shrugged. ''Just the heat.''

The double dose of losing both Woll and Cappelli, combined with the storm I knew would break when Woll's involvement became common knowledge, was hardly grounds for enthusiasm. Furthermore, it heightened my sense that I was losing control of this investigation. It had been three days since we had found Charlie Jardine in the dirt, and I was plagued by the thought that while some play was indeed being acted out, we were all crowded into the wrong theater.

It was therefore with mixed emotions that I saw Gail sitting in my office as I entered the detective bureau. Usually, the sight of her lifted my spirits, brightening me like the proverbial breath of fresh air. This time, however, I would've had to have been sleepwalking not to know the reason for her visit. Indeed, in my present state of mind, her being here was as inevitable as the pain following a twenty-foot fall from a ladder.

"Hi." I bent to kiss her and was met with a cold look. I settled for positioning myself warily behind my desk. "What's up?"

She stared at me darkly. "I'm not sure what to call it. Breach of trust comes close."

"On whose part?" I was groping, badly, for appropriate lines.

"Why didn't you tell me the Police Department was shielding one of its own during a murder investigation?"

"We weren't." It never ceased to amaze me how fast and inaccurately information was passed around in this town.

"You're denying there was evidence against John Woll from the moment you found Jardine's body?"

"I'm not denying there was some; a lot of it pretty skimpy until about an hour ago."

"I've been told Jardine was having an affair with Woll's wife, that the two men had fought over her since high school, that Woll was seen at the grave site just before Jardine was found, and that he was possibly burying the man at the time."

"He claims he was investigating a road flare someone had thrown over the embankment."

"A road flare no one has found."

I placed both my hands behind my neck and looked at her for a moment in silence. "You're well informed."

"Not by you."

Despite my earlier misgivings, her almost officious rage made me toe the party line. "Gail, you sound like I'm to blame for not keeping you up to date on the latest police business."

"I don't expect you to tell me everything you're up to. But I thought you were sensitive enough to warn me of the time bomb you were sitting on before Jackson, Nadeau, McDonald, Katz, and everybody else in the world opened fire. You asked me yesterday if things ever got tough because of our relationship. Well, today I felt like an idiot, because you let me be blind-sided."

The inevitability of this conversation pained me worse than I'd imagined. I got up and circled my desk, reaching for her shoulder. "I apologize for not warning you about John Woll's involvement. I've been carrying this around inside me like heartburn from the start. I should have told you; I almost did last night, but I guess I kept hoping it would go away. You know, even with the shit hitting the fan, we still don't know if John had anything to do with Jardine's death. He and his wife might just be patsies. Brandt and I only kept quiet because there was so little to go on; we knew John would be put through the wringer regardless of the evidence. We wanted to make sure of what we had before he was fed to the lions."

"You could have warned me." The refrain was the same, but the tone of voice had softened.

"What did Jackson say?"

"It got very personal. I don't want to repeat it, Joe, but it hurt. I guess I thought it would have hurt less if you'd told me what you were up to."

I put my arm around her and held her, glad to have her accept the gesture. "I am sorry. I had no idea you'd get flattened like that."

She looked at me then, her eyes worried. "He actually frightened me, Joe. Remember when I told you he seemed overly interested in all this? Well, it's more than that; I've never seen him so worked up. It's like he's gone around the bend almost."

I'd seen Luman Jackson under full sail, filled with bluster and egotism, and I'd seen Gail handle him with her usual cool aplomb. Her distress disturbed me deeply, introducing a personal, threatening element to an investigation already tinged with some dark and vengeful psychology.

How far would Jackson go in pushing the selectmen and the Police Department to satisfy his private needs? And, perhaps more to the point, why?

CHAPTER
22

I looked down the length of the conference table. There were none of the usual wisecracks or paper shuffling, no muttered one-liners. The assembled faces of the detective squad looked back at me, silent and glum. Now that the press conference had come and gone like a long-awaited storm, they were more resentful than ever.

My own mood hadn't improved much either. The encounter with the press had been like standing before a firing squad. Not only had preempting his scoop incensed Katz, but his colleagues from the surrounding area's newspapers, radios, and two regional TV stations had grilled Brandt, Dunn, and to a lesser extent me, with equal vigor.

What was frustrating was how overblown the reaction had become. From the time Brandt had almost casually decided to keep Woll's name under wraps, both he and I had known there was an element of risk. On the other hand, most investigations cause names to pop to the surface like corks, and only a few of them eventually prove worthy of attention. Ours is usually a process of elimination. That one of those leads should be a cop had struck us as sensitive, certainly, but hardly as a deliberate cover-up. We'd been dumb perhaps, but not treasonable.

I leaned forward, splaying my fingers on top of the table, a little irritated at my present audience. "I gather we have

222

problems here among ourselves. Or, more to the point, you have a problem with me.''

There was a stifling silence, broken only by a few self-conscious chair creaks.

I let the discomfort hang in the air. Sammie finally spoke up, her voice slightly belligerent. "I don't have a problem."

Heads swiveled from her to me. I turned to her, trying to staunch any impressions that she might be trying to cozy up to me; her honesty didn't deserve that kind of abuse. "Okay. What don't you have a problem about?"

"About what you and Brandt did."

"Which was what, as you see it?" I asked them all.

Tyler tossed his pencil contemptuously onto the pad before him. "Oh, Christ's sake. You guys sat on part of an investigation we were all supposed to be sharing. You didn't trust us."

DeFlorio nodded, Ron didn't move, and Sammie frowned.

I sat down heavily and leaned back in my chair, suddenly exhausted, no longer interested in debating the fine points. Tyler's words echoed in my head. "Okay—I screwed up. We thought if we could eliminate John from the list of suspects quickly, we could avoid unnecessary bad publicity. We had no idea he would end up at the top of that list, and when he did, it was too late."

DeFlorio nodded, seemingly satisfied.

Tyler, however, wasn't so simply bought off. "It might have helped if you'd included us."

I shrugged, but Sammie spoke up for me. "I think they had a point; the more people you bring in, the more chance there is of a leak. Besides, we don't reveal to the press everyone we're investigating; we'd get our butts sued inside a week."

Tyler shook his head. "This isn't the same. It made the whole department look bad. I'm not after you personally, Joe, but you and Brandt played god and got caught. It was a dumb move, insulting to us and ready-made for the media."

"That's too rough," Ron finally muttered.

"Yeah," DeFlorio added. "I didn't feel insulted, just surprised. Wasn't that big a deal."

"It was a security thing," Sammie reiterated. "And

we've had problems there from the start. Look what happened to Milly Crawford after you announced you'd nailed his prints to the baggie in Jardine's house.''

Tyler smacked the table with his open hand, surprisingly upset. ''Now just wait a goddamned minute . . .''

I stood up, both arms held high, startled at the sudden rise in emotions. ''Hold it, hold it.''

Tyler was still glaring at Sammie, who was holding her own. Silently, I gave her the debate. She'd hit J.P.'s one sore spot, a spot he, along with the rest of us, had obviously been contemplating since Milly's untimely end. She'd also burst his self-righteous bubble, which, I suspected, had been inflated more by exhaustion than by true outrage.

''Okay. We're tired, we're frustrated, we've made mistakes. Sammie grabbed the wrong bum off the street; Mark Cappelli is suing us 'cause Ron and I didn't ID ourselves before he opened fire. The bottom line is we have a bitch of a case, we're understaffed, we don't have a lot of experience, and we're under a microscope. I don't want to ignore any real unhappiness here, but we can't let this get the better of us.''

J.P. rubbed his eyes with his palms. ''No . . . I'm sorry. Maybe Milly getting whacked worked on me more than I thought.''

''That and the fact that you've probably had six hours sleep in the last three days,'' I added.

Tyler sat back and waved one hand. ''Yeah. Okay, look, I've had my little fit. Let's get back to business.''

''Which,'' I picked up, ''might have suddenly become a little less complicated. We no longer have to worry about John or Rose Woll. If any of us picks up evidence tied to them, we simply pass it along to Dunn's office.''

''That only works in our favor if the Wolls are innocent.''

That was Tyler again, back on track, applying the logic he held so dear.

I nodded in agreement. ''Good point. Let's put the Wolls on the table and see what we've got. J.P., were you able to do anything with the stuff you found in their apartment before Dunn's people took it over?''

''Nothing solid; impressions, really, and only about the

two items you know about. The baggie looked exactly like the ones in Milly's apartment. But that doesn't mean much unless the SA can lift some prints off it. The gold watch was engraved on the back, 'To Charlie with Love,' and it looked as clean as a whistle. I looked at it under the light and it was polished, front and back. I don't know about you folks, but my watch always has prints on the face of it.''

Instinctively, and feeling a little foolish afterward, we all consulted our own watches. No one commented on having a polished crystal.

"Of course," Tyler added, "that doesn't prove anything either.''

"But it does imply something," I picked up. "It strikes me that the case against John Woll has been awfully neat and tidy—almost gift wrapped.''

I held up the fingers on one hand to tick off the items I had in mind. "John is seen at the grave site, lured there, he says, by a flare we never find. Negative implications are: He was there burying Jardine, and he lied about the flare to cover himself.''

I bent down a second finger. "Rose and Charlie were having an affair, a continuation of some romantic triangle they formed in high school. John is a boozer with limited career goals and a low sex drive, going nowhere while Jardine is suddenly a high flyer. Implication: John whacked Jardine out of jealousy, envy, or vengeance.''

"Third, in Milly Crawford's apartment, Ron found a list of telephone numbers, one of which belonged to Mark Cappelli. The others, as you all know by now, belonged to three others we have yet to chase down. There was, in addition, a fifth number, which belonged to John Woll.''

I waited for the bristling body language to settle down before going on. "I told Ron to keep it under his hat. You can add that to the general apology I made earlier. Nevertheless, the inclusion of John's number indicates that John was somehow tied to Milly's drug business.''

"And now," I concluded, placing my hand back on the table top, "we have Jardine's watch and possibly Milly's cocaine in John's apartment. The implications there are obvious.''

Sammie shook her head in wonder. "If it is a setup, it's very good."

Pierre Lavoie's voice was tentative, torn between curiosity and the fear we might throw him out for speaking up. "I don't understand why the SA hasn't arrested him, if he's got all this evidence against him."

Ron Klesczewski spoke up for the first time, grateful for an opportunity to take control. I wondered how long it would take him to risk sticking his neck out again, now that the political knife-wielding had caused him to pull back. "For one thing, the evidence isn't all that strong, and for another, once an arrest takes place, you've only got so much time available before you have to wrap the case up and present it in court."

"Besides," I added, "Dunn's got time on his side, if he ignores all the pressure. Right now, the implications I counted off establish a motive, an opportunity, and a bag of circumstantial evidence, all of which cropped up within three days. Chances are, if there's proof to be had, it'll surface before long. Then Dunn'll be able to waltz into court with an airtight case."

There was a long pause as each of us considered that possibility. Dunn's record was very good; he rarely "waltzed" anywhere without getting results. So, the last and final implication had to be that if he did go to court with this one, it meant John Woll had killed Charlie Jardine.

"So if John killed Jardine, who killed Milly Crawford?" Ron asked in a barely audible voice.

No one answered immediately. Then Sammie spoke up. "And if John killed Milly to silence him, then why leave a baggie of Milly's dope taped to the toilet?" No one had to add that leaving Jardine's watch in a sock drawer also seemed pretty implausible. With questions like that floating around, Dunn's apparent answer to who killed Jardine could never ring absolutely true.

"Find that out," I finally answered, "and a whole lot'll fall into place—probably more than Jardine's killer intended."

I began pacing the back of the room. "Ron, where in Milly's apartment did you find that phone list?"

"Behind the dresser, on the floor."

I mulled that over for a few seconds. "An inconvenient place to hide something, but a suitably obscure place to plant one, especially if you were in a hurry. Now, we're pretty sure Milly was knocked off on the spur of the moment, to stop us from talking to him. Without having time to get fancy, the killer must have figured that any planted evidence would be better than none, especially if it linked Milly and John."

Tyler looked at me, both smiling and doubtful. "Christ, we're going around and around here."

But I could tell he was intrigued. "True, so, since we're not allowed to investigate the Wolls, let's assume they're innocent, just for the sake of the investigation, and pursue all our other leads. Considering the doubts we have about Dunn's case, we might even be right."

There were a few more chuckles around the table. The incongruity of assuming a suspect innocent out of pure convenience might have seemed laughable, but I'd raised a legitimate point. Furthermore, it cleared the smoke away, allowing us to see both homicides in a new light, perhaps a light we were intended never to see by. That possibility alone was enough to recharge the batteries of every person in the room.

I sat back down, content the squad was back on track, newly braced against the turmoil that had briefly derailed it.

• • •

I stopped DeFlorio as he was heading out the door. "I hear the court order was delivered on Jardine's business records."

He made a face. "Yeah; piss me off. We spent hours on that junk, all for nothing."

"You didn't find anything?" I knew that if Dennis didn't understand something, he tended to throw it out.

He conceded the point indirectly. "None of it made any sense to me, anyway; stuff's all Greek. Tell you the truth, I was tickled pink when the court order arrived. Talk to Willette. He might have picked up something."

I decided to do just that, walking down Main Street to the

south side of the public library and a large, clapboard, century-old building that had been converted into a mini-office building. Justin Willette's two-room suite was at the top of the stairs on the second floor.

Willette grinned and pushed his glasses high up onto his head as I walked in. He rubbed his eyes with both stubby hands. "I wondered when I'd see you. I take it you heard the bad news."

"That Arthur Clyde got his papers back, or that there was nothing to find in the first place?"

He chuckled. "Is that what Dennis told you? I'm not surprised; he was looking a little microwaved toward the end."

"Then you did finish?" Willette's desk was actually a seven-foot-long dining table he'd moved in from his house. I sat down opposite him, as if preparing to make a meal of the stacks of paper between us.

The glasses stayed parked up on his broad, pink forehead, giving his face an odd, four-eyed appearance. He settled back into his chair and linked his hands behind his neck. "Well, we finished the short course. Jardine having been in operation for only a year made it a whole lot easier. Still, all I got were impressions. To do it properly would've taken days and corroboration from other data sources."

Justin Willette had never lit the world on fire as a financial high roller. He had not come to Brattleboro after a career on Wall Street or from advising the yacht-owning set on how to screw up American business through LBOs. He had stuck to doing his homework, had worked long hours with firms in Boston getting the basics down, and was now a registered rep of one of the big national stockbrokers. He had the reputation of guiding the little guys through the investment maze with integrity and a minimum of smoke and mirrors.

He also liked a puzzle, and had helped us in the past to unscramble a few. Although there was no evidence of it now, I knew he and Dennis had spent the entire day poring over buy and sell tickets, market-trend charts, financial newsletters, business correspondence, and God knows what else, all with frequent referrals to the computer glowing on the counter behind him, and all, I had no doubt, at no cost to us.

"So you smell something fishy?" I asked him.

He pursed his lips. "Yeah. That's a pretty good way of putting it. Nothing definite, but something wrong. Not court-of-law material, though; keep that straight."

"Okay."

He nodded, reassured. "Okay. Small lecture on trading, then. The National Association of Security Dealers, called NASD for short, and the New York Stock Exchange, monitor all trading, as does the SEC, which oversees both of them. Also, with national firms like Merrill Lynch or Prudential-Bache or whatever, senior partners of regional offices tend to keep an eye peeled. What all of them are looking for are patterns, since there're way too many transactions conducted every day to analyze every one.

"What is a pattern, you ask?" Willette continued, although I had done no such thing. "It's something like buying AT&T stock one week before a merger is announced, and then doing the same kind of thing with another company a few days or weeks later, cashing in both times. That catches people's attention, especially if it keeps happening and involves a fair amount of cash."

"Insider trading?"

"Possibly. That's the tricky part. There's a lot of analysis that goes on in this business, and there're a lot of smart people doing it. Look at "Wall Street Week" on TV sometime and you'll see them in action. They study the trends, look at the figures, sometimes even interview the principal players, and then they make a buy. If the stock then suddenly goes through the roof, is that insider trading? Nope. So the watchdogs have got to tell the difference between a sharp guy with an honest track record, and a crook."

"So what makes you suspicious of Jardine? That he was too new in the business to be any good?" I paused. "How good was he, by the way?"

Willette chuckled. "I don't know about him, but ABC Investments was off to a healthy start. If they'd been wooing me as a customer with their track record, I would have listened. What do you know about Arthur Clyde, by the way?''

It was an embarrassing question, considering the effort this man had expended on our behalf. ''Not much, I'm afraid. We would have had more if it hadn't been for this double homicide; our manpower's been stretched to the limit. Basically, you've been our only Clyde investigator up to now.''

Willette smiled and shook his head. ''Didn't mean to put you on the spot. I know you're ass-deep in alligators. I did a check on Arthur Clyde. He was cited and suspended by the NASD two years ago for what I'd call irregular paper-shuffling. It's not that rare; people get caught in the rules all the time, and usually it's no big deal, at least as far as the public is concerned. Unfortunately, the broker can really get pinched, depending on how tough the bureaucrats want to get.''

''How tough did they get with Clyde?''

''Well, that's the interesting part. It was just a little thing—I called a friend of mine who did some digging. Clyde apparently goofed on some paperwork having to do with a client's discretionary account. From what I understand, he put things right within a single work day, but the milk had been spilled and NASD was called in to supervise the cleaning up. Normally, that means a hearing, a certain amount of bowing and scraping, a slap on the wrist, a small mountain of paperwork, and that's it. Only this time, it didn't work that way. Clyde, with a squeaky-clean record going back God knows how many years, got pissed. He told the NASD boys to screw themselves and refused to attend the hearing. So they found him in contempt, slapped a fine on him, and gave him a six-month suspension; not that it mattered, since he'd already quit his job.''

''Wasn't that a problem when he went in with Jardine?''

''No. The fine had been paid off and the six months had long since elapsed. As far as NASD was concerned, it was ancient history.''

''Until now.''

Willette wobbled his head from side to side. ''Maybe, just maybe.'' This was what he got in return for his labors:

the joy of being the oracle, if only briefly, in the midst of a major case. The man knew enough of the world to realize I wouldn't be in his office if I wasn't in need of his knowledge. Finally, he laughed. "Okay, I'll concede. But keep in mind it's all pretty subtle and will need lots of supporting evidence, none of which I have."

"Gotcha."

He propped his elbows on the arms of his chair and built a steeple of his fingers. "I do suspect some insider trading, but not on the order to which we've become aware in the news."

I could feel the crease growing between my eyes.

"The trick to this game, as a retail business, is to show people you're a consistent winner. It's nice to hit the jackpot, of course, but unless you do it frequently, you're quickly seen as a flash in the pan. And if you do hit it frequently, pretty soon your place of business is crawling with investigators all wondering how you did it. Word of that gets out fast, too, and can be as bad for the bankbook as unemployment. So you work for a middle ground, enjoying the peaks as they come, but going for solid, respectable returns."

I kept my mouth shut at the end of this primer, knowing the punch line would come in good time.

"The first thing that caught my eye with ABC was that they hit this steady, predictable stride right off the bat." He paused.

"And that's pretty rare?"

"As a snowball in hell. It's like any other business; it takes you a while to find your sea legs."

"But what about Clyde? Didn't he have years of experience and contacts he could bring to bear? And there was Wentworth in the background, too."

Willette wagged his finger at me, delighted. "All true, but Clyde's contacts would be on the investment side, not the investor. You can have a great product, but you need clients to buy it; that's why an operation like this usually takes time to show a profit. As for Wentworth, he'd have the same problem in reverse. He might have the local appeal, but any clients he could round up would want to see a solid track record before they signed on. It's like a Catch-22; you can beat it, but not easily, especially with a partner like Jardine, whose résumé would look good only on an application to Taco Bell."

"But they did it nevertheless."

"That they did, largely on one account."

He paused again, and again I played along. "Okay. I give up. Which account?"

"They landed the Putney Road Bank Trust Department almost as soon as they'd hung out their shingle."

Mention of the Putney Road Bank made the short hairs on my neck tingle. Two of the names on Milly's list were employed there.

"In your digging through ABC's paperwork, did you run across either Kenny Thomas or Paula Atwater, in connection to the bank?"

For once, Willette looked blank. "Nope, doesn't ring a bell."

I tried a more general approach. "Why would a bank put that much money into a new outfit like ABC? I mean, what wou.d the pitch be to the board of directors or whoever?"

Willette thought about that for a moment before answering. "It would have to hinge entirely on connections—the credibility of the person making the pitch. ABC wouldn't have anything else."

"And that would've been Wentworth, since Clyde's a newcomer and Jardine's a nobody, at least in the bank's eyes."

Willette shrugged. "Sure, Wentworth. But not him alone. The real enthusiasm would have to come from within the bank, from officers carrying Wentworth's torch, and that's something I don't think they'd do without some real incentive."

"Like a kickback?"

"Kickback, payment up front, drugs, sex, or rock 'n roll; who knows? You know what they say: 'Money talks and bullshit walks.' A lot of bankers I know are either stupid, greedy, or both. If Wentworth paid off a fat sum to the right people, then that, mixed with his own reputation, might do the trick, especially with an outfit like Putney Road Bank.

It's hardly Chase Manhattan, after all; it's more like a one-horse barn, but perfect to get ABC off to a nice start."

"You implied ABC got a few other lucky breaks."

"Yeah, equally intriguing, and again only because of the suspicions it raises. Traditionally, in this business, the slow hard road to success is attained through old-fashioned hustle. You get a tip, you offer it around; people turn you down but watch to see what happens to the stock in question. If it goes up, you don't make any money, but you gain a little credibility. So you do it again, and again. Eventually, if you keep hitting base hits, and especially if you hit the occasional homer, people start paying you for your advice. It's pretty elementary.

"The trick, of course, is to come up with enough winner suggestions to get enough clients to keep you from going bankrupt. The hassle, in other words, isn't just in trying to locate customers, but also in locating juicy investments. Here again, I found ABC to be remarkably well blessed."

"Reflecting Clyde's abilities to choose stocks, Wentworth's influence and number of contacts, and Jardine's salesmanship in putting the two together."

Willette chuckled. "Very good—just what they'd want you to think. Old-fashioned American know-how at work."

"Well, couldn't it be?"

"Sure, it could be, but not probably. See, Joe, I live in this part of the jungle. On the face of it, you'd be right, maybe. A lot of guys, mostly in the old days, did get to the top à la Horatio Alger. But it took a lot of work, and I mean real ball-busting, year-after-year stuff; not very appealing to either the young modern male or the old guy in his twilight years who still has a greedy twinkle in his eye."

I sighed, a little depressed at how cannily accurate it all sounded. "So how do you think they did it?"

"It's a little off the wall—really just a guess on my part—but I'd say they were giving license to a moral difference of opinion with the law."

I shook my head, not even bothering for an explanation. He was now in his role of alchemist, turning the lead weight of Wall Street number crunching into the gold of human nature, unfortunately in one of its least appealing aspects. I got up from the table and crossed over to the window which looked down onto Main Street and the drive-in bank opposite. The people on the sidewalk strolled back and forth like bedouin wanderers: slow, dehydrated, flattened by the postsunset heat.

Justin Willette continued with his treatise. "The laws against insider trading are seen by many investment types as an unrealistic, knee-jerk political reaction catering to a bunch of socialist bleeding hearts. They were designed to give everyone a fair shot at grabbing the gold ring, from the little guy with enough change for a stock or two, to the corporate giants investing the assets of entire countries. Problem is that nowadays, most everybody uses the same outfits to buy and sell; both the little guys and the giants give their money to say, Merrill Lynch, or Shearson, or Kidder Peabody to invest. So who's getting screwed by the insider-trading laws, these people ask? Everybody, big and small."

"And you're saying Wentworth and/or Clyde followed that line of reasoning?"

"I have my suspicions. But I think they were very subtle about it. Too subtle for me to nail down their exact technique with the little I've seen, and maybe not even then. After all, neither one of them needs to land in the slammer at this point in their lives, nor do they appear to need any more money. The trick was to play the game just enough to get ABC on its feet. After that, it would be Jardine's baby, with the two older guys in the background, giving him perfectly legitimate advice now and then."

The frustration was making my head pound, even with the air-conditioning. "But why, Justin? That's what bugs me. Why the hell take the risk at all? You steal a hundred bucks or you steal a million; it's still stealing, and if you get caught, you still get the book thrown at you. I understand why it all made sense for Charlie Jardine, but Clyde and Wentworth are a total mystery to me. Could Clyde have been ignorant of the whole thing?"

Willette shook his head. "Not a chance. Wentworth might have been. I didn't find any documentation linking him financially to ABC. There were a lot of letters from and to him in the files, but they were all legit. Morris, McGill, after all, drew up the papers that created ABC. As for motivation, I can only take a shot at Clyde; the other two are too murky for me."

I left the window and faced him, still standing. "So what's your shot?"

"Revenge. I think he got back into the game to stick it to 'em. He felt he'd been nailed for some paperwork screwup after a lifetime of minding his p's and q's, and that this was the perfect payback."

I couldn't keep the skepticism from my face, not that it fazed him in the slightest. "Hey, it's just an idea—an educated one, I might add. Old-timers like Clyde have a tough time retiring, and from what I heard from my sources, he was pissed something royal by the treatment he got. Guys like that can be competitive as hell; it's what keeps 'em on top. Revenge is as natural to them as Velveeta is to you."

"Thanks a lot."

"Joe, I know it's not much, certainly nothing you can bring to court, but it's all I could glean. Maybe if you could get another warrant and get a whole team to really give ABC a microscopic look, you might find your smoking gun, but I kind of doubt it. It was too small an operation, run by some canny old farts. They wouldn't have left too much lying around."

"Then why the court order to return the papers to Clyde?"

"Instinct. We like to see ourselves as riverboat gamblers, secretly, of course. It's bad form to let someone see your cards, even if you're about to fold."

I thanked him for all his time, energy, and insight, and left. The image of a circle of card players stuck with me, though. It brought to mind again the notions of calculation and manipulation. The further I progressed into this case, the more I felt the pressure of vested interests at work—of egos bruised, ambitions run amuck, and of minds working overtime toward specific, malevolent ends.

CHAPTER
23

THE phone startled me, shattering the late-night stillness of the empty office. It was Sammie Martens.

"What's up?" I asked.

"Someone I'd like you to talk with, on Elliot Street." Sammie gave the address in an obviously strained voice. "He's a little reluctant to leave home right now."

"Be right there."

The address she'd given belonged to one of the most notorious of our city's flophouses. The entrance was a narrow doorway, wedged into the far-left side of the building. The rest of the first floor was occupied by a series of ever-changing storefront businesses. I climbed the dimly lit wooden staircase, keeping my hands away from the stained and rotting smashed plaster walls, acutely aware that I was ascending into a closed and poisonous atmosphere of urine, sweat, and years' worth of unwashed bodies. The stench, sharpened by the saunalike conditions, made my head swim. It also made me think that Sammie Martens had been crawling these halls, and others like them, for days now, in search of her elusive bridge-dweller. For her sake, if for no one else's, I hoped she'd hit paydirt.

I reached the top floor, walked down the corridor, stepping around a pile of something that looked vaguely organic, and stopped before the open door of number 33.

Sammie Martens, pale, exhausted, but obviously exultant, was standing in the middle of the room. Sitting on what passed for a bed was our odorous friend Milo.

I nodded to them both, although Milo, either depressed or half comatose, was staring at the floor.

"Thanks for coming, Lieutenant. Milo here has something he wants to get off his chest."

There was dead silence in the room, apart from Milo's breathing, which sounded a little like air escaping from a water pipe.

Sammie kicked him in the shin, hard. "Don't you, Milo?"

He grabbed for his leg and slipped off the bed, howling in protest. Normally, I would never have tolerated such a move by a cop, but I also knew Sammie Martens well, and realized that what I was witnessing must have been the culmination of a lot of back-and-forth between these two, in which Sammie had probably been receiving the short shrift. It was an angry outburst I would let pass, but just once.

She was down on her knees in front of him now, her face inches from his. "Come on, you son of a bitch. I've looked like a jerk once because of you, and it's not going to happen again."

Her face was shining with sweat, which matted her hair at the temples and streaked the back of her shirt. Whatever Milo had told her could have been put in a report, or she could have brought him to me, as she had done before. But that would have been under normal circumstances, and right now, I realized, not much was normal about Sammie's behavior. I'd let her overextend herself, hadn't reassured her enough about her earlier mistake with Milo.

I knelt down next to them. "Milo, what've you got?"

"I got a fuckin' broken leg is what I got."

Reluctantly, I reached out and lifted his chin until we were looking straight at one another, from so close I thought my eyes might water. "Concentrate, Milo. Talk to us now and we'll get out of your hair."

His one good eye blinked at me a couple of times. "Toby paid me off to lie to you people."

I looked sharply at Sammie. "Toby? Wasn't that the same

guy who was offered five hundred bucks to identify the bridge bum?''

Her expression was bitter. "The one and only. Talk about coincidences.''

Milo shook his head free of my hand and snorted. ''Coincidence, bullshit.''

"What do you mean?''

"I was the one got offered the five hundred. I told Toby about it, and he came up with the idea to switch places.''

"Why?''

"How do I know? He paid me twenty bucks. If he's stupid enough to pay me to jerk you around, I'm not gonna ask why. I wasn't gonna get no five hundred, 'cause I didn't know who'd been under the bridge.''

"Where'd he get the money?''

"Beats me.''

"Where's Toby live?''

This time, he actually chuckled, or made a noise like it. ''Shit, he lived in a goddamn dumpster once. How the hell am I supposed to know that?''

Sammie shoved his shoulder to get his attention. This time, I grabbed her hand, which she ignored. "You knew his dumpster address, didn't you?''

"If you don't know, then who might?'' I tried.

He stared malevolently at Sammie, as if I weren't even in the room. "Try Mother Gert's.''

Sammie scrambled to her feet and headed for the door. I patted Milo on the shoulder and put a ten-dollar bill into his hand. "Thanks.''

I caught up to Sammie in the hall. "Hold it.''

She turned and faced me. "What?''

I let a moment of silence elapse, during which I just looked at her. She stared back, defiantly at first, and finally she let her gaze go to the floor.

"How much sleep have you had in the last three days?''

She didn't answer at first, as if choosing from a selection of answers, some of which she knew she'd regret upon utterance. Suddenly, her shoulders slumped and she let out a sigh. "Guess I messed up.''

I couldn't resist smiling. "Christ, no—you got him to

talk. Of course, if you'd kicked me that hard I would have talked too. Don't do that again, okay?"

"No," she muttered. "You going to pull me?"

I squeezed her shoulder and steered her down the hall toward the stairs. "No. But I am going to give you a sit-down job for a while; you're working on half a battery."

The air outside was no cooler, but its mere cleanliness was a relief. "Go back to the Municipal Building and get me some help. Toby might be at Gert's, but I'm not counting on it, and if he's not, we better find him fast. If what Milo says is true, maybe Toby did see something, which means his life is hanging by a thread. Make some calls—the Retreat and the hospital and anywhere else you think he might have gone to ground. I'll let you know what I find out at Gert's."

• • •

Mother Gert's, on Western Avenue, was located between the twin municipal clusterings of West Brattleboro and Brattleboro, in a kind of no-man's land, neither suburb nor city. Its geographical identity was linked to the Interstate, which sliced through the map like a meat cleaver.

Gert's was a privately funded halfway house for society's rejects, mostly the homeless and alcoholics. It dated back to the altruistic sixties, and was presently run by a no-nonsense, lapsed Catholic nun named Gertrude Simmons, who lived in a room on the top floor of what had once been an almost statuesque Greek Revival mansion.

I parked at the front of the building, locked my car doors, and went around to the rear entrance, the official entryway. A tough-looking young woman wearing a Hard Rock Café T-shirt and camouflage combat trousers walked down the central hallway into the reception room I'd just entered.

"Hi, Joe."

"Suzanne. How're you?"

"I'm doin'. What'd you want?"

Suzanne didn't like cops, having spent many of her prereform years in and out of our detox cells in the Municipal Building's basement.

"Is Gert around?"

"Maybe. Why?"

"I'll let her tell you."

She scowled at me and jerked her thumb down the hallway. "In her office."

"Thanks." The hall was lined with doors leading to bedrooms, dormitories, and small counseling rooms, all catering to the various needs of the establishment's frequently strung-out clientele. It wasn't fancy; it was run on a shoestring. But if I'd been in need of advice, comfort, or simply a place to spend the night, Mother Gert's would have been my first stop. I obviously wasn't alone in my appreciation—every open door I passed revealed one or more tenants.

I found Gertrude Simmons in the glorified closet they called her office, pounding away at an ancient manual typewriter.

"Hi, Gert."

She got up and gave me a hug, a greeting I'd seen her give most everyone she met, and no less personal for that. "Hi, Joe. Long time. I was sorry to hear of your troubles."

I parked myself on the only other chair in the tiny room, which put me right up against the side of Gert's desk. "It's mostly media fanfare. We'll sort it out."

She looked at me closely. "I hope so. But I sense it's more than fanfare."

Gert was as instantly intimate and comforting as her Attila-at-the-door, Suzanne, was combative. It was, of course, the perfect combination for this kind of place, for if you survived Suzanne's scrutiny and actually gained admission, you became highly appreciative of Gert's motherly attention.

Nevertheless, I didn't yield to the unspoken invitation to spill the contents of my heart. "I gather one of your regular customers is a man named Toby."

The motherliness was replaced by the seldom-seen steel I knew was necessary to run a place like this. "Joe, you know I'm not happy with that kind of inquiry, not without just cause. And the proper paperwork."

This was why I'd decided to come here myself, instead of having Sammie simply call. "Gert, he's not in any trouble from us, but he may be the target of someone who has a lot to lose if Toby gets conversational.''

A crease appeared between her eyes. ''Toby saw something?''

''Maybe. Someone is looking for a bum who may have seen the burial of Charlie Jardine from under the Elm Street Bridge. Toby paid a guy named Milo to feed us some cock-and-bull story about Milo being that bum. It sounds like a run for cover to me. I want to find Toby before the other guy does.''

It was the kind of condensed information for which McDonald or Katz would have killed, but I had no qualms about sharing it with Gert. Not only did I trust her discretion, I also knew that unless I was utterly straight with her, she'd wish me a nice day and escort me to the exit.

''Where does your policeman fit into all this, the one whose wife was having an affair with Jardine?''

''Maybe he did it, maybe he didn't. But we won't know if someone kills Toby first.''

''How do you know his life's in danger?''

I had to admire her determination to gather the facts. It showed how highly she rated privacy, even that of a street bum. ''A man offered Milo five hundred dollars to lead him to the guy who was under that bridge.''

''And this Milo didn't turn in Toby, not for five hundred bucks?'' Her incredulity showed how far she'd come from believing in the milk of human kindness.

''Milo didn't know who'd been under the bridge; nor do we, for that matter. It's just that Toby is being suspiciously slippery. In fact, he told one of my officers that he was the one who'd been offered the five hundred.''

Gert shook her head, a gesture with which I could sympathize. ''Why would he do that?''

''I think he may have switched roles with Milo to cover his tracks as completely as possible. On the other hand, it may be more complicated than that. Maybe he's involved somehow in Jardine's death.''

Gert shook her head. ''I don't believe Toby's involved. His one ambition in life is to be left alone. He doesn't want help, as we call it. He just wants to be free, to do as he wishes. If he did see something, he'd do what he could to deny it. You know, he may not be in as much danger as you think. He may have just left town.''

"How would I find out?''

Satisfied with my motives, Gert stood up and opened the top drawer of a tall filing cabinet that crowded the other side of her desk. She pulled out a folder and began leafing through it. "Like I said, Toby was worse than most about staying put. He wandered around.''

She finally stopped at a single sheet of paper and studied it for a while. "Well, it's a bit of a long shot. He had a girl friend once, named Melanie Durocher, lived up on Spring Street, behind the Fire Department. That was about a year ago, which was the last time I saw him. From what you tell me, I guess they broke up, which doesn't surprise me.''

I shrugged and stood up. "If I come up dry, I'd like to circulate a description of him. You wouldn't have any historic details, would you? Place of birth, parents, military service, anything like that? A photograph?''

She smiled and shook her head. "I'm afraid not. I can give you a description, though—he looks just like Ernest Hemingway as an old man.''

"White beard and fondness for turtlenecks?''

"The spitting image. If you copy Hemingway's photo from *The Old Man and the Sea*, you'll have Toby exactly.''

"What's his real name?''

"That's the only thing I do know. He's quite proud of it, in his quiet way, although I may have been the only one he ever told. It's Tobias A. Huntington.''

* * *

I stood in the middle of Spring Street, looking up at the lit windows above a locked auto-repair shop, wondering where the front door was. As far as I could tell, the building was boxed in on both sides by its neighbors, and was built almost flush against the hill behind it, in true Brattleboro fashion. I'd already checked out the narrow alley back there, as best I could in the gloom, and had found nothing aside from several decades' worth of junk, piled up almost to the second floor.

I was about to resort to hurling pebbles against the window panes, like some latter-day Romeo, when I noticed not only that all the windows were open, but that someone's shadow was moving about inside, which would have made my contemplated gesture appear considerably more hostile.

I fell back to a less subtle, but less damaging approach. "Hello—you in the second-floor apartment. Could you come to the window?"

The shadow paused, grew larger, and finally blocked one of the windows. Spring Street, being at best an aggravated alleyway, squeezed between the hill and the back of the looming Elliot Street Apartments, had no lighting to speak of, so the figure that addressed me remained a one-dimensional black void, for all the solidity of its voice.

"Who the hell are you?"

"I'm a policeman. My name's Gunther."

The shadow didn't respond.

"I was wondering if I could ask you a couple of questions."

"Got a warrant?"

I couldn't make up my mind on the sex of my quarry, since her, or his, voice hovered somewhere between both possibilities, as did the size of the shadow. "I'm just after some information, about someone you might know. Could I come up?"

"No."

That stalled me for a moment, until I realized he or she wasn't moving away from the window. The implication held some hope: I could still hold an interview of sorts, from the street. I glanced around. The street looked deserted.

I gave a mental shrug and cleared my throat. "I'm looking for Toby."

"Don't know him."

Ah, I thought, I hadn't followed the proper protocol. "Mother Gert sent me. Said he used to live here. You Melanie Durocher?"

There was a pause. "Yeah."

"Seen Toby lately?"

"Not since he moved out."

"When was that?"

"Soon as the weather got warmer."

I smiled at that. "Do you know where he might be now?"

"Shit, I don't know. Lived in a dumpster once. Could be anywhere."

The dumpster had obviously made history in certain circles. Unfortunately, Melanie Durocher was right: Toby could be living anywhere, including, as Gert had suggested, out of town.

"Said he once had a room with a view."

"What?" The comment had come after a moment's contemplation, and jarred oddly with my images of dumpsters and bridges. "Where?"

"Don't know. Said it was real small, had a window on each wall, like a lighthouse."

"He didn't identify the building itself?"

"Nope. All he said was that it was hot shit when a storm came in."

"But in Bratt, right?"

"I guess so."

"Do you know how long ago this was?"

"Nope. I gotta go, okay?"

I opened my mouth to answer, but the shadow had already left. I stood there for a few seconds, enveloped by the gloom, hearing the town's nocturnal hum all around me. I half wondered if I'd made the entire conversation up. I scratched my head and walked back to my car, hoping to find out what Sammie had dug up with her calls.

As I drove back toward the Municipal Building, I turned Melanie Durocher's last words around in my mind, trying to match Toby's cryptic description of his "room with a view" to some recognizable piece of architecture in town. Simple logic dictated certain givens: It was high up, for upcoming storms to be impressive; it was small; it had windows on all four walls.

I had stopped at the red light on the corner of High and Main streets, feeling like the one idiot in a game of charades, when I suddenly stuck my head out the car window, and looked straight up at the one place in town that fit Toby's lair like a glove.

I pulled over in front of the Paramount and radioed Dispatch.

"What's up?" Sammie asked, once she'd been brought to the radio.

"You had any luck?"

"Negative. You?"

"Maybe. Can you meet me at the Brooks House Main Street entrance right away?"

"Sure."

I parked my car in a legal spot and got out, eyeing what I was increasingly sure was my goal. The Brooks House, built as an upscale red-brick hotel in 1871, as announced by a large bas-relief plaque on its wall, filled the southwest corner of the intersection like the bow of a masonry ocean liner. Its first floor was entirely made up of retail businesses, and the three floors above were residential, unremarkable in both price and appearance. But at the corner, on top of the illusory prow of the building, was a single, squatty, fifth-floor Victorian tower room.

Sammie Martens parked her car in front of Brown and Roberts Hardware and crossed the street to join me. "What are we looking at?"

"I hope it's a lead." I led the way to the entrance hall, checked out the names over the mailboxes, and pushed the button for the elevator. The manager's apartment was on the third floor.

"You found Toby?"

"No, but I think I may have found one of his hideaways."

We wandered down the dark hallway in search of the proper door. The Brooks was a high cut above where Milo had been festering, but it was still no home for the faint-hearted. As with most American cities, large or small, the downtown dwellings, despite their convenience, didn't cater to a high-class crowd.

I pounded on the door. There was a brief silence, followed by some shuffling footsteps, and the turn of a lock. A young man, thin, narrow-chested, and sallow-faced, wearing a T-shirt, jeans, and a sour expression, pulled open the door.

"What?" It was less an inquiry than a challenge, making me aware not only that it was getting late for house calls, but that managers of low-rent buildings seemed, for the most part, to carry their burdens with remarkably little grace.

"Are you the manager?"

"Who wants to know?"

I pulled out my badge and made the introductions.

It had a remarkable effect. The young man's face turned fuchsia. "Oh, for Christ's sake. What is it with you people? The guy was a guest, all right? As far as I know, it is not against the law to have a guest in your house. He's just a poor son of a bitch who wants to be left alone. Like I do."

Sammie and I looked at one another and then back at the manager. I spoke first. "I think we're missing something here. We just dropped by because we're looking for someone."

"Who?" The voice was no less hostile.

"His name's Toby."

Again he exploded. "Who the hell you think I been talking about? What did he do, anyway, rob a bank? I know nothing about it, all right? So get off my back."

He began to close the door. I stuck my foot out and stopped it.

"Watch it, man. I don't have to talk to you."

I held up both my hands in surrender. "That's true. But we're investigating a murder and we would appreciate any help you could give us."

He looked at me in astonishment. "You're shitting me. Toby was tied in to those murders?"

I remembered the name from the mailboxes downstairs. "Look, let's back up a bit. Are you Mr. Weller?"

"Yeah."

"We're looking for Toby because we think he may be in danger. All we want to do is talk to him. We have no hassles with you at all; in fact, we'd appreciate your help."

I left it at that. He looked at both of us, finally shrugged and let the door swing back. "All right; come on in."

It was a small apartment, in which he apparently lived alone, accompanied by the bedlam and odor of smelly socks and stale food that most young bachelors seem to find inescapable. The one detail of interest to me, however, was the sight of a narrow, metal circular staircase leading up.

Weller headed off into a living room, swept some clothes off the bedraggled couch, killed the television, and sat in a straight-back chair. Sammie and I both remained standing.

"So what do you want to know?" Weller said, looking up at us uncomfortably.

"When did you last see Toby?"

"A couple of months ago. But I heard him yesterday."

I could hardly believe our luck. "Why the distinction?"

"He lives upstairs, in the tower. He comes and goes through the back window, over the roof—uses the fire escape."

"He's living here now?"

"He was. I went up there this morning and found he'd cleared out. He does that, though; comes and goes. Usually he stays longer."

"How long had he been here this time?"

"I'm not really sure, but it couldn't have been more'n a couple of days."

"How do you know him?" Sammie suddenly asked.

Weller actually smiled. "I'm a writer, or I'd like to be. I started putting this idea together, a biography of the home-less. I'd interview as many of them as I could, get them to tell me their stories—a Studs Terkel kind of thing. I met Toby way early on. He was a real tough nut to crack, but he interested me, you know? I was finding out that a lot of the people I was talking to really didn't have anything to say, or they couldn't say it 'cause they were too tanked, or screwed up, or whatever. But Toby wasn't your average drunk bum; he doesn't drink, as far as I know, is pretty well educated, and is tidy, given the people he hangs out with."

"Could we see where he lived?" I interrupted.

"Huh? Oh, sure." Weller walked over to the circular staircase, at last the affable host. "Watch your step on this thing. I don't think it was designed for adults."

We followed him up gingerly, arriving at a room fitted with only a table, a chair, and a bookcase.

"That's where I do my writing." Weller didn't break stride but continued up the stairs.

"Here we are," he announced at the top, with a one-handed flourish, purposely leaving the lights off.

The room matched his own recent change of attitude. Its dim interior wasn't much: low, stained ceiling; walls seriously in need of paint; and a floor covered with trash and a bare mattress. But the impression it made was magical. More than a room with a view, as Toby had described it, it gave the impression of being a crow's nest above Brattleboro. Each window dominated the wall it inhabited, exhibiting at this time of night a sparkling urban vista of lamp-lit streets, buildings, and roofs. I felt utterly on top of the town.

Weller understood our silence. "Pretty neat, huh? I tried putting my office up here at first, but I couldn't take my eyes off the view. Had to give it up."

"How did Toby come to live here?" I asked.

"It was kind of an exchange. At first, he wouldn't talk to me—real reserved, almost hostile. He was that way with everybody. But then, I don't remember how, the tower room came up, and he saw it might be to his advantage to have a cubbyhole available when he needed it. I promised to leave him alone, let him come and go as he pleased. As payment, he agreed to talk to me, and introduce me to a few people. It was a pretty fair exchange; I learned a lot."

I located the light switch near the stairs and turned it on, flooding the room with a garish brightness that both diminished the view and revealed the starkness around us. There wasn't much to look at. Other than the mattress, there was no furniture, and the floor was littered with food wrappers, old newspapers, and a couple of rags. I stepped carefully over to a tin ashtray that was parked under one of the windows.

Squatting down, I pulled a pen from my pocket and flicked a balled-up candy wrapper out of the ashtray. Underneath, instead of cigarette butts, there were several enormous wads of chewing gum. "Likes his gum, huh?"

Weller laughed. "Oh, yeah. Chewed that stuff like other people chew tobacco. Used to put three sticks in his mouth at once. Made him look like a cow."

I looked back at the wads of gum, perfect matches for the ones Klesczewski had found under the Elm Street Bridge.

Weller shook his head, his face growing serious. "Is he really in trouble?"

"I think so. If you see him, you better tell him to get hold of us. I'm afraid someone else is looking for him." I straightened up. "We'll want to put some coverage on this place, just in case he does come back. Is that a problem with you?"

"No, not at all. What's this other person look like, the one looking for Toby?"

His tone of voice sent a chill down my back. "We don't know. Why?"

"That's why I bit your head off earlier; you're the second guy today asking about him."

I felt Sammie become very still next to me. "Who was it?"

"I don't remember his name. He pounded on the door late this afternoon, saying he was the building inspector or something; said he'd heard I was running a hotel for bums up here, letting them run up and down the fire escapes and over the roofs. He was real obnoxious about it. I denied it, of course, which didn't make things any better. Real asshole. I thought he'd sent you guys."

I turned the light back off and found myself staring down Main Street, five flights below, thinking about a question Brandt had asked me on Milly Crawford's roof the day he was killed.

"His name wasn't Fred McDermott, was it?"

"Yeah, that's it."

"What did McDermott tell you?" Brandt had asked. "DeFlorio mentioned he was here when the shooting started."

I'd forgotten all about McDermott. A cold ball began to form in my stomach. It had been an unforgivable oversight.

Sammie caught my change of mood. She touched my elbow. "Are you okay?"

I stared at the street in silence, wondering where Toby had gone. "No, I don't think I am."

CHAPTER 24

IT was almost midnight. I hit the "off" button on the small dictaphone I'd been using to record my daily report. I popped out the microcassette and chucked it into the wooden *out* tray. Harriet Fritter would retrieve it in the morning and have it transcribed and circulated within an hour. A frighteningly efficient woman, I thought. A hell of a lot more efficient than I was.

I sat back in my office chair, the dictaphone still in my hands, and stared at the fan, shaking its head sadly on the corner of my desk, as if in sympathy with my own self-assessment.

The odd thing was that Fred's name surfacing in the context of Milly's murder was not as earth-shattering to me as the fact that I'd initially overlooked it. The priority of both revelations had been switched by my wounded ego.

I am not by nature a vain or self-glorifying man. I've met too many people whose minds are far superior to mine to have an overly inflated view of myself. But I have my pride. I have taken the time on occasion to glance back and consider my progress through life, if only to ascertain that my own standards, however modest, were not being reduced through laziness or self-contentment.

In general, that kind of cursory introspection has yielded acceptable results. I've made retrievable errors now and then, stepped on people's toes unnecessarily once in a while, but overall, I could live with that. If nothing else, I could at least look at myself and see a certain predictable steadiness.

But not this time.

We all overlook things, sometimes important things. I knew that, and indeed I'd done it before. Gail would have claimed that I'd done it quite recently by not warning her of an approaching political hurricane. Still, whatever pain and confusion those occasions caused were nothing to what I was feeling now.

Fred McDermott was the kind of man you assumed had a niche in appointed town government. Short, round, with pale, thinning hair and a fondness for TV bowling tournaments, he had the slightly portly, bland-faced quality of the unimaginative bureaucrat, enforcing the rules as they were passed onto him, without challenge or critical judgment. He agreed with those in power, less because he believed power and wisdom were synonymous, and more because power hired and fired. It was an attitude designed to keep his pension-focused mind riveted to his assigned task.

That I had dismissed this man in the context of a case as easily as I had in day-to-day life was bad enough; that by so doing I might have endangered the life of Tobias A. Huntington bordered on criminal stupidity.

I didn't delude myself into thinking that just because McDermott had surfaced twice in the context of an investigation, it automatically made him a killer. But overlooking him caused me to wonder how much else I had missed.

It was this unhealthy combination of self-doubt, guilt, and embarrassment that had consumed me since leaving the Brooks House tower room. I had dropped by McDermott's house, a pleasant, middle-class split-level ranch on Wantastiquet Drive, near the Connecticut River, but had learned from neighbors that he and his wife were out to dinner. That had probably been for the best; to interview him now, when I was emotionally off balance, would have been to compound my error. I needed to think, to take the time necessary to see how McDermott might fit in as a major player. I knew I had time; his office was directly over mine, and he would be appearing, as usual, bright and early, with a briefcase and paper in one hand, and a lunch box in the other.

From one body, a few footprints, and a cigarette butt, I had amassed a fortune in possibilities, plus an additional corpse.

And, to make sense of it all, I had four detectives and a few borrowed patrolmen whose cumulative experience could have been matched by one New York cop with a month on the job.

Still, I was convinced there had to be some logical pattern. McDermott's appearance had startled me; he'd been in the right place at the right time. He worked in the Municipal Building and often came downstairs to share the Police Department's coffee and to shoot the breeze, and thereby pick up information. But for now he was also, like all the others, merely a loose strand.

The phone rang. I picked it up and answered.

"Joe? Are you okay?"

It was Gail, the wrong person at the wrong time. Instead of finding comfort in the gentle tone of her voice, now I found she merely reminded me of another area where I'd recently dropped the ball.

"You sound depressed."

"Just a little behind on my sleep."

"How's it going?"

"Slowly." I tried willing myself to be more conversational, to lighten my tone, but I didn't have it in me.

"I tried calling you at home, but when I got no answer, I thought I might find you there. Would you like to come over after you're through?"

I hesitated before answering. "I'm not sure how long I'll be, plus I have to talk to someone at the crack of dawn."

"You've got to sleep sometime."

"I know." A long silence stretched between us. "I'm sorry I caused you trouble with Jackson."

"To hell with him. He just surprised me, that's all. I'm not sure it would have been any easier even if you had warned me."

I was glad to hear that, but I still remembered the sting of her accusations. I was both surprised and disappointed to find my self-doubt being replaced by resentment; it revealed to me that I, like many of my colleagues, had slipped into a siege mentality.

"Gail, I'll take a rain check on tonight. I'm too bushed and too swamped. But thanks for the offer. Maybe once this mess is over, we can make up for lost time; go away for a weekend or something." They were all mechanical phrases, and sounded tinny even to me.

Her voice echoed with disappointment. "Sure. Well, I just wanted to say hello . . . Don't stay up too late."

I thought she was going to add something, but after a long pause, which I only later realized I should have filled, the line went dead. I swore to myself and hung up. I couldn't have devised a better way to further damage my pride.

I heard the bang of the hallway door being kicked open. I leaned forward over my desk to look through my interior window and saw Buddy wrestling his armload of janitorial paraphernalia into the squad room. He glanced up at my movement and wiggled a couple of free fingers at me in greeting. Through my half-open office door, I heard his muffled, "Hey, Lieutenant."

I returned the wave and sat back down, uncertain of how I felt about the interruption. He was sensitive enough that if I merely picked up a folder and pretended to be reading, he'd let me be. But I wasn't sure I wanted that.

When he did gently tap at the door to retrieve the wastepaper basket, I made a point of not appearing overly occupied.

He smiled shyly and nodded toward the fan. "Still doing the trick for you?"

"Yeah. Thanks again."

"No problem. It was a pleasure."

He pulled a plastic garbage bag from his pocket and snapped it open, preparing it to receive my refuse. He paused, and then said tentatively, "You folks sound like you're in pretty hot water."

I shrugged. "Sounds worse than it is. That's what sells newspapers."

"So you're doing all right?" he asked, as he reached for my wastebasket.

"Not too bad," I answered, thinking of McDermott.

He beamed. "That's good. I was talking to a friend of mine, and he kept saying you didn't know what you were doing. I said you did, but you couldn't say so 'cause of security reasons."

"You got it, Buddy."

There was an awkward pause. I picked up a folder and opened it. Buddy quickly replaced my empty trash basket. "Well, I got to get back to work, Lieutenant. I'll close the door on my way out so the vacuum don't bother you."

"Thanks, Buddy."

"No problem." He smiled awkwardly. "Stay cool."

I returned the smile as the door shut and he passed in front of the glass panel. Stay cool. That's what my nemesis was doing: taking care of business until I could find a way to stop him.

CHAPTER
25

I was waiting outside Fred McDermott's door when he walked in at seven forty-five.

He looked surprised to see me, perhaps even startled. "Hi, Joe, long time. How's the investigation going?" He fumbled to extract his keys from his pocket, dropped them, and let out a nervous laugh as he bent over to retrieve them. "Oh, oh. Sign of a bad day coming."

I followed him inside. "That's what I wanted to talk to you about."

The dimensions of his office were almost precisely the same as mine, but he still had the older, taller ceiling, and no window to the reception area. The mad renovator had yet to cast his hellish spell on McDermott's corner of the building. Indeed, he even had an air conditioner, which he switched on before putting his briefcase on the desk. The initial blast of warm air smelled dusty and oddly electrical.

He motioned me to sit, as he did so himself. He looked quite pleased at my comment. "Bringing me in as an expert witness?"

"No. I'm interested in what you were doing on Horton Place the day Milly Crawford was killed." I'd picked my words carefully, fully intending their implied suspicion.

His face went through a fast series of expressions, from very still to bemused, to mournful. "Yeah, can you believe that? Talk about bad timing. You guys scared the hell out of me."

"What were you doing there?"

He blinked at me several times in silence, as if slowly getting the gist of my question. "I went there to meet someone . . ."

"Who?"

"Well, I don't know exactly. I got a phone call from some guy, telling me he was working on that new motel going up near the *Reformer* building, and that there were a bunch of violations he thought I should know about."

"He told you to meet in Milly's building?"

"In the alleyway out back."

"When did you get the call?"

"Just before. He sounded real nervous, said he'd been sitting on this a long time, trying to get up the nerve to tell someone. I drove right over and got there just as everything went crazy."

"If the guy was on the motel job, why wasn't he working then? It was the middle of the day."

McDermott's mouth was now half open. "I get calls like that all the time, piss-ant stuff, like when some tenant gets mad at a landlord."

"You get a similar call to go to the Brooks House yesterday?"

The mouth fell all the way. "Have you been following me?"

"Let's say we've been bumping into you. What did the guy sound like who called you out to Milly's neighborhood?"

He gave a small shrug. "I don't know. Intense—talking about how people were going to die if the motel went up the way it was being built."

"Didn't any of that strike you as unusual?"

"Well, sure, but if what he was saying was true . . . I mean, I wasn't going to tell him to call my secretary for an appointment."

"Did you hear or see anyone or anything unusual?"

He loosened his tie. "No. No one showed up."

"Anyone enter the building?"

"A couple of kids left just before all hell broke loose, but that was it. I never heard any shots or anything."

"You never heard from the guy who'd called you?"

McDermott shook his head. "I went out to the motel site; checked it over with a fine-tooth comb. Place was as clean as a whistle; it's being built closer to code than my own house."

"Who called you about Brooks House?"

He held up his hand at my renewed, colder tone of voice. "Joe, do you think I'm up to something? 'Cause if you do, maybe I shouldn't be talking to you."

Good move, I thought, too much naiveté could be as bad as too little. "Do you feel the urge to call your lawyer?"

He loosened his already tortured tie some more. "The urge? I want to know if there's a need. What the hell is going on?"

His voice had finally gained an edge. "We have a lot of people out there right now, looking under every rock they can find. If a name pops up, we check it out. Yours popped up twice, once at Milly's place, and again when we were speaking with the manager of the Brooks House. What brought you out to Brooks House, Fred?"

"Again, I got a call, from somebody telling me—"

"Same guy as before?"

"Huh? No, this one had an accent."

"But it was a man?"

"Yeah."

"Could the accent've been faked?"

He paused, his brow furrowed. "Well, I . . . maybe. I don't know; I hadn't thought about it. I mean, I hadn't put the two voices together before."

"What did the guy tell you?"

"He said Weller was renting out his tower room to a bunch of bums, that they were using the fire escape as a front door, and that, quote-unquote, 'weird shit' was going on in the apartment that the town ought to know about."

"This caller didn't leave a name or number?"

"No, but when I went over there, I had a feeling there might be something to it. The fire escape has obviously been used, and a few of the other tenants admitted hearing people going over the roof. And Weller was very belligerent. Still, I can't do anything until I catch them at it, which isn't likely. I don't have the staff."

"You didn't see any of them?"

"No. Of course, Weller wouldn't let me into his apartment. He might have had an army of bums in there, for all I know. I looked around from the outside, you know, checking out the fire escape, but I didn't see anything that caught my eye."

I let a few seconds of silence pass by. Now was the time for him to flaunt his innocence again, to bring up lawyers and the appearance that he felt he'd been falsely accused.

He remained quiet.

I got up and moved toward the door.

"Joe," he blurted out, like an actor missing his cue.

I paused at the threshold.

He gave me an awkward smile. "I'm not in any trouble, am I? You're not thinking I had anything to do with people dying?"

I hesitated. Nothing he'd told me had diminished him as a suspect, which meant he was either as pure as fresh snow or very clever. "I don't know what to think, Fred. Sure as hell somebody killed those people."

•   •   •

I had left a note with Harriet to schedule a staff meeting at eight, after I'd finished with McDermott. I therefore entered a detective bureau that was fully manned and waiting. Everyone followed me into the meeting room.

I waited for them to sit. "We found Charlie Jardine in the ground four long days ago. That's not good for our side. Assuming John Woll's innocent, then the scent that might lead us to Jardine's killer is getting colder and colder. That means we're going to have to depend on each other like never before. This is the first time the entire squad has had to work on a single case. We all have different styles, different paces, and I know that can cause problems."

No one debated the point. "If you start running into each other, I want to hear about it. Maybe we can arrange it so the friction is reduced. But keep in mind, there aren't enough of us to go around, so there'll be some head butting."

There were some barely discernable nods around the table.

"Okay, in case anyone is keeping score, we now have three lawsuits filed against us and a fourth pending. Mark Cappelli and the motorist who almost got swiped by one of our guys have been joined by the bridge-repair people, and Arthur Clyde is still scratching his head on whether to join the crowd or not."

I paused to let the bad news settle in. "The point to all this is: forget it. Let everyone else focus on the fireworks. The more we stick to our job, the more likely it is we'll come out ahead. Let's go over what we have so far."

I filled them in on what Willette had dug up on Jardine and ABC Investments, underscoring what I'd put in my daily report.

Klesczewski cleared his throat. "It sounds like hard evidence might be a little difficult to come by on that."

"Maybe. We may not need it if we can get other people to corroborate Willette's suspicions. Ron, you were looking into the names on Milly's list, what've you got so far? Do the two Putney Road bankers have a connection with ABC?"

Ron looked a little uneasy. "Well, I don't know. The ABC angle didn't surface until your talk with Willette last night, which occurred after my check on them. All I found out was pretty routine: what they did, how long they'd worked there, did they have any criminal history... I did find out that Kenny Thomas was reputed to be fond of an occasional toot of cocaine."

"Reliable source?"

"I think so."

"But you didn't interview Thomas or Atwater?"

"No, they weren't there. I plan to do that today."

"What about Jake Hanson? You told me he owned two warehouses on Birge Street. How does he check out?"

Klesczewski looked at his notes. "He does have a record. Got nabbed a couple of times hauling goods across the Canadian border illegally. Fish and Game got him once for slipping out-of-season venison into the legitimate market. He was buying from a bunch of poachers, most of them up north, and then selling the meat in Boston and New York, where it was trendy and no questions were asked. He copped a plea and turned in most of the hunters to avoid doing time.''

"Friendly fella," DeFlorio muttered.

"Any narcotics?" I asked.

"No. The list goes on, but it's mostly along the same lines; nothing violent, nothing hard-core."

"Did you check out the warehouses?"

"Yes. Seemed on the up-and-up. He's got them divided into sections. Some he rents to businesses, like a mail-order outfit, others he just rents the space for storage. There's a tree surgery business that parks its trucks in one part. I interviewed several of the tenants. Most of them had never met the man, and those who had reported that Hanson was your typical old chummy type, full of bad jokes and easy talk."

"What about Mark Cappelli?"

Ron pulled another sheet of paper from the folder before him. "Got an armed robbery conviction; several assaults; he's done time. It's a grab bag, but it's all violent, and he seems to keep it up to date."

I leaned back in my chair and locked my fingers behind my neck. "So what do we make of Milly's list so far?"

Tyler addressed Ron. "No connections between any of them?"

"Nope—except for Thomas and Paula Atwater, the bankers. They work in the same building. Of course, this is all preliminary. If we dig deeper, we may find something."

Sammie tapped the table top with her pencil. "A guy with a warehouse, an ex-con who drives trucks, two more who handle money, one of which does cocaine. It's got potential, you have to admit."

I smiled at that—Sammie had made the same connections I had, especially concerning Thomas's drug habit. "I agree. I want you and Ron to look for the connection. And keep the ABC angle in your sights, too. It might be pure coincidence that ABC landed the Putney Road Bank's pension fund, but it also might be that the bank is the link between Jardine, Wentworth, and Clyde on one side, and Milly and his list of folks on the other."

I looked at Dennis. "What's happening with your efforts?

Both the Jardine and the Crawford canvasses have been dumped in your lap. Anything new?''

Dennis cleared his throat. ''Well, technically, it's no longer our jurisdiction, but I did find someone who claims to have seen John Woll at the embankment the night Jardine was killed. A woman who lives in the Elliot Street Apartments, complete with a pair of binoculars. She says a bright flame first caught her attention. That's good news, of course, but she also says she thought the policeman was acting 'very suspicious,' to use her words, and that he was lighting the flare, not putting it out.''

''But it was a policeman?'' I asked.

DeFlorio gave me a lopsided frown. ''I have my doubts. That's what she claims. She may have seen something, but I think the policeman thing came to her after the press reports. There were a few other details that sounded fuzzy, too. Anyhow, it's out of our hands now.''

''Anything else?''

''Nothing much. Jardine was seen going to work the morning of the day he was killed, but that just corroborates what Clyde told us. He wasn't seen coming home, although he must've to change clothes and turn on the air-conditioning. I couldn't find any restaurant that served him dinner, or any store owners that saw him. I did find his car, by the way, in the lot by his office, covered with parking violations.''

''I took a look,'' Tyler interrupted. ''Nothing.''

DeFlorio resumed. ''As far as I can tell, the guy vanished as soon as he left work.''

''Assuming he did leave work, at least under his own power,'' Sammie interjected.

I turned to Pierre Lavoie, the temporary member of our group. ''Pierre, what about the background searches into Jardine and the Wolls?''

Lavoie glanced around uncomfortably. Not only was he low man on the totem pole, but the recent fireworks in the room had made him a little gun-shy. ''I've found several people who knew all three of them. I didn't find much new—the Wolls were an item, but Rose had eyes for Jardine, as well. It turns out that wasn't too unusual for her . . . I mean, Jardine wasn't the only one.''

"You haven't found anything about Jardine that might tie into his death?"

"He did a lot of drugs. I was hoping I could track the drugs to a supplier, but so far, it's been no luck."

I turned to J.P. and raised my eyebrows.

He started right in. "One of the reasons I checked Jardine's car was I had found some dirt on his shoes that didn't correspond to the grave site. Turns out it's got a lot of fuel oil in it, along with some old brick dust; totally incompatible with any dirt in or around his house. None of it was ingrained, and beneath it was soil that did fit the soil outside the house."

"Which tells you what?"

"That he picked it up at the time of his death, in an area where number-two crude oil is handled, like around a furnace in a dirt-floor basement somewhere."

"But not his own basement?"

Tyler shook his head. "No. That's paved and clean as a whistle. I think it was an older building, possibly one with an old brick foundation where the brick is beginning to erode. I also think either the feeder pipe from the oil storage tank to the furnace is leaking, or maybe the tank itself, because a healthy system doesn't have that much oil around it. The delivery pipe is almost always outside the building, not only because it's convenient, but also so no oil can spill inside. One other thing," he added, "the high concentration of oil also made me think the building's owner is probably broke or sloppy, or maybe that the building is badly maintained. Otherwise, a serviceman would have been called in to stop the leak. Of course, that last point is pure guesswork."

"You mentioned searching the car," I reminded him.

"Right. No oil-tainted dirt, which would have been there if he'd driven at all. Proof again that he got that dirt sometime between when he left his car and when we found him. That means he either drove home, changed, and drove back downtown to meet someone, leaving his car in the lot, or he hitched a ride home with someone straight from work."

"That's it?"

He shrugged. "That's it for the car. I compared the gum

you found last night in the Brooks House to the stuff we found under the bridge—it's a match. Otherwise, we don't have much to show."

Kleszewski spoke in a cautious voice. "It's possible the murderer forced Jardine to drive back to the lot after grabbing him at home, to confuse us."

I conceded the point. "Maybe we ought to expand the canvass to include the parking lot for that night. You up to questioning a whole new batch of people, Dennis?"

DeFlorio shook his head and grinned. "I've done half the town already. Why not?"

"I spoke to Billy Manierre last night," I resumed. "Every one of his people are on the lookout for Toby Huntington, as are the State Police and Sheriff's Department, so I hope we'll get lucky there. What about Jardine's phone records?"

Ron pawed through his notes until he located the right paperwork. "The phone company was very helpful. I talked to some of the most frequently called numbers, male and female friends of his. It's a little awkward, of course: no eye-to-eye contact, no way to check their stories without help from other departments. I didn't get anywhere on the drug angle, but I did get a feeling that he played both side of the fence sexually."

"He was queer?" DeFlorio burst out.

"I think so." Ron emphasized the *think*. "No one flat out said as much, but that's the impression I got."

"I'll be damned," Sammie muttered.

"Yeah, it does open up more possibilities," I said. "—blackmail being the first of them. What about Jardine's bank files?"

Sammie raised her pencil. "I looked them over."

"Anything unusual?" I asked her.

"Nothing obvious. I tracked down the parents' will, to see if he really did inherit eighty-five thousand dollars; it looked legit to me. Also, I bugged Willette a bit while he was going through the ABC material to see if Jardine's investment claims matched the income he was reporting. Again, he came out looking clean. If he was collecting blackmail money, he was subtle about where he put it."

I nodded at Ron. "Any other leads on the homosexual angle?"

He shook his head. "The phone records were all long distance. If Jardine made local calls, we don't know about them. The two people who implied Jardine was gay were old high-school connections—but they wouldn't stick their necks out far enough to actually name names."

"The obvious choices are Wentworth or Clyde," DeFlorio said. "The two guys with big bucks."

"Assuming Jardine was blackmailing anyone," I added. "I plan to see Wentworth today. He was supposed to have returned last night from a trip out of town."

"What did you learn from McDermott?" Sammie asked.

I glanced at DeFlorio, who along with me had forgotten McDermott's appearance at Horton Place. He was intensely studying the bottom of his Styrofoam coffee cup. "On the face of it, not much. It sounds like he was at both Milly's and the Brooks House through sheer coincidence, or because he was set up. But he could also be lying. J.P., go after him, okay? Check out his background, likes and dislikes, finances, and anything else you can."

Tyler nodded.

I stood up. "Okay then. I guess we're all set. Anyone feeling underworked?"

There was a general groan around the table.

"There is one more thing," I added, "and normally this would go without saying, but I think we have to be especially discreet from now on. There've been too many leaks from this department already. Things are tough enough without shooting ourselves in the foot."

The implication that the source of some of those leaks might be sitting in this room left a sour note in the air, one I hoped they would all take to heart. I wanted not only to put an end to the idle chatter, but to plant a reminder that the heat we were beginning to feel the most had nothing to do with the lack of air-conditioning, or with the complexity of the case we were trying to solve.

CHAPTER
26

THE Hillwinds development on Upper Dummerston Road, also known as Country Club Road, was an unsentimental farmer's dream come true. For all those exhausted tillers of the soil, rich in land and poor in cash, bruised by climbing taxes and falling milk prices, the erstwhile Hillwinds Farm was an inspiration. Located on a high ridge overlooking the West River Valley between Brattleboro and the county seat of Newfane, twelve miles away, this prime acreage had been gracefully converted into one of the highest-priced exclusive pieces of real estate in the area.

The houses placed along the winding ribbon of road that ran the length of the ridgeline were, for the most part, rural architectural showpieces, natural wood and glass confections, most often seen and envied in the pages of *Fine Homebuilding* and at the back of the *New York Times Magazine*.

It was not a place to find a surfeit of resident native Vermonters.

It had, on the other hand, managed to avoid looking too much like a wealthy suburb, despite an unnatural absence of free-growing trees and a preponderance of overly manicured lawns. The saving grace was in the setting, for no matter how Aspen-like the buildings or Greenwich-like the grounds, the politely distant trees, the sense of the river far below, and indeed the entire valley, was pure, unadulterated Vermont.

I turned off Upper Dummerston Road and drove up the steep, clean macadam of the main entrance road, emerging from a shielding line of trees onto the ridge. At the stop sign, I had a choice of going left, back into the trees and the older, more modest section of the development, or right, where the overpriced prima donnas had been placed for all to see. Following Jack Plummer's directions, I turned right.

I wasn't sure whether Wentworth would be back yet, but I figured I would take my chances in the hopes of catching him by surprise.

Crawling north at ten miles per hour, craning my neck like some visiting rube, I found the hilltop broadening and dipping slightly, until I came to a gentle crest, below which the ridge concluded in a soft, rounded promontory. On either side of me were two stone pillars guarding the road, one of which carried the warning, Dead End—Private Road. Ahead, crowning the promontory and commanding a vista of the entire valley, was a clustering of outbuildings arranged admiringly around a central main house of truly regal proportions. Two days earlier, Jack had described the view from Wentworth's house as a jawbreaker. It had not been an overstatement. Whatever else Tucker Wentworth might have been, he was obviously not one to either ignore his creature comforts or to hide his means of begetting them. Seeing this estate from above, and identifying what had to be Blaire Wentworth's two-thousand-square-foot "cottage" off to one side, helped me to better understand some of the guarded, patrician undercurrents that I'd noticed in my conversation with her the day before.

I rolled down the driveway and parked in the traffic circle before the main house. It was Greek Revival in mimicry, with white clapboards, corner pediments, and a porticoed entrance, but it yielded to modern tastes with its skylights, huge windows, and a gigantic down-slope deck off the back—all highlighting a style meriting its own architectural label: Ostentatious.

My knock on the door, however, was not answered by the expected female domestic in a broad-striped aproned uniform, but rather by a tall, thin man, dressed in worn gray slacks and an open-necked, button-down shirt with frayed cuffs and collar. His eyes were bloodshot and he needed a shave.

"Yes?"

"Mr. Wentworth?"

"Yes."

"My name is Joe Gunther; I work for the Brattleboro Police Department."

His face was unchanging. "I was wondering when you'd come around."

"I'd like to talk to you, if I may."

We stood there, eyeing one another for several seconds, a cool, air-conditioned breeze sweeping past him and pleasantly drying the warm sheen on my forehead.

He moved aside. "All right."

I followed him inside, through a grandiose lobby, across an immaculate, almost sterile living room with a breathless view of the West River Valley, and into a book-lined, mahogany-paneled office with overstuffed leather furniture and antique lamps. He settled, indeed almost collapsed, into an armchair placed beside a pair of French doors, and fixed his gaze on the scenery outside, ignoring me completely.

I looked around for a moment, analyzing the contrasts I'd witnessed so far. The house, as much as I'd seen of it, had been store-bought from very exclusive sources. The drapes in the living room matched the fabric of the furnishings, the wall-to-wall carpeting was ankle-deep and softly off-white, tastefully highlighted with carefully placed, small Oriental rugs. The paintings on the walls were ersatz, expensive Impressionist, the light fixtures ran to either fake-antique brass or modernist cutting-edge. It was as if someone had taken ten of the most expensive catalogs available and had organized the contents of this house from their pages. Looking at this disheveled old man, with his eyes fixed on the distant hills, and remembering his cool and elegant daughter, I had no doubts as to the designer.

I sat in the armchair opposite him, enjoying the tangy odor of the leather that enveloped me as I leaned back. It was a chair of almost womblike comfort. "I gather you've been away for a few days."

He didn't answer at first, but just sat there, staring. Finally, he turned his head and looked at me. I was struck by the pallor of his blue eyes, which made them look almost blank, and also by the fatigue etched into his heavily lined face.

"You left the morning Charlie Jardine's body was found. Is his death the reason why?"

He lifted one long, thin, patrician hand, and rubbed the side of his nose with his index finger. "Yes," he said, after a pause.

"Where did you go?"

A small crease appeared between his eyes. "What?"

I knew he'd heard me. The house was quiet as a tomb. I decided to take his lead and remain silent, forcing him to pick up the conversation.

He merely sighed gently and went back to gazing out the window. It occurred to me then that we were not playing power games, nor was he recovering from a hangover or a bad night's sleep. What I was witnessing was a man with little regard for his surroundings, no interest in idle chat, and, perhaps, no hope for the future; a man in deep mourning.

"Charlie meant a lot to you, didn't he?"

This time, he just barely nodded.

"Can you think why someone would murder him?"

He still didn't look at me, but at least I got a full sentence out of him. "No. That's what I keep asking myself; I don't understand."

"What did you know about him?"

"Know about him?" He hesitated, scratching his forehead, as if realizing for the first time who and what I was. "You mean his past?"

"Sure. That's a start."

"He was from around here; went to school here; was orphaned here. He was an only child, like Blaire . . . I don't know; I guess he'd been unruly as a teenager, a little aimless, trying to find his way. He was very bright . . . quick to learn; eager."

"Was he ever involved in drugs?"

Wentworth's expression blackened with both pain and anger. "Oh, my God. Is that what you think? He had long hair once, so that makes him a drug user? I am not unaware of the pressures being brought against your department; that one of your own policemen might be involved in Charlie's death. Wouldn't it be convenient to drag in a drug connection and write the whole thing off as just another turf battle?"

I kept my voice calm and assured. "Mr. Wentworth, there is something you may not know, since we withheld it from the press. Charlie Jardine was first rendered helpless, tied to a chair, and then slowly strangled to death over a period of some minutes. That technically categorized his murder as torture/execution. It was not a crime of passion."

Wentworth persisted in trying to depersonalize his friend's violent death. "There are lunatics everywhere. Look at Ted Bundy, or that poor woman who was assaulted in Central Park."

I leaned forward in my chair to make my point. "Your friend was not the victim of a spontaneous crime. He was killed because of who he was and what he'd done. He was a specific target. If we could find out more about him, we might also find out why he was killed, and by who."

Wentworth was breathing fast, his mouth partly open, making him look even older than his age, which I guessed was somewhere in his late sixties. "I never knew him to have anything to do with drugs," he finally answered, calming down and faking a strong voice. "On the few occasions the subject came up, he had only scorn for both users and dealers."

"When did the subject come up?"

He waved his hand impatiently. "On the news; it was nothing personal."

"What do you know about his private life?"

Again, there was a slight scowl of irritation, although I sensed it was less directed at me, and more at his own ignorance being exposed. "I knew enough, Mr. Gunther. Charlie was not a very complicated man. He was neither old enough nor well traveled enough to have become overly complex. He was still driven by his ambition and his desire to learn. If someone did target him, as you say, it was not because of some deep, dark secret in his past. It would seem to me your best suspect is the policeman the papers wrote about; isn't jealousy the standard stimulus for violence?"

I ignored the question. "Did he have a lot of girl friends?"

Wentworth was becoming increasingly restive, or maybe embarrassed. "I wouldn't know. He was an attractive, engaging individual, fully capable of appealing to any woman."

Or man, I thought, but kept my mouth shut. "You were a great help to Charlie."

He was quiet for a moment, and then smiled slightly. "I don't know how helpful I was. I just happened to be in the right place at the right time. Charlie's time had come. Indeed, he sought me out, full of questions. I never would have noticed him otherwise."

"But there was more to it than just helping a guy on the fast track; you took a liking to each other, didn't you? Wasn't it your friendship that fueled your sponsorship, rather than the other way around?"

He chuckled, his face lighting up for an instant, before the wear lines, the pain, and the loss redescended. "You're right, of course. Had it not been for his personality, I wouldn't have much cared about his ambitions. It didn't hurt, though, that he was so keen, and that he focused so much attention on me."

"And he was a quick learner."

"Extremely. He had an amazingly analytical mind, which is imperative in this business. He didn't get sentimental about many of the issues that slow other people down."

I waved my hand at him to interrupt. "I'm not sure I understand."

"Oh, you know. Dealing in the market sometimes takes a hard heart. There are all sorts of people out there, breaking their backs to get something going, pleading for support. You know their intentions are pure, but you also know they don't have a chance in hell of putting the deal together. You have to be able to steel yourself against making decisions based on sentiment, or on other people's enthusiasm, which can be just as disastrous. Charlie was a natural at that; while gentle, he also knew exactly what he wanted. That's a natural ability, not something you learn."

I thought back to what I'd learned about Charlie Jardine during the last four days. Wentworth had chosen to admire what he liked in the man, as had Rose, Jack Plummer, Arthur Clyde, and the others, all of whom had held him to the light and been dazzled by a slightly different facet.

But it was that manipulative element that kept tugging at me, the growing conviction that Charlie, he of the "analytical mind," had only allowed each of these people to see what he'd wanted them to see. Of course, as with any camouflage, the illusion was never quite perfect. Apart from Rose, whose needs were too desperate for clear-sightedness, the others had caught a glimpse of something else, something a little less appealing. The difference with Blaire and Tucker Wentworth, however, was that they didn't care. They, who had apparently liked him the most, and had understood him the best, had each taken what they'd wanted of the man. Tucker happily embraced the hardhearted strategist, Blaire the artist as lover, while both secretly longed, I suspected, for more of the entire man.

It occurred to me then that there was a perverse symmetry at work in the life of Charlie Jardine, whose complex need for attention demanded he always be part of a triangle, whether it be emotional, as with Rose and John Woll, practical, as with Tucker Wentworth and Arthur Clyde, or a bit of both, as with Tucker and his daughter.

"Mr. Wentworth, did you ever feel that Charlie was using you?"

He actually burst out laughing, throwing his head back and tapping himself on the chest. "Of course he was, as I was him. My God, man, why else do people do what they do? Why else are you in this house, or am I employed by Morris, McGill, or does my daughter live in my backyard, decorating and redecorating this whale of a house? We're all using one another; that's how society works."

My silence following this outburst was misinterpreted as rebuke. Now Wentworth leaned forward in his chair, his face animated by the nondebate. "Come, come, Mr. Gunther, surely a man of your profession can't be that naive. Besides, no one says that friendship can't play a part in it. I love my daughter; why should I care that while she's loving me back she's also protecting her inheritance?"

It was an interesting viewpoint, revealing more than I

think was intended. Could Blaire, forever attentive to her self-interests, have seen Charlie as a challenger? Did she seduce him to keep him under control? If so, would she have resorted to extreme measures if she felt she'd lost that control?

It did seem that Tucker's affection for Charlie transcended the mentor-protégé model. I didn't know yet if their relationship had a sexual side to it, but even if it didn't, some emotional bonding, almost like a father and son, had apparently taken place. That sure as hell would have given me sweaty palms, had I been Blaire Wentworth.

"Did you see something of yourself in Charlie?"

"I guess I did," he answered slowly. "There were vast differences, of course, more than there were similarities, but I found him so remarkably receptive to ideas."

"What were some of the differences?"

"Well, he was better with people than I am; he had an uncanny ability to make them open up. Most people, myself included, like to talk about themselves. You know, you ask someone what they do for a living, not because you're interested, but because you want them to return the favor and allow you center court for an hour or more. Well, when Charlie asked, he was genuinely interested; he did everything but take notes. It made him very easy to like."

"And hard to get to know."

The smile of reminiscence stayed on his lips. "Yes. He kept his cards close."

"Did your daughter ever meet him? What did she think?"

"Blaire? I don't know that she thought much about him either way. We spoke business mostly, when he came over. She has little interest in that. I must tell you that my daughter and I do not have much in common. We spend a lot of time together, mostly over meals, but I don't think either one of us is very interested in the other."

I nodded without answering. I disagreed, of course. From what I'd learned over the past four days, I thought both Wentworths had quite a bit in common.

I decided to drop Blaire from the conversation and concentrate on her father and Charlie again. "So whose idea was it to create ABC?"

He seemed instantly more relaxed. "His. Actually, I

should say it was his ambition, and perhaps my idea. He had shown himself so good at the game that I thought it would be a waste to see him disappear down some huge corporate black hole on Wall Street. Communications being what they are nowadays, there was no reason why he couldn't set up shop right here and be a successful independent. The idea didn't really take shape until I heard Arthur Clyde was looking to get back in the game.''

"Why was he such a factor?''

Wentworth raised his eyebrows at my lack of knowledge. "Oh. Well, Charlie could never have done it all by himself. I mean, he was bright and ambitious and a real go-getter, but he was no magician. No one man can both drum up business and watch the market, not as an independent operator. If you're a Shearson or an IDS rep, you can do both because those companies supply your research; all you have to do is be a good salesman and have a thorough grasp of the basics. But Charlie couldn't do it all alone.''

"You were there.''

He smiled, but I could tell there was no humor. "So was Arthur, and Arthur is a born analyst. I'm not. The trick here is to know your limitations.''

It was a straightforward statement, but I couldn't help feeling it also contained an element of warning. Throughout this latter part of the conversation, I'd wondered how much he knew of our recent activities concerning ABC. Surely his buddy Arthur had called him first thing after hearing of Charlie's death, and definitely after we'd walked out with all his business files. And yet Wentworth hadn't spilled a drop of all that.

"Was your involvement with ABC limited to introducing Charlie to Arthur?''

"That was the jist of it. Of course, I was free with any advice I might have had.'' He chuckled briefly. "Much to Arthur's dismay. I'm sure he kept wishing I'd go on a long vacation.''

"You didn't put any money into setting it up?''

He waved the notion away with his hand. "Oh, no. That would have been just the wrong thing to do, as I saw it. Charlie had an inheritance, and lord knows Arthur is no pauper; I felt it would be best if the two of them put their own money at stake. I've always felt it's the element of risk that makes the real artist in this business. If you're not betting your own money, then why should you care if you win or lose?''

I kept watching his eyes, which had told me much of his pain and loss earlier. Now they were clear and cool and calculating, his body language relaxed and almost jovial. I couldn't believe a man could so overpower his own grief, unless he had a dire need to focus on something more important, or more threatening.

Since his guard was now so blatantly up, I felt I had little to lose in the chess game I'd been imagining a while back. "You probably heard we subpoenaed all of Charlie's business records and correspondence."

The smile remained in place, but barely. "Yes. I believe Arthur told me. He was quite upset."

"That he was. He even had a court order issued from the bench, not that there was much point."

"No?"

"Not really. We'd pretty much gone over what we wanted by the time the order was served. You actually did more than just introduce Clyde to Jardine, didn't you? In fact, after they set up ABC, you steered quite a bit of business their way."

"That's true, I did. Are you saying I did something wrong?"

"No, no. I do feel I ought to warn you, though, that the ABC records we studied will be subpoenaed again, Mr. Wentworth, with an eye toward your involvement in that operation. We don't for a minute believe it was pure paternal benevolence."

He rose to his feet, pale, tight with fury, and stared down at me. "I challenge you to find a single scrap of evidence that I benefited from Charlie's business. He was a friend; moreover, he was the son I never had, unless you find that too maudlin to believe. If you carry this idea too far, I will add to your string of lawsuits, only mine will have the balls of an elephant. It will ruin the Police Department, the town, and you personally, because it, unlike your insinuations, will be based on facts."

I too got to my feet. "I never said you'd benefited from ABC. In fact, I think just the reverse. I think ABC's success was based entirely on your priming its pump. It's true that Charlie had an inheritance, and that the paper trail indicates he put it all into the business, but I don't think he did, not really. You didn't let him. You told him that, win or lose, he wasn't risking that eighty-five thousand dollars; that even if the business went belly up, the money would reappear in his account."

He stared at me for a long while, his eyes searching mine. He glanced briefly out the window, a jerky, awkward movement. His voice, when it came, was muted. "There's nothing illegal in that."

The decent thing then would have been to leave. Unfortunately, that wasn't an option. Being softhearted had not been Wentworth's only offense, and I had to tell him I knew that.

"Maybe not, but making money through insider trading is, even if the beneficiary is somebody else. And there's the matter of the Putney Road Bank's pension fund, and how it came to be entrusted to the care of a fledgling investment firm, one of the founders of which had until recently been washing cars and waiting tables. And what about Arthur Clyde? He wasn't fool enough to throw his money in with the likes of Charlie Jardine—Christ, he could barely stand the man. What did his involvement cost you?"

Wentworth didn't answer. He stood mutely before his expensive armchair, surrounded by his daughter's taste for opulence, his head turned toward the extravagant view.

I showed myself out. There was no hard evidence of the allegations I had just made, and maybe there never would be. The man, after all, was no novice. But it was clear that Tucker Wentworth, for all his cynical philosophy, had become a sentimental old man, and may have broken a few laws to prove it. But I doubted he was a murderer.

On the other hand, I could no longer say the same of Arthur Clyde or Blaire Wentworth.

CHAPTER
27

I pulled out of the lunch-hour traffic into the parking lot of the Putney Road Bank. Ron Klesczewski was leaning against his car, looking morose. He'd called me on the radio as I was driving back into town from Wentworth's place, asking me to meet him here. His tone of voice had not been encouraging.

I glanced around as I got out of my car, looking for Sammie, with whom Ron was supposed to be working. "What's up?"

He read me correctly. "She's not here. We had a bit of a run-in."

I suppressed a sigh. The combined pressures on us were beginning to spread. "What happened?"

His face was oddly still as he spoke, his emotions rigidly under control. "I screwed up, I'm afraid. I may have let the birds fly the coop."

He and Martens were supposed to have researched and interviewed Hanson, Atwater, and Thomas. "All three of them?"

He nodded. "Yup. Hanson for sure. We checked his home, neighbors, business addresses, the works. Nobody knows where he went. All we know about the other two is that they didn't show up for work today and that neither one is picking up their home phone."

Part of his depression became clear to me now. Had he been more aggressive yesterday, he might have been grinning in victory instead of standing here empty-handed. I didn't doubt the hard-charging Sammie Martens had driven that point home, perhaps deeper than usual, in compensation for her own screwup with Milo.

"That's not all," he added mournfully. "Sammie also found out that Hanson owns several businesses, not just the warehouses, like I thought. None of the others are in his name, but he's majority owner in all of them."

"Anything directly relating to this case?" I asked.

He shrugged. "Who knows? Nothing on the surface."

"So where's Sammie?" I repeated.

"She went after Kenny Thomas. We did the basic background research on all of them early this morning, in preparation for the interviews. But after we discovered Hanson had taken a powder, I thought we should regroup, maybe talk things over with you. Sammie wanted to go after the other two without wasting any more time."

He was doing this well, keeping his tone neutral, his account unprejudiced, but I suspected Sammie and he had actually had quite an argument.

"So, anyhow," he concluded, "I thought I ought to let you know what was up, in case it was mentioned later."

I nodded. "Fair enough. What's your plan now?"

He looked toward the bank. "I thought I'd talk to them first, find out what I could about Atwater and Thomas, and then go over to Atwater's place."

I smiled despite myself, stimulated by Ron's unremitting gloominess. "Lighten up, it feels worse than it is. We've all messed up at least once so far in this case. If Sammie still has a chip on her shoulder when you see her later, sort it out; but I think you'll find it's blown over."

I opened my car door and slipped behind the wheel. "Look, why don't we cut it three ways? You take the bankers, I'll take Atwater, and we'll leave Sammie to chase after Thomas, okay?"

He smiled weakly and began walking toward the building, a living monument to how a major case could be undermining to one's self-confidence.

Atwater lived on Organ Street, parallel to Birge and lined up against a long row of ancient Estey Organ warehouses. Typically, however, while only a couple of hundred feet separated the two streets, Organ was some forty feet higher in elevation, perched along the edge of a treacherous slope.

The building I was after, like many in the center of town, dated back before World War I: boxy, two stories tall, with a one-windowed half–third floor tucked in under the gables. It had originally been sided with pine clapboards, but was now surfaced with those oddly shaped, fluted composition tiles that some demented designer decades ago had apparently thought were the spitting image of cedar shakes, "only better." I found Atwater's doorbell on a mailbox by the front door and pushed it.

"She's not home. Left yesterday."

I stepped out onto the sidewalk and looked up. Leaning precariously out of a window was a large woman with a voice to match, wearing a tentlike cotton dress and a headful of brightly colored plastic curlers.

"I know you; you're Lieutenant Gunther, aren't you?"

"Yes, ma'am."

"Ma'am?" She let out a bellow of laughter. "Just like 'Dragnet.' I've read about you in the newspaper. What's up?"

"I'd like to speak with Paula Atwater."

"She in trouble?" The woman sounded like she didn't care one way or the other.

"Not with me. You know where she went?"

"Nope. She took off in a big rush late yesterday with a suitcase. You want to look around her place?"

It was a tempting offer, but I had to watch my step. "I don't have a warrant."

The woman laughed again. "Oh, hell, that's no problem. I got the key. Come on up. I own the place."

Still I demurred. "Can't do it. Legally, that apartment is her property; we'd be trespassing, even though it's your house."

She scowled at me. "I'm not so sure it is her property. Her rent was due three days ago, and she blew out of here saying she didn't know if or when she'd be back. Even gave me her keys, which she usually doesn't do. I was thinking of throwing her out anyway—too noisy."

Without knowing it, she had opened a small legal loophole, implying that Paula Atwater had terminated her lease. "So you don't expect her back?"

"I was going to give her the benefit of the doubt, maybe a few days, but the rent is overdue and I'm not a wealthy woman."

I smiled and bowed slightly. "Then I'd be charmed if you'd show me her apartment."

I climbed the central staircase and met my hostess on the second-floor landing. She stuck out a large, sweaty hand I felt obliged to squeeze in greeting.

"I'm Shirley Barrows . . . Lieutenant Joe Gunther. Damn, you're a real hero. My girl friends and I are real fans of yours, ever since that ski-mask murderer. We would get together and read the paper out loud; it was just like watching the soaps." She paused. "You got your hands full with this one, though, huh?"

"We're working on it around the clock."

Her eyes lit up. "And you think Paula's tied in somehow?"

I made a sad face and started to mouth the usual platitudes, but she plunked me on the shoulder with her ham-sized mitt and took me off the hook. "Don't say it. You can't talk, I know; confidential, right?"

I smiled in relief. "Right. Sorry."

She fished a key ring out of a large pocket on the front of her dress and waddled up one more flight to what had been originally designed as an attic. She fiddled with the door lock on the narrow, dark landing, barely wide enough to hold us both. Her moon-round face looked as grim as a judge's. "No sorries about it. You take your time in here, and just pound on my door on your way out."

She turned the key and stepped aside so I could squeeze by. "I can tell the girls we met, can't I?"

"Absolutely."

The silence was deafening following her departure. I

stood motionless in the living room, looking, smelling, and listening to the muted sounds from outside, trying to absorb initial impressions.

It was obviously a young single woman's apartment, hung with suggestive posters of Axl Rose and Slash, a Leland and Gray Union High School pennant, and a personality dart board where the target rings had been replaced by a black-and-white photograph of a serious-looking older man in a tie and rimless glasses. I recognized him as the CEO of the Putney Road Bank, a regular at Rotary lunches and benefit affairs for the museum. His bland face had been pockmarked by the passage of darts, three of which now resided in his nose.

There were stuffed animals, open cassette tapes, pillows, and dirty clothing strewn about, but it was not the disarray of a hasty departure. Rather, it looked to me like the residue of a sloppy housekeeper. The air smelled slightly of seeped-in marijuana. The few books that were scattered about were all romances, soft-porn bodice-rippers with beautiful, half-naked people on the covers.

The living room doubled as kitchen, with a small fridge, sink, and counter set into an alcove. Opposite me were two open doors, one leading into a tiny bathroom, the other into a bedroom of barely greater dimensions.

I looked around the living room first, mostly getting a feel for Paula Atwater's life-style. Her music collection ran to heavy metal, the stereo and TV were inexpensive and well used, the food was sparse, prepackaged, and unhealthy.

The bathroom was unremarkable: the usual cabinet supplies, with toothbrush, paste, and blow dryer missing; a hamper with dirty underwear; a couple of mildew-rich towels; tissues, sanitary napkins, Q-Tips, and Clearasil; the empty box of a one-shot pregnancy test. It was hard to tell from these leftovers how long their owner planned to be gone.

The bedroom looked like any unsupervised teenager's: cyclone-ravaged, dirty, smelling of used clothes, and, in this case, stale sex. The unmade sheets were stained in the right place, the wastebasket under the nightstand had wads of crusty tissues, and crumpled up on the floor was a black, sheer, lacy garment of a type I'd once seen featured in a Victoria's Secret catalog. In the closet, alongside a limited collection of severe-looking skirts, dresses, and blouses, was a mass of colorful, abbreviated, leather-and-metal-adorned clothing, suitable for the average aspiring punker. It made me wonder with a smile how many other presumably demure people we saw in banks and lawyers' offices were equally rebellious on their own time.

I sat gingerly on the edge of the water bed and began to go through the waist-high chest of drawers. Working from the bottom up, I found mostly clothing, costume jewelry, and a single spare blanket. The top two drawers, however, held some old bank statements, a small fistful of bills, a photo album, and some letters and postcards, all mixed in with several pieces of old candy, a broken comb, an unopened box of condoms, some spare change, a few colored feathers, an obscene bumper sticker, and a tube of fluorescent lipstick.

I looked through the correspondence. The letters were signed by her mother, and the postcards were addressed to "Pebbles" from "Kenny." The postmarks on the latter were all from Hartford, Connecticut, scenes of which graced the fronts, and were dated over a one-week period eight months earlier. Despite the fact that the postcards were open to casual scrutiny, their contents were intimate to the point of pornography, detailing Kenny's longing for his Pebble's specific body parts. Passing references were also made to the "banking conference" being "a total drag." Assumptions are a dangerous habit in police work, but I had few doubts this Kenny was the same one Sammie was hunting across town.

The letters detailed Paula's mother's daily activities in a chatty, over-the-back-fence style. It took some reading, however, to figure out her locale. There was no letterhead, and no attached envelopes, and it was only through references to the new Union Hall clock, the deli department at Morse's Store, and the fund-raising efforts of the NewBrook Fire Department that I finally figured out that mom must live in Newfane, twelve miles up Route 30 from Brattleboro. That discovery also helped explain the Leland and Gray pennant in the living room: located in Townshend, it was Newfane's designated high school.

The photo album confirmed my guess, providing me with graduation group shots showing Paula and several family members in front of the Windham County Courthouse. From the date on the senior-class banner in the background of one of these, I figured Paula Atwater couldn't be more than nineteen years old. From her photos, she looked friendly and outgoing, neither chubby nor thin, with a tangled mop of curly brown hair and a mild case of acne. In several of the nongraduation pictures, she and several friends or family members were clowning around on the front lawn of a one-story brown house with a bay window to the left of the front door.

I reached out to the phone on the floor by the side of the bed and dialed the Windham County Sheriff's Department, headquartered in Newfane. I asked for Lieutenant Norman Powell.

"Hey, Joe, long time no see. What's up?" Powell and I were old friends, but primarily on a professional basis. Whenever we talked, it was usually business that brought us together.

"I'm looking for someone down here, and I think she flew the coop into your neck of the woods. I have a few pictures with a house in the background. If I drove up there right now, could you take a shot at identifying the building and maybe the family?"

"What's the name?"

"Paula Atwater, about nineteen, Leland and Gray graduate."

There was a short pause. "Doesn't ring a bell offhand. Sure, come on up. I'll see what I can do."

I hung up, pulled some sheets of paper from my small notebook, constructed a couple of quasi-legal forms, and left the apartment with the photo album under my arm. Shirley Barrows's door opened before I'd knocked on it twice.

She instantly spotted the album. "Oh, hey. You got something."

"Yeah. I was wondering if you could do me a big favor and sign these two documents. One states that you voluntarily invited me into Paula's apartment, since you now believe she's left for good and the property's yours again, and the other is your acknowledgment that I have removed one item, a photo album, from that apartment."

She signed both pieces of paper eagerly, her sweaty hand leaving a damp patch at the bottom of each. "This is great. Wait'll I tell the girls. Just like the movies. Do you think I'll get my name in the papers?"

•　•　•

Route 30, heading northwest toward Newfane, parallels the Upper Dummerston Road, which I'd traveled earlier that day to visit Tucker Wentworth. But where the latter is a narrow, winding, country road, blocked in by trees and homes on either side, the former is a legitimate highway: broad, flat, smooth, and built for speed. It is also one of the prettiest roads in the county, running along the bottom of the West River Valley, matching the water's serpentine bends, a paved mirror image of the broad, sparkling, rock-strewn waterway so attractive to dozens of weekend tube-floaters and sunbathers during Vermont's brief summers. The valley walls, steep, verdant, punctuated by occasional cliffs and feeder streams, embraced and soothed me, despite the hot breeze that lashed at my face through the open window.

The Sheriff's Department and the County Courthouse face one another across the enormous Newfane Village Common. However, as if by design, any suggested fraternity between the two has been tempered by Route 30, severe and barren, which lies as a no-man's land, slicing the common in two. It's a sad and occasionally traffic-choked modern intrusion, upsetting a near-perfect mix of historic architecture and manicured nature.

I swung right, around the edge of the common and toward the old jail house, marveling at the play of light on the grass and the shimmering white of the one-hundred-and-fifty-year-old buildings.

Norman Powell stepped out onto the concrete porch of the old jail as I stopped my car before it. Gray-haired, tall, and lean, he was an ex-army sergeant who'd joined the department after he'd found retirement at forty not all it was cracked up to be. He nodded at me, his hands on his waist, vaguely reminiscent of some uniformed Texas Ranger, squinting into the sun. "Hey, Joe."

I brought the album out of my car and laid it on the hood. He came off the porch and stood next to me as I flipped through to the shots of the family on the lawn. "Know where that is?"

"Yup. If it weren't for the buildings in between, you could see it from here. Mrs. Adams's house. That's not the name you gave me."

"Paula Atwater?"

He scratched the gray stubble at the back of his neck. "Right. Could be same family, different last names. Glenda Adams was married once before, a long time ago; that might explain it. I'd forgotten about that." He extended his hand to point down Route 30, the way I'd come. "Glenda lives in Rolling Meadows, behind W.W. I'll show you."

We got into my car. He could have just given me directions. W.W. Building Supply, which straddles the entrance road to the long, circular drive that constitutes the Rolling Meadows development, was barely two hundred yards back down the road. But there was a jurisdictional politesse being followed here. While a policeman in Vermont carries his authority with him throughout the state, regardless of which turf he actually calls home, it's best for him to check in with the locals. Failure to do so usually results in ruffled feathers, unnecessarily tense explanations later, and the inconvenience of frosty relations in the long run. It's also a dumb move strategically; if something goes wrong, and you send out a call for backup, it takes a while for the locals to figure out who you are and what the hell you're screaming about.

The house in the photo album was the first on the left-hand branch of the circle. It looked wrong to me somehow, as I parked in the driveway, and it wasn't until I got out of the car that I realized I'd so cemented Paula's photograph of this house in my mind that I'd come to expect a lawnful of laughing people to be permanently gathered before it, as if that joyful day had just gone on and on and on.

Powell and I crossed the now-empty lawn and I worked the heavy brass knocker on the front door. The young woman I'd come to know solely through her possessions opened the door, her expression falling at the sight of Norm's uniform.

"Yes?" Her voice caught in her throat.

"I'm Lieutenant Joe Gunther, of the Brattleboro Police Department; this is Lieutenant Powell of the Sheriff's Department. Are you Paula Atwater?" I used my best official voice and showed her my badge.

"Yes." Now she was barely audible.

"And you work as a teller at the Putney Road Bank?" She nodded.

"May we come in?"

She stood aside and we filed by her into the darkened house, not air-conditioned, but surprisingly cool nevertheless.

"Is your mother or anyone else home?" Norm asked.

"No. Mom's at work." She led us into a pleasant, comfortable living room and curled up on an armchair, her legs tucked under her, her arms instinctively wrapping themselves around a large pillow she clutched to her stomach. She looked worse than her picture, paler, more drawn, her acne now in high relief, her hair unbrushed and bedraggled. I doubted she'd slept at all last night. I was hoping to use that to my advantage to speed this up. Grilling bewildered teenagers was not my idea of recreation.

"I guess you know you're in deep trouble," I said, hoping she'd help me out.

She hugged the pillow tighter, looking from one of us to the other. "I don't know what you mean."

I inwardly sighed. "Why aren't you at work? You didn't give the bank any explanation. You didn't tell Shirley Barrows."

The mention of her landlady made her eyes widen; it told her how thoroughly I'd been hunting for her.

"Who told you and Kenny to get out of Brattleboro, Paula? Cappelli?"

"No," she answered in a whisper.

"You know, you're all on your own now. They're all long gone. They left you holding the bag."

She bent over the pillow, her eyes fixed on her lap, her face invisible to us. She shook her head.

"Kenny got you into this, didn't he?"

Her head shot up. "No."

"Paula, we're not talking smoking in the bathroom here. I'm running a murder investigation."

She didn't move for a couple of seconds; I doubted she even breathed. Then she stared right at me, plainly frightened. "We had nothing to do with that."

"That's not what the evidence tells me. It was our investigation of Milly Crawford that led us to you."

She was beginning to look slightly panicky. "I didn't kill anyone."

"How long have you known Kenny Thomas, Paula?"

"He's not a killer. We love each other." She struggled unsuccessfully for more words that might convince me.

"Where did you meet? At the bank?"

She nodded.

"What's his position there?"

"New accounts, customer service."

"But he's not a teller. He doesn't handle money or put it into people's accounts, the way you do."

I'd begun this conversation as a man in the dark, groping for recognizable objects, hoping they would tell me more about my environs. Now, judging my progress both by her reactions and the instinct I'd formed of Kenny Thomas through his postcards, I sensed I was getting close.

"Kenny came on to you strong, didn't he? Lots of flattery, gifts, nights on the town. Swept you off your feet, right, Pebbles?"

She flinched at my use of his nickname for her. "We loved each other." But the tone was softer, more doubtful.

I could almost feel what I was after under my hand. "When did he tell you about his get-rich-quick scheme?"

Again, she was silent.

"Paula, the law holds you as accountable as he is. In fact, I have to tell you that, while you're not under arrest, you might want to stop talking to us until you can get hold of a lawyer. That's your right. Do you understand?"

I stopped, hoping I'd planted enough seeds of doubt to make her open up. I let a long silence creep by.

"Do you understand?"

She nodded slowly.

"Then talk to us, Paula; it'll work in your favor."

She sighed. She didn't look up from her lap, but she did begin to speak, softly, like a child. "He told me he'd been waiting for someone like me for a long, long time; someone to share his dream with. We fell in love. He *was* in love with me. A woman knows things like that."

I quelled the cynic in me. "I can accept that. What was the plan?"

"Kenny was getting money from someone, maybe it was drug money, I don't know. He would open different accounts, and I would divide the money between them."

"How did the cash get into the bank?"

"We brought it in with my lunch. Then, during the day, at odd moments, I would enter it in, never too much at a time."

"What were the names in those accounts?"

"It didn't matter. We made them up."

"Did you ever open accounts under the names Jake Hanson, Mark Cappelli, or Charles Jardine?"

She shook her head, I thought a little too quickly.

"But you knew Cappelli; you all but admitted that a minute ago."

Her face tightened, but she finally nodded slightly.

"How did you know him?"

"I saw them once. Kenny always picked up the money on his own, usually the night before we would bring it into the bank for deposit. Well, one night, something must've gone wrong, because they came by my place late, when Kenny was staying over, and he went down to talk to them. I followed him and saw them, and later I asked Kenny who they were."

"They?"

"There were two of them."

"Did he tell you?"

"He was mad at me at first, but he finally did. One of them was Cappelli; the other was Jake Hanson."

I suppressed a contented smile. Now we had more than a simple list of names linking the four together. "Didn't Kenny tell you where the money was coming from?"

Still she denied it with a shake of her head.

"What happened to the money after you put it into the phony accounts?"

"Usually it was taken out by wire transfer to another branch of the bank."

"By who?"

"I don't know, but they used the names we'd made up. Kenny took care of all that. I don't know exactly how it worked."

"How did you and Kenny get your cut?"

"Kenny took care of that, too."

"Did you ever see any of it?"

"No. We were supposed to wait, so as not to get anybody suspicious."

I seriously doubted Kenny had waited for his share. "Who told you to get out of Brattleboro?"

"Kenny. He said that we should split up and that he'd contact me later."

"Do you know where he went?"

"No."

"Does he know how to get in touch with you here?"

"No." Her head had slumped so far forward by now, we could only see the top of it.

"Then how could he have contacted you later?"

There was a long silence, during which, from the dark, liquid spots appearing on the pillow against her stomach, I knew that Paula Atwater was crying.

Norm and I exchanged glances. "Paula, you realize you've broken a few laws; that you'll be held accountable?"

She nodded wordlessly.

"Tell your mother what we talked about when she gets home. The two of you can find a lawyer and maybe something can be worked out so you won't have to go to prison. But listen to me." I crossed the room and squatted down before her, forcing her to look at me. "You're going to have to concentrate on saving yourself. Kenny and you are over, not just because you got caught, but because he set you up.''

She began to respond, but I held up my hand. "Don't talk, just think. Regardless of how you feel now, you'll find out Kenny was more interested in the money than in you, and that he played you for a loser. The only way you can save yourself is to prove him wrong. Remember that, okay?''

She stared at me, her eyes red and swollen, her face expressionless. I held her gaze a few moments longer, wondering if my words would have any effect later on, when she'd need them most.

But there was no way to tell.

I rose and headed for the door, leaving her to soak in her newfound puddle of reality.

CHAPTER
28

THE smoke in Brandt's office hung in the air like a veil, the still box-fan in his window a silent rebuke to the computer repairman's recommendation. I'd been wording a warrant for Kenny Thomas's apartment with the reunited Ron and Sammie when the chief's summons had come through on the intercom. His tone of voice had left no room for delay.

Brandt was clearly irritated. "What the hell is going on? I spent half the afternoon getting my ass chewed off by Luman Jackson and Tom Wilson again. Not that I'm not getting used to it, but I don't expect to be left in the dark by my own people. Why the hell are you hassling the god-damned building inspector? And apparently Tucker Wentworth has complained to Jackson that you accused him of impro-prieties regarding ABC Investments."

I stared at him in stunned silence. My mind was too busy playing connect-the-dots to be offended by Brandt's tone of voice. Besides, since I hadn't updated him, he had a right to be pissed off. What worried me was that somehow every move we made, every lead we pursued, became public knowledge within hours. It was as if we were conducting an investigation under a microscope.

I parked myself on the low filing cabinet by the door. "I interviewed McDermott this morning. He'd been in Crawford's building at the time of the killing, and poking around Toby's hideaway just before he disappeared. It was a legitimate inquiry. McDermott claims he received anonymous phone calls luring him to both places. He may be telling the truth. On the other hand, it's awfully convenient that, both times, the callers refused to identify themselves. As for Wentworth, I didn't accuse him of anything, but I sure as hell asked him to explain his connection to Charlie Jardine and ABC Investments. It is true he got a little pissed off at me, but it sounds like you got the *National Enquirer* version of both stories.''

He took his glasses off and rubbed his eyes with his fingertips until I thought he might do himself some damage. He finally slouched way back in his chair. He sounded exhausted. ''Jackson blew in here, spitting nails about Wentworth. I guess they talked on the phone or something right after you left him.''

I shook my head. ''I didn't think he was in the mood to talk to anyone when I left him. How did he and Jackson become such pals?''

Brandt shrugged. ''Beats me; small town. In any case, Jackson's now convinced we've totally lost our minds, running around accusing prominent citizens of being horse thieves and ax murderers. He said we're exposing the town to lawsuits that'll bury us; he even dragged in Nadeau at one point to quote me some legal mumbo-jumbo.''

I could now understand why Brandt was upset. I knew Luman Jackson all too well, and could read between the lines of Brandt's abbreviated account. Jackson's style was like that of a hell-bent bible thumper, full of spittle and rhetoric, shifting from accusation to innuendo. He also had a blood-thirsty appetite for other people's throats. The few run-ins I'd had with him had left me breathless.

Brandt got up and paced around his office a bit. ''Look, this may not be the end of it. Jackson said he was going to assemble the selectmen for a closed-door meeting, presumably to fry the Police Department. He has to get three out of the five selectmen to play along before it'll happen, but it still might, so be prepared.''

I rose and opened the door. "I'm prepared now. They can kiss my ass anytime they want."

Tony stopped me just as I was about to close the door behind me. "Joe?"

"What?"

"Sorry I jumped down your throat."

I smiled at him. "Don't worry about it. Occupational hazard."

Our little chat had thoroughly shaken me. Increasingly, throughout this investigation, I'd felt control being wrested from our grasp, first by events and the lack of manpower, and then by the attending publicity. But the growing political pressure was making it difficult to maneuver at all.

Initially, my plan had been to refocus on Blaire Wentworth and Arthur Clyde, to see if the knowledge I'd acquired since my first chats with them might be used to further crack their shells.

Now, however, I had but one idea in mind. In the time-honored tradition of an attacking force trying to destroy a strong, largely unknown defensive position, I was going for a secret weapon. I was sick and tired of having everyone know what I was doing.

I left the Municipal Building by the front door and cut to the right along a walkway that led to the town library's rear entrance, which, because of the steep slope down to Main Street, was also their top floor.

Inside the library, I traveled the length of the building, down one flight of stairs, and out onto the second-floor mezzanine. Standing slightly back of the railing to avoid attracting attention, I surveyed the large reading room below me, looking for the man I was after. From my vantage point, I could see the typing room, the microfilm tables, most of the first-floor stacks, and the reference desk. I didn't see him anywhere.

I walked along the balcony to the glass door of the local-history room, normally kept locked to protect the archives shelved inside. There was no one at the reading table in the front room, but a light was on in the stacks beyond. I turned the door handle and entered.

The local-history "stacks" amounted to just one moderately sized, windowless room divided into rows by several floor-to-ceiling shelf units. The aisle directly opposite the door was empty, but I could hear sounds off to the left.

There was the sudden loud slap of a book hitting the floor, followed by an equally explosive, "Fuck."

I knew I'd found my man.

Willy Kunkle was in his early forties, of medium height, with a muscular, barrel chest, a head of thick, black hair, and a permanent scowl. A tough New York–born Vietnam vet who'd brought with him more emotional baggage than he could civilly carry, he'd moved to Brattleboro, married a local girl, and joined the Police Department as a patrolman. The armed forces had trained him well; he rose quickly through the ranks to join the detective squad within two years, and in the process had become one of the most difficult men to work with I'd ever known. Indeed, it had often occurred to me during his tenure that many of the people he busted were kinder and more compassionate than he was.

Nevertheless, despite his soured, cynical, and angry soul, and the spousal abuse that had quite properly cost him his marriage, he'd been a cop's cop, a man with an unrivaled sense of the street.

Perhaps predictably, his career had come to a premature end. In helping me and several New Hampshire State Troopers pursue a suspect in the ski-mask case, he'd caught a high-caliber rifle bullet in the left shoulder, shattering it beyond repair. Several operations later, his entire arm permanently disabled, he'd been given the option of retiring from municipal service or taking another town job at comparable pay. He'd stunned us all by choosing the latter, thereby beginning a minor reign of terror within the library.

I knew it wouldn't last in the long run. His style had been tough enough on his fellow cops; its prolonged effects on a group of peaceable librarians was guaranteed to end catastrophically. But he'd been working here less than six months, and, as far as I knew, his co-workers so far had managed to find him isolated nooks and crannies in which to work, far from them, and from any potentially horrified member of the public.

I rounded the corner of the bookshelf and watched him heft a gigantic leather-bound tome off the floor with one hand, and wrestle it onto a shelf. His left hand remained, as always, deep in the side pocket of his trousers, giving his body, if not his facial expression, an incongruously nonchalant appearance.

"Hey, Willy."

He barely gave me a glance. "Well, if it isn't Typhoid Joe. Come by to share some of the heat you been gettin'?"

"Only if they catch us."

That got his attention. He glared at me. "Us? To hell with you. I got enough shit on my plate without that."

"Working you hard, are they?"

"If assholes could fly, this place would be an airport." He turned his back to me and began flipping through a card-catalog tray he'd placed on top of a cabinet lining the wall.

"What've you heard about the case?"

"I read the papers."

"What'd you think?"

"I think you're fucked. The SA's ID'd the watch as Jardine's, and nailed down the time and place that Rosie Woll bought it for him; plus, they found Jardine's wallet in Woll's car, under the mat in the trunk. I think you guys better prepare for Johnnie Boy's going-away party."

He riffled through the card catalog with his dexterous right hand. I had to smile at the pretense: Willy Kunkle was still so wired to the street he had information the state's attorney's own staff probably didn't know about, much less the newspapers.

I resisted pointing that fact out. If I was to reel him in, I'd have to pique his interest enough to make him bite. "That's not enough to prosecute; they could've been planted."

He shrugged. "Maybe."

"Why did Cappelli pull a gun on us?"

"Guilty conscience."

"He says he thought we were bad guys."

"Bullshit; he thought you were about to fry him. It was only when you didn't press charges that he started getting imaginative."

"What was he up to?"

He still had his back to me. "Hey, what do I know? Rumor had it he was running dope for some new guy."

"Milly Crawford?"

Now he turned to face me, his expression quizzical. "Did you guys really find that big a stash at Milly's, or was that all smoke?"

"It was there, and he'd been playing with it; his prints were all over it. We're pretty sure one baggie made it to Jardine's house."

He shook his head. "I don't know who was running Cappelli, but it wasn't Milly; the man was a jerk-off. And I never heard a peep about him on the street, not tying into that kind of action."

"Who would have supplied him the money?"

Kunkle thought about that for a moment. "I know Cappelli. He and Milly wouldn't mix."

During his years at the department, as Ron had pointed out earlier, Willy Kunkle made the local drug trade his specialty, getting to know the players, the supply routes, the money sources. Little of his knowledge ever resulted in direct busts, but it was an invaluable tool when it came to leveraging information from people.

"We found out Cappelli and Hanson were handing money to two Putney Road bankers, apparently for laundering. You hear anything about that?"

Kunkle chuckled. "Found out about Jake, huh? He and Cappelli definitely connect. In fact, I think Cappelli used to be married to one of Jake's daughters."

"Did Hanson have a specialty?"

"You know about the warehouses?"

I nodded.

"That was it, pure and simple. Mark was the transporter, Jake the storage man."

"Neither one of them sold?"

Willy shook his head. "That's one of the reasons we never nailed 'em. There was nothing to be gained trying to sell that shit in this town. I mean, we nailed a few small-timers, but there was a whole lot more moving through here than we ever saw, heading upstate to Rutland, Burlington, and mostly to upper–New York State, where the big market was. We never got anywhere because it just passed through. By the time I heard about it, it was history.''

"So why the change?''

He gave a knowing smile. "New players. Plus more riffraff is beginning to stick to Vermont's famous 'Gateway.' We've not only got the best welfare check around, we're just a short piss away from the Mass border, where the economy's going to hell in a handbasket. That all creates a market for dope.''

"It was a lot of dope all of a sudden.''

He chewed on that for a bit. "Yeah, that's what makes me think new players. Had it been the old crowd, they would have penny-anted their way up, and would have gotten nailed before long. How'd you tumble to Hanson and Cappelli?''

As usual, he'd identified the correct button to push. "We found their phone numbers on a list in Milly's apartment, along with those of two employees of the Putney Road Bank, and John Woll.''

There was a slight break in the conversation, which caught us both looking at our feet. Kunkle snapped out of it first. "So why're you here?''

I hesitated. "I was wondering if you could chase this down a little further.''

His eyes widened. "You mean Milly's list of numbers? You're shittin' me.''

"Nope.''

He slapped his forehead with his hand. "You've got to be out of your friggin' mind. You want me—a town librarian—to go poking around in official police business, right after you and Brandt have already had your asses fried for withholding evidence?''

"No one ever mentioned withholding evidence.''

He shook his head. "Oh, well, pardon the hell out of me. Why in Christ's name should I put my butt on the line for you?''

"I need your help.''

He stared at me, his mouth half open. "This is bullshit.

Klesczewski and your other Keystone Kops can chase down four stupid names. Why do you need me?"

"I've got a leak in the department. I can't go to the bathroom without everyone in the building knowing about it. I need someone on the outside, to gather information only I get told about."

He hesitated, looking doubtful. I glanced at my watch. It was close to quitting time for him. "Let me tell you what I've got so far. Then decide."

It took over an hour, still standing in the stacks out of sight, to sketch in the convoluted cast of characters and the twisted strings that tied them all together. Much of it Kunkle obviously already knew, either by intuition or by reading the paper, but mostly he kept silent, apart from an occasional question.

"You think McDermott's your man?" he asked, when I was through.

I shook my head. "Call it a pecking order, with some names higher up than others, but none of them highlighted in neon. Look, the way I'm seeing it now, some son of a bitch has spent a lot of time and effort arranging his pile of rocks just right, so that when the first one—Charlie Jardine— fell into our laps, all the others began to follow, until now we're getting buried in an avalanche. Maybe McDermott's being targeted just to keep us off the scent, maybe he's the guy orchestrating this entire thing and hiding in plain sight. I haven't the slightest idea. All I do know is that I can't move without being seen."

"And I can," Kunkle muttered.

"Yeah. If you can find some hole in his camouflage, maybe we can get the bastard before someone else gets killed."

"Like me."

It was said quietly, without rancor, but it hit me hard. I hadn't actually considered myself or any of my people at risk in all this. Willy's fatalistic comment was a brutal reminder that whoever the killer was, if cornered, he wouldn't hesitate to use his teeth. I looked at Kunkle's useless, shriveled arm. He needed no reminder of how lethal these contests could become.

I leaned forward, propping my palms against one of the steel shelves, and hung my head between my shoulders, suddenly exhausted by the weight of it all. Busting petty crooks and calming domestic quarrels was poor preparation for dealing with a full-blown homicide investigation. Murders were so rare in Vermont that the State Police had put together a single five-man flying squad to investigate all homicides within their jurisdiction, just so they'd gain the experience. Police Departments like Brattleboro's tended to shun the State Police if they could, but their exposure to such crimes was even more limited.

I straightened and let out a sigh. "Forget it, Willy. You're right. I guess I'm losing my grip."

He tilted his head to one side and said coldly, "So this is where I say, 'Bullshit, my heart never left the service; let me do it one last time for you, boss, just like the good old days,' right? Well, you got the bullshit part down okay. I stuck my neck out once for you guys; peaceful old Vermont's done me a hell of a lot more damage than 'Nam ever did. You can get somebody else to get their ass shot off for you."

I knew he was right, but I couldn't suppress my own growing sense of futility. Somewhere, I knew, there was a weak spot, some fissure in the dam confronting me. I had hoped Willy Kunkle might be the dynamite I needed to turn that weak spot into a gaping hole. But that apparently was not to be.

As I exchanged the library's cool embrace for the hot and soggy air outside, I found some of Willy's anger caught in my own throat. He'd been absolutely right, of course. Enlisting him would have been a foolish risk, for him personally, for me politically, and for the legal integrity of the case. But none of that was going to stop me from kicking this case open, one way or the other.

Whoever was pulling the strings was privy to a lot of inside information, and was counting on us to work within the rules. The trick would be to deny him the first, and to play a little loose with the second.

CHAPTER
29

THE phone call caught me after hours again, alone at my desk, poring over the growing pile of transcribed interviews. I was taking longhand notes, a tissue under my right hand so it wouldn't stick to the page.

It was Dispatch, on the intercom. "I think you better get over here."

I did so at a half trot, peeling bits of tissue off my hand. Dispatch's tone of voice had not been encouraging, and I wondered what new bombshell was about to land at our feet.

"What've you got?" I asked, as I turned the corner.

"An MVA on the Canal/Main Street Bridge."

An MVA was a motor-vehicle accident, and the location was a four-road, two-parking-lot intersection with no traffic light—the town's OK Corral for opposing automobiles. "So?"

"It's John Woll."

I borrowed a patrol car and played the blue lights down to the scene. Rescue, Inc.'s, boxy orange-and-white ambulance was just pulling up from the other direction. The short concrete bridge spans the Whetstone Brook where Main nominally becomes Canal in a dip between two hills, right across from the Brattleboro Museum, where I'd met Blaire Wentworth earlier. In the dark of night, the whole area was alive with lights, flashing blue, red, and white off the buildings, the trees, and the pale faces gathered around the wrecked car.

I parked just short of the congestion and walked over to the driver's side of the car. Its nose had become one with a cement pillar securing the south end of the bridge's railing.

John Woll was sitting at the wheel, his face covered with blood, bubbles of which ran gently from his mouth and down his shirt front. His eyes were open and unmoving, staring straight ahead out the shattered windshield. Beyond him, on the car floor, I saw the glint of an empty bottle.

"John?"

He didn't react, which was just as well. I was immediately eased out of the way by several Rescue personnel, who went to work quickly and quietly, putting on a cervical collar and an oxygen mask, wrapping his upper torso in a bracelike vest, and then transferring him to a long wooden backboard.

"You going to the hospital?"

I turned to see Billy Manierre's concerned, fatherly face over an open-necked sport shirt.

"I'd like to, but I don't want to get in your way."

"No problem. Ride with me."

I arranged to have another officer return my borrowed patrol unit to the lot, and Billy and I followed the ambulance in his car.

"What happened?" I asked.

Billy sighed. "He was alone, I guess he fell asleep at the wheel."

"You saw the bottle?"

He nodded. "I saw several more in the back, too."

I shook my head in frustration. "I should have known this would happen, or something like it. Did anyone call Rose?"

Billy turned the car into Belmont Avenue, in front of the hospital, and from there nosed his way into the parking lot. "Rose left him."

I was surprised at that, her words of idealistic support still echoing in my head. "They have a fight?"

"Don't know. The only three words I got out of him were, 'She left me.' "

He parked and we got out of the car, hearing the ambulance's back-up alarm beeping in the night air as it edged toward the emergency room's loading dock. "He's in a world of hurt, Joe."

His voice had the pain of a grieving father.

We sat watching a muted TV in the waiting room while they tended to his needs, giving him X-rays, IV medications, and neurological tests. A nurse came in at one point and asked if we'd like the sound turned up. We both immediately declined, preferring the silence.

A half hour later, a middle-aged woman with an enormous purse stepped into the room from the lobby. She was small and trim, with shoulder-length straight red hair, parted down the middle and held back in a ponytail. She paused when she saw us.

"Are you Lieutenant Gunther?" she asked me.

"Yes." I rose and shook her hand.

"Barb Southworth."

I gestured behind me. "Billy Manierre." Billy half rose and waved.

"John's told me about both of you. He thinks very highly of you."

"Glad to hear it. You're a friend?"

She smiled. "More like a war buddy. I'm an alcoholic, too. John had one of the nurses call me. He wanted me to talk to you."

A nurse appeared from the hallway. "Did one of you want to interview the police officer?"

Billy stood up and tucked his clipboard under his arm. "I'll handle the paperwork. You two chat."

Southworth caught the tone of his voice. "How far is John in trouble?"

"Tonight's little trick alone is a criminal offense, and the papers are going to have a ball with it. How long have you known him?"

She sat in the chair next to mine. "Several years. We met at the Retreat."

The Retreat, along with being a mental-health center, also treated for substance abuse. "AA?"

"Yes, but we were there at different levels. I was on the

bottom, and had little left to lose except my life. John had a long way to go. He was there because his job depended on it."

I caught the implication, as well as the time reference. Their meeting would have been right after John had been caught drinking on the job at the elastics factory. "Didn't he kick the habit?"

She shook her head. "How well do you know John? I mean, really know him?"

"Not well. I know his history somewhat; I know what I've seen as one of his co-workers. This investigation has brought a lot into the limelight."

"He's self-effacing, neat and tidy, eager to please, almost a workaholic at times, right?"

"Close enough. He obviously doesn't have much self-esteem. I suppose that makes him overcompensate somewhat."

"You think part of it is because he's trying to pull himself up by the bootstraps?"

"Sounds reasonable."

She snorted, stood up, and began pacing before me. The gesture revealed a screwed-down nervousness I hadn't focused on earlier. Behind the demure clothing and quiet demeanor was a bundle of energy.

"I kept in touch with him over the years, after he'd dropped out of the program. He liked me, trusted me, and he used me as a sort of miniature AA, which doesn't work, of course. You can't solve this kind of problem by confiding in one person."

I thought back to when I'd found him at home, the glass balanced on his stomach. I described the scene to Barb Southworth.

"You didn't test his blood alcohol?"

I was surprised at the question. "No. We had no cause to. It was ginger ale."

"Well, if you had, I'd lay odds you would have found him fully loaded, or damn near. You saw the glass, jumped to the right conclusion, and then went into full retreat when you found out it wasn't booze. That's what he counted on. I guarantee that if you'd looked for it, you would have found an empty bottle hidden somewhere. He was lying there with a full glass of ginger ale either because he saw you coming, or because he'd run out of the real stuff.''

I was shaken by what she said, not least because it revealed I'd been as gullible as all the rest. I'd come to pride myself on my powers of observation. To discover that a drunk had persuaded me he was sober was a humbling experience.

And yet, I felt there was still something missing, something more important than just being told that John had never been on the wagon.

"Why are you telling us this? Why did John want us to meet?''

"John is still too self-absorbed to make that an easy question to answer, but I think he wanted me to interpret something for him, something he can't put into words himself.''

She paused, as if to gather her thoughts. "Alcoholics . . . all addicts, for that matter . . . are driven by just one desire, and they will do anything to gratify it. On a street level, where appearances don't matter, that means they'll lie, cheat, steal, and even kill to get what they want. At our level, appearances are paramount to survival: We can drink ourselves into the grave as long as no one finds out about us. But, in both cases, it's the addiction that controls everything.''

"So what does that tell us about John Woll?'' I asked.

"That he couldn't have done the things they say he did in the papers, because those things had nothing to do with either satisfying or disguising his addiction.''

"His wife and Jardine were cheating on him.''

Her voice was quiet and calm. "If you were him, being a cuckold might come as a comfort; it would reinforce your rationale for drinking, maybe even make it more acceptable to others. Plus, your self-esteem would be so lousy anyhow, that your wife taking a lover might be exactly what you thought you deserved.''

In an abrupt but fluid movement, she picked up her handbag and walked toward the door, as if suddenly irritated at her role in all this. She paused on the threshold. "I've said what I think John wanted me to say. You've got the wrong man, and while the evidence for that may be psychological, it's hard evidence all the same. Good night.''

I followed her to the glass door and watched her walk away, her red hair highlighted periodically by the lamp posts she passed under. I believed what she had told me. I knew the state's attorney would have to complete the dance he'd started, and that McDonald and Katz and everyone else with a press deadline to meet would play the story until the business office told them it was no longer selling air-time or issues. But for me, the John Woll aspect of this case was over, not just because it had been taken from me physically, but because Woll himself was innocent.

I'd assigned him that position before, of course, but only because my hands were tied. Now, truly believing it, I found the entire case taking a different shape in my mind, as if, by removing John, I'd also removed one of the rocks of the avalanche I'd envisioned burying me earlier, and by doing that, I'd shifted all the others, revealing aspects of them I hadn't previously noticed.

For the first time in days, I felt enlightened. I'd beaten the shadow player who was behind all this, by making a lie of his very first premise.

CHAPTER
30

IT was almost two in the morning when I drove up Gail's steep driveway. Climbing out of the dark embrace of the tree-shrouded road, I was so taken with the vastness of the shimmering, starlit sky that I killed my headlights halfway up to the house and drove the rest of the way without them. It was an almost mystical experience; instead of missing the intense brightness of the car lights, I was overwhelmed by the sky's generosity. I could see everything without shadow, without glare, and, most impressive of all, without color. The landscape's chromatic vitality had been drained to a mere hint, making me feel as if I were intruding upon the huge and empty stage of a long-closed theater.

I got out of the car, closing the door quietly, letting the sensation carry me for a few moments longer. It was fitting that I should feel ethereally suspended; I'd had so little sleep over the past few nights, my brain felt like warm mush, and I was here to reach back through time and to make amends.

"Joe?"

I peered along the length of the deck above me. About halfway down, outlined in black against the sky, I saw Gail's slim shape standing at the rail.

"Hi."

"What are you doing here?"

I was suddenly embarrassed and tongue-tied. How to

explain that watching Barb Southworth walking away, her tale of misery, duplicity, and sorrow in my ears, had made me miss Gail, and regret the tensions that had recently wormed their way between us?

I fell back to the mundane. "I needed to tell you something."

"About John Woll crashing his car?"

I shook my head, beat out by the grapevine again. "No."

Her arm beckoned against the stars. "Come on up."

I climbed the outer staircase to the deck. She remained at a distance, facing me. She was completely naked, her body glowing white in the starlight. In the blackness of the building beside her, she looked as if she were floating.

"It was too hot to sleep inside." Beyond her, shining dully under the stars, I saw her mattress laid out on the deck.

"Take your clothes off."

I hesitated, not wanting to lose sight of why I had come.

"I feel at a disadvantage," she added.

The gentleness of her voice persuaded me.

I pulled off my clothes, feeling awkward and self-conscious, and walked over to her. We didn't touch, but stood side by side, our elbows on the railing, facing the dark slope below and the glow of the city beyond.

"I wanted to apologize for the way I've been acting."

She opened her mouth to respond, but I kept going, wanting it out in the open. "I've used you to comfort myself, but I haven't paid enough attention to how all this has been affecting you."

"It's been affecting all of us, and there's not much you can do about it."

That stung slightly. I wanted her to accept my offer, not remind me of my limitations. But maybe that was her point: I wasn't responsible for everything that had happened.

"Has Jackson kept it up?"

"You'll soon find out for yourself. He's called for a closed-door session of the selectmen with you and Chief Brandt, first thing tomorrow morning."

I hung my head with weariness. "Terrific. Can he do that?"

"Legally? I'm not sure; normally, the town attorney would check on something like that, but I seriously doubt Gary Nadeau's going to stick his neck out." She paused and then let out a short, mirthless laugh. "That's an option, by the way; if it turns out the meeting's illegal, you and Tony could try suing the town."

I whistled at the mere thought. "That might be fun."

She didn't react.

We had been here before, Gail and I: Each of us could see the other's viewpoint, often with empathy, but our responsibilities were frequently at odds. The stress of a mind going down a road not of the heart's choosing could take its toll. It could even border on the absurd. I found it sadly disillusioning to stand next to an attractive, naked woman, under a sparkling-clean sheet of stars, only to ponder the coolness that kept us apart.

"I met a woman who's acted as a kind of unofficial counselor to John with his drinking problem; someone he met at the Retreat."

"What did she have to say?"

"That he's been a closet drinker from the start, that he never did get on the wagon like we'd thought when we rehired him."

"Jackson's going to love that."

"He may not find out about it. The point is, this woman thinks it plays in John's favor. She says an alcoholic like him is so focused on getting his next drink that he doesn't take time off to go running around torturing people."

Gail didn't seem impressed. "Well, if Luman doesn't find out about it, it won't matter, and if he does, he won't care. He'll just say it's self-serving, psychological bullshit. I wouldn't be able to argue the point; a lot of addicts are violent."

I was a little irritated at her narrow view. "The point is, I think John didn't do it; I don't give a damn about Luman Jackson."

"Maybe you should. John Woll isn't the one who's going to drag you over the coals." She paused, reflecting on that very point. "Why has Jackson become so unstrung over this?"

"I've been wondering the same thing. Under different circumstances, I think I'd try to find out."

"How do you mean, different circumstances?"

"I don't have the manpower, and he has the spies, or at least some information pipeline I haven't been able to track. Something came up this morning at a squad meeting which was handed to me on a plate by Brandt this afternoon, right through Luman Jackson."

This time, she showed some interest. "How could that have happened?"

"There was a rational explanation, but I don't know if it was the truth." I ran down the conversation I'd had with Brandt earlier.

She chewed that over for a while in silence. "I guess it's not so hard to figure out why he called tomorrow's meeting. I didn't know he and Wentworth were acquainted, but he sure as hell toadies up to the higher class in this town. It's the only time I ever see him bow and scrape; it's a real stomach-turner, in fact." She let out a long, deep sigh. "What a mess this is."

I moved closer to her and placed my arm around her waist. She reciprocated, and drew me close. I was filled with a sense of relief. Somehow, obliquely, we'd managed to clear the air. Knowing the tough times we'd survived, and the presumably grueling session we were to share in a few hours, I was particularly grateful for this hiatus. With so much general animosity and tension around us, I needed to know that our friendship was sound.

"Thank you, Gail."

She turned and kissed me, her breast brushing my arm. "For what?"

I hesitated, trying to put it right, knowing it would fall short, and that it wouldn't matter anyhow. "For your spirit."

She patted my bare hip. "Come on, let's stare up at the stars for a while."

CHAPTER

31

I had just been handed my mail, my phone messages, and the daily report by Maxine Paroddy through Dispatch's freshly hung door when Tony Brandt left his office diagonally across the room and grabbed me on the way by.

"Ready for the slaughter?" He headed for the back stairs up to the second floor where the selectmen held their meetings.

I was both trying to follow him and go through my correspondence, with more or less success. "I wouldn't mind a cup of coffee first."

"No can do, unless they have some in there." We walked down the upstairs hallway to the front of the building. Ahead of us, clustered in front of the doors leading to, respectively, the town manager's office, the town attorney's office, and the board of selectmen's meeting room, were Tom Wilson, Gary Nadeau, and Brandt's secretary, Judy. Off to one side was James Dunn, whose face looked like he was standing barefoot in manure.

Brandt swept by them as he had me earlier, marching toward the far-left door. "Hi, boys and girls." By his tone and demeanor, he struck me as the happiest of Hannibal's soldiers, off to conquer Rome. I just hoped the results weren't the same.

He led the way into a large, newly redone room, smelling of fresh paint, cut wood, and new carpeting. The back of the room, from where we entered, was filled with metal folding chairs, arranged in rows. Facing us, their backs against the sunlit windows, the five selectmen sat at a long semicircular table, looking like a half-baked imitation of the Supreme Court.

By instinct, we clustered in separate groups: Brandt, Judy, and I off to one side of the center aisle; Wilson and Nadeau to the other. Dunn stayed disdainfully in the rear, by the door, as if planning to leave discreetly as soon as the lights dimmed and the play began.

Indeed, the lighting was theatrical, coming mostly as it did from the windows. It forced us to squint slightly, and made the faces of those across from us dark and slightly menacing. Brandt muttered something to Judy. She looked doubtful but, with a little more prodding, finally got to her feet again and walked around to the back of the selectmen, lowering the blinds of each of the windows with a snap. Dunn, for his part, hit the switch by the door for the overhead lights. Suddenly, the room was bathed in bland, even, artificial light.

Luman Jackson, tall, hawklike, and furiously scowling, twisted in his chair, hoping perhaps to burn Brandt's emissary with the heat of his glare. It almost worked; the poor woman returned to Tony's side looking diminished in stature.

Brandt merely smiled at Jackson. "Sorry. Hard to see."

I noticed Gail was hiding her smile behind her hand.

Jackson was not amused, and pointed at Judy. "What is she doing here? This is an executive session."

"This is my secretary, Judith Levine. I invited her here to take a verbatim transcription of everything that's said today."

"We already have someone doing that." He nodded toward the most recent member of the board, a pale-faced accountant named Orton, who was already scribbling furiously.

"Good," was all Brandt answered.

There was a pause, during which I guessed Brandt was supposed to give Judy her marching orders. He just stared at Jackson, waiting for the meeting to begin. Judy looked like one of the vestal virgins about to be thrown on the fire. I seriously doubted that any notes she took following this would be readable.

Jackson tried a more direct approach: "I'm requesting that you ask your secretary to leave before we begin, Chief Brandt."

"I don't think so, Mr. Chairman, but thank you all the same."

The silence was thundering. I thought I could hear my watch ticking on my wrist. Mrs. Morse, who'd been ineffectually holding her chairman's gavel from the start, slowly leaned over toward Jackson and muttered into his ear. His expression didn't change, but his mind apparently did. He nodded once curtly, and announced as if nothing had happened, "This meeting is now in session."

Gail cleared her throat gently and pointed delicately at Mrs. Morse. Jackson looked from one to the other with irritation and then flushed slightly. Indeed, Mrs. Morse, no shrinking violet herself, looked ready to use the gavel on Jackson's head.

Jackson muttered an apology and Mrs. Morse banged the table top loudly. "Now we are in session."

James Dunn immediately stood up. "Madam Chairman, might I inquire why I was asked to be here? My understanding of the town charter is that executive sessions are held primarily to discuss personnel matters, like salaries and such."

Luman Jackson, whose own frostiness could rival Dunn's, cocked an eyebrow and shut Mrs. Morse up just as she opened her mouth to respond. "Mr. State's Attorney, I can sympathize with your wanting to go back to your office, but to pretend this meeting was called to discuss salaries doesn't do justice to your imagination. We are here to discuss John Woll, who is not only a town employee, but is also being investigated by your office—"

"And as such not a subject for conversation in a setting like this, at least not with me here," Dunn finished for him. "If you, Madam Chairman, or anyone else in this room, wants to know what the state's attorney's office is doing about John Woll, you will just have to wait until that investigation has been concluded."

With that, Dunn turned on his heel and left the room, closing the door behind him with a bang. Jackson was looking less and less like the vice-chairman he was, and more like an angry, frustrated caricature carved in stone. We hadn't been here five minutes, and already the air had enough electricity in it to power the town for a week.

Brandt chose that moment to clear his throat. "Madam Chairman, with the departure of Mr. Dunn, I suggest that any further discussion of John Woll be tabled. As you are aware, the Police Department has been cut out of that investigation and has handed over all its files to the SA's office. I'm sure Mr. Nadeau would agree with me that any official discussion of the case without Mr. Dunn might well be treading onto very thin legal ice."

Mrs. Morse, not bothering to compete verbally, merely pointed her gavel at a pale and nervous Gary Nadeau, who nodded, also without a word.

"Let it be noted that the town attorney is in agreement with the chief," she intoned, pleased at last to be heard.

Tom Wilson, who was no Richard the Lionhearted, but who also disliked Jackson with a passion, raised his hand. "That brings up the advisedness of this entire meeting, actually. Mr. Dunn mentioned the town charter; if indeed we are to deal with personnel matters in any detail, it is my understanding that I as town manager am supposed to be the board's agent in these matters, and that the board should be called together to discuss such a case only after I've completed my own investigation."

Jackson whacked the table before him in irritation with his open hand. "I've had just about enough of this. You bureaucrats can run for cover all you want, but something stinks here, and I intend to find out what it is. I don't give a rat's ass what's in the charter, and nobody's going to tell me that I can or cannot ask certain questions while the whole goddamn town is falling down like a house of cards."

"That may be overstating the case a bit," Gail said levelly, from her end of the curved table.

Jackson flared. "Maybe from your vantage point, Miss Zigman, but not all of us share your source of information, or your obvious bias." He shifted his attention back to the rest of us, allowing Gail to redden angrily more or less in private. "My phone is ringing at all hours of the day and night; I'm getting calls from newspapers in California, for Christ's sake. 'Is it true that Brattleboro has become the chute for Massachusetts's dirty laundry?' That's what one of them asked me. That's not good for business or morale, and by allowing it to continue, it might just become true."

Gail sailed back in. "What's the point, Mr. Vice-Chairman?"

It seemed to me Jackson's frustration was so real he could barely give it voice. Despite my antipathy for the man, I began to feel slightly sorry for him. "The point is: I want to know what's happening here. I hear our building inspector is being investigated for no good reason. I hear one of our most eminent citizens is suspected of fraudulent financial dealings. I hear a perfectly respectable businessman had all his records removed by the police, again for no apparent reason. There've been shootings, high-speed chases, and now a DWI involving a cop who's also suspected of murder. It sounds like our Police Department is both corrupt and stupid. And the result, I might add, will be more lawsuits than this town has ever seen. I'm sick and tired of looking like a moron to everyone who asks me what's going on, and I want some answers. Now."

There was a general rustling following this, as everyone either shifted through paperwork or squirmed in their chairs, figuratively looking for some sort of cover. Tom Wilson glanced at Brandt, who merely smiled and extended his hand in invitation; these people were more Wilson's bosses than Brandt's, the gesture said, so be my guest.

Wilson sighed and addressed the board. "Madam Chairman, I wish I could accommodate you and your colleagues here, and I'll certainly do the best I can, with Chief Brandt's cooperation, of course. Despite the setbacks, the confusion, and all the press, the Police Department is doing its job. Progress is being made, and the instances you mentioned of what looked like random police activity all have clear and reasonable explanations——"

"Of which we can give you only the barest outline," Brandt added.

"I'll start with that," Jackson said. "God knows I don't have a damned thing now."

I sensed from the tone that things were settling down slightly, entering a purely informational phase. Wilson and Brandt were to become, for the next several minutes, the feeders at the lion cage, doling out morsels to a beast with an appetite for both their arms. I turned my attention to the wad of papers that Maxine Paroddy had handed me earlier.

It turned out Jackson hadn't been the only one to get calls from reporters in California. I gave up on the phone messages about halfway through and turned to the daily report to see if anything new had surfaced during the night shift. Apart from the usual array of domestic disputes, a barroom brawl, and a foot chase after a teenager who'd been trying to pry open a bank's night-deposit box with a crowbar, the report told me nothing I wanted to know. I wished to hell I'd been able to get to my office before I'd been dragged in here, so I could have had a peek at our own inner-office report.

Disappointed, I returned to my mail, dimly aware of the back and forth goings-on at the front of the room. Wilson, with little help from Brandt, was trying to explain the necessity of checking into everything and everybody in a case like this, even at the risk of stepping on toes.

My mail was also unenlightening: equipment brochures, official junk mail from the state capital, notifications of various classes being offered to police officers, from first aid to SWAT tactics. I went back to the phone messages, this time starting from the bottom of the pile.

The fifth one up froze me in my seat: Isador Gramm, Beverly Hillstrom's forensic toxicologist, had called with "interesting news." The message indicated he'd called just five minutes before I'd been dragged into this kangaroo proceeding.

I snapped out of my reverie at the mention of my name.

"—been up to, nosing around like some damn tabloid reporter?"

Brandt answered. "His job, Mr. Vice-Chairman, which he can't do sitting here."

"He is the one heading this investigation, is he not?"

"He is, but he will not be allowed to speak on that matter."

Jackson bristled. "What the hell does that mean?"

"Please," Mrs. Morse muttered, looking at Jackson.

"It means I won't let him. I am head of the department, and everything Lieutenant Gunther does is cleared through me. I will be his spokesman at this meeting and I think you'll find that doing otherwise will only get all of us into more hot water if and when the press finds out about this little get-together."

"I do not intend that they find out."

Brandt didn't argue the point. "May Lieutenant Gunther be excused from these proceedings?"

It wasn't, from his tone of voice, a debatable question.

As Mrs. Morse said, "Of course," Jackson barked out, "No." They stared at each other for a long moment, the lady's knuckles white where she was gripping her weapon of office. Jackson, either cowed or mollified that Brandt himself had no intention of leaving, finally nodded and muttered, "Oh, all right."

I gathered my wad of papers, smiled back at Gail's quick and tiny thumbs-up gesture, and left.

Outside, on the landing, I met Stan Katz coming up the stairs. He looked as exhausted as I felt. We eyed one another warily. "Hey there, Stanley."

"Hey, yourself. See the paper this morning?" The question was asked neutrally, even tentatively.

"Nope. You take John to the cleaners?"

He sighed and his shoulders sagged slightly. It made me wonder for the first time about the toll this kind of story took on the man reporting it. It was a jarring thought, and not one I enjoyed; things were tough enough without wondering if Stanley Katz had feelings.

"I wrote about the accident and put it in context," he said tiredly. "How're they doin' in there?" He motioned toward the room I'd just left.

I feigned ignorance, Jackson's claim that the press would never hear of the meeting still echoing in my ears. "They?"

"The selectmen. The executive session."

I played with the idea of giving him the standard "no

comment,'' but thought better of it suddenly, realizing I had nothing to lose here. "How'd you hear about it? Jackson thinks the meeting's top secret."

Katz grinned, the carnivore in him resurfacing. "Really? Maybe I ought to call Ted and the others to fill up the hallway. That would startle him."

I shrugged, resigned to his not revealing his source. "Be my guest."

He chuckled, the idea growing on him. "I think I will. Why're you out here, by the way?"

"Brandt cut me loose. Told 'em he wouldn't let me talk to them—that they'd have to go through him."

This time, he laughed outright. "Damn, your boss has balls."

"Dunn walked out at the start; said he'd talk when he was good and ready."

"Christ, how's Jackson taking it?"

"Hasn't blown a fuse yet, but Mrs. Morse is about ready to kill him. Might be worth sticking around."

He shook his head, still grinning. "I gotta get to a phone." He stopped suddenly, his eyes narrowing to their familiar suspicious squint. "Why'd you just tell me all that?"

I laughed, heading for the stairs. " 'Cause I don't give a damn and I'm in a good mood."

I didn't even pause to turn on Buddy's stolen fan before dialing Isador Gramm's number.

He answered on the fourth ring. "Dr. Gramm."

"This is Joe Gunther, down in Brattleboro. Sorry I wasn't in earlier."

"Oh, nice of you to call back. I think I may have found something in your case. It was one of those brain teasers, you know? I kept coming up with reasonable possibilities and getting nowhere. Had it not been for the tissue sample Dr. Hillstrom let me have, I'd probably still be barking up the wrong tree."

"So what was it that killed him?"

There was a deadening pause. "Killed him? Cerebral ischemia; I thought you knew that. Dr. Hillstrom didn't tell me I was to determine cause of death."

I swore softly under my breath at the literalness of the scientific mind. "Sorry, I meant what was injected into him?"

"Tubocurarine chloride."

"What the hell is that?"

I shut my eyes at my own outburst, but Gramm merely laughed. He was obviously so pleased with his own detective work, nothing was going to dampen his spirits. "In layman's terms, curare."

My mouth fell open. "Curare? As in South American Indians and blowguns?"

He was still chuckling. "Pretty weird, huh? It's a quaternary amine, the bane of toxicology, a real pain in the butt to analyze, unless you know what you're looking for, or you just get lucky. I guess I benefited from both."

I was still having a tough time mentally transplanting tribal tranquilizers into a Brattleboro setting. "Why curare?"

"Well, that's it exactly. Actually, you helped in this discovery. It was your comment to Dr. Hillstrom about the dichotomy of the presenting evidence that started me thinking along the proper lines. The hypothesis ran that the victim was positioned so that he could witness his own death, both visually and, since the method chosen was so specifically painful, sensorially. And yet, while his limbs had been taped to inhibit movement, there were no signs of his having struggled against those bonds, despite the pain he experienced during the terminating process."

I winced at the phrase "terminating process," but Gramm went happily on. "That turns out to have been the watershed deduction, steering me away from the narcotics which, while subduing the patient, would have also subdued his sensitivity to pain. It was in thinking about that seemingly contradictory requirement—to numb the muscles but not the neurological sensitivity—that I suddenly remembered an extraordinary experiment I'd read about that took place in the late 1800s.

"There was this doctor who had his colleagues overdose him with curare to test the drug's properties. Back in those days, it wasn't as exotic as it seems today, but it also wasn't very well understood. They were standing by, of course, ready to give him artificial respirations if he needed them, and it was a lucky thing, too. He had the most horrible experience. He couldn't move, couldn't breathe, couldn't do the slightest thing. He felt like he was gagging to death, feeling his saliva running down his throat without being able to swallow. That was the first experiment to clearly identify the full range of effects of curare on a human being. Crazy thing to do, of course, but scientists tended to be that way back then; real adventurers."

I was running his words through my mind, translating them to fit my notion of how Jardine died. "You said he couldn't breathe."

"Ah, right, but he'd been given a series of escalating doses, to determine the various stages of the drug's effects. The respiratory muscles are the last to go, as it turns out, and the first to recover. So, if the injection came to just below that effect, the victim would never suffer from respiratory arrest. He would just be rendered totally motionless. In retrospect, it fits your case like a glove."

Gramm sounded positively delighted, for which I couldn't really fault him. The closest he'd come to Charlie Jardine had been a tiny chunk of meat in a test tube.

"But the victim would feel pain?"

"Oh, absolutely. Remember I said that doctor felt the saliva running down the back of his throat; that indicates his neurological antennae, if you will, were still perfectly functional. It's the muscles that are affected. The patient can still hear, see, and feel normally."

I was still half stunned by the oddness of this discovery, and becoming hopeful that its uniqueness might eventually be the killer's undoing. A knife, after all, could be gotten almost anywhere. But curare?

"So where can you get this stuff? South America?"

Gramm laughed again. "Good lord, no. I mean, you can, of course, but it's a lot easier to locate than that. It's not as rare as it sounds, and it's not a regulated drug, so no DEA license is needed. It's not in everyday use, but it's still handy in surgery where the patient's neurological receptors need to be intact. Hospitals carry it, and so do most decent-sized veterinary clinics."

"As in animal vets?"

"Yup. Of course, the doses they carry are smaller, as befits the size of their average customer."

I was wracking my brain, trying to come up with the right questions, the answers to which might point me in the proper direction. "How do you administer the stuff? Is injection the only way?"

"Yes, that's why the Indians can eat the birds they kill with their famous curare-tipped arrows or darts. It has no effect when injested."

"You mentioned the doctor took it in progressive doses, until he couldn't breathe. Doesn't that make it tricky to administer?"

Gramm sounded pleased. "Ah, very good. Yes, that's true. The recommendation accompanying tubocurarine chloride is that it be administered only by a trained anesthesiologist. Of course, that's only true when you're out to benefit the patient; clearly, that doesn't apply here."

"It may not apply, but presumably the killer didn't want Jardine to die on him before he was ready."

Gramm's voice was suddenly doubtful. "Jardine?"

Again, I was reminded of the man's distance from the case. "That was the dead man's name."

"Oh, sorry, I wasn't told. Well, anyway, I suppose you're right. Still, the injection could have been administered gradually, so that its effects could be monitored. That would account for the victim being bound. On the other hand, the drug only lasts ten minutes or so, then it has to be boostered with another dose, half the strength of the first. That part's important, since curare is additive."

"But there was only one injection site."

Gramm mulled that over for a while. "True. Well, there's always the element of dumb luck, especially if the dose was secured from a vet."

"Because it's smaller, you mean?"

"Right. The killer could inject the entire dose at once and get away lucky. Chances are a full-sized, healthy man could survive that, if just barely. And I guess the killer wouldn't be too concerned either way. I mean, the worst thing that could happen is that the victim would die. It wouldn't be painful, but it would still be a terrible experience, tantamount to suffocating in the midst of fresh air.''

Terrible maybe, but the victim hadn't died of curare. The dosage had been perfect. I wrapped up the conversation with my thanks and a few pleasantries, and hung up.

I stuck my head out the door and yelled for Ron Klesczewski. He appeared from around the cluster of cubicles in the middle of the room and followed me back into my office. I scribbled "tubocurarine chloride" on a piece of paper and handed it to him. "That's the fancy name for curare. That's what was injected into Charlie Jardine to keep him still while he was being strangled."

Ron stared at the name. "Holy shit."

"Apparently, this stuff's available in hospitals and vet clinics, and maybe by prescription. I want you to check out every source around here and find out if any of it's either gone missing, say within the last year or two, or if anyone has bought any legally."

As he started to leave, I grabbed his elbow. "Ron, if we can nail this down, we might find out who was behind this mess. I don't want anyone to know what we're up to, okay? When you're doing your inquiry, make up a story of some kind—an animal poisoning, anything to throw people off."

Ron nodded. "Gotcha."

I sat back in my chair and closed my eyes for a moment, thinking hard. A rare drug, requiring careful administration. Which of my suspects had that kind of training in his or her background? And why be so eccentric when any number of more mundane drugs could have been used? I was dealing with an ego here, someone consciously leaving a signature.

Harriet appeared on my threshold, holding another pink phone message. "Thought you'd like this right away, pretty mysterious."

The message I took from her read, "Drop by the library."

• • •

I found Willy Kunkle back in the local-history room, sorting through his card catalog. "Don't they ever let you out of here?"

He ignored any preliminary niceties, continuing to flip through the index cards as he spoke. "Jake Hanson, Mark Cappelli, and the two bankers were in cahoots, but as far as I can tell, the girl was played for a patsy by her boy friend. He needed a teller and sucked up to the dumbest one he could find."

I remained silent.

Kunkle finally raised his head and smiled at me. "The catch is, they were not working with Milly."

I stared at him, my mind trying to place this new fact in order. "But what about all that coke? You saying it wasn't his?"

"I don't know, but the people sure weren't. Nor was Johnnie Woll, if that's any comfort. I think he was thrown in because it was an easy frame."

"Who were the other people on the list? Rivals?"

"You got it."

"Working for who?"

"Flatlanders from Boston. They aren't anymore, though. That's why all you got was the girl. After Cappelli jumped to conclusions and took a shot at you, the publicity caused the Boston boys to end the relationship. Too bad for Hanson; he'd been working with them for years."

I shook my head slowly. "So the list was a plant, sending us in two wrong directions at once."

Kunkle grinned. "Yup. It got John Woll into hot water, and it got you guys to close down a rival dope ring."

I looked at him closely. "You're sure about all this."

He held up three fingers. "Scout's honor."

"All right. Let's break this down into segments. If we cross off everyone on the list, who do we have working with Milly? He's the connection to the streets—the seller. In fact, he may have sold that baggie to Jardine."

"Or it may have been a freebie to Jardine for having supplied the money to buy the stuff in the first place."

I nodded. "Okay, which makes Charlie the money man. You think either Charlie or Milly had any big-time dope connections—someone who could supply them with a stash that large?"

"Hanson and Cappelli were supplied out of Boston. I

don't know much about Jardine, but I can guarantee you, nobody in Boston would look twice at Milly, much less sell him a kilo of coke.''

"So the supplier was either Charlie or a third guy.''

"I like Wentworth as the money man. He's got lots of it. Didn't you check on Charlie's finances?''

"Yeah, and they came up clean. He inherited eighty-five thousand dollars and put it all into ABC Investments. In fact, I'm pretty sure Wentworth made him a guarantee of sorts—that if Charlie lost his shirt, Wentworth would make up the losses; ABC was the old man's idea, after all.''

Willy was obviously enjoying himself. "Sure, what the hell, make Wentworth the money man, maybe unknowingly, and Charlie the pimp in between, turning the money into dope.''

I put my hands to my temples. "Let's slow down. We've got nothing on these people. Except for Milly, this is all pure guesswork.''

Willy shrugged. "Go back to Milly, then.''

"Right. Why was he killed?''

"Because you were about to talk to him.''

"Come up with another reason.''

Willy shook his head. "Like you and the killer were there at the same time by coincidence? No way; the thumbprint identified Milly, so Milly had to die.''

"But why?'' I repeated.

"Because Milly could identify the killer.''

"As what? Were they partners?''

"Maybe; maybe not. If they weren't, then the dope wouldn't be the first priority; the killer might not have even known about it.''

"All right. That's one explanation for why the dope was left behind. What's another?''

"No time; you and the killer were minutes apart at most.''

"But it took time to plant the list of names. You don't carry phone numbers like that around in your head.'' I snapped my fingers. "Try this: You have a small amount of time available to you, only enough to do one of two things. You can go to a phone book and construct a phony list of numbers to plant, or you can go straight to Milly's apartment, knock him off, and take the time to steal as much dope as you can.''

Kunkle was tapping his foot nervously. ''And the killer opted for the list. What does that tell us?''

''That framing either John Woll or the rival drug ring was more important than the dope, and worth the risk of getting caught while killing Milly.''

Kunkle whistled. ''So we're talking serious motivation, something way beyond just protecting an identity.''

''Right. You implied the Woll frame was an extra, thrown in because it was easy. Why even go to that trouble?''

''Because it's personal. He's too low-ranking a cop for it to be anything involving the department.''

''Which makes the list an insight into the killer's personality. That list, with its flimsy frame of John Woll, is the only evidence combining the two tangents here: the drugs and the Charlie-John-Rose triangle, which has roots ten years old.''

Kunkle scowled impatiently. ''I can't deal with the triangle; it's too complicated, and you've got nothing concrete to go on. I think if you follow the dope, you'll find the shooter.''

''But he didn't touch the dope. You said yourself he might not have even known it was there.''

Kunkle waved that away. ''I know, I know; I don't believe it, though. You want a gut reaction? People kill each other over dope, even small amounts of it, and I think that's why Milly got whacked. Why was the dope left behind? It wasn't only a time problem; otherwise, the shooter would've killed you and Dummy both and had plenty of time to pack up. It was left behind because it was small potatoes. That's the big question here; it's not whether Wentworth knew about the money, or whether Jardine was or wasn't a partner of Milly's. It's what's the story behind the dope?''

I looked at his impassioned face, radiating an enthusiasm I hadn't seen in over a year. ''Will you find out the answer?''

He pulled back a little, flexing the hand he'd made into a

fist during his last speech. He made it sound nonchalant.
"Yeah, I can ask around."

I couldn't suppress a smile. For the first time, I felt we
might have gained an advantage, and with it reached a
turning point. If I was right, the manipulator would become
the quarry, and the hunt would begin in earnest.

CHAPTER

32

DESPITE Kunkle's lack of interest in the subject, the money angle continued to prey on my mind as I returned to the Municipal Center. It galled me not knowing for certain whether Milly's stake had come from Jardine, or from a source I knew nothing about. The irritant was the coyness of those involved: Wentworth, Arthur Clyde, and Blaire, while all affected more or less by Jardine's death, nevertheless seemed preoccupied with details they wanted kept well out of sight.

I was therefore startled when Sammie Martens intercepted me at the Municipal Building's front door. "I think I found something," she said, her face flushed with excitement.

I looked at her, not bothering to hide my surprise. It had been a while since I'd touched base with her. "What?"

"I discovered Fred McDermott has an anonymous bank account."

"McDermott? I thought J.P. was checking into him."

"I had the contact at the bank, so he let me have a crack at it."

I smiled at her irrepressible ambition. "How much did you find?"

"Fifty thousand, built up over the last year or so."

I sat down in the shade on the uppermost step, stunned. Below me, I saw the traffic trying to sort its way through another of the town's onerous intersections. "What do you mean by 'anonymous'?"

"It's under his middle name. The money only goes in; it doesn't go out. Desposits have been large, and regular as rain. I thought I'd poke a little into his finances, not so much that I'd need a warrant, but just kind of chatting with a friend of mine in the bank. She volunteered that she'd stumbled over this thing a while back—had figured out that the account was really McDermott's—but hadn't given it much thought until I brought up his name."

"How did she make the connection to McDermott?"

"The address. McDermott doesn't bank there under his real name anymore, but he used to, and his address was still on file. She was checking some accounts, hit the wrong entry on the computer, and discovered the same address under Ellison, which is McDermott's middle name. And McDermott's lived in the same place for twenty-five years. I checked."

"Do you know about this account for a fact?"

She smiled. "No. I didn't go digging through his files. This was purely conversational. If we can get a subpoena, it'll hold up in court."

I shook my head. "I don't see how we could get one, not at this point. For all we know, he has some investments that've been paying off, or some rich aunt who died and left him a fortune."

"We could ask him."

"I don't think so. If he's dirty, he already knows we're sniffing around. There's nothing to be gained by tipping him off we found his nest egg. We'll have to come at him from another direction. Nice work, though."

She grinned. "Hey. I got lucky."

Lucky, indeed, I thought. Just when I want to find a sizeable amount of clandestine money, it falls into my lap. Kunkle and I had not worked McDermott into our equation, but now that he was there, he presented some interesting possibilities. His office in the building behind me allowed him casual scrutiny of the Police Department, his demeanor and general blandness made him a person most people overlooked, and his job as building inspector, if properly manipulated, could be made a large producer of under-the-counter cash.

It occurred to me suddenly that perhaps we'd been too clever by half in our investigation of this case, constructing elaborate schemes involving millionaires, stockbrokers, and rival drug gangs. What if dull Fred McDermott, without fanfare and fuss, had been doing business on the side?

I sat there for thirty minutes, plugging him into the question-and-answer game I'd come to know by heart over the past few days. The results were as unsatisfying as ever. As a suspect, McDermott had his place, along with half a dozen others, it seemed, but it still wasn't a perfect fit.

I remembered when we were kids, my brother Leo and I would lie on our backs of a sunny Sunday afternoon, watching the clouds float by overhead. He would claim to see some form or another in a cloud, and I would try to come up with something completely different. Sometimes, we managed to conjure up four or five different shapes apiece out of a single lumpy cloud.

Was I doing the same thing with this case, I wondered? I sighed, shaking my head, and retreated into the Municipal Building.

• • •

My depression did not last long. I hadn't even reached the detective bureau's door before Maxine called over to me that Ron Klesczewski had requested I meet him at the West River Veterinary Clinic. Mention of the location alone gave me an enormous lift. Dr. Gramm had said curare might be available at hospitals or veterinary clinics. If Klesczewski had indeed managed to tie a supply source to the curare Gramm had found in Charlie Jardine, we'd taken a giant step toward finding out who had wielded the syringe.

The West River Clinic was located in the North Shopping Plaza, the second of three malls lining the overcommercialized Putney Road. The plaza, despite its name, was not an open square of shops, but rather a gargantuan spread of black macadam, lined only at the back with one solid wall of stores. I parked next to Klesczewski's unmarked car.

Ron met me on the sidewalk in front of the clinic's front door. "I think we hit the jackpot. Aside from the hospital, this is the only source of curare in town. The hospital's supply is tiny: one bottle, buried in the back of a locked cabinet in a very secure area; they never use the stuff. Also, this place was burgled about nine months ago. At the time, nothing was reported missing, but today, after I asked them to check their stock, the people here think that about four vials of curare are missing from a total of ten."

Inside, Klesczewski introduced me to a middle-aged woman in a white lab coat, who led us to a back room, half stock area, and apparently half laboratory. The woman's name was Dr. Thelma Richie.

"We don't use this room too often," she explained. "It's mostly storage. Almost everything is prepackaged these days, and we send out most of our lab work."

She looked from one of us to the other, her hands in her coat pockets, as if making sure we thoroughly understood.

"In other words, while we come in here fairly frequently, it's mostly just to grab something, which is why we overlooked the missing tubocurarine."

Ron added, "Dr. Richie explained that at the time of the burglary, they focused their attention on some destruction in the filing room and one of the offices."

"Nothing was taken, though," Dr. Richie interjected. "I mean, that's what we thought at the time."

Ron continued. "I figure it was a smoke screen, that the curare was the target all along."

I gestured to a glass-doored cabinet mounted on the wall, its shelves crowded with rows of small bottles and colorful cardboard containers. "It's kept in there?"

"That's correct," she answered.

"Has anyone used the cabinet since the burglary?"

"No. Your sergeant asked me that, and I've checked with the staff."

Ron and I exchanged glances.

"Want me to get Tyler in with his evidence kit?"

I was about to answer when Dr. Richie interrupted. "You mean to lift prints off the cabinet?"

"Yes."

She shook her head. "I wouldn't bother. It gets wiped down regularly, along with everything else. Helps customer confidence if everything looks shiny, even back here."

Ron pulled a long face, prompting her to add, "but not the contents of the case."

I crossed over to it and pulled its doors open. "Not locked?"

She looked sightly embarrassed. "Well, none of these are regulated drugs, but, to be honest, I lost the key a few years ago."

"Which is the curare?"

She pointed to the top shelf, where the normally neat rows of bottles had been disturbed. "If you're after prints, that's where they'll be. They pack some of these things in sawdust or plastic peanuts for shipping, so we wipe them off as we unpack them. That should help."

I couldn't resist smiling. "Hope springs eternal. Can I use your phone?"

I tried calling Tyler at the Municipal Building, but he was out and didn't respond to his pager. Unfortunately, that came as no surprise. His pager was ancient and had been slated for replacement for two years, but at five hundred bucks a whack, we'd been told to make do. I hung up and returned to the back room, explaining the situation.

Dr. Richie gave a wide smile. "Is an evidence kit just a way to collect things, to keep them uncontaminated until analysis?"

We both nodded.

"Well, remember, I said we ship most of our lab work out. We probably have most of what you need."

Indeed they did. Within a half hour, using rubber gloves and tweezers, we'd tucked all the bottles we thought relevant into separate plastic bags, which in turn we placed in a rugged cardboard box filled with packing material. The end result, I thought, would have made Tyler proud.

We gave Dr. Richie our thanks and a receipt, and headed out to the slowly dimming parking lot, shading our eyes against the sunset's reflection in the car windows aligned ahead of us.

We were some forty feet from our cars, with Ron carrying

the box in his arms, when I sensed rather than heard a vehicle coming up behind us.

I interrupted Ron, who was remarking on our good fortune. "Better shove over; car coming."

We glanced over our shoulders and ended up frozen in mid-step. Bearing down on us, with a sudden, tire-squealing burst of acceleration, was a dark, rust-spotted van. The driver was wearing a mask.

Instinct taking over, Ron dropped the box, and we both dove to either side, the van cutting between us with inches to spare, or so I thought until I heard Ron's shout of pain. I'd landed on my side between two parked cars and quickly swiveled around to see Ron curled up in the middle of the traffic lane, both arms wrapped around his left knee. Between us, the box lay unharmed, the wheels of the van having neatly straddled it.

Just as I turned to check on the van, hoping to make at least a partial ID, I heard again the squeal of its tires and saw it tearing back down on us in reverse.

"Ron, look out."

Klesczewski began scrambling awkwardly toward the opposite row of cars, and in the split second it took for me to gauge his chances of success, I realized the van wasn't coming for him. It was aimed diagonally across the lane at the box.

Without pausing for thought, I knew instantly that the contents of that box must be what we'd been looking for from the moment we'd found Charlie's body in his grave; the one mistake that would link his murder to the man who had committed it. Starting from all fours, only dimly aware of the onrushing vehicle to my right, I flew out from between the cars, my body pitched forward as in a dive, and slapped the box as I sailed over it, my momentum sending both it and me skidding across the asphalt toward where Ron was staring at me openmouthed. The van roared by, just grazing my foot as it was still in midair.

There was a shrieking, metal-crumpling crash as the van's rear end piled into the parked cars near where I'd been hiding.

"Get the box. He's after the box."

Ron spun around, sweeping the box up with one arm, and half rolled, half dove between the far row of cars, with me close on his heels. In our ears, for the last time, we heard the van's burning tires scream past, as our pursuer gave up and blasted out of the parking lot.

Lying there, dirty, bruised, and bleeding from various cuts and scrapes, I instinctively groped for my radio. Ron reached his first, pulling it from his belt savagely enough to tear the metal clip off its back. He reported an approximately ten-year-old, black and rusting van with no side windows, and two unreadable bumper stickers on the rear, heading north out of town on the Putney Road. He paused, after a glance at me, and he added that both Vermont license number and driver identification were unknown.

After receiving acknowledgment, he dropped the radio on the ground and lay back against one of the cars.

There was a long pause, filled only with our rapid breathing, before I asked him, "How's the leg?"

"Hurt's like a bitch."

"Can you move it?"

He tried, and winced.

I reached for the radio and added, "You better send Rescue for an injured leg—the North Shopping Plaza parking lot."

I pulled the box toward me and opened its top. Ron looked at me, his face red and soaked with sweat. "How is it?"

I poked around gingerly and grinned. "Couldn't be better."

•   •   •

As it turned out, we both made a trip to the hospital, Ron to have his leg X-rayed and treated for what turned out to be a severe sprain, and I to have some of the gravel dug out of my palms and knees.

J.P. Tyler met me in one of the treatment rooms in the Emergency Department just as I was pulling the tattered remains of my pants back down over my bandaged knees. The box from the veterinary clinic was sitting safely by my side on the bed.

"What the hell happened?"

"Attempted hit-and-run. And that was the target." I jerked my thumb at the box and explained about the curare and our hopes that the thief had left his prints behind on some of the other bottles. J.P. gingerly opened the box, shaking his head in wonder at my description of how the drug worked.

"If my guess is right," I continued, "that holds the major key to this case, or at least the killer thinks it does. Which brings up another point, something I want kept just between the two of us for the moment."

Tyler reclosed the box and looked at me.

"I want you to sweep my office for a listening device."

"You're kidding."

"This morning, I brought Ron into my office and told him about the curare; the only other time I mentioned the stuff was on the phone when I first heard about it. I haven't written anything yet in the reports, I haven't even brought Brandt up to date. Yet someone knew enough to ambush us outside the vet's office. I'm beginning to wonder whether someone hasn't placed a bug in the office. With all the construction going on, it's not inconceivable. And it would explain some of the other leaks we've been having. It would also explain how the killer knew about my attempt to talk to Milly. We'd thought his killer had just tailed me to Horton Place and then gotten the jump on us, but a bug could've given him an even bigger edge. You got something you could sweep my office with?"

He nodded. "I have an AM radio. It'll work as long as the device isn't too fancy."

I tried to keep the skepticism out of my voice. I was expecting something higher-tech than an AM radio. I pointed at the box. "All right. Check this out for prints first, and guard it like Fort Knox. We'll do the sweep after hours. And keep this to yourself, okay?"

"You got it."

I slid off the hospital bed and shuffled painfully down the hall to the nurse's station.

A young woman in white with a small pink teddy bear pinned to her collar looked up at me and smiled. "All set?"

"Yes. Could you tell me what room John Woll's in? I just want to poke my head in to see how he's doing."

She gave me a pleasant shrug. "Better than you, I guess. He checked out."

"Already? I thought they'd hold him for a while."

She shook her head. "He just looked bad. Once the alcohol wore off, he was fine. Facial cuts do that sometimes—they look much worse than they are. Lucky guy."

I thanked her and left, the irony of her last words like a bitter taste in my mouth. Tomorrow, I thought, Dunn or no Dunn, I'd go by John's place to check up on him.

• • •

Tyler was unpacking what indeed looked like a large transistor radio from a briefcase when I limped into the squad room at nine, after dining on a steaming, limp, microwaved ham-and-cheese grinder at the convenience store across from the Courthouse. He turned to greet me, but I silenced him by putting my finger to my lips and motioning to him to follow me outside.

"What'd you find?" I asked him in the parking lot.

He wobbled his right hand from side to side. "Good news, bad news. The bottles had prints, enough good ones to make a match, but not from my files. If the guy has a record, it's not with us. I Fed-Exed what I got to both Waterbury and the FBI with a red flag on both. So we're going to have to wait and pray."

"How about ruling anyone out?"

"I'm working on that. The easy exclusions are Charlie Jardine and Milly Crawford, and the entire staff at the vet clinic. All their prints were either on file or easily accessible. I don't know how you're going to get any from the Wentworths or Arthur Clyde or even Fred McDermott without a legal fight. The biggies, of course, are John and Rose Woll. I called the state's attorney's office to see about getting sample prints from them. They said they'd call me back." His expression told me how much credibility he pinned on that happening anytime soon.

"By the way," he added. "I took a little time to check on

Fred McDermott's whereabouts at the time you and Ron were being run over. He was out of his office all afternoon. They found the van, too, in Dummerston, clean as a whistle. It'd been stolen.''

I was disappointed about the prints, but I thanked him for his speed, complimented him on taking the proper initiative, and led the way back inside. Outside the veterinarian's, with the squeal of the killer's tires still in my ears, I was convinced I had my hand on the prize. Now I had to face the possibility that the killer's prints were not on file at all—leaving us with something, but not the jackpot. Still, I thought as we reentered the squad room, at least we could eliminate some of the suspects, even the dead ones, and narrow the field a bit.

McDermott, of course, seemed the obvious number-one choice, but what stuck in my craw there was that, if he had been clever enough to present such a sterling facade all these years, why had he been dumb enough to set up an illicit checking account under his own middle name and address? It was an inconsistency that had been tugging at me for most of the day.

Also, that afternoon, Sammie had reported on her search through McDermott's past. Hours of digging through files at the town clerk's and the tax-assessor's offices had revealed the man's life to be as bland as his appearance.

I pointed at the radio on Tyler's desk and raised my eyebrows. He nodded and switched it on. Tinny music filled the room before he tuned it to soft static between two stations. Shaking my head in doubt, I followed him into my office.

For about three-quarters of an hour, I sat on the edge of my desk and watched him pace slowly back and forth, the extended antenna on his radio hovering like a nervous hummingbird over the phone, the desk, the fan, the carpeting, the walls, the radiator, the wall switch, the filing cabinet, even my office chair. Throughout the entire process, the slight hum emanating from his speaker never altered. Until he reached the false-ceiling panels.

He was standing on a chair by then, working in a three-foot-square grid near two intersecting walls, when the static gave out an ever-increasing howl of protest, affronted by what it had found.

He quickly killed the power switch and looked down at me in the now-accusing silence, his face questioning. I motioned him down and took his place on the chair.

Gently, the fingers of both my hands splayed, I carefully exerted pressure on the white-foam panel directly overhead. It resisted at first, but then, with an almost imperceptible pop, it freed itself from the surrounding metal framing. I slowly moved it to one side and peered into the semidarkness captured between the real and false ceilings. There, two feet away, dangling from a wire above and twinkling in the half-light, was a small microphone.

I replaced the panel, descended from my perch, and pulled a sheet of paper from my desk. On it I wrote, "One bug, coming from above. Let's try to trace it without being seen."

He nodded, reached into his pocket, pulled out a key, and mouthed, "master key."

I chuckled softly and gave him a thumbs-up. Leaving his detector behind, we both headed out the door and one flight up.

Avoiding detection was no great feat. Only the Police Department was manned at this time of night, so the janitor remained our sole other concern.

Nevertheless, we proceeded like cat burglars, walking on the balls of our feet, keeping to the walls, furtively looking about. Had we run into Buddy, he would have thought we'd lost our minds.

We didn't meet anyone, however, and arrived on the floor over our squad room half embarrassed, and half triumphant. We were standing amid a cluster of town offices which clung like satellites to a central reception area. In the corner, directly over my own office, was an approximate clone with a locked door. At eye level was the label: Building Inspections—F. McDermott.

"I'll be damned," Tyler whispered.

I resisted telling him of Sammie's discovery that McDermott, on top of all the other suspicions gathering around him, was rumored to be holding an anonymous fifty-thousand-dollar bank account.

Tyler used his key to get us into McDermott's office. It was dark, of course, and the remaining coolness of a day's worth of air-conditioning still lingered. I shook my head at Tyler's gesture toward the light switch, and instead made my way across the room by the reflected glow from the parking-lot lights filtering through the windows.

Directly over where I'd seen the microphone dangling, near where the two walls met, was a low-profile filing cabinet covered with a neat row of housing-regulation reference books. I shifted the books to the floor, lifted one end of the cabinet, and held it as Tyler slid several of the books underneath to keep it elevated. Then we both got on our hands and knees and followed the beam from my pocket flashlight. What we saw, nestled in the cavity of the cabinet's three-inch base, was a small black box with two wires coming from it, both of which vanished through the wall-to-wall carpeting into the floor. Tyler slipped a cotton glove on and gingerly reached in and manipulated the box slightly, studying it in the flashlight's harsh but narrow glare.

He finally withdrew his hand, turned off the light, and waited for me to lift the cabinet so he could retrieve the books and return everything as we had found it.

Outside, back in the reception area, he handed me back my flashlight. "It's a transmitter, wired right into the building's electrical supply. Did you see any wires above the false ceiling downstairs?"

"Sure. There were several of them. Looked like they were part of the overhead lighting."

Tyler nodded. "Probably were. Anyway, it allows him to eavesdrop for as long as he likes without ever having to worry about batteries running low. Very slick. I looked for a manufacturer's ID, but it'd been melted off, probably with the tip of a soldering iron. With that kind of care, I doubt we'd get fingerprints off it. Anyway, if I dusted it, he'd probably catch on. It's hard to leave everything exactly as you found it."

There was a distant clattering outside. I carefully stuck my head out into the hallway and saw Buddy's assortment of cleaning supplies piled up outside a door at the far end. As I watched, the supply-closet was kicked open and a foot pushed a pail with a mop in it out into the corridor. I ducked back inside before Buddy saw me.

"We better get back downstairs." We waited until he'd moved all his things into the office he was cleaning, and then we tiptoed back to where our presence wouldn't seem odd.

"How far does it transmit?" We were standing in the rear lobby, near the back entrance, and yet I still found myself whispering.

"I don't know specifically, but given its size and simplicity, I wouldn't say much beyond a couple of hundred feet, farther if it was outside."

"So, the receiver's inside the building?"

"Probably, but we won't know where unless we either tear the place apart from top to bottom, or we hire some specialist out of Boston or somewhere, whose equipment is fancy enough to trace the signal's path to the receiver."

"The State Police don't have something like that?"

Tyler chuckled. "Only in their dreams."

Nevertheless, I was pleased. Whoever our quarry was, we now had his prints, which I still was convinced would yield something, and we knew he was listening, which I hoped I could use against him. Also, Fred McDermott had rung the bell again, this time twice in one day. It wouldn't be long now before we had enough against him to possibly make something stick.

I grinned at J.P. in anticipation. "Go home; get some sleep. First thing tomorrow, we'll see if we can't jerk this guy around a little."

CHAPTER
33

AS things turned out, none of us got much sleep that night. I worked at home until midnight, writing instructions in preparation of the next day's game plan, and hadn't been asleep two hours before the phone jarred me back awake. Billy Manierre's sad rumble filled my ear. "Joe, you better come on over to John Woll's place. Been a shooting."

In the moment it took for that information to sink in, Billy had hung up, leaving me in silence and despair.

I didn't know who had shot whom, or if John or Rose Woll were even involved, but as I drove through the dark, abandoned streets, I didn't have many doubts. Billy's tone had told me more than his words. There had been a death, and I was all but certain that John's problems had finally ground to a halt.

The familiar chaotic twinkling of emergency lights greeted me at the beginning of Brannen Street. I parked at the bottom of the short hill and climbed on foot, walking past a string of patrol cars. Everyone on the force was by now aware of this address. The mere mention of it by the dispatcher had been enough to gather us all, as for a dress rehearsal of the funeral that would soon follow.

Billy was waiting for me at the top of the exterior staircase.

"John?" I asked him.

"In the bedroom."

The tiny apartment was harsh with the mutterings of police radio speakers, and the shuffling of heavy, regulation shoes. I asked Billy to evacuate his people, and I wended my way through the narrow hallway, watching the glum, almost embarrassed expressions on the downcast faces I passed. These were not hardened cops; where the sight of a fellow officer, bloodstained and lifeless, might have been a familiar enough sight to veterans in New York or Boston or Miami, it wasn't to the Brattleboro force. The hurt and confusion on their faces, the utter lack of a practiced professional reaction, was telling.

John was sitting in the rickety rocking chair opposite the bed, the one I had used when I'd last talked with him. He was dressed in his undershorts and a T-shirt, his bare feet sightly pigeon-toed. One arm hung like forgotten laundry, its fingers dangling just inches off the floor, reminding me of Kunkle; the other lay nestled in his lap, curled around the butt of a black and menacing semiautomatic pistol. He'd shot himself in the heart, the blood of which had turned most of the front of his entire body a dark, still-glistening red. The entrance wound appeared raven-black and jagged in the half-light, ringed by a charcoal halo of burned gunpowder.

I felt Billy standing beside me and was suddenly aware of both the tomblike silence inside the building and the muted noise of a large, shuffling crowd outside. I wondered, just for a moment, if that's what a body could hear from the inside of its coffin, had its hearing not been silenced.

"How did it come in? Gunshot?"

"No. Rose called it in. She'd been trying to get hold of him, not getting an answer. She came over and found him."

"She still here?"

"No. I sent her to the hospital with one of the boys. She was out of control; I thought for a while she might try to do herself in. She may yet." He paused, looking at John as he might a troubled, sleeping child. "What a waste. I've never understood suicide."

"Did the neighbors see or hear anything?"

"No, and there were several of them around."

I frowned at that and looked again at the gun. "You'd think they would have heard something."

Billy shrugged. "Maybe. Judging from the hole, though, it looks like he made a silencer of his own chest."

It was true. The wound looked like it had exploded from within, as would have happened when the explosive gases from the shot reflected off the shattered sternum, but that scenario snagged on something in my mind and made me look about the room.

"Who was the first one here, besides Rose?"

"I was. Couldn't sleep, and I heard it over the radio. Only took me a couple of minutes to get here."

"How'd it look?"

Billy frowned. "Like you see it, pretty much."

"Nothing to make you think anything other than suicide?"

His expression didn't change, but his eyes cooled and flattened. He, like I, was now wary of where we were headed. The element I'd introduced not only added to the pain he was already feeling, but it carried a sting along with it, an implication that assumptions had been made too quickly, and that a possible homicide scene had been altered by almost a dozen patrolmen tramping through the apartment. We both knew instinctively that we were balanced on opposite edges of a threatening pit; I, after all, had asked to have the premises vacated, while he, reaching back to more trusting, compassionate instincts, had taken what he'd seen at face value, which the rule books stridently warned against.

He didn't answer my question immediately. "I made sure only a couple of us got this close. Course, I don't know what Rose might have touched."

I nodded, and allowed him his out. "Good. I'm sure everyone was careful. It's a hard impulse to step on, rubbernecking."

"Especially when you know the guy," Billy agreed, but his voice betrayed him. He'd been at this too long not to know he'd committed a major blunder. Any forensics expert will attest that on a microscopic level, a scene as trespassed upon as this looks like Main Street after a parade. Any hope of separating and identifying hair samples, stray fibers, or shoe impressions vanishes.

We would do this by the numbers from now on, but my only real hope at this point was that John himself, through his autopsy, might tell us something of the few minutes preceding his own death.

I rubbed the side of my nose with my finger and turned toward the hallway. "Well, let's put a lock on the place until the assistant ME and Tyler get through with it."

Billy followed me out without saying a word.

• • •

The usual morning banter was lacking in the squad room a few hours later. The greetings were muted, questions about one another's progress went unasked. I sat in my room, looking out the interoffice window, and watched my professional family coping with a combination of grief and anger. The newspaper had run the story with banner headlines, as expected, and while Katz had stuck to the facts as he knew them, keeping as neutral a voice as possible, the effect simulated the turning on of a bright, hot spotlight, aimed at people who had already been feeling the heat for too long. I was worried about the department's ability to bear the load for much longer, and I wondered what form the first sign of their collapse might take.

On the other hand, their muffled demeanor would make my bit of planned theater that much easier to enact, and would lend credibility to their reaction.

I went to my door and waved them into my office, an unusual but not unprecedented event. I wanted to be sure that what I was about to say would be picked up by the bug. There were just four of them: Tyler, Martens, DeFlorio, and Pierre Lavoie. Ron was under doctor's orders to remain at home with his leg elevated and wrapped in ice packs.

"I got some news last night that might brighten your day a bit. I talked to a snitch who swears he's got a witness to the Jardine burial."

"Where's he been hiding?" DeFlorio interrupted. "I thought I'd turned over every rock in this town."

"Well, you missed this one. From what I heard, this guy may well have what we're after. He's not going to be an easy witness, though. He only wants to meet with me, alone, and only late tonight."

"Where?" Sammie asked.

"I don't know yet. I'm supposed to get a call later today; I guess so we can't seal the area off."

"Why's he so nervous?"

"It seems we've been trying to put a roof over his head, courtesy of the state, for some time now. He's also scared shitless that the same guy who came after Jardine and Milly may come after him."

DeFlorio was shaking his head. "So why talk to us? Why not just lay low?"

"Because keeping out of our sights was getting difficult enough without worrying about getting his tail shot off. I think he's looking for a deal—he'll finger the bad guy if we drop what we've got against him. That way, he gets to walk around in plain sight again."

"Can we figure out who it is by going over our fugitive warrants?"

"We could try, but he may be wanted under some other paperwork. Besides, we'd still be guessing. For all I know, the guy's full of it and we're just getting our chains yanked. I think we should wait for the call, give the meeting location a very loose net, if we have the time, and otherwise just wing it. There's no indication of anything risky here; it's just a meet with a snitch." I stood up and moved to the door, the sheaf of papers I'd worked on the night before in my hand. "Given the events of last night, I'm going to give a pass to this morning's usual meeting. Let's just hit the streets and see if we can beat this snitch to the facts."

I received several odd looks. If anything, an event like John's death would guarantee a gathering of the minds, not the reverse. The looks got even odder as I handed out the sheets of paper, pausing each time to place my finger to my lips in a sign of silence. Only DeFlorio ignored me. "What's this?"

Everyone stared at him, since the first line on the pages

they were all now holding read, "Watch out—the office is bugged."

I shook my head, but answered in a nonchalant tone. "Just a copy of the press release on John's death, in case a reporter ambushes you."

DeFlorio's face reddened as he reread the first line, and the others beneath it. His embarrassment was such I could tell he was about to apologize, so I patted him on the shoulder and gave him a gentle shove out the door.

●   ●   ●

We reconvened two hours later in the medical director's office overlooking the truck bay at the Rescue, Inc., ambulance service. I'd chosen it because it was remote, tucked under the high ceiling and accessible only by a single wooden staircase leading down to the bay, and because it was as unlikely a meeting place for us as I could imagine. The legal occupant of the room had been only too willing to help me out for an hour by taking his paperwork elsewhere. I'd been here once before, to discuss some public-awareness event in which the Police and Fire departments were to put on a show with Rescue, and it was the one place I'd thought of last night that would be well-nigh impossible to bug on short notice, unless one of the people entering it carried the bug in with him.

There was no chitchat from any of them as they filed noisily up the stairs. The note I'd given them had pointed out the need for discretion, both in the office and on any department phones. It had also dictated their times of departure from the Municipal Building to arrive here so that our eavesdropper wouldn't become suspicious at our all leaving at once. Their silence was a testament to their understanding of how fragile a functioning unit we'd become.

I waited until the last of them had found a seat in the tiny crow's-nest of an office. I stood by the long, rectangular window looking down onto the trucks below, noticing that the gleaming shininess of all four ambulances didn't extend to their otherwise invisible flat roofs.

I nodded over to J. P. Tyler, who was holding his AM radio. "You all set?"

He nodded, switched it on, and began to play the antenna around the room, and the people in it, much as he had on the day before. I addressed the stunned expressions before me. "This is only to protect us all. If this bastard could bug my own office, he could sure as hell find a way to slip a bug into one of your pockets, so please bear with me."

After some twenty minutes, he sat back down and turned off the quietly hissing radio. "Okay."

I cleared my throat, relieved. "In case you haven't figured it out by now, tonight's meeting with a snitch is bogus. I'm hoping that when whoever's at the other end of the bug in my office hears he's about to be blown, he'll try to cover his tracks, just as he did when he killed Milly Crawford."

"And John Woll?" asked Tyler.

It was a legitimate question, if a bit theatrical. I'd spent all night watching Tyler work, and the State Police Mobile Crime Lab, which I'd insisted should join us. They had all examined the crime scene in detail and hadn't found anything out of place, except, as the state boys were quick to point out, what Billy's people had trampled. Hillstrom hadn't contacted me yet about John's autopsy, a fact Tyler knew, so I was curious what had prompted his rejoinder.

"John was murdered?" Sammie asked, an incredulous look on her face.

Tyler crossed his arms. "I think so."

"Based on what?" I asked.

He let out a sigh. "Just before I came over here, I got a visit from Dunn's investigator. The SA decided—a little late—to let me see John's fingerprints. They don't match what I lifted from the curare bottles."

A general muttering filled the room.

I raised both my hands. "Okay, hold it. Let's talk about John a bit. I don't argue that his death might have been a homicide; the state crime lab is looking into that, and so is Beverly Hillstrom. But I also don't see where it would have benefited anyone to kill him. On the face of it, he was a prime candidate for suicide, and I think we all ought to admit that's a strong possibility. None of us likes to think a friend, much less a colleague, could be pushed that far; maybe there's an element of guilt here. I do know, though, that we can't let it derail us. It's just possible, at long last, that we've gained an advantage; sure as hell, the attempt to destroy those curare bottles proves we're giving this guy a hotfoot."

I held up my index and thumb and held them a half-inch apart. "We might be that close, folks. Let Hillstrom and the state boys do their job and report back to us. In the meantime, let's see if we can nail the son of a bitch."

I watched my small, grim audience. I understood the pressure they were under, and I shared their grief. Nevertheless, I fully believed what I'd told them; we had turned a corner, and we were getting closer to the end. To disintegrate now would be to literally let a killer slip between our fingers.

Tyler helped stabilize the boat he'd just rocked. "So where's tonight's meeting?"

I pulled a schematic map from my pocket. "This is a layout of the Brattleboro Union High School. From the viewpoint of our fictional snitch, it's the perfect rabbit warren in which to disappear if things go wrong. It's got dozens of exits and a million nooks and crannies."

The map showed an almost random clustering of rectangles, surrounding two open-air courtyards. Some parts of the overall building, which had grown over the decades, addition by addition, were two stories tall, others were one, and the auditorium was about two and a half. It was a huge, convoluted, labyrinthine structure, a classic case of pragmatism over form.

I poked my finger at one corner of it. "This is the main cafeteria. It's got about seven exits, direct or roundabout. To a real-life informant, it's custom-made. Given short notice, we wouldn't have the time or the manpower to adequately seal it off and trap anyone inside."

"You're not gonna have a real snitch?" DeFlorio interrupted.

I looked up at Pierre Lavoie and smiled. "I'm going to have a real person play one." Everyone chuckled and he reddened slightly, obviously pleased. "Compared to the rest of us, Pierre has been pretty low-profile. Once we dress him up and slap a fake beard on him, he should do just fine.''

I returned to the map. ''The point is, what looks to be a custom-made layout for escape will actually be a locked box. At night on the weekends, the school is divided into sections, either by heavy internal gates that come out of the walls or by padlocked chains run through the handles of interior double doors. It allows them to limit total access in case they're broken into. The implication will be that the snitch has at least one passkey, and thus access to part of the building. In fact, we'll use the gates to our advantage and surreptitiously guard the other supposedly open passages. The idea is to let our eavesdropper into the cafeteria, and then lock the place up behind him. And just to make sure we don't end up on the wrong side of a locked door or gate, should something go wrong, I've had passkeys made up for all of you.'' I handed them out.

Even as I laid it out for them, it sounded a little slim. If Lavoie and I were playacting in the cafeteria, that only left Sammie, J.P., and Dennis to block all those potential exits. I added as an afterthought, ''Of course, some of the doors will be jammed so they can't be opened from either side; that'll help slant the odds in our favor.''

Sammie was clearly underwhelmed. ''We going to have backup on this?''

''I don't think it'll work if we do,'' I told her.

I was not the only one aware of how information had been gushing out of the department. The hidden microphone in my office was one obvious explanation for that, but everyone in the room knew the problem was much larger. Where there was one mike, there were probably more, a fact we couldn't risk exploring without showing our hand. And the strong possibility existed that the man pulling the strings had a backup system in place, maybe even a cop on the dole.

Involving our Special Reaction Team, normally the thing to do, would be inviting disaster, which brought up another question, this time from Tyler. ''You're setting yourselves up as sitting ducks. I mean, if this guy does take the bait, it'll be to kill this supposed snitch, and you with him.''

"Pierre and I'll be wearing armor and we'll be wired for sound. But the whole thing hangs on all of us working within very close tolerances. I also want to pull in the chief on this—give him a little street exercise—so we'll have one extra body to put in place."

I also had an additional card to play, but I didn't show it here, no more than I had since I'd first thought it up. Willy Kunkle, as irascible, deformed, and illegal as he was on paper for an operation like this, was my ace up the sleeve. Not to share my thoughts with my colleagues was a flagrant breach of faith, and probably good grounds, if I was caught, for my dismissal. The risk of being caught and fired, however, was secondary to the shocked response I knew I'd get from my own squad. Pulling in Kunkle without telling them, especially after the stunt I'd pulled with Woll early on, would prove I didn't trust them. And that would mean the end of my effectiveness as their lieutenant, now and forever.

And yet I was still going to attempt it, to try to entice Kunkle to join the operation. An obsessed and devil-driven paranoid, he had always been a trustworthy cop. I wanted him as my hidden floater in this game plan, the guy whose training and outlook wouldn't allow for a last-minute screwup.

I'd tried to tell myself at first that I was keeping Kunkle to myself because he was an illegal in this, a handicapped civilian involved in an undercover police operation. But in my heart, I knew that, especially with John Woll's death, I wasn't sure I trusted my own people anymore. I didn't want to believe that, but I had to consider it, and I wasn't about to risk Pierre's life and mine just to spare a few hurt feelings.

For now, Willy Kunkle would remain my little secret, one I planned to share only with Brandt. I did my best to shove the moral debate to the back of my mind as I spent the next ninety minutes going over our plan of attack again and again until everyone knew their roles by heart.

I was able to secure a warrant for Fred McDermott's bank records, much to Sammie's delight. The evidence against him had built up like the incoming tide, gradually, with little fanfare. It hadn't been at all like the case against John Woll, complete with footprints, cigarette butts, incriminating personal ties, and a shiny gold watch in a sock drawer. McDermott was being painted into a corner almost by innuendo. He was in the wrong place at the wrong time; he wasn't around when he needed an alibi the most; his office held the transmitter but not the receiver of a listening device; he had an unexplained bank account.

Cumulatively, it satisfied Judge Harrowsmith, especially when given the proper slant in the affidavit, but I was not as sanguine as Sammie Martens. I couldn't overlook how many times we'd been led down the wrong path in this case, nor could I ignore the price John Woll had finally paid for that. I didn't want another falsely accused man on my conscience—nor did I want a guilty one to get away because of my timidity.

I was about to invite Brandt out into the Municipal Building's parking lot to discuss some of this, when Dispatch buzzed me on the intercom to inform me the State Police had dug something up they thought we'd find interesting.

Their meaning was quite literal. With J.P. in tow, I followed directions to West Brattleboro, to a lonely field off Ames Hill Road, and to a well-dug grave containing the decomposing body of Tobias A. "Toby" Huntington. He had been shot in the head.

A good half of Brattleboro's legally defined geography is unadulterated countryside: verdant hills, small lonely streams, and meadows grazed by horses and cows, all looking as remotely pastoral as their country cousins one hundred miles into the boondocks.

Toby's last home emphasized that fact, tucked as it was under the shade of the first row of trees bordering the lower edge of a field. As a young and proper Vermont State Trooper explained that the body had been uncovered by a local farmer's overly curious dog, I was intensely aware of the silent shimmering heat radiating off the burnt-blond grass beyond the shade. I could hear, above the insects and birds, the sound I'd been hearing all too often as of late: the squawk of walkie-talkies and the distant wail of sirens, signaling yet another homicide. I began wondering what it was that had prompted me as a young man to pursue a line of business so dedicated to exposing society's least-attractive habits.

Tyler conferred with the trooper on how his own evidence-gathering should coordinate with that of the state's Mobile Crime Lab. I moved to the edge of the scene, and leaned against the burning metal of a parked patrol car.

"So this is the guy you've been looking for."

Tony Brandt had quietly crossed the field and stood before me.

"Yeah." The enthusiasm I'd felt at my meeting this morning had evaporated with this latest discovery. Watching homicide-scene technicians yet again at work, measuring, photographing, collecting, I began to question whether we'd made any progress at all.

Although I'd never met him, Toby's death hit me as hard as John Woll's. I had been concerned for his safety, had considered the darker possibilities for his disappearance, but I had always hoped he'd be able to avoid the man stalking him as well as he had us. Four people were now dead, and I had no idea who might be next. That thought depressed me as few things had before.

Brandt seemed to know what was going on inside me. He, more than anyone on the force, had traveled the same path for as long as I had. And he, more than I, had done battle with politicians, press, and public, all opponents who were never easily satisfied. Who better could recognize in a fellow cop the telltale warnings of impending burnout?

He asked me the kind of deductive question that could bring me back to the scene before us: "Why was he buried here?"

It was said casually, and it took a few seconds to sink in, like a rock seeking the bottom of a well. But when it touched home, I began to play back the events leading to this grave, as well as to another I'd stood over just days before.

"Because he—unlike Charlie Jardine—wasn't meant to be found."

Charlie's burial had been an arrogant challenge, put forth by a mind that believed itself in control. It had been the first overt move in a carefully thought-out campaign. Toby Huntington had been killed by a man scrambling to cover his tracks, just as when he'd attacked Ron and me in the parking lot, and even earlier, when he'd shot Milly Crawford. With Milly, he had taken the time to salt the trail with red herrings. Lately, however, that subtlety had begun to evaporate, replaced, I realized, with a propensity to make mistakes.

As a living potential witness, Toby had been an elusive, uncooperative failure. Now, I became increasingly convinced, he might help us far more from his burial place.

I walked to the roped-off edge of the scene. "J.P."

Tyler, on his knees, his evidence kit beside him, looked up at me.

"It's just a feeling, but don't get too lost in the details here. I think our man is running for cover, and I don't think he's taking time to be overly neat and tidy."

"You mean, look for the killer's wallet under the body?"

"You can dream if you want, but make sure you tell Hillstrom to compare any bullet fragments recovered here to what she dug out of John Woll."

Tyler sat back on his heels and flashed a smile. "Wouldn't that be sweet?"

I walked back to Tony Brandt, my earlier depression blown away as by the wind, the smell of the scent again fresh in my nostrils. I took him by the elbow and steered him away from the small crowd, out into the privacy of the open field. "I've got something cooking that should scare the hell out of whatever political ninth life you have left."

* * *

Willy Kunkle had apparently organized the local-history room until it could stand no more. We were now on the first floor, in the back corner of the research section, in a twenty-by-five-foot room filled with racked back issues of magazines like *Consumer Reports* and *Road & Track*.

Kunkle was savagely jamming weatherworn issues back

into their proper places after a day in which the periodicals had seen more than their fair share of use.

I was patiently waiting for his reaction to my invitation.

"Why the fuck should I help you guys?"

"You have so far."

"I was curious; it was total self-interest."

"It was also useful, and it's beginning to flush this guy out."

"You could fool Toby."

"Toby may yet tell us things."

He didn't answer, and I watched him for several minutes at work, his muscular right hand working as fast and sure as a hawk talon. After he'd left the department, I'd heard he'd begun lifting weights and exercising with his usual obsessive drive. Indeed, aside from the withered arm, I'd never seen him fitter.

"I found out a little more on the drug angle."

I went with his change of topic. "Oh yeah?"

"Turns out the guy I told you about, the one in Boston who had Hanson and Cappelli on the payroll, he's been approached by someone else."

"Who?"

"Don't know; real secretive, but the base is supposed to be here in Bratt."

"Same action, new players?"

"Looks that way. I'd say whoever you're up against has both scores to settle and big ambitions."

I watched him work some more in silence. "How much longer do you see yourself filing books?"

He stopped in mid-motion and glared at me, his face twisted. "Fuck you, Joey-boy. I want career counseling, I'll hire it."

"We might be able to get you back on the force."

He became very angry, very suddenly. "Look, you bastard, you want me to cover your ass in some bullshit commando crock tonight, that's fine with me. I'll do it. With any luck, I'll get a little action, and you and Brandt'll get your asses handed to you on a platter—good for everybody. But don't blow in my ear, okay? Don't pretend you give a good goddamn what happens to me. I'm the biggest pain in the ass you ever had in the department, and it's goddamn insulting that you think I'll swallow your wanting me back."

"I didn't say I liked you, Willy—but you were the best at what you did. My only problem was I wished I could keep you under a rock until I needed you."

He smiled slightly, perhaps with perverse pride. "So what the hell are you saying?"

"There's a new federal handicap law, one of those antidiscrimination acts. You could use it to get back on, whether you help me tonight or not. It would be better than this, and you'd get the pleasure of making my life miserable again."

He shook his head and turned away. But he didn't resume filing magazines. Instead, he just stared at the shelves, lost in thought. Finally, he looked back at me and scratched his head. I thought for a split moment that he seemed faintly embarrassed. His voice, however, remained predictably hardbitten. "I'll think about it."

He stuck his hand out. "You said you had some blueprints for tonight's dog-and-pony show."

I shook my head, doubting my own sanity, and pulled them out of my pocket.

CHAPTER
34

THE high-school cafeteria was a sterile place at the best of times: linoleum floor, pale cinderblock walls, fluorescent strip lighting. The only colorful spots were the dispensing machines along one wall, a few socially conscious posters across from them, and a bolted-to-the-floor army of garish blue-and-red, picnic-style tables and benches in between. Now, however, late at night, with only maintenance lighting leaking in from down a distant hallway, the illuminated soda and snack machines dominated the place, glowing as from some inner life-force, spreading the hues of their chaotically clashing logos across the huge, ghostly quiet room.

Pierre Lavoie and I sat facing each other at one of the picnic tables, I with a legal pad before me, he with a small knapsack. The pad was for show only, the sack to hide his portable radio. Our budget did not allow for the fancy hands-off communications systems the Secret Service seems to favor. We made do with standard patrolman radios, tucked out of sight and hooked to a small earphone and a somewhat larger clip-on lapel mike whose side button had to be manually depressed for the user to transmit his message. The gloominess hid most of the extraneous wires from sight, as did the long-haired wig I'd forced Pierre to wear. The mikes were clipped to the armored vests inside our shirts.

Pierre, his voice disguised, had placed the rendezvous telephone call to my office thirty minutes ago, giving the high school as the meeting place. He'd then gone straight there to wait for me. Around us, out of sight and in place for an hour already, were Sammie and J.P. along the "open" corridors; Dennis and Tony Brandt outside the building; and, his exact location unknown even to me, Willy Kunkle.

The cafeteria was right off the building's main southern entrance, which Pierre had unlocked with his passkey, and which I'd walked through to join him two minutes earlier. Three hallways radiated out from this general area: One continued north from the entrance into the heart of the building, the second took off at a ninety-degree angle to service the east side, and the third, far shorter and narrower, almost inconsequential, led from the back of the cafeteria, around a corner to the west, to a few isolated rooms, two staircases leading up, and a side door to the outside.

"Where do you think he'll come from?" Pierre muttered.

I arranged the pad before me and began to write, pretending to take notes. Most of the room was windowless, but one wall of it was made of glass and looked onto another, equally large dining area which often doubled as classroom space. On its far wall, along with one of the doors I'd chosen to jam shut, there were windows. If this guy was going to come for us, I wanted to make damn sure he believed what he saw until it was too late.

"He's got three obvious choices. The way we came in, the door at the far end of the east hall, and the one out the side, around the corner. If it were me, I'd take that one; it'd allow me to sneak up on us the best. The other two are too wide-open."

"Shit. That's what I feel—wide-goddamn-open."

He was sweating badly, but then so was I. Armored vests are cool-weather defenses; plus he had the wig on.

I surreptitiously reached under my jacket and keyed the radio mike. "Hi, boys and girls. Everybody in place?"

Over the earpiece, I heard a tinny chorus of acknowledgments.

"You see anyone when you came in?" I asked Pierre, more to keep him occupied than anything else.

He was about to answer when he stiffened suddenly. It was Brandt's voice on the earphone, reporting from outside. "Someone driving up to the front door."

"Christ, so much for subtlety." Pierre let his hand drop casually off the table near his waist, where his gun was hidden.

I stayed the way I was, pretending to take notes.

"One occupant; short-haired male." Brandt's voice was calm and detached, reminding me of those jet jockeys who announce they've taken a missile and are corkscrewing in.

"He's parked. Getting out. Pale striped golf shirt, dark slacks, no visible weapons." There was a pause. "It looks like Fred McDermott."

I keyed my mike. "Everybody stay put. Let's see what he does."

Sammie Martens, who was behind a door in the hallway leading away from the main door, peeked out. "He's approaching the south entrance."

We both heard one of the large glass doors rattle as someone tugged at it.

Sammie's voice again. "Trying to get in locked half of the door."

The rattling stopped and was followed by a door swishing open. Footsteps sounded in the lobby, slapping against the linoleum. Pierre dropped his hand entirely into his lap and I heard a small click as he snapped the safety off his automatic.

The dark outline of a man appeared at the corner where the lobby expanded into the cafeteria. "Hello? Is anyone here?" McDermott's voice was absurdly loud, ringing off the cement walls.

"What the hell?" Pierre whispered.

I spoke into the mike. "I'll deal with it. Keep sharp; it may be a setup."

I rose from the table. McDermott whirled at the movement, surprised, and Pierre pulled his gun, slid off his bench, and took aim at McDermott's chest.

"Put it away," I snapped at Lavoie, "and sit back down."

"What's going on, Joe?" Fred asked anxiously.

I walked over to him, watching his hands, which stayed open and still by his sides. "What're you doing here, Fred?"

His brow furrowed. "You asked me here."

Suddenly, the radio interrupted over the earpiece. "Someone at the—" It had been Dennis's voice, abruptly interrupted.

"Dennis? Dennis, come in."

"I'm checking on him now," reported Brandt.

McDermott, who could hear none of this, was looking more and more confused.

Pierre Lavoie, his nerves stretched as far as they would go, stood near the table, his gun still out, his wig torn off, swinging his body back and forth, trying to cover all possible avenues at once.

"Pierre," I shouted at him, "cover the—"

The words "back hallway" were still in my mouth when another figure appeared at the entrance to the corridor. Pierre brought his gun to bear, there was a blinding flash and a terrific explosion, and Lavoie went flying backwards like a puppet pulled by a string. He sailed across the table and crumpled into the gap between tabletop and bench, his legs sticking awkwardly in the air.

I grabbed McDermott by the neck and threw him down to the floor. "Stay low." I tore off my jacket and pulled my gun, keying the mike with the other hand. "We have a man down. Shooter's in back hallway behind kitchen."

As I ran toward Pierre, I could already hear Sammie throwing open her door and the pounding of feet as J.P. ran down the east hall to join us.

Pierre's eyes were closed, but he was breathing. There was a bullet hole in the middle of his shirt. I tore it open and checked for blood. Apparently, while the armored vest had done its job, the flight across the table and into the bench had knocked him cold. I quickly straightened him out so his airway would stay open.

Brandt's voice: "Nobody's at the door. He's still inside. I

found Dennis. He was knocked on the head but he'll be okay.''

"Switch frequencies and call for backup."

"Ten-four."

I moved to the entrance of the crooked hallway and waited for Sammie and J.P. to join me. "Okay, remember the layout?"

"Isolated two-story segment, about nine rooms downstairs, same above, two staircases, hallway like this upstairs."

That, in Tyler's staccato nutshell, was it. This was the only two-story section in the school's southwest corner, which meant the upstairs windows gave out onto a lot of flat, open roof.

I looked at their two sweat-sheened faces. Both of them held handguns pointed safely up, ready for use. "Okay. Brandt's got the exit. You two work the downstairs. I'll go up. Remember, he may have a key, so don't trust a locked door. And take your time; I'd sooner let him get away than have one of you killed. Deal?"

"Deal," Sammie muttered, her voice half strangled by adrenalin.

I began working my way up the near staircase, feeling the risers with my toes and keeping my eyes, and my gun, trained up above to where the stairs doubled back on themselves to link up with the top landing. I took my time, moving slowly and quietly, my concentration not only on what I was doing, but also taking in what I could glean from the radio. In the back of my mind, I wondered what Kunkle was up to.

I reached the top without mishap and moved quickly to the angle where the landing turned the corner into the hall. There I removed the earphone to better concentrate, and found myself suddenly alone.

I strained to listen for anything unusual, and heard nothing but distant sirens fast approaching; movements from Sammie and J.P. downstairs; and the distinct rasp of a chair being pushed, ever so slightly, out of the way, as by somebody groping in the dark.

That last one grabbed my attention. It had come from nearby.

I wiped my forehead with my sleeve. The additional disadvantage of my position, aside from being far removed from everyone else, was that the entire second floor of this small section was dark. There were no vending machines, no exit signs, and no windows, since the hallway was lined with classrooms. The doors leading to those rooms, however, did have windows, and gradually, as my pupils adjusted, I could just grasp the outline of the corridor from the dimly filtered streetlights outside.

That allowed me one discovery: There were no chairs in the hall, so the sound I'd heard had come from one of the rooms.

Whoever I was stalking knew the building. The door he'd entered hadn't been jammed, but it had been left locked, so as not to appear suspicious. Since Dennis had been put out of action just seconds before Pierre had been shot, no time had been wasted picking a lock. Therefore, the gunman did indeed have at least one of the building's four passkeys. In addition, he'd known that particular door led to the most discreet approach to the cafeteria and that McDermott's arrival through the main entrance would encourage us to face the wrong direction at just the right time. Ironically, had Pierre not lost his cool, it might have worked.

But what did all that tell me? That he had to be in one of the north-facing rooms, the only ones which gave out onto the roof, and which were invisible from the ground level.

I looked out into the corridor again. Using that logic, I had two choices, both of them almost directly facing me: the two doors of the only classrooms whose windows afforded the access my quarry was seeking.

Crouching, I slipped across the hall and placed my hand very gently on the doorknob of the first door. Slowly, hoping that perhaps in his haste he'd forgotten to lock it behind him, I twisted the knob. The sweat began to pour off my forehead, stinging my eyes.

The knob fully over now, I positioned myself on the balls of my feet and gave a little push. As I did, the door released a loud mechanical snap.

I instantly yielded to instinct. Rather than pulling back and surrendering my hard-won surprise, I threw my weight against the door and dove in to one side of the room, covering my head with my arm to ward off any chairs or tables that might be in the way. The room blew up with the sound and light of a single gunshot, and I heard the sharp splat of a bullet hitting the door I'd just used.

I rolled on the floor, trying to find a target against the slightly pale windows lining the opposite wall, but my eyes were still blinking away the white star left behind by the muzzle flash. There was the sound of glass shattering, of feet scrambling for a toehold, and of a distant thump as something heavy landed on the roof outside.

I staggered to my feet and punched the button on my microphone. "He's on the roof, he's on the roof." Against the night sky, I could see a shadow running, and hear his feet slamming on the gravel as he made for a distant rooftop greenhouse.

Not wanting to fire indiscriminately, I made to follow, and placed my hand right on a jagged shard of glass. I swore and stepped back, using my gun barrel to sweep the window frame clean. "He's making for the greenhouse. Close in on him from downstairs."

I tried again and this time jumped cleanly to the roof. It was higher by two feet than the pale rubber-coated roof on which the small greenhouse stood, so I quickly moved to the lower level where my footsteps would make no sound.

There I paused to reassess. The greenhouse, a small fifty-by-thirty-foot student-research facility, was a penthouse of sorts, with an interior metal staircase leading down to a cavernous forestry and horticulture classroom, a part of the career-training school. I couldn't see the door of the green-house from my vantage point, but I was betting that was where the gunman had been heading. Unfortunately, if he was on his toes, he now knew what I knew, and had therefore probably changed his plans; that meant I was either staring at an empty structure and he was long gone in another direction, or he was waiting around the corner to plug me as soon as I became visible.

I began circling the small glass building from a distance, my eyes on its sharp-edged silhouette, watching for any crouching form, waiting for an ambush. As the narrow end came into dim view, I could see the flimsy metal door was half open. Encouraged, I began closing in, slowly, cautiously, still balanced and poised to duck to either side. The first three feet of the greenhouse walls were aluminum, so I kept almost on hands and knees for cover as I peered around the edge of the doorway and looked down the short cement-floored aisle. Warm, fetid air hit my face, tinged with the slight sweetness of confined vegetation and damp earth. I listened and heard only the faint hum of some overhead fans, along with voices and the sounds of people gathering down below, no doubt preparing to make an assault up the narrow stairs.

From where I crouched, I could see a light switch just inside the door. I reached in quickly, turned it on, and slipped back to see what would happen. The building lit up like a jewel in the night, but not a sound or a movement followed suit.

I gingerly poked my head back around the corner. What I saw made me laugh. I straightened up, crossed the threshold, and after a brief final glance around the place, walked to the middle of the aisle, keying my radio as I went. "All clear. I've got him in the greenhouse."

Stretched out before me, spread-eagled and unconscious on the floor, his gun several feet beyond his reach, was the inert body of Selectman Luman Jackson.

Willy Kunkle, his part done, was nowhere to be seen.

CHAPTER

35

"THIS is an outrage. Take these off."

Sammie Martens checked Jackson's handcuffs and gave him a contemptuous shake of the head. "I don't think so."

She crossed the room to where Brandt and I were talking with Billy Manierre. "He's still bitchin'."

"Okay, thanks Sammie. Did you read him his rights?" She nodded.

"Great. Why don't you pile him into your car and take him downtown, but don't bring him into the building till we get there. I want to keep this under wraps for a while."

We all waited until she'd escorted Luman Jackson out the door, ignoring his protests as he passed. "What's your game plan?" Brandt asked.

We were still in the high school, off the cafeteria in a small, windowless dining room. Jackson had been checked for the thump on his head, which all but Brandt assumed I had given him. The troops had been sent home with no explanations and without having seen either McDermott or Jackson. Brandt and Billy had been concocting a properly vague press report to explain all the lights and sirens. The shots were now firecrackers, the whole affair ascribed to "probably teenage vandals," pending a further investigation.

I answered Brandt with a smile, lightly fingering the

bandage I'd wrapped around my cut hand. "I'd like to talk to both of them tonight, before they start thinking too much. Maybe put Jackson in Dunn's office, for privacy, and have Fred cool his heels in Interrogation. Is Dunn coming himself, or sending a deputy?"

Brandt chuckled. "Not hardly; he's hooked on this case. Said he'd meet us at the Municipal Building."

I looked around at the empty room. "Then I guess it's show time."

•   •   •

Brandt was driving while I looked out the passenger window at the still city passing by. We were rolling down South Main Street, toward the center of town, following the patrol car carrying Fred McDermott. When I'd been on the graveyard shift, many years back, this had been my favorite time of night—the long, quiet pause between the last of the rowdies packing it in, and the first stirrings of the early-morning crowd.

Brandt cleared his throat. "So, any wild guesses?"

"I have a question first: What happened to Dennis?"

"Someone snuck up behind him, slapped a black cloth bag over his head, brought him down like a ton of bricks, and tied his hands and feet with wire, all in seconds flat."

"Just as he was about to report someone coming in the side door."

"Yup."

I let that rattle around my head for a minute. "If you were riding shotgun for a buddy on a break-and-enter job, knowing the place was guarded, you'd try to nail the guard before your buddy was spotted, wouldn't you?"

"Sure, unless I'd had trouble finding the guard."

"But you'd take the time to find him; otherwise you'd be risking the whole thing. That'd be stupid."

"Not if there was a timing problem."

"Like Jackson having to appear at the back hallway just as McDermott walked in the front?"

"Yeah, especially if each didn't know the other was there. McDermott sure looked like Mr. Innocence himself."

I mulled that over. "He told me he showed up because someone had phoned him and told him I wanted a meet. That's possible. Jackson obviously had a fairy godmother watching his back. I wonder if he knew about it?"

Brandt pursed his lips, as interested as I was to kick a few ideas around before interrogating our two suspects. "So, you have two people showing up for a meeting because they were both invited by a third."

"That looks like it, although 'invited' might not work in Jackson's case. He had a gun, and I suspect Dennis was taken out so he'd have an opportunity to use it."

* * *

Dunn was waiting for Brandt and me on the third floor of the Municipal Building, in the reception area of his small nest of offices. Despite the hour, he looked as dapper as if we'd called him out of a banker's meeting.

He looked at us without expression. "I gather you hooked a curious fish."

Brandt smiled. "You could say that."

"Where is he?"

"In a car downstairs," I answered. "I wanted you to call the shots on how big we should play this."

Dunn smiled thinly. "Very diplomatic of you. Why don't you give me some background before we invite him in?"

Bringing James Dunn up to date, and determining what interrogation strategy to use on Jackson, consumed about twenty minutes, during which the state's attorney sat at his polished antique desk and covered the top sheet of a yellow legal pad with small, carefully scripted notes.

Only when he was thoroughly satisfied with what we'd told him did he give me the go-ahead to radio Sammie in the car and have Luman Jackson brought upstairs.

What arrived on the SA's threshold three minutes later was not an attractive sight. Jackson was disheveled, red-eyed, and oddly out of sorts, as if torn between being angry and frightened. I hoped we could use that displacement to our advantage.

Dunn bowed slightly and waved to a small conference

table, surrounded by hard, wooden chairs. "Please, Mr. Jackson, have a seat."

Jackson twisted his body around, showing his manacled wrists. "For God's sake, James, these handcuffs are completely unnecessary."

Dunn made a conciliatory gesture. "Of course; a necessary formality. Lieutenant?"

I pulled a key from my pocket and set Jackson free. He made a theatrical show of rubbing his wrists as the rest of us gathered around the table. Dunn pointed to one of the chairs and placed a tape recorder before it. "Luman?"

Jackson stared at the recorder as if it were a snake and gingerly sat before it. With a loud click, Dunn turned it on and announced the date, the time, the location, and the identities of the other people in the room.

Then he sat at the end of the table and nodded to me, directly opposite Jackson.

"Would you please state your name?" I asked.

Luman's face darkened. "Luman J. Jackson."

"Mr. Jackson, have you been apprised of your rights?"

"Yes."

"And you fully understand those rights?"

"Of course I do. Look, this is absurd—"

"Do you wish to speak with us now, or do you want an attorney present?"

"I don't need an attorney, for Christ's sake. This whole thing is a misunderstanding."

Dunn spoke up. "I guarantee you, Luman, before this is over, you will need legal representation."

"However," I added, I hoped not too hastily, "if you do wish to talk to us now without a lawyer present, you'll have to sign a waiver."

I slid the waiver across the table to him and waited, holding my breath. There were times I had no doubt of the outcome of this ritual legal dance, but this man, normally so belligerent, was muted and confused enough to keep me guessing.

He signed the waiver.

I glanced at it before sliding it over to Dunn. "Thank

you. What were you doing at the Brattleboro Union High School tonight?''

Jackson glanced across the table at James Dunn briefly and then concentrated on staring at his knuckles as he clasped and unclasped his hands.

"Mr. Jackson?" I repeated.

He sighed and wrestled some more internally. "I went there to meet someone."

"Who?"

"I . . . I can't say."

"You were carrying a gun. Do you do that normally?"

"No, of course not."

"Then why tonight?"

"I was nervous."

"I noticed that you had the gun already drawn as you appeared from the hallway; that's how you got the drop on Officer Lavoie. Why was your gun out and ready to fire?"

Jackson opened his mouth to speak, thought a moment, and then closed it again.

"You entered the building through a locked door. How did you do that?"

A flash of the old Luman crossed his face. "With a key, of course. I had it from when I used to teach there."

"You were last employed by BUHS five years ago. Weren't you supposed to hand in all your keys on your last day there?"

He hesitated. "Technically, I guess. I forgot."

"Were you alone tonight?"

"Of course. Look, instead of all this back and forth, why don't you just let me tell you what happened?"

"Please do."

But having made the offer, Jackson looked momentarily stuck. "Well, I . . . I was supposed to meet someone—a private meeting, perfectly legal—but the time and the location made me . . . nervous, so I took my gun along, for security."

His voice slowly gained confidence as the tale weaved itself in his mind. "As I entered the building, I heard voices, and since I was only supposed to be meeting one person, that made me very uneasy, so I drew my gun from my pocket. Then, as I turned the corner, there was a man aiming a gun at me. Naturally, I fired in self-defense, after which, seeing several more people in the room, I fled for my life."

"You didn't recognize me?" I asked.

"Of course not. All I saw were guns."

"If your meeting was perfectly legal, Mr. Jackson," Brandt interjected, "then why won't you identify the other party?"

Luman looked around at us, the coy smile on his face contrasting with the sweat on his upper lip. "It's a matter of discretion. A romantic situation. I'm sure you understand."

"Your date showed up. Didn't you see Fred McDermott by the front door?" I asked.

Jackson's face turned livid. "That's disgusting."

"You're denying you were there to meet with McDermott?"

"Of course I am."

He was full of bluster, but I thought I'd heard a catch in his voice. "Mr. Jackson, at the moment, we're considering charging you with at least illegal trespass, reckless endangerment with a firearm, and attempted murder. This is not a great time to get cute. It is up to the state's attorney here to determine what we do with you tonight. Your cooperation will play a large role in that decision."

There was a moment's silence in the room. Jackson finally muttered, "I am cooperating."

"Then tell us who you were planning to meet."

I could almost hear the wheels going over in his head, considering the options, weighing the risks. It proved to be more than he could handle on short notice. "I refuse to answer."

I glanced at Dunn and raised my eyebrows. He nodded slightly. I switched subjects. "In your years as a teacher, did you ever have Charlie Jardine as a student?"

Jackson let out a small laugh of surprise. "Jardine? What the hell? . . ." He looked around at us quizzically.

"Answer the question, please," Dunn said quietly.

Jackson shrugged. "Sure, let's say he attended a few of my classes. Biggest troublemaker I ever had, which is saying a lot, given the competition."

"Memorable, was he?"

"He was a dope-head and a sex maniac, as far as I cared to determine. Halfway through the year I demanded the principal have him transferred to another class."

"I didn't know you could do that."

"It was done."

"What about John and Rose Woll? Her name was Evans then. Ever have them in class? They would've been in the same grade."

"I remember John Woll; very good student, albeit too quiet for his own good. He won a grant to attend college at the end of the year; very prestigious award. Turned it down, the idiot. I think there's truth to what they say about education being wasted on the young. They've abolished the award since, of course, along with anything else having to do with education."

Jackson was visibly gaining speed and self-confidence on this new ground, the arrogant swagger returning to his voice. "You'd think that meant he had brains, but he was no different from the others; when the time came to decide on the rest of his life, he let his cock do the thinking."

I smiled at him, encouraging. "You're kidding. He dumped the scholarship for a girl?"

Jackson gave me a contemptuous look. "I thought you'd been conducting an investigation on the man. Don't you know anything about him? I shouldn't be surprised, of course. I don't doubt you were bending over backwards to sweep the whole thing under the rug, you and your police fraternity."

"Who got the scholarship instead?"

"No one did. Woll didn't back out until it was too late to assign another recipient; selfish as well as stupid."

"Who was the girl that got him sidetracked?"

"Oh, for Christ's sake, Gunther, how the hell would I remember that?"

Again, Dunn's soft voice floated down the table. "Let's try to stay cooperative, Luman."

But we'd lost our advantage; no longer unsure of himself, he tilted his head back slightly and stared at us in contempt. "You people don't know what you're after, wandering all over the map, asking me about old students. Did you really think you could tie me in with Jardine's killing? You must be scared to death of me to try something like that."

Brandt's voice was tight with anger. "You shot a police officer tonight, Jackson; would've killed him if he hadn't been wearing armor. Shot at Joe, too, for that matter."

Jackson's face reddened. "Just a minute; you never identified yourselves as police. I was defending myself, in fear for my life. I could probably sue you for reckless endangerment."

Dunn rose and looked down at him. "That's your privilege, certainly."

"Good. That's what I'll do, then. I want to call my lawyer."

The state's attorney smiled thinly. "You can call him on your own time, Luman. Right now, I'm recommending you be formally cited for attempted murder and released pending the appropriate judicial proceedings."

Jackson looked at us, his nose wrinkled in disgust. "Fuck you, Jimmy boy. You want to get in a pissing match with me? That's fine, but be prepared to lose a lot more than this bullshit case. And that goes for the rest of you, too."

Dunn reached over without a word and turned off the tape recorder.

* * *

By the time I got downstairs to the tiny interrogation room tucked into a corner of the detective bureau, Fred McDermott had been waiting for over an hour. Despite the coffee that Sammie Martens had supplied him, he looked utterly beat, his face drawn, his eyes at half-mast, and his hair tousled where he'd run his fingers through it countless times.

I paused before actually entering the room, and stepped inside the observation cubicle adjoining it. A one-way mirror separated the two. Sammie Martens appeared at my side, sipping from a cup.

"What do you think?" I asked her. "What's his role in all this?"

She shrugged. "Who's to know? Normally, you get as much evidence against a guy as we have against Fred, he ends up fitting the part. But Fred hasn't budged from looking as innocent as the first day we focused on him, which in my book either makes him one hell of an actor, or the victim of one hell of a frame."

"What is the evidence so far?"

"He was at Horton Place when Milly bought the farm, he was dogging Toby's last residence just before Toby disappeared, he has no alibi for when the van almost ran you over, the bug was found in his office, he's got a nice, fat secret savings account, and he showed up tonight at the high school."

"And on the plus side?"

"His wife supplied him with alibis for the nights Jardine and Woll died, and he looks like my uncle, who's a priest. Also, he's got no record and has never displayed any obvious signs of wealth. As far as we can tell, that bank account has only received money; nothing's ever been taken out."

I nodded. "The chief's still upstairs with Dunn doing paperwork. Tell him I'm going to interview Fred in the parking lot, just for safety's sake."

Sammie glanced up at the ceiling as if it were dripping microphones. "Kind of gives you the creeps, doesn't it?"

Fred McDermott was obviously delighted to get out of the small interrogation room. He paused on the edge of the parking lot at the back of the Municipal Building and filled his lungs with air as if we were camping by the side of a mountain lake.

It was still dark, but just barely. The first half-light of dawn was beginning to slip between dark objects and their backgrounds, bringing them into relief. I led the way to a grassy slope under some trees and sat down. McDermott joined me, awkwardly placing his hands on his chubby knees. He didn't ask why I'd brought him out here.

"Fred, you said you got a call telling you to meet me at the high school, is that right?"

"Yes, that's right." His head bobbed several times too

many, a reflection of just how baffled he still was after the night's activities.

"Did the voice sound familiar at all? Did he identify himself?"

"No, I didn't know who it was. He just said he was calling from the Police Department with a message from you."

"Did he specify the time and location?"

"Oh, yes; the middle school entrance on the south side at midnight."

"And you were to go inside the building?"

"That's right; go inside and wait."

"You didn't ask why? It was kind of an odd request, wasn't it?"

"Well, I was curious, but I didn't really get a chance. He just made sure I had it right, and then he hung up. Oh, and he said it was confidential and to keep it to myself."

"What time did he call?" I asked.

"It was late, around ten-thirty."

I paused at that. If he was being truthful, that was right after Pierre's bogus call to me setting up the meet. Apparently, our elaborate hoax had been a failure from the start. Our eavesdropper must have been standing around, knowing what we were up to, just waiting for the location so he could put his game plan into motion.

"Fred," I resumed, "do you have any particular bone to pick with Luman Jackson, professionally or otherwise?"

He shook his head. "I barely know the man."

"But you came to him complaining that we were putting pressure on you."

He looked surprised. "Oh, no. He came to me. He said he'd heard about it someplace and wanted to know if it was true. I told him we'd talked, that it had startled me a bit, but it hadn't particularly bothered me. I'd just figured you were doing your job."

"He didn't identify his source of information?"

McDermott paused and his face furrowed in concentration, but I knew what he'd say before he said it.

"No, I'm sure he didn't say."

I shifted focus abruptly, trying to catch him off balance.

"What're you doing with almost fifty thousand dollars in the bank, listed under a phony name?"

He looked at me blankly for a moment, then blinked and stared harder, as if my nose had suddenly sprouted flowers. "What?"

I plowed on, despite his blatant incredulity. "We found a listening device in the ceiling of my office, hooked to a transmitter under your filing cabinet. Combining that with your always showing up at the wrong place at the wrong time with these killings, we got a search warrant and dug into your bank records. It wasn't hidden too well."

He shook his head, his mouth partly open. "I don't know what the hell you're talking about, Joe. I've never had fifty thousand in the bank. I've never had that kind of money anywhere."

"Regular deposits, nice fat ones, made out to Fred Ellison, who happens to have your home address and your first and middle names."

He spread his hands out to each side in symbolic surrender. He was so taken aback by the suggestion, he wasn't even irritated at our invading his privacy. "I swear to God, I don't know anything about it. I know I keep saying that, like when I showed up at that murder scene just as it was going off, but I'm innocent. I don't know why, but somebody must have it in for me, 'cause I haven't done a thing, honest."

His eyes were wide and soft, devoid of the calculation and malice I'd seen in Jackson's just a half hour before. I stared off over the parking lot, now lit by an anemic pale-gray sky, plugging what had occurred over the last few hours into what we already knew. McDermott stayed quiet and still beside me.

I finally looked at him again. "Have you ever had anything to do with the Brattleboro Union High School?"

He half shrugged. "Sure, I have to inspect it every once in a while, just like I do all the other schools."

"How about in some other capacity? Did you attend school there?"

"No. I lived in Rutland as a kid."

"Ever have any problems in your role as inspector?"

"Nothing out of the ordinary. Everybody slips up now and then. When I found something out of line at the school, I just told the assistant principal and it was taken care of."

"A few years ago, they had to tear a lot of asbestos out. Did you catch any flak for that?"

"No. People were unhappy; said they'd lived through it fine and didn't see that their kids were doing any worse, but that was just normal complaining. I mean, hell, it hit my taxes, too. I wished like crazy I could have told them it was no problem."

I thought about it some more. "How about any of the people there? Ever get into a tangle with one of the teachers or maintenance staff?"

He just kept shaking his head.

I saw Brandt appear at the back door of the building and look around. I waved to him and turned to McDermott. "Hang on a sec, would you? Be right back."

Brandt nodded toward McDermott as I approached. "Getting anywhere?"

"Not yet. I just started fishing for a high-school angle."

"You really think that's where it all ties together?"

I looked back at the round building inspector, perched on the slope like a soft boulder. "I don't know... A hunch. I keep thinking all this begins a long time ago, like when Jardine and Rose and John Woll first met up."

"In high school," Brandt finished.

"Yeah, the same place Jackson taught."

"And the same place you chose for your wishful-thinking bushwhacking tonight. You do that on purpose?"

I tilted my head to one side. "I don't know. Maybe subconsciously. It was the only other place besides the Municipal Building in which a few of the players had a common link."

Brandt shook his head. "I don't know. We've known three of them were connected through high school from the start of this thing. You've had people checking into that for days with nothing to show for it."

"Maybe the fact that we knew it early on made it unremarkable; we knew John and Rose had to have met somewhere, so Jardine having been their classmate was the only coincidence. And in a town this size, it wasn't much of one. Then came Milly. There was no school connection there, but it introduced the whole drug angle, which introduced us to Cappelli and Atwater and the others. We lost sight of the original connection."

"Which Luman Jackson has just revived."

"Yeah; there's something else, though. Look at who we're dealing with. It's not some guy discovering his partner was skimming the profits, or his wife was fooling around. We're after someone with some serious anger here. Jardine was executed with amazing forethought. His killer thought for a long time, years probably, about the best way to do it. He researched it like a guy building an atom bomb, fantasizing about how he'd like to do it, then finding a way to make the fantasy real. He found out about curare, God knows how, and then discovered how he could get his hands on some. He stole just enough, months in advance. See what I'm saying? This guy was burning like a long, slow fuse."

"No argument. So how does it connect to high school?"

"Because that's their common ground. We saw this as a triangle at first—two guys falling out over a woman—but once we figured John Woll was being framed, or at least put it in our calculations, that meant a fourth person had to be factored in. Combine that with the way Jardine was killed, with a calculating hatred, and the way John was framed, and you've got someone who must have been a part of the high-school crowd; someone who'd been wounded by Jardine especially, but also by the other two . . ."

"Joe, down boy. My God, you're laying this whole thing out like it wasn't entirely your own imagination."

"But it fits. If you accept that John was framed and that the list we found in Milly's apartment was planted, you've accepted that the guy we're after is no dummy. He's smart; he's a planner; he's a puzzle master, if you like. What we've been doing is trying to fit the pieces to the puzzle he arranged for us. What we need to do is find the pieces of the puzzle he's a part of."

Brandt sighed and shrugged. "Hey, why not? Lead the way."

We both walked back to McDermott and sat on either side of him, the three of us looking like spectators waiting for a parade.

"Fred," I picked up, "we were talking about any connection you might have had with the high school."

He nodded. "I don't really have any. I've been thinking about it while you two were talking. I never worked there, never had any major problems with them as inspector. My wife and I are childless, so I didn't have any kids go there. I can't think of a thing."

Brandt spoke up. "How about something less directly connected? A run-in with someone who worked at the school, or some outfit with a major contract with them, like a roofing contractor or something?"

McDermott kept shaking his head.

"Maybe a more personal angle," I said. "A friend, an enemy, a lover?"

McDermott chuckled. "My wife?"

But I persisted. "How about before her?"

His face reddened slightly. "Oh, you know... Well. There is no connection."

"What?"

"It's a little embarrassing. It did happen before I was married, almost twenty years ago. I had an affair with a married woman, but there's no connection there to the high school."

"What happened?"

"It didn't work out; I suppose those things rarely do. I did love her, but it became too complicated. The husband was very angry; it ended in divorce. She doesn't live here anymore; I think I heard she'd died a year or two ago."

"Were there any kids involved?"

"One, a small boy. You know him, in fact. Buddy Schultz."

"The janitor?" I said.

"That's right."

I pictured Buddy in my mind, a tall, skinny, shy loner with a fondness for books and isolation. He was about the same age as Jardine and the Wolls, just under thirty. I glanced at Brandt.

He got up. "I think Ron has a copy of the school yearbook in his desk. I'll go get it."

McDermott and I watched him go.

"How did his parents' breakup hit him?" I asked.

"Pretty hard, I guess. He was kind of a strange kid anyway, moody and withdrawn. Very attached to his mother; the two of them had a special bond. She could make him come out of his shell like no one else. Then he could be really sweet. He's still like that, kind of hot and cold, although I barely see him anymore. He doesn't start work till after I've left, most of the time."

"Does he hold you responsible for his parents divorcing?"

McDermott tilted his head. "I don't see how he couldn't. They probably would have broken up sooner or later anyhow, but I was right in the middle of it."

"And Buddy knew about you."

"Oh, yes, I was around, trying to give Mary support."

"How's he react to you now?"

"Buddy? We don't have much to say to each other. It was a long time ago. We mostly just say hi to each other in the hallway, once in a while."

He paused and shook his head as Brandt came out of the building and headed back in our direction, the yearbook in his hand. "It's odd when you think about it; if things had turned out differently, I might have been his stepfather."

Brandt stood before us, holding the book open so we could both see its contents. Under the picture of a younger, more sullen-looking Buddy was the caption, "Wendell Schultz, Jr."

"What do you think?" Brandt asked.

"I think the tables just turned."

CHAPTER

36

WE met in a twenty-by-twenty-foot meeting room at the Quality Inn on the Putney Road, just across from the enormous C&S warehouse. I had booked the room in person, and had spread the word to everyone to gather there, just twenty minutes before, using the lobby telephone. I was hoping this spur-of-the-moment planning would assure me of absolute secrecy. J.P. had swept the rest of the Police Department by now and had found two other bugs, but I still wasn't convinced his battered AM radio had caught them all; nor had he made that claim.

I stood up at the head of the long, broad table. Going down either side, with plenty of empty space between each of them, were Brandt, James Dunn, J.P., Sammie, Dennis, Ron with his leg parked on the chair next to him, and now, Willy Kunkle. Willy, predictably, had chosen to sit at the other end, so that we faced each other like estranged parents at an awkward family get-together.

"I appreciate you all coming here on such short notice. I think our security breach is known to you all by now, but, in addition, there have been some recent developments I think we should all be aware of without resorting to telephones or memos. Although we think we've located the bugs that were in the department, we don't know if any of our other means of communication have been compromised."

I stepped away from the table and began to walk back and forth across the front of the room. "First off, I'd like to reintroduce Willy Kunkle. You all know him from the old days. His expertise when he was employed by us was in narcotics, and his knowledge of the local players in that game is still very up-to-date. The docs have told us that Pierre Lavoie sustained a bruise right over his heart, from where the vest stopped Jackson's bullet, so we've been advised to put him on sick leave till that clears up. As a result, we've now hired Willy as a temporary special officer, just until we see this thing through."

I paused and looked especially at James Dunn. "What we've been examining during the last twelve hours is the possible breakthrough we've been hoping for from the start of this case. We have evidence that the man who killed Jardine, Milly Crawford, Toby Huntington, and John Woll is Wendell 'Buddy' Schultz, the Municipal Center janitor."

There was a shifting of bodies around the table. Only Dunn had still been in ignorance of this fact by now, but saying Buddy's name in the open came like a breath of fresh air. Not only had about half of us gone sleepless for the last twenty-four hours again, but we'd been reduced to either working in virtual silence when in the office, or escaping to parked cars and restaurant booths around town in order to have secure conversations. The strain, and the increasingly fragile tempers, had begun to show toward the end.

"We came up with Buddy's name in the early hours of this morning. The trick, however, was to pin the evidence to him, item by item, to see if it stuck. We began with his fingerprints. J.P.?"

Tyler scratched his temple, taking a few seconds to organize his thoughts. "We had a set of prints we lifted off the bottles of curare . . ." He stopped suddenly and gave me a questioning glance.

I nodded. "The curare is common knowledge; no need to explain."

J.P. resumed. "I tried the FBI and the State Police, as well as our own files, but no bells went off. After Joe pegged Buddy, though, that gave me something to go for.

Trouble was, how to get Buddy's prints legally without letting him know?''

"Raid the janitor's closet," Dennis muttered.

J.P. smiled. "I thought of that, but he's not the only person to handle that stuff. Anyway, the Lieutenant remembered that when Buddy stole him a table fan to keep the heat down, he wiped it off before putting it on Joe's desk. I checked it out, got a perfect set, and made a match with the prints from the curare bottles.''

"You ruled out Lieutenant Gunther's prints, of course?'' asked Dunn, who by now was taking notes.

"Yes, sir.''

I picked it up from there. "That connected Buddy to the curare, but it didn't necessarily make him the man who used it on Jardine. So we began digging deeper into the similarity between the deaths of John Woll and Toby Huntington. J.P.?''

"What caught our attention was that they, like Milly, had both been shot, and that, as the autopsies revealed, Toby had died first by a day or so. The bullets Hillstrom recovered weren't in great shape—one of them was in fragments—but the crime lab still managed to make a comparison, and came up with the fact that all three of them, including the only good one recovered from Milly, had been fired from the same gun, the gun we found in John's hand.''

"That,'' I broke in, "wasn't necessarily a mistake on the killer's part, by the way. Buddy knew that John was still a prime suspect in Charlie's murder, and a lesser one in Milly's; the gun would have been concrete evidence linking John to their deaths. The scenario would have been that John shot both Milly and Toby, and then used the gun on himself.''

Dennis snorted derisively.

"The mistake he did make was discovered by the crime lab: All three bullets had passed through the same silencer, an item we didn't find attached to the gun in Woll's hand.''

Dunn held up his pen. "Hold it. Explain that about the silencer.''

"Most silencers aren't in perfect alignment with the barrel, so they'll mark each bullet slightly on the way out, which means that you can match a bullet to a silencer just like you can match it to an individual barrel. The first tip-off to the lab boys was that, while the gunpowder marks on John's T-shirt were proximity burns, they were inconsistent with an open barrel.''

As Dunn continued taking copious notes, I broadened the scope somewhat. "Right now, pinning the tail on Buddy is still theoretical; we don't have enough to get a warrant for him or to search his place, even with the fingerprints. He could, for example, claim he'd been at the vet's a year ago, and had handled those bottles out of curiosity. So we've taken a background approach, rechecking all the evidence we've accumulated so far, with Buddy's name plugged into the equation as the bad guy. The results have been encouraging. Ron, you spent most of the day reinterviewing some of your more competent, and discreet, high-school sources. What was the bottom line on Buddy?"

Like J.P. before him, Ron took his time before speaking. "Moody, introverted, bookish, quick to anger and slow to forget, got very good grades but was too broke to go on to college without help. He was a competitor for the scholarship that John won in his senior year, but grades were only a portion of the award's criteria. John wasn't straight-A, but he was considered 'well-rounded.' Buddy was just the reverse: never a B in his career, but a real oddball. From what I heard, he was resentful as hell when John got it over him."

"And no doubt doubly so when John threw it away to get married to Rose," I added.

Ron pulled out another sheet of paper. "More than we guessed. I found out that Buddy's mother checked him into the Retreat right after graduation. He stayed there for a year, but I don't know what his diagnosis was. We'd have to get a subpoena for the files.

"Rose might have played a part in his breakdown, in fact. Buddy had a thing for her in high school. Apparently, he and Rose had tried out the back of Buddy's car, and according to my source, things didn't go too well. Buddy mooned over Rose for a long time afterward, but by that time she was going with Charlie Jardine. Buddy never forgave Jardine for 'stealing' his girl—although the choice for Rose had obviously been easy."

Dunn broke in. "That's all too vague. Will your source be any good in court?"

Ron nodded without hesitation. "I think so. I didn't give him much time, since we were all trying to cover a lot of ground fast, but he implied it was no deep, dark secret. We should be able to tighten up his testimony, and get others to back him up."

Dunn nodded without comment.

"While we're on the psychological angle," Ron added, "I did a little checking into what might have triggered Buddy to flip out ten years after getting out of school. Turns out his mother died about a year and a half ago, which is when he began laying the groundwork for his mayhem. I talked to a psychologist friend of mine, who said that if the mother-son attachment had been intense, her death, coupled with Buddy's long-standing mental problems, might have been enough to push him over the edge."

"One other background item," I added, and I described Fred McDermott's connection to Buddy's mother. When I finished, I sat back down. "Again, none of this will secure a warrant, but it reveals bad blood between Buddy and several of the victims."

"What about Jackson?" Sammie asked.

I turned my palms up in a shrug. "Don't know yet."

Ron responded. "I heard a rumor that long ago, like twenty years or so, Jackson almost got into serious trouble. I couldn't get any details, but something sexual was implied."

"With one of his students?" Dunn asked.

Ron shook his head. "I can't be sure; that's the feeling I got. I asked a couple of his contemporaries and got nowhere. But if something was hushed up, surely a retired principal or administrator might know."

"What do we care, if it happened before Buddy's time?" Dennis asked.

"It may have given Buddy ammunition," Brandt explained. "Since the beginning, Luman Jackson has displayed an extraordinary interest in this case, above and beyond what might have been expected, even for him. It's possible somebody was putting the squeeze on him, for whatever reason . . ." He suddenly stopped and looked at Ron. "Did Jackson ever teach Buddy?"

"Yes."

"Any feedback on that?"

"Not particularly with Buddy. The general consensus was that Jackson treated all his kids like shit, attacking their weak spots and humiliating them in front of their friends."

Brandt made a face. "Charming. Still, that would supply Buddy with an ax to grind. What he had on Jackson, I don't know, but it must have been pretty bad."

Sammie had been staring at the tabletop through all this talk of Jackson. Now she finally blurted out, "What went wrong at the high school? Why didn't our trap catch Buddy, if he was the bad guy?"

I hesitated. J.P. and I had already discussed this privately, and while I was going to enter our conclusions in the final report, I thought I'd sit on it within reason until then.

Tyler got me off the hook, however. "Because I screwed the pooch. When Joe told me he thought his office was being bugged, I knew we'd probably have to wander around the building, looking for its source. So I went to Buddy for a passkey to all the offices. He must have had a good laugh listening to us later, trying to set him up."

There was a long, embarrassed silence.

I finally cleared my throat. "I think you're in good company when it comes to screwing pooches. I'd like to move on to something else, a major facet of the case we haven't mentioned yet. In the middle of this whole mess, we stumbled over the biggest single stash of dope we've ever seen in this town. We were pretty sure from the start that it was tied into the homicides somehow, but we didn't know how.

"Initially, as you recall, we thought Jardine and Milly might have been partners, with Charlie the money man—perhaps using Wentworth's money—and Milly handling the street contacts. That had a variety of holes in it, not the least of which was: Who killed them both? Since then, we've come to believe Charlie was a peripheral party. It all makes better sense when we make Buddy and Milly partners and have Charlie simply as a customer, which explains how that baggie ended up in his house.

"This new scenario gains credibility because of a few things Willy Kunkle discovered through his sources. We'd thought initially that the names on the list found in Milly's apartment might be Milly's colleagues. In fact, except for John Woll, they were all from a rival operation; therefore, the list was a double frame, implicating both Woll and Milly's competition. It worked, of course. Our suspicions of John did increase, and our pursuit of Mark Cappelli led to the collapse of the ring he worked with.

"Another problem we had were the drugs. Why had the shooter—Buddy, for the sake of clarity—killed Milly, planted the list, but left behind a fortune in dope? The simplest explanation was time. Buddy didn't have enough of it, and it was more important for him to set up the double frame than it was to collect the inventory. But that didn't make sense to us; by killing his partner, Buddy put himself out of business.

"Now we could see where Milly had become a sudden liability. He knew Buddy, and what he was up to, and he'd sold a baggie of coke to Charlie. He was the bridge that could have led us straight to Buddy. Also, in Buddy's eyes, he was replaceable.

"But what about the dope? By abandoning it, Buddy not only sacrificed its potential value, but also whatever it had cost him in the first place. That remained our thickest stone wall. We fooled around trying to connect various money sources to Buddy, plugging in Jardine, Wentworth, McDermott, and Luman Jackson as blackmail victims, but all of them had problems.

"The debate was finally ended, again through Willy Kunkle. This morning, Willy discovered why Cappelli started shooting before Ron and I identified ourselves as police officers, and why the rest of his gang have gone so far underground. It turns out Cappelli and Hanson were ripped off several months ago of the exact amount of dope we later found in Milly's apartment. The Boston people were unhappy, perhaps even suspicious of their Brattleboro colleagues, and Cappelli and Hanson were as nervous as cats on a highway.

"Having therefore secured his drugs at no cost, Buddy was less concerned with abandoning them, and more interested in giving his competitors a final shove. We have recently heard that the Boston suppliers have been approached by someone wishing to replace Hanson et al. Even with our breath on his neck, Buddy is still trying for the gold ring.

"Obviously," I concluded, "Buddy would have preferred to keep both Milly and the drugs in place. But our finding Milly's prints on the baggie in Jardine's house had all the potential of disaster. It's proof of Buddy's weird brilliance that he could not only plug a sudden leak like that, but turn it to his own advantage."

"Assuming Buddy is the killer," Dunn declared with emphasis, dropping his pen on his pad. "Look, I think you have something here, but watch out for the 'maybes.' If you want to badly enough, you can turn Buddy into the man who really shot Kennedy. You've got some good stuff; chase it down, make it something we can take to a judge. If we can get just enough for a warrant, the rest might open up like a flower, so don't waste your time running all over the place. Focus."

He stood up, gave us all a curt nod, and left the room.

•   •   •

A half hour later, we were all following Dunn's suggestion, gathering our notes, preparing to head out again and chase down the ideas we'd discussed at the top of the meeting; all of us except me. I stayed slumped in my chair, my chin cupped in my right hand, buried in a debate I'd held earlier with myself.

Willy Kunkle was watching me from his end of the table. "What's on your mind?"

"Curare."

The bustling and movement in the room abruptly stopped. "What about it?" he asked.

"Why curare? Why not just put a plastic bag over his

head? The fun of watching would be the same; so would the final result.''

People drifted back near the table. "And the answer is?'' Willy asked.

"Because curare shows you're smart. It's a signature. It's not only exotic, it's tricky to administer, hard to find, and most people don't even know what it is.''

"So we got a big ego on our hands.''

I shook my head. "We have a high-school graduate needing to prove he's brighter than everyone else. He reads a lot—he's always carrying a book in his back pocket—so maybe he's aware of curare, but he needs to know all about it, to do research—''

"At a library,'' Kunkle finished for me, a grin spreading across his face.

I gave him a nod. "You got it, Sherlock.''

"Curare.''

CHAPTER
37

THE library was closed. We found the head librarian at home, and, keeping Kunkle out of sight, Brandt persuaded her of his need to gain immediate access. In fact, her reluctance played to our advantage, since what she finally did was give us the keys and permission to use them, instead of accompanying us personally, as she was no doubt supposed to.

Kunkle's usually dour mood lightened immediately as soon as he, Brandt, Tyler, and I entered the gloomy building, lit primarily by the ever-changing lights and shadows thrown through the building's twenty-foot glass front wall by the moon and the vehicles prowling back and forth on upper Main Street. Until we found the main bank of light switches and returned the world to normal, the high-ceilinged room, with its clusters of half-seen furniture and aisles of stacked books, reminded me of a grade-B horror movie from the thirties.

Kunkle hurried over to the card catalog and began pulling out drawers and riffling through their contents, his well-muscled fingers a blur. I'd seen him in this hyper-driven mood before, and knew better than to ask him if we could help.

After some fifteen minutes, he'd filled both sides of a small square of scrap paper with Dewey decimal figures, and we followed him into the stacks. There, one by one, he began pulling down large, heavy tomes and checking their indexes, all to no avail. Finally, highly irritated, he crossed over to a desk near the middle of the reading room and dialed out on a phone there.

"Doug? It's Willy. How the fuck do I find out about curare in this dump?... I know it's closed, just answer the question, okay?... yeah... yeah... no shit, really? I'll be damned... same to you, asshole."

He slammed the receiver down and smiled. "You'll love this: The reference librarian says that Buddy Schultz asked him about curare around six months ago."

Kunkle led the way up the narrow metal stairway to the mezzanine stacks and pulled the biggest book yet from its shelf, the *Physician's Desk Reference*, known throughout the medical profession as the *PDR*. Gripping it against his chest, he took it out to one of the tables lining the balcony overlooking the reading room and slapped it down with a bang.

"This bastard ought to have it; it's what Doug recommended to Buddy." He flipped to the back, ran his finger down the list of entries, and muttered, "Bingo."

Without a word, unconsciously slipping into old cooperative habits born of prior years of working together, Tyler dropped a cotton glove onto the book, which Kunkle pulled onto his hand with his teeth. He then turned to the appropriate page near the front of the book, flattened the page by tugging gently at its corners, and quickly scanned its contents.

"That it?" Tyler asked.

"Yup."

Tyler withdrew a foot-long cylindrical object from the evidence case he'd brought with him. "You realize this 's a shot in the dark. Any prints have to be less than two weeks old for this gizmo to work."

"Christ's sake, J.P., just do it. You can run for cover later."

In official terminology, what J.P. was preparing for use was called a "disposable iodine fuming gun." Fat and short at one end, long and thin at the other, it looked like a straightened-out bubble pipe. Tyler took the fat end between his fingers and rolled it back and forth, crushing the iodine crystals within and releasing a small amount of gas. He then bent over the page Kunkle was holding open, and blew through the slim end of the pipe, using his breath to wash the gas over the surface of the paper. Slowly, as he swept the operating end back and forth, two clear ochre-colored prints began to appear. He concentrated on them, no longer moving about, until they were sharply revealed. He then put down the fuming gun, quickly pulled a fingerprint card from his pocket, and held it next to the two already fading prints he'd uncovered.

There was a noticeable stillness in the small group around him. "It's a match."

"You're absolutely sure?" Brandt asked.

Willy slapped Tyler on the back once, an uncharacteristically jovial gesture for him. "Course, he's sure; son of a bitch never says anything unless he's sure."

We all looked at the page while the prints quickly faded from view. Later, up in Waterbury at the State Police Crime Lab, they would be made to appear permanently through a different process. But for now, this was all we needed. Tyler prepared a cardboard container for the book from materials he'd brought with him.

"All right," I said. "We've got a murder victim with curare in him, a report of missing curare, bottles with Buddy's prints that were near those stolen bottles, and now we've got his prints on an article dealing with curare. Enough for a warrant?"

Brandt nodded. "Certainly enough to try for one."

Tyler was still troubled. "If the curare was stolen months ago, Buddy must have consulted the *PDR* back then. Why was I able to find fresh prints?"

Kunkle wasn't worried, predictably. "Who cares? Maybe he came back to refresh his memory on how to inject the stuff. Point is, when the state lab guys do a real job on that page, I bet they'll find a bunch of prints, dating way back."

"Including a few extras from other people," Tyler muttered.

Kunkle shrugged. "I doubt it. It's a recent edition, and I bet there aren't too many people brushing up on South American poisons around here."

Brandt chuckled. "In Brattleboro, who knows?"

Buddy Schultz lived on Prospect Street, the single inhabitant of the only run-down, weatherbeaten, one-and-a-half-story clapboard building on the street, perched on the edge of a sixty-foot, heavily wooded, almost precipitous incline that overlooked Clark Street and, beyond it, Canal Street. Buddy's home loomed almost directly over the erstwhile grave of Charlie Jardine.

By the time we reached the building's sagging front stoop, it had been surrounded by officers, and Tyler and DeFlorio were near certain the place was empty. Under normal circumstances, that would have come as no surprise; it was late at night, when Buddy normally was supposed to be carrying out his janitorial duties at the Municipal Building. We hadn't been able to locate him tonight, however. But standing here, waiting for the door's lock to be forced, I had the creepy feeling that he wasn't far off, and was probably watching us now.

Dennis, J.P., Sammie, and several members of the Special Reaction Team entered first, guns drawn, fanning out inside like a release of lethal, armored locusts.

I stayed outside, listening to the sound of boots pounding throughout the building, enjoying the first hint of coming coolness in the night air. The forecast for tomorrow was for temperatures in the seventies, with an eighty percent chance of rain. The weather, like the investigation, looked about ready to break.

"Scene's secure."

I entered a central hallway, with a small living room to one side, a spare bedroom to the other, the kitchen straight ahead. Even with the lights on, it had a dingy, dark, forgotten feel to it. The wallpaper bellied out from the walls, the wooden floors had been ground into a uniform gray, the light fixtures were bare bulbs. It wasn't a dirty place, but definitely forlorn.

"Joe?" Tyler stuck his head out of a doorway farther down the hall.

I joined him at the entrance of a bedroom/office combination, really just a room with a bed at one end and a desk at the other. But it was obviously the heart of the house and, aside from the bathroom and kitchen, probably the most used room of them all; unlike the rest of the place, it looked, if not cheerful, at least comfortable. There was an ancient, overstuffed armchair, a well-placed black-and-white TV, stacks of well-thumbed paperback books and periodicals reflecting an eclectic and surprisingly intellectual range. I reminded myself that the inhabitant here had once been a grade-A student, with hopes of college and presumably a great deal beyond. It was a sobering reminder of how potentially poisonous the mixture of brains and a damaged psyche could be.

I stepped back into the hallway and whistled loudly. "Yo, people. Your attention for a second."

Heads appeared from various openings.

"Just a few reminders: One, we have a warrant for curare only; two, if you find it, let out a shout so J.P. can deal with it; and, three, if you find anything else that catches your eye, let us know. If it's juicy enough, we can try to expand the warrant to include it, but do not look in places where a bottle of curare obviously wouldn't be."

There was a general murmuring of assent and most of the heads disappeared.

"I think I got something here," I heard Sammie announce from behind me.

I reentered the bedroom and crossed over to where she had removed the drawers of the desk; she was flashing a light inside the cavity.

"Looks like one of those soft-sided briefcases."

I stuck my head in next to hers and saw what she was describing, wedged high up against the back of the desk, just shy of where the drawer back would end up when the drawer itself was closed. "Looks like it could hold a bottle or two. J.P.?"

Tyler came over, took a photograph of the desk, then a close-up of the case in its hiding place, and finally gingerly removed it, wearing his cotton gloves. He unzipped the top and poured the contents out onto the floor. Fanned out before us were a sheaf of documents, notes, and letters, and, rolling a short distance away before coming to a stop in the middle of the room, was a long black metal cylinder. A silencer.

None of us moved for a moment. I quickly scanned the top sheet, and another that poked out farther than the others. The first was a bank account showing Fred McDermott's address but using the same false name we'd found his slush fund hidden under. The second was a plaintive note from Luman Jackson, agreeing to "the terms you set forth," but demanding, typically, that "this must have an end or I will damn the consequences."

I turned to Sammie. "The silencer is ours, since it's illegal in this state, but we're going to have to get a judge in on the rest of it. See if you can round one up, will you?"

"Roger," she said, and headed out to the hall to find a phone.

Borrowing a pair of gloves from J.P., I carefully began sifting through the rest of the documents, feeling as I did that I was being slowly sucked under by the intrigue and anguish that Buddy Schultz had set in motion. What he'd secreted in the desk was more than just the ammunition we'd seen him use, like the bank account and the blackmail of Jackson. There were other items, little gems whose potential spoke for themselves, like the copy of a receipt for the watch Rose had bought Charlie. It hadn't been used—the planting of the watch among John's socks had done the trick—but obviously Buddy was a man who liked more than one option at his disposal.

The material concerning Jackson was less blatant. I had to make assumptions in order to piece it all together, and then I knew I'd have to talk to Jackson to have it all make total sense.

I stuck my head out into the hallway again. "George?"

George Capullo, the senior shift man here, appeared from around a corner. "What's up?"

"Pick up Luman Jackson at his home and bring him here, would you?"

"Just like that? What makes you think he's not going to piss on my boot?"

"Tell him I've got the paperwork that's been costing him so much. And do it code-three. I want him here now."

"You got it."

Sammie gestured to me from the kitchen. She was holding the receiver of a wall phone in one hand. "I've got Harrowsmith," she mouthed soundlessly.

I took the phone and began talking. Harrowsmith, for all his intimidating ways, was a cop's judge. His demeanor, helped by that enormous hawk nose and bushy eyebrows, imparted a fierceness he was well capable of demonstrating, but it was only provoked by sloppiness. It was his desire to see the bad guys in jail that stimulated him to be tough on us, for he knew that if the case was lost in court, or never got there to begin with, it was usually because we'd screwed up our homework.

Twenty minutes later, I'd made my case and had received his official sanction. He'd made it clear, however, that to really make him happy, we should make every effort to locate the only item that did appear in the written warrant: the ever-elusive curare.

I saw flashing lights draw up to the house through the open front door. As I walked through the house to greet my reluctant visitor, Tyler's voice drifted up the basement stairs. "We're off the hook; I just found a couple of the bottles, plus I'm pretty sure the dirt down here will match the samples I got off Jardine's shoes."

I poked my head through the door. "Great; what was the vet's count on the total missing?"

"Four."

"Okay, assuming one was used on Jardine, that leaves one more to find."

Tyler, the wind strong in his sails, sounded optimistic. "We got a couple of rooms left to go."

My own good mood was further enhanced as I stepped outside. The air was cooling down rapidly, bringing with it the return of the grouchy, brittle, northern weather we knew so well. I took the first deep breath I'd allowed myself in over a week.

Capullo nodded to me as I approached the car. "I told him to sit tight; figured you two would enjoy the privacy."

"Thanks."

Luman Jackson was sitting bolt upright in the rear of the patrol car. He glared at me as I entered and settled down next to him. "What the hell do you mean by rousting me in the middle of the night and having me dragged over here with some nonsensical threat note?"

"If it was nonsensical you wouldn't be here," I said flatly. "You came of your own free will. Look, we have two ways of doing this: We can either chat here and now, and get everything out in the open so we can do our best to save your butt on the murder charge, or you can pretend to be outraged and above it all and watch James Dunn turn you into a roman candle, with Stanley Katz lighting the fuse."

"You *are* threatening me," he said in a shocked voice.

I remembered the name I'd read in Buddy's private document collection. "Who was Cheryl Jacobson?"

He didn't actually stiffen, but I felt as if he'd suddenly turned to cement.

I waited, and finally put my hand on the door handle.

"She was a student of mine." His voice was a monotone.

I arrested my faked exit. "When?"

"Many years ago."

I remembered the scuttlebutt I'd heard from Ron at our meeting at the Quality Inn. "You got her in trouble?"

He nodded.

"And you were being blackmailed."

Again, he nodded.

"You know by who?"

He sighed. "I thought I did."

My mind flashed back to last night, his pistol instinctively aimed at Pierre Lavoie's chest. "Fred McDermott?" I tried to keep the incredulity out of my voice.

"Yes."

"Why him?"

"Recently, we talked a couple of times on the phone. He disguised his voice, but there were certain mannerisms, turns of phrase I'd heard before. It didn't click until I heard you were sniffing around McDermott, that he'd been at the murder scene on Horton Place. Then I knew who it was . . ."

"How long ago did this start?"

"Over a year."

"You said you spoke on the phone recently. How were communications handled before?"

"By letter, always."

Of course, I thought. Buddy held off implicating Fred until he was good and ready. "And last night at the high school? Were you gunning for Fred?"

He moved for the first time since we began talking, twisting his body around to face me. "I didn't go there to kill him. I only wanted to talk."

Presumably, Buddy had needed Jackson's money both to finance his criminal ambitions—buying listening devices, for instance—and to implicate Fred McDermott, whom he resented for busting up his parents' marriage. That done, what better conclusion than to have Jackson shoot McDermott? Jackson would be ruined, and McDermott's slush fund would surface to sully his good name. A nice double play and a monument to Buddy's late mother.

Jackson let out a deep sigh and looked out the side window at the darkness, not realizing how lucky he was. Still, I felt most of the bluster had gone out of him. "Come on, Jackson, don't make me pull it out of you word by word. Let's have it all. Now."

He rubbed his forehead. "All right." But he remained silent.

Exasperated, I hit the door handle and swung half out of the car, stopped only by his anguished cry. "I'm trying, all right? It's hard. I've carried this son of a bitch around inside me for decades."

I relented, moved by the unprecedented intensity of his emotion. I had no problem imagining how the burden of his secret had worn him down over the years. Nevertheless, I left the car door open as a warning.

The fresh air seemed to wash the rest of his reserve away. "She died trying to self-abort. She literally used a coat hanger, like in some bad melodrama. She left a note, naming me, blaming me even, for what she'd done to herself. I couldn't believe it. Her mother was a conniving old bitch; got hold of the school, put on the pressure. I had to settle with her just to keep my job."

"They didn't fire you?" I asked.

"They had no grounds. She backed off after I paid her; told them it was a mistake, that her daughter had been a hysteric with a long history of blaming her problems on people she didn't like. I'll give the bitch that much: She was convincing. Still, I was under a microscope for quite some time. It was hell, and it became hell again."

"How did the blackmail start?"

"There was a warning—a note—telling me 'the shit was going to hit the fan,' a phrase I've always despised, and that if I didn't mind my 'p's and 'q's all this ancient history would be given to the press."

"What were you supposed to do?"

He laughed shortly. "Pay, of course."

"How much?"

"Damn near everything I had; about seventy thousand dollars overall." He softly hit the back of the driver's seat with his open hand, an oddly effeminate gesture. "Talk about a nightmare. When I finally figured out who it was, I wanted to tear his head off."

Or shoot him in cold blood, I thought. "You mentioned you figured out it was McDermott from his slips of the tongue. But how did you know where to find him that night? Somebody must have told you."

He hesitated just enough that I knew he was about to lie. "I had an informant."

"Who?"

He gave me his superior look; he was starting to pull back, trying to cut his losses. "Sorry, Lieutenant, I have to protect my sources, too."

"You've been played for a complete sucker, Jackson: blackmailed on the one hand, and set after us like an attack dog on the other. Your 'informant' used some of your money to fake a slush fund in McDermott's name."

Jackson stared at me, his mouth partly open.

"He also told you the blackmailer was going to be at the high school that night. You never wondered how he knew that. Maybe you thought he was a cop, privy to everything. But you took off, gun in hand, to lay your personal devil in his grave. He made a fool out of you, and you cooperated every step of the way. You screwed yourself by paying him off, and you fucked us over by getting in the way."

His cheeks flushed red. "Now just a minute. You can't..."

"The hell I can't. How many times did you listen to your informant, so greedy for the shit he was doling out, you never once wondered how true it might be?"

"I don't..."

"Even while you were being blackmailed, you never guessed the information you were fed came from the very man who was sucking you dry. What's it like being that vain, Luman?"

I got out of the car and leaned back in. "This'll all come out, one way or the other, and I hope like hell they ride you out of town on a rail." He began to speak, but I quieted him with an abrupt hand gesture. "And if you throw that I'll-sue-you crap at me again, I'll make sure that rail is labeled with Cheryl Jacobson's name."

I slammed the door and left him with his mouth open.

IT was four in the morning. I was alone in my office. The window was open, the suddenly chilly predawn air actually lifting goose bumps across my bare forearm. I was filled with the exhaustion that follows hard, rewarding manual labor, content in the knowledge that, while Buddy Schultz was still on the lam, his being so was the only loose thread of the case.

Under Judge Harrowsmith's demanding judicial guidance, we had gathered enough evidence to satisfy even James Dunn. The work had been painstaking and tedious, however, and I had finally told everyone to go home for a few hours' sleep. Not that I was going to be alone for long; Ron Klesczewski had called to say that he couldn't sleep, didn't want to miss out on the kill, and that his leg would be perfectly content propped in a neighboring chair while he pitched in on the paperwork.

I took advantage of the lull, therefore, to make a phone call.

"Where have you been?" She didn't even sound sleepy.

I put my feet up on my desk and leaned back in my chair. The weather, and Gail's voice, was like the calm after the storm.

"I've been crossing t's and dotting i's."

My satisfaction was obviously bordering on gloating. She laughed uncertainly. "You mean it's over?"

"Not over over, but we know who's behind it all. We have to hospital-tuck the corners and actually put our hands on the guy, but at least we know which way is up now."

She hesitated slightly before asking, "Can you say who the killer is?"

"Deep background? Buddy Schultz, our night janitor."

There was a stunned silence, as if I'd invoked the butler instead of the janitor. "You're kidding."

"Nope. Pretty driven guy. Lot of hate, lot of envy, a long memory, and sharp as a tack. Bad combination."

She sighed. "Well, congratulations, Joe. You must feel a thousand pounds lighter."

I chuckled. "Hell, no more than you. By the way, you might find certain changes on the board; no guarantees, but I'd lay money on it."

I'd rarely heard her so elated. "Jackson?"

"Yup. Closetful of skeletons; keep Katz busy for a week. I had the distinct pleasure of feeding him some of his own medicine."

"My God. Tell me more."

It wasn't the right thing to do. Indeed, it emulated the very same nasty habit I bemoaned in my fellow police officers, but for the next fifteen minutes, I gossiped. I told her of all our pitfalls and false trails, of all the people we'd suspected of one crime or another, from Paula Atwater, who'd told Dunn she would turn state's evidence against Hanson, Cappelli, and the smooth-talking Kenny Thomas, to the Wentworths, father and daughter, once so high on the list, whom I imagined would continue sharing breakfast in isolated splendor.

I hypothesized that Arthur Clyde would be forced to tend to his wife's garden, that Rose Woll would find some other human island to latch onto like a shipwreck survivor, and that James Dunn would do everything in his power to throw the book at Luman Jackson. Fred McDermott, I thought, although momentarily startled by what had happened, would plod on toward retirement and pension like the desk-bound soldier he was.

I'd been looking out the window, at nothing in particular, enjoying the sound of Gail's laughter in my ear, when a slight sound at my door shifted my attention. Standing there, his clothes dark with sweat, his face unshaven, his eyes bloodshot and narrow with fatigue, was Buddy Schultz. He was holding a Colt .45 on me, its barrel looking big enough to stick my thumb in. He nodded at the phone.

"Got to go," I said, and hung up on Gail in mid-sentence, hoping to hell she'd guess something was wrong.

"Get up. We're going on a short walk."

My feet were still on the table, so I had to shift around a bit to do what he asked. In the process, my left hand dropped to the arm of my chair. The sudden pain in my hand reminded me of the deep cut I'd suffered pursuing Jackson through the classroom window. Instinctively, not knowing precisely why, perhaps thinking of Ron's imminent arrival at the office, I ground my palm down hard on the point of the chair arm, reopening the wound and causing a small trickle of blood to course along my little finger and drip onto the floor. Buddy didn't notice.

"What've you got in mind, Buddy?"

He smiled that absurdly friendly smile, all the more bizarre etched across that now blighted face. "I thought I'd kill you first, and then worry about my next move."

"Why?" His answer was so senseless, my curiosity almost overtook my rising fear, but not quite.

"You messed me up, man." He moved next to me, grabbed my left elbow like an escort, and began steering me toward the door. His gun was half buried in my back, making any evasive move a suicidal gesture.

"Buddy, you messed yourself up. You should have just killed Charlie and made his body disappear, instead of trying to pin the murder on John."

He swung me left, away from the tiny corridor leading to the exit, and toward the deadend conference room.

"Where're we going?"

He stopped me in front of the row of cabinets at the back of the conference room. Manipulating some mechanisms in the small gap between the cabinets and the side wall, he caused an upper portion of one of the cabinets to swing open on invisible hinges, like the top half of a three-foot-thick Dutch door. Behind it, instead of unpainted wall, there was a man-sized hole revealing a huge vertical air shaft, a remnant of the old building's original heating system. A wave of hot stale air poured over us, a bottled-up memento of the past week's hellish weather.

"Climb up."

"How? That's a four-foot threshold."

He kicked over a chair, as I'd hoped he might. I positioned it against the lower cabinet, let a surreptitious drop of blood hit the seat, and immediately put my shoe on it as I stepped up. I put my knee on the edge of the square opening, smeared a tiny bit of blood where it could be seen once the secret door was shut again, and crawled halfway in.

He had climbed up behind me to keep me going, not taking time to look around at the trail I'd left behind. "Keep moving."

"It's hard to see." That part was true. Beyond the hole at the end of the three-foot tunnel, it was just a dim void with an odd, empty resonance to it.

"Put your leg over and reach down. You'll find the bottom; it's even with the floor."

I did as instructed. As soon as I gained solid footing, I turned to see if I could catch him off guard, but he was already next to me, having closed the cabinet behind us and leapt down in one easy, practiced movement. Again, I felt the gun's hard nose nuzzle my spine.

"Straight ahead, there's a ladder."

The air was suffocating, as bad as the heat wave of the past week—worse in the total blackness surrounding us. There was a rancid odor of decay, and of something akin to old, moldy wool. My bloody hand located the rungs of a ladder.

"Start climbing, and don't try to hit me with your heels. I'll be out of the way."

The thought had crossed my mind, along with dozens of others. I had seen situations like this in the movies, and I, along with everyone else, had been critical of the hero for not being more aggressive. After all, I'd always reasoned, you're dead anyway, why not fight for your life?

The problem with all that, I now knew, was that you didn't really believe you were dead anyway. Despite what he'd told me, I knew there had to be a way out of this; it became too irrational otherwise. I started climbing.

"Where's this lead?" I asked.

"Up."

We'd been trained about hostage situations, about creating a bond with the kidnapper, making it harder for him to kill someone who was hell-bent on becoming a friend. But I knew it wouldn't work on Buddy.

"How far up?"

"You'll know."

I had no feeling of my surroundings. I might as well have been climbing into the night sky above a boiling cauldron, swathed in its cloying, invisible steam. I tried focusing on something more tangible. I knew I was climbing one of the four air shafts; there were no other available empty spaces in the building. During the remodeling, there'd been some discussion about taking over the hundred-year-old shafts to create more floor space, since their original purpose had been replaced by modern, less cumbersome technology. But the engineers had vetoed the idea—something about structural integrity. The shafts had stayed.

"You do this during the remodeling? Cover your noise with the carpenters?"

There was no answer. Despite his warning, I tried kicking back with my heels a couple of times, but all I hit was air. I was sweating profusely, not only from the heat, but from the exercise. I felt I'd been climbing a half mile straight up.

Suddenly, I ran out of rungs. My hand reached up in what was becoming an automatic grasp, closed on nothing, and threw me completely off balance. My foot, in mid-air, hesitated, missed its placement, and rattled by several rungs as I almost fell backwards into the darkness, arrested only by my throbbing left hand. I heard Buddy grunt below as he ducked to avoid my swinging, kicking feet.

I latched back on and rested, panting hard.

"Reach the top?" Buddy's voice was sarcastic.

"What the hell was that? You gonna drop me into a goddamn black pit?"

"I have something better in mind for you. Know where we are?"

I looked around, feeling aimlessly for something solid with one outstretched arm. "The attic?"

"Yeah, the bat cave. That's what we call it in maintenance. Climb to the top, take one step forward, and freeze. It's not all floor, so don't get fancy."

I stepped off the ladder, but then immediately turned and waited, all my energy directed at sensing when Buddy would come even with the floor so I could kick back at his head.

Instead, I heard his voice slightly off to one side and level with me. "Waiting to send me back down the hard way?"

I had no idea how he'd done it. He seemed totally oblivious to the pitch black of our surroundings. Indeed, everything about him had metamorphosed, including his slightly hesitant, boyish speech. A tingling spread across the nape of my neck; a small reminder of panic awaiting.

There was a scraping sound and abruptly a dim shaft of murky light sliced into the void, outlining the large square hole before me, the top of not one, but two ladders, and the dim perception of a room the size of a closet. Buddy's shadow stood by the side of the narrow door he'd opened, the gun in his hand shining dully.

"Step right this way." The gun waved in invitation.

I edged around the shaft hole and stepped through the door. I was on a narrow catwalk, suspended from cables that disappeared into the gloom overhead. Beneath me was a gridwork of floor joists and support beams, the square gaps between them filled with musty, dark snowdrifts of rockwool insulation. I looked to the sides. Nearby, I could make out the forty-five-degree slope of a couple of immense rafter beams, along with another catwalk angling off into the dark. The air was almost literally suffocating, rich with the stench of bat dung, rotten wood, and damp insulation, fragments of which I'd smelled at the bottom of the shaft.

"Go down to the end, turn left, and keep going to the platform."

I reached out tentatively to steady myself. Each catwalk had but one handrail, also made of cable. The other side was left free, presumably to make it easier for workmen to lower ladders to the joists ten feet below. It was a practical idea, but not great for one's sense of balance. At best, the catwalks were two feet wide. In my present state of mind, a tightrope was no wider.

I followed Buddy's directions, my earlier thoughts of leaving a trail long gone. The length of the climb, the darkness, the near-unbearable heat, had all combined to make the attic as alien to me as the far side of the moon. Only a few dozen feet below, the night-shift policemen were loitering around the coffee machine, or chatting with the dispatcher. Ron Klesczewski was probably hard at work, awkwardly poised over his paperwork, having totally missed my feeble message. Up here, suspended between a pitched roof I couldn't perceive and a floor that looked like a wood-strewn, blackened sea, I felt utterly abandoned.

The platform he'd mentioned was two steps up from the catwalk and about six feet square. There were no handrails at all here, the area serving as a junction for four catwalks, one branching off from each side. A single chair stood before me, placed near one edge, overlooking the entire attic's only source of light: a dim, dirt-covered skylight that hung over the building's top-floor corridor. In the days before electricity, this skylight had matched a similar window cut into the roof above, allowing Mother Nature to illuminate at least a portion of the building's interior. The outer skylight had long ago been sealed over, leaving its quaint and functionless mate to gather dust. I stepped up onto the platform and looked down onto the grimy glass rectangle, noticing, outlined against the dim glimmer coming from the corridor's fire-safety lighting, the stiff and tiny body of a sparrow.

The first possibility of escape occurred to me then, justifying in my own mind my docility so far. If I were to merely step off the platform, I could crash through the skylight to the floor below it, and maybe get away. From this elevation, it was probably twelve feet to the glass, which in turn was some ten feet above the floor. A long way to go, but survivable, which was more than I thought my chances were with Buddy. Besides, I continued thinking hopefully, even if I broke both legs, I might still be able to crawl to a fire alarm and summon help. I took a small step toward the edge to get into position.

"Cute," was all I heard from behind me before the back of my head exploded into a painful flash of light and I felt my entire body go weak. My hand flew to the point of impact and was grabbed by Buddy, who pulled me backward off balance into the chair. I landed heavily, my head still swimming, and was only half aware of him quickly handcuffing my wrists behind my back, to the outside rails of the chair back. He ran off two long strips of duct tape, and fastened my legs to the front legs of the chair.

If there was one image that had dogged me throughout this case, and had served as a continual reminder that the man we were after was both determined and crazed, it was the picture of Charlie Jardine, bound and helpless, having to watch his own death like a spectator. Superimposing that image on my own situation, I suddenly came face to face with the true meaning of the word "horror."

I worked my mouth several times, trying to get the words to come out, fighting the fearful nausea and the pain from the back of my head. "Buddy, for Christ's sake. Why do this?"

He laughed, putting the finishing touches on his handiwork. "This has been my home away from home. No one knows where we are. I'm going to end this the way it began and then I'm history."

He pulled a small bottle and a packaged syringe from his pants pocket and began preparing an injection.

"Buddy, we went through your house; we found the silencer and the curare. We know you killed Jardine. Killing me isn't going to help you."

He was meticulously measuring how much curare to pull into the syringe barrel, holding it against the skylight's dim glow. He sounded almost bored. "It doesn't matter. If I am caught, I'll be able to get off on an insanity plea, especially after killing you."

He tapped the syringe with his fingernail and shot a little

of the fluid out the end of the needle, to eliminate any air bubbles.

I made a single, convulsive leap against my bonds, hoping for a flaw in the duct tape or a weakness in the chair. I barely moved, though the pain and nausea from my head wound doubled in intensity.

Buddy looked at me and shook his head. "That reminds me: I better tape you down a little better before I stick this in. Wouldn't want you bouncing around, messing my aim up."

His words had the proper undermining effect. Had I waited until he was just poised with his needle, I might have been able to knock it out of his hand with my shoulder.

I closed my eyes as he set about taping my elbows painfully together, pinning my upper arm against the back of the chair so tightly I could barely move.

"There we go," he said happily. "Trussed up like a hog."

He picked up the syringe from the floor and held it ready. "Any last words? Words become a little difficult after this stuff goes in; that's what Charlie found, anyway."

"Yeah, Buddy, I'd like to know why? Jardine didn't steal Rose from you, and losing a scholarship couldn't have been the end of the world."

He paused for a long time, giving me a faint touch of hope. "Let's say I thought it was poetic justice, and leave it at that."

He did it then with astounding quickness. One moment he was smirking down at me, the syringe held delicately in his hand, and the next it was over, the needle had been withdrawn, and he was carefully putting the small plastic sleeve back over it before slipping the whole thing into his pocket. "Gotcha," was all he said.

I felt for a moment that my heart had stopped. I turned my head away from him and looked down at the shape of the small, dead sparrow, all my focus turned inward. After a half minute, I realized I needed to start breathing, and I took some of the hot, stale air into my lungs, no longer resentful of its poor quality.

"I envy you a bit, you know. I'm curious about how it

feels. With Charlie, it was almost like he was going into a trance, until I grabbed his attention, that is. Did you guys figure out exactly how I did it?"

I was beginning to feel very odd. I tried to answer, mostly to see if I could do it, but the effort seemed too much. I wasn't numb, which was how I'd imagined Charlie had felt. Instead, it was just the opposite. I could sense everything that was going on inside me: the air moving in and out, the blood rushing through the vessels in my neck, the regular thumping of my heart, the sweat pouring down my face. But I could not will myself to do anything, wiggle a toe, or move my tongue, or even swallow. It was if all the body's automatic systems had taken over, and all the voluntary ones short-circuited.

Buddy was still chatting, fooling with something beyond my scope of vision, but I no longer listened. All I had left was my ability to concentrate, and to spend what time I had left paying attention to Buddy seemed a waste. At first, though, I didn't actually know what to think about. The case came to mind, the irony of it ending this way, questions about how they would deal with my death. I wondered if Ron would be made lieutenant, and if Willy Kunkle would bother trying to get back on the force without me goading him.

Gail eventually pushed all that aside, as she often did in real life. I found myself regretting how little time I'd given her this past week, and how I'd allowed the tensions of the investigation to come between us, if only temporarily. I remembered holding her close just recently, having patched up those differences, and the warmth of her voice on the phone a mere twenty minutes ago.

Buddy thrust his face before my own, cutting off my view of the skylight. "Hi, Joe. You haven't been paying attention. I invented a new toy, something to help me in my work." He dangled a thin nylon strap in front of me, on which two empty wooden sewing spools had been taped, about an inch and a half apart.

"See, when I killed Charlie, it was hard work; it took a long time and ended up being painful—for me, that is. My thumbs hurt for a couple of days. So this is my new experiment." He disappeared and I could hear him moving behind me. The strap, held horizontally, reappeared before my eyes, the spools side by side, in the middle.

"It goes around the neck, each spool over an artery, so that when I pull it tight, you can still breathe, but the blood gets shut off. It's no wear and tear on me, 'cause I just work a tourniquet stick from the back. What 'ya think? Neat, huh?"

I felt his hands around my neck, adjusting the strap, fitting each spool into the depression on either side of my trachea.

"Of course, if it doesn't work, I'll just go back to using my thumbs, but let's give it—"

Silence fell like a cleaver. The strap went slack. I couldn't move my head, but I shifted my eyes from the skylight and scanned what little I could see of the darkness beyond. Behind me, I could hear Buddy quietly pulling the hammer back on his gun. Whatever had caught his attention was quiet now.

He moved as gently as a cat, sliding into my field of vision from the right, his gun in his hand, gliding down the two steps from the platform to the one catwalk I could see in my frozen state, the same one we'd traveled from the air shaft.

My heart beat faster, the hopeful memory of the trail of blood drops springing back to mind. Gail must have done something, called someone. And told them what? That I'd hung up on her and wouldn't answer when she called back? She had done something, I was utterly convinced. She had set salvation into motion. I knew, just as Buddy obviously knew, that that one sound, whatever it had been, had come like a knock on a door. It had to be answered, or the door would be kicked in.

Buddy vanished into the gloom and I tried willing myself to see further, surprised to find I could actually squint a little. I remembered then what Hillstrom's toxicologist had told me, that curare only lasted a few minutes, and that without booster injections, its effects wore off quickly. The simple act of squinting gave me hope I was on the upswing.

If Buddy could be taken out, I'd survive, even without medical intervention.

But this was no textbook assault by a police SWAT team. In fact, it might be no more than an animal scratching at some rotten wood. If that were true, Buddy would satisfy his curiosity, retracing our steps to the air shaft, perhaps checking out parts of the maze of catwalks he knew more intimately than anyone, and then he'd return to conclude his little fantasy.

There was a sudden, blinding, conical stab of light. I saw Buddy arrested in mid-step, like a tightrope artist at the circus, trapped by a spotlight in the gloom above the audience. There was a double explosion accompanying two long, fiery, swordlike muzzle flashes, one from Buddy's gun, the other from the darkness beyond the source of the light. That light, obviously a flashlight, spun out of control, landed with a thud on the catwalk, rolled over the edge, and, in a final end-over-end sparkle, vanished into the soft, absorbing insulation below.

There was a long moment of silence, punctured only by the rasping of my own breathing. Then I heard movement, slow, cumbersome, no longer stealthy. I kept my eyes on the distant end of the catwalk, as intent on it as a gambler on the flip of a coin. A shadow moved there, too vague to decipher, a man using the one handrail for balance, lurching, fighting for control, half dragging himself along, the glow from the skylight still too weak to pick out his emerging features.

Finally, almost mercifully, the dim light picked up Buddy's twisted face, his eyes screwed tight in pain, one hand clutched across a blood-soaked chest, the other, still holding the .45, sliding uncertainly along the handrail. I breathed a sigh of relief, the suspense over, the outcome no different than it had been five minutes earlier. Whatever hope I'd had vanished without complaint, having never been of much substance to begin with.

Buddy paused some fifteen feet away, his body swaying, his breathing a ragged string of gurgles. He tried once to let go of the railing, failed, tried again, and half succeeded, holding his gun hand only a foot away from the cable, testing his balance. Satisfied, he finally looked up at me, his eyes glistening with a malevolence I wouldn't have thought possible in another human being.

The hand with the gun slowly rose and leveled out, the black eye of the barrel seeking my motionless forehead. But the white-orange blast, when it came, came from behind, and it threw Buddy up like a leaf caught by the wind, and tossed him lightly into the air. Spread-eagle, he landed with a crash on the skylight, his weight taking the entire pane of glass with him to the floor below, where it blew apart with a crystalline shattering. The cool air from the hallway beneath washed up and surrounded me like the after-splash from someone leaping into a pool.

Ron Klesczewski appeared out of the darkness, his stiff leg making him look like some peg-legged sailor of old. His face was both quizzical and lined with pain. There was a crimson gash on his forehead, but no blood to speak of; "a scratch," as they say.

I looked back through the skylight opening. Buddy's corpse lay as a child's in sleep, half curled up on itself, its fetal memories still strong. Near his face, like a prized possession, almost cupped in one hand, was the dead sparrow.

In the quiet, soothed by the cool air pushing by me, I closed my eyes for a moment, once again aware of my own breathing and heartbeat. I felt a drop trickle down my cheek and fall away soundlessly, but whether sweat or a tear I didn't know.

Archer Mayor has been variously employed as a scholarly editor, a political advance man, a theater photographer, a newspaper writer/editor, and a medical illustrator. He lives twelve miles northwest of Brattleboro, Vermont, with his family, and where his alter ego Joe Gunther is about to face a baffling new case.